THE FEASTS OF LESSER MEN

THE **FEASTS** OF **LESSER MEN**

STEPHEN PARRISH

LASCAUX
BOOKS

Cover design by Wendy Russ.

ISBN-10: 0985166606
ISBN-13: 978-0-9851666-0-1

This is a work of fiction. Character names, locations, and incidents are either the product of the author's imagination or are
used fictitiously, and any resemblance to actual persons, living
or dead, business establishments, locales, or events is entirely
coincidental.

Lascaux Books
www.lascauxbooks.com

To the feasts of lesser men
the good unbidden go.

—Plato, Symposium

For everyone ever assigned MOS 11B

And for Sarah

BOOK ONE

*Out of timber so crooked as that from which man is made
nothing entirely straight can be carved.*

—Kant

Chapter 1

I IDLED THE TRUCK down Alzeyerstrasse to the cemetery gate, where I pulled up on the sidewalk and parked. Cybulski sat uncharacteristically still in the passenger seat, staring through the windshield, watching a long line of stubbornly optimistic street lamps recede in the vacant and indifferent darkness. I punched him on the shoulder. He blinked a few times, then reached for the door handle. We unloaded the tools, slipped through the gate, and navigated the gravel paths, taking care not to bang the tools against one another.

Shepherd's lamps embellished many of the graves. Whether the candles were lit depended on how dedicated the relatives were to their dead. In the dark mist the lamps flickered like jack-o'-lanterns.

We checked one recent burial after another until we found the one we were looking for, a simple rectangle of fresh soil heaped with flower arrangements. Behind the plot, hidden by the flowers, was a granite headstone.

First the flowers had to be cleared away. We placed them on an adjacent grave. Then we dug with our spades, tossing the soil into a pile on the gravel path. The going was easy because the burial had occurred only hours before. Within minutes we heard the hollow, muffled thunk of stainless steel striking wood.

"There," I whispered to Cybulski. "Help me clear the dirt away from the sides."

"Are we going to lift the whole thing out?"

"Not the coffin. Just the contents. Keep digging."

We had to climb into the grave to reach the remaining dirt; it was packed more tightly and the going was slower. I wiped the sweat from my face and looked at Cybulski. The moonlight was just bright enough that I could see the disquiet in his eyes, a glint of the fear of the end of things we all carry inside. I resisted the urge to yell "Boo!" He stopped once to lean on his shovel and look nervously around, but we were the only entrepreneurs working the beat.

The low moon projected gnarled oak branches across the cemetery, exaggerating their reach. Stilled to lethargy by the muggy air, the branches gripped the earth with their shadows. The same chestnuts and pines that lent an atmosphere of tranquility during the day only deepened the darkness of night and created a low-lying layer of mystery.

Cars whizzed down nearby Alzeyerstrasse. Nocturnal creatures rustled among the pine needles, and once in a while a twig snapped or a pine cone fell. From across the cemetery we heard the faint wail of a grieving woman.

Footsteps crunching in the gravel, just a couple of rows away, made us freeze. We crouched and held our breath until they passed. When we stood up again, Cybulski's head darted to and fro, scanning the shadows for movement. He looked at me and swallowed hard.

We continued digging in silence. When we got the level down to the surface of the lid we brushed away the remaining soil with our hands.

"Good," I said. "Now hand me the crowbar."

Headlights flashed briefly across the cemetery.

"Down!"

The car hugged the fence, its lights illuminating the polished granites and marbles in rapid succession. The stones crowded the fence like convicts gazing forlornly through their cell bars. *Hier ruht in Gott,* HEIKO KAUFMANN, 1916-1990; *Unsere liebe Mutter,* SIGRID SPREYER, 1891-1990; *Der Herr nahm zu sich,* THOMAS WOLFF, 1950-1990. As the car turned the corner and drove out of sight we stood up from our crouched positions.

Cybulski handed me the crowbar. "This is the part I hate," he croaked.

"Funny. This is the part I like."

I nudged the hook of the crowbar between the lid and front side and pulled hard. The wood groaned and splintered.

Cybulski blurted, "Jimmy, I don't want to touch it."

"Why not?"

"It's got AIDS."

"It's dead!"

"Yeah, but it died of AIDS."

"Look, I brought you here to help me. If I didn't need you, I wouldn't have brought you. You can't stand there now and tell me you're not going to touch it."

"I did a lot of the digging. Isn't that enough?"

"No."

"Well, I'm not going to touch it."

"Then you're not going to get your cut."

I moved the hook of the crowbar to one side of the lid, then the other, jerking, splintering, until the lid was free.

"Maybe I could pull some on the rope," Cybulski said.

"Fine. You pull on the rope. I thought taking away your cut would change your mind."

"This is already the seventh one we've done. How long are we going to keep doing it?"

"What do you mean?"

"I mean, the law of diminishing returns. The more we get, the less each one is worth. Sooner or later we'll be caught."

"The law of diminishing returns," I repeated. I sat down on the lip of earth and rested my feet on the box. "Look, if it's worth doing the first time, it's worth doing the last time. It's worth doing *every* time. We have to take advantage of what we've got while we're stationed in Germany. Do you know how hard this is to do when the caskets are made of aluminum?"

"Oh Jesus, Jimmy."

"Besides, how could we possibly get caught?"

"Doesn't it give you the creeps?"

"Nope. I'm not hurting anybody. Least of all her."

I pushed myself back on the grass and kicked the lid open. It was funny how they looked so content in a place they'd so dreaded entering. This one was dressed in white satin. Her hands were clasped across her stomach. On one of her fingers was something glinting in the moonlight.

"God it stinks," Cybulski said. "Why don't they embalm the fuckers?"

"Hand me the flashlight."

"Here, it's all yours now."

"Check for ankle bracelets."

"Fuck you."

I shined the flashlight on her face. She had not been an attractive woman, even in her more animate days. Her nose was too long and her chin was recessed. Now the cheeks had sunken and the skin had dried and shriveled, promoting the apparent growth of facial hairs. Retracting lips exposed her front teeth; she looked like a snarling Chihuahua.

"Sleeping beauty," I said.

"Come on, Jimmy. Get on with it."

I slipped on a glove and stuck my finger in her mouth, pushing her lips up and away from her teeth and shining the flashlight around. Two gold teeth shined back at me.

"Jackpot," I said.

The glinty object on her hand was a common wedding band that slipped easily off her shriveled finger. I put it on my little finger, then checked the fingers of her other hand but there was nothing. I looked for earrings and necklaces. Nothing.

"Cheap bastards."

"Aren't you done yet?"

"The family owns a vineyard bigger than Vermont, for Christ's sake."

"Jimmy, *please.*"

"All right, all right. Let's take her out."

I scanned the woman once more. Particles of dirt had trickled into the coffin, soiling the white satin bedding. It didn't matter. She was vacating the premises.

"Do you need the rope?" Cybulski asked.

"Nah. She's real light. Come on, sweetie. We're going for a ride."

I lifted her out of the box and laid her on the grass next to the grave. "Close it," I ordered Cybulski, but he was already dropping the lid. He grabbed the shovel and tossed soil back in as fast as he could. I took the ring off and examined it in the moonlight.

"What was gold today, Chuck?"

"Jimmy . . ."

I put the ring back on, picked up my shovel, and helped Cybulski fill the hole. The moon continued to rise and the shadows grew shorter. Church bells rang from far off in the Altstadt. I checked my watch; it was four o'clock.

More of the cemetery's wooden crosses were visible now, posing like scarecrows. Row after row of headstones resembled a crowd in an open air arena. In the darkness I couldn't read the names on the stones, and the anonymity made the crowd seem like a mob.

Alone in a cemetery in the daytime you never get the feeling anyone else is around; everyone else in your immediate vicinity is dead. But at night you never convince yourself you're alone. The tombstones, innocuous by day, seem more alert, watchful, and somehow *present* at night.

We leveled off the surface and patted it down. Cybulski took the broom and swept the grass next to the stone, then hurriedly replaced the flowers.

The stone was easier to read now: HANNELORE SCHNEIDER, 1954-1990, *Dem Auge fern, dem Herzen ewig nah.* A pair of angels, naked but for flimsy marble cloths that barely covered their genitals, embraced the words like parentheses.

I picked up the woman and stood her on her feet. She was stiff and only needed balancing. Because her arms had been clasped and I had unclasped them, they projected awkwardly in front of her like a mannequin.

Cybulski picked up the tools and trudged back between the monuments to where the truck sat. I put my arm around the woman, lifted her a few inches, and followed him.

"Give us a kiss," I said, bumping into Cybulski.

"Stop it." He threw the tools in the back of the truck.

"Come on, give us a smooch."

"You morbid motherfucker." He went around and got in the passenger seat. I lifted the stiff and slid it into the truck like a board. Then I climbed into the driver's seat and started the engine. Cybulski stared sullenly out the window.

"You know," I said, "you can get AIDS just by looking up their skirts."

"Asshole. I didn't look."

"I *saw* you looking."

"I didn't, goddammit."

"Hey, I just thought of something. When you kick off I might be able to sell you to Dr. Fuchs too!"

"You're a piece of work, Jimmy."

"Got any dental problems I should know about?"

"A piece of fucking work."

*

I PARKED THE TRUCK in the empty AAFES gas station one block from the Kaserne gate, and Cybulski made a beeline for the barracks. He would have just enough time to take a shower and maybe eat breakfast before roll call. If I hurried I would have enough time to shine my boots.

I climbed into the back of the truck and turned on the battery-powered lamps. The woman exuded the sour odor of an orchard whose unpicked fruit has overripened. Using a chisel to pry her mouth open, I forced a couple of rubber erasers between her front chops to keep it open. Then I slid a roll of acetate under her neck to lean her head back. But the neck was too stiff to bend. It would have to do.

The flashlight revealed three gold teeth, not two. I wriggled them out with a pair of needle nose pliers and sealed them in an envelope.

All in all it had been a profitable night's work. I was happy; Cybulski was happy, whether he knew it or not; Dr. Fuchs would be happy when he took delivery of the stiff. The stiff was not any less happy than it had been the day before. I removed the erasers from its mouth and drove the truck to the university neurology clinic in Frankfurt.

Fuchs was already waiting at the ambulance entrance, his arms crossed, his weight shifting from one leg to another. "Do you never arrive anywhere on time?" he asked.

"Good morning to you too, Doc. How's the research going? Found a cure yet?"

"And must you always come in an army truck?"

I backed the truck into the entrance and Fuchs climbed into the rear to examine the stiff. He had long hair and crazed eyes that made him look like a stand-up comic impersonating a doctor.

"Okay," he said, and motioned to two assistants who put the stiff on a stretcher. Then he turned to me. "Several teeth are missing."

I shrugged. "Since when did you become a dentist?"

"You bring them as you find them. Lord knows what else you've done to her. Now get this truck out of here."

He turned to leave. I grabbed him by the arm and spun him around.

"Tell me again," I said. "What is it you cut out of their brains? The anal commissary, or something?"

"The anterior commissure. You idiot."

"Listen, fucker." I poked his chest with my finger. "You pay me. For the last one, too. Or someone'll be cutting out *your* anterior commissure. And shoving it back in through an entirely different opening."

Chapter 2

"YOU'RE LATE."

Sergeant First Class Pendergrass was always grumpy in the morning. By mid-day he was palatable and by late afternoon, when he'd sampled from a bottle of cherry-flavored brandy he kept in his desk drawer, you began to doubt the rumors he pulled wings off flies for fun.

"I was helping someone relocate."

"You can move furniture on your own time, we have a problem." He pointed behind me to the map board on which we had planned the next field exercise.

"What's the problem?"

"The Old Man wants different colors. Doesn't like orange and blue. Has this wild hair up his ass he wants orange changed to red and blue to green."

The Old Man had been nominated for a third star and was thus required to begin acting as if he already wore it, which meant more stupidly. He had mastered the eccentricities of a two-star and I was confident he would do justice to three and enjoy a clear shot all the way to chief of staff.

"That's no problem," I said. "I'll just redo the acetate."

"It's not that simple. Look."

He lifted the acetate and sure enough, Cybulski had drawn with his blue and orange markers directly on the map sheets. The whole job would have to be redone.

"Well," I said, "I guess what the Old Man *really* wants is to leave the colors the way they are now."

"What are you talking about?"

"He told me: leave them the way they are."

"When did he tell you that?"

"In ten minutes, when I get around to asking him."

Pendergrass laughed. "You're nuts."

"He likes me."

Pendergrass shook his head. "Like I said, you're nuts."

Sergeant Pendergrass had little right to accuse anyone of a mental disorder. When filled with enough cherry-flavored brandy he would claim he had traveled in time to the present from the near future. He was a capable enough sergeant, and with his fifties-style flattop and mug-handled ears, looked like one. Which was no doubt why he had been promoted to sergeant first class. But word was out on the time travel thing and he probably wouldn't be promoted again. You didn't get promotion points for time travel.

Once I asked him how it worked. He recited a proof of its theoretical possibility written by a mathematician named Kurt Gödel and explained that a Bell Labs mathematician had solved (*will* solve, mind you) the crucial nonlinear differential equations. A University of Illinois electrical engineer subsequently built the machine.

It was classified, naturally, but secrets like that could not stay secret, and soon every country was trying to make one, much as they did nuclear weapons after World War II. The White House was afraid that if others got "the device" they would use it to alter history and topple the American Empire.

For example. One might travel back to Valley Forge with a squad of fifty caliber machine gunners and turn George Washington into a leaky sieve. Of course, the United States Army would send an even bigger squad back in time to arrive even before the turn-George-Washington-into-a-leaky-sieve squad. Wars would spread in time as well as space. Who can possibly imagine what George Washington would think when he wakes up on the bank of the Potomac to find an A-10 strafing his horse?

I gave Pendergrass the benefit of the doubt for a time. But when he refused to share his knowledge of the next few Kentucky Derby winners and plainly failed to capitalize on that knowledge himself, I concluded his story was bullshit. If time travel ever became possible the technology would eventually become available to everyone, and every "now" would be filled with wing nut time tourists and anti-Darwinists coming back to set matters right. That Hitler wasn't smothered at birth is proof time travel is and always will be impossible.

"If you think you can get the Old Man to change his mind," Pendergrass said, "knock yourself out. Frankly, I think you're insane."

He knocked on Major Skelton's office door and asked the major to come out and give his opinion. The major's opinion didn't matter one way or another, but Pendergrass thought the man's rank earned him the right to consultation.

"Oh God," Skelton said, when he saw what Cybulski had done. "Oh shit." Major Wayne Skelton was a nervous and absentminded officer with a cadaverous face. His exclamations of dismay always contained the nomenclature of both divinity and excrement, as if to define the vast disparity between what ought and ought not be.

"What are we going to do?" Skelton asked.

"Fisher here is going to take care of it," Pendergrass said. "Unless you have another idea . . ."

"No no no. By all means, Fisher, take care of it."

"Yes sir. I appreciate your confidence, sir."

Skelton looked at his watch. "Where's Cybulski? Shouldn't he be in by now?"

"The replacement detachment has a roster of fresh meat," Pendergrass said. "I sent Cybulski over to pick out a new clerk for us. He should be back any minute."

"Oh?" Skelton raised his eyebrows. "Why wasn't I consulted about this? Doesn't a section OIC have something to say about the staffing of his section?"

"Of course, sir. I merely anticipated your wishes. You always pick the soldiers in the detachment with the highest aptitude scores, so I sent Cybulski to do just that. Surely he's competent enough, and you don't need the distraction. If you want us to cancel the selection . . ."

"No no no. By all means, allow Cybulski to take care of it."

"Yes sir," Pendergrass said. "I appreciate your confi-dence, sir."

Skelton went back into his office and glanced into his empty inbox, then sat down heavily in his chair.

"Cybulski knows what he's doing," Pendergrass whispered to me. "At least he did the first time he lived these events. Watch, he won't bring back a fag with earrings, like the last guy."

The "fag with earrings" had been the senior Plans clerk. No one, not even the clerk himself, knew why he got his port call two months early. Chuck Cybulski and I were junior Plans clerks. We were privates first class, and I was hoping Chuck wouldn't bring back a corporal because I wanted the job. In fact he would bring back whatever the replacement detachment gave him—whoever had the highest aptitude scores—which is why Pendergrass didn't bother doing the "selecting" himself.

Pendergrass gave me some routine filing jobs, then went into the war room to conceptualize, which is to say, to take a nap. I went down the hall, through the security doors, and asked the Old Man's secretary whether I could see him. While we were arguing about it the Old Man himself poked his head out and told me to come in.

Major General K. Carson Bundy's office smelled like it had been hosed down with furniture polish. He was an old foot soldier who preferred to spend his office hours in the field. The pencil holder, stapler, and memo pad on his desk were evenly spaced and perfectly lined up; they'd never been used.

On the wall behind him was an expensively framed crayon portrait of a balding man with a rim of white hair, round wire rim glasses, and a straight line across the face representing neither a smile nor a frown. This on the neck of a stick figure with a body that was disproportionately small under the head. The caption read "Grandpa." The portrait bore a striking resemblance to the man behind the desk.

"Come come come come come!" he said, pointing to a chair. "How are you, son?"

"Fine, sir. Fine fine fine."

"Good. Good!"

I got down to business. I tried to forget that the man before me could, if he got the itch, send forty thousand grunts to their deaths.

"Sir, I just wanted to commend your decision to change those colors from orange to red and from blue to green. It not only demonstrates your subtle artistic . . . flair . . . but the red is definitely more suggestive of a communist attack—or a counterattack against one, we won't quibble about that—and of course the red and green together having their own connotation which, it being the month of June—"

"Fisher."

"Sir?"

"You can leave them the way they were."

"Oh, thank you, sir. I appreciate your confidence."

"Was there anything else?"

"Yes sir, indeed there was."

13

I gave him my stock list of complaints. He had heard most of them before. He listened patiently, sometimes smiling. When you've made general you can take the corncob out of your ass. You have a limo and a driver and an aide and somebody to shine your boots and more pay, probably, than you can spend. You don't need to step on the people below you. Which explains why a junior enlisted grunt can have the breeziest conversations with the officers who outrank him the most.

That was then. Nowadays I have as much chance of redressing my grievances with a general as does a crab on the general's balls. For the United States Army had unwittingly concocted a simple recipe for getting its young soldiers in trouble:

Take one army private. Pay him less than minimum wage. House him in crowded barracks and exact ridiculously demanding standards of his housekeeping. Work him twelve hours a day, including weekends. Order him to clean latrines, scrub pots, and peel potatoes. Punish him for every minor infraction, and perceive everything he does as an infraction of something. *Then give him a security clearance.*

I'm a celebrity, I suppose. But my fortunes are entirely circumstantial. I didn't rise to an occasion so much as an occasion lowered itself to me.

Chapter 3

BACK AT THE PLANS office Cybulski was already showing the new guy the ropes.

His name was Shane Garrett. He had a strong, boyish face and intelligent eyes. His hair was more than an inch long, which was unusual, since he was fresh out of training. He was not, as Pendergrass had promised, wearing any earrings. Most importantly, the rank on his collar indicated he was a Private E2.

"Welcome to the monkey house," I said. "What kind of name is Shane?"

"My father's favorite novel," Shane Garrett answered. "And maybe his sense of humor, too."

"Anything in particular you want the greenie to do?" Cybulski asked me.

"No, you're doing fine."

Cybulski took two keys from Pendergrass's desk drawer and handed them to Garrett. "Here's a key to the inner door," he said. "And here's one to the padlock on the vault door. The vault door is locked at night, on weekends and holidays, and the inner door is locked at all times. You can open it from the inside by pressing this buzzer under the desk—after first looking through the window to see who's there."

Cybulski pressed the buzzer and Garrett nudged the door open. He smiled. When the buzzer stopped Garrett tried again and the door wouldn't open.

"It's low tech, but effective. There's also a combination lock on the vault door, the same kind you'll find on all the safes. We've programmed the combinations in a series to remember them more easily. The first two numbers are the same on every lock." He gave them to Garrett. "The third number varies for each lock, starting with seven on the vault door and increasing by increments of seven for each safe, top row first, right to left, then bottom row, left to right."

Garrett nodded.

"Okay," Cybulski said. "Open safe number nine."

Garrett walked over to the safes and mentally counted locks across the room, starting at the door. He turned the dial a few times and the safe door popped open.

"See?" Cybulski said. "You'll never forget them. And you don't have to write them down."

"What about the top secret safe?" Garrett asked.

"It's not in the sequence. Only Sergeant Pendergrass and Major Skelton have TS clearances, so only they know the TS combination."

This was true, theoretically, but Skelton had the memory of a gnat. Probably the TS safe combination was just another iteration in the sequence, but nobody but me suspected it because nobody but me believed field grade officers could be so careless about security or could have such poor memories. Skelton often forgot how to open the safes and had to ask me to open them for him, even in front of the Old Man. I always pretended the drawer was stuck and made jokes about uncooperative inanimate objects to avoid embarrassing the major. The truth was, Skelton had a mental disability: he was an officer.

*

IT WAS TIME TO take Garrett down to the basement for a security clearance. The moment we entered the G2 executive office, Colonel Leslie "Redeye" Riddell cleared the top of his desk as if to make room for something important. Garrett sat attentively in front of the desk with his knees close together. I had a sudden fear, and dismissed it, that Riddell would ask him point blank whether he'd ever had sex with animals.

Riddell tapped his fingers. He'd lost part of the ring finger of his left hand in a freak grenade accident, and since that was the hand he tapped with, the rhythm was disrupted by the periodic soft pat of the stump. The effect was not a soothing one; the interviewee became mesmerized by the stump, which wiggled in turn with its companions, like the runt of the litter trying to keep up. Riddell's face had a peculiar lumpy quality, as though it had once been flattened by a truck and subsequently reinflated with a tire pump.

"Have you ever fucked a sheep?" Riddell asked Garrett.

The boy leaned forward impulsively. "Sir?"

"You can't get a clearance if you've done it with animals. Well?"

"Ah, sir, I can assure you I have never had sex with an animal. However, I'm told by some that my last girlfriend was something of a dog."

The attempt at humor was in vain. Riddell had been staring more or less absentmindedly at the top of his desk, but now his head rotated slowly upwards and he leveled his porcine glare on the boy.

"Druggie?"

"No sir."

"Faggot?"

"No sir."

"Love your country?"

"Yes sir."

"Would you turn your grandmother in if you caught her shoplifting?"

No one, not even the most scrupulous of men, would turn his grandmother in if he caught her committing an illegal act. But Garrett had gotten the gist of the interview and answered without hesitating.

"Yes sir. In a heartbeat."

"Excellent."

The interview thus over, only the paperwork remained. The candidate was required to explain his whereabouts and activities for the past ten years. Theoretically, security personnel would then comb his background, corroborate his statements, and interview his former neighbors in the mobile home park, even the fat ones in sweaty t-shirts whose cars were hopelessly disassembled in the yard. In practice, however, there were too many people applying for security clearances and too few investigators to conduct background checks, so the candidates below top secret got a cursory glance at best. I was putting Garrett in for secret, which was all he would need to do his job. Probably they would run a routine FBI check and that would be that. Which is why we went ahead and gave him access to the Plans office before his clearance came through: it would come through regardless of what his third grade teacher thought of him.

"By the way, Fisher," Riddell said. "The tactical assembly area you gave Echo Company, it's under water."

Echo Company was the military intelligence battalion's electronic collection and jamming company. It was a pet of Riddell's.

"I admit it's a little damp in that neck of the woods," I said.

"It's a fucking swamp."

"There is some high ground," I said. "It's not all swamp."

"There isn't enough high ground to support a jeep, and you know it."

"Sir, the plan's finished, the acetate's all marked up, the tracings are done. I think it's a little late to suggest changes."

"Suggest, your ass. You did that to me on purpose, because you enjoy pissing me off. You stay up all night trying to figure out new ways to piss me off. What's it going to be tomorrow?"

"Now, sir . . ."

"Tell me!" His eyes bulged out of their fleshy folds. "Tell me *now* so I can prepare myself for it. I got your goddamn tracings minutes before you walked in here. No shit it's a little late to 'suggest' a change. You didn't supply a scratch-n-sniff with your plan, so I have to find a cow pasture somewhere in which to read it."

"Sir, what is it you want me to do? The general has already signed off on it."

He closed his eyes. The wrinkles on his face smoothed out. Either he was calming down or his head was expanding with hot gas. "I want you to look at this," he said. "You see this?" He pointed at the rank on his collar.

"Yes sir, I see it."

"You know what it means?"

"I do." It meant he was a colonel.

He pointed to a patch above his shirt pocket. "You see this? You know what this means?"

I did. It was his master parachute badge, something of which he was infinitely proud. It meant he was a fool, one of only two things that fall out of the sky. The other being birdshit.

"Get the hell out of here."

As we retreated down the hall Garrett said, "He's an unhappy man."

I nodded. "He's an officer. But he's right about one thing. I'm going to have to stay up late tonight trying to figure out how to piss him off again tomorrow."

19

Chapter 4

THERE WAS NOTHING ELSE for me and Cybulski to do now but take Garrett out and get him fermented. As Beetle Baileys such behavior was expected of us, and we were not about to start a revolution. We went to the Netz 14, a popular American hangout, and ordered Hefeweizen. You can get drunk on this beer, and because the yeast isn't filtered, you can get sick too. Cybulski, Garrett, and I did both.

Garrett told us his theory about Aristotle's urine. Aristotle, Garrett said, had lived a long life and throughout that life had of course urinated many times. The total volume of his urine was unknown, but it could be estimated and was nevertheless sizeable. More to the point, the number of molecules in that volume was astronomical. The molecules had in the two millennia since Aristotle's death been dispersed around the earth, via evaporation and precipitation, via the water table and the rivers and oceans. Thus there was a statistical likelihood that at least one of the molecules was contained in the beer we were drinking.

"Think about it," Garrett said. "What you're pouring down your throat right now was once pissed onto the ground by Aristotle."

"God, that's deep," Cybulski said.

"The interconnectedness of things is awesome, ain't it?"

I nodded sagely. "Fuckin-A."

"Want another one?"

"Not yet. Talking about piss makes me need to take one."

"Well, why don't you?"

"I'm not sure I can stand up. I'm afraid if I do I'm going to be sick."

"Don't talk about sickness," Cybulski said.

"Beer always makes me sick," I said. "It always wants to come back up. I don't think it's going to wait for me to take a piss. I think it's on its way now."

"Don't talk about it. When you talk about it, it makes me sick."

"I never could drink Weizen in quantity. Everything I put into my stomach comes right back out."

"I told you—don't talk about it."

"I've even had it spew out through my nose."

Cybulski leaned over and got sick on the floor. It came out in a transparent golden stream, slightly frothy, as if it were being poured from the tap. I laughed at him and called him a pussy. Then I got sick too. So did Garrett. Since we were all drinking the same thing, our respective sicknesses were not differentiable on the floor.

Garrett said he had to go piss some Aristotle. He stood up, slipped in the puddle of sickness, and fell.

"Help me," he said.

"No," I said. "I don't want to get it on me."

But I had to get up too, because I couldn't hold my Aristotle any longer, and when I tried to walk I slipped and fell alongside him. Cybulski lent me a hand, which I used to pull him down to the floor. The three of us then contributed additional volume to the mess while kneeling in it, retching like dogs that had swallowed too much grass.

21

"Where can a guy get horizontal refreshments around here?" Garrett asked.

"There's Amy's," I told him, "across from the barracks."

He stood up shakily, suds dripping from his elbows. "Let us not tarry."

*

CYBULSKI AND I HAD to help Garrett up the groaning staircase. The girls' rooms were on the second floor, on either side of a long hallway painted solid pink and furnished with second-hand church pews. We sat on a pew and waited for one of the doors to open. After a few minutes a drunken sergeant stumbled from a room at the end of the hall. He passed us, oblivious to our presence, his fingertips scraping the wall to guide his path. Remaining in the doorway of the room was an excruciatingly pretty girl adjusting her skirt. She smiled at us.

"That'll do," Garrett said.

Cybulski and I had to dig the change out of our pockets because the whore required an extra ten bucks to work without a raincoat.

"There's none that will fit me," Garrett slurred contemptuously.

"You'll be lucky to get it up at all," I warned him.

As soon as the door had closed behind Garrett and his whore, Cybulski tucked in his shirt meticulously, inspected a couple of soil flecks on his sleeve, then leaned out the window and rent the night calm with wracking heaves.

It would be a while before Cybulski was in any condition to go home, and before Garrett was in any mood. So I went down to the other end of the hall and took a peek into Melina's room. Melina was my regular whore, the one to whom I was steadfastly faithful, unless she happened to be absent, in which case I fucked one of the others. I found her alone, leaning over her vanity with her face in her hands, crying.

"What's the matter, sweetie? Did somebody hurt you?"

She shook her head and wiped her eyes. "I went to confession today. The priest told me I was damned because I'm a whore."

"Is that all?"

"Don't diss this one, Johnny. It's serious."

"Jimmy."

"Jimmy, sorry. The church is important to me. I grew up in the church."

"It's just that, in this country whoring is *legal*."

"Yeah, and most politicians are going to roast in Hell for all the legal acts they've committed."

She had me there. Melina was a spunky brunette with big brown eyes, full lips, and a deep throat. She could take three guys at once, with room left over for politicians.

"But listen," I said. "You just told me you went to confession. Doesn't that mean your past is erased?"

"Not according to the priest. It only means my *future* will be clean if I stop scrogging. My past stays like it is—and it's enough to do me. I've been busting my head over this all evening."

"But your past isn't so bad. Shit, honey, I know more whores than I do officers. And I'd rather have the company of a whore, any day."

"Yeah? And how many whores do you know get down on their knees in the HHC day room, with all the company-grade officers lined up to make a deposit?"

"You confessed that to the priest?"

She blew her nose and nodded.

"No wonder he thinks you're damned."

She started crying again. I made her sit down and poured her a shot of Jägermeister from a bottle she kept in the nightstand. After a couple of minutes I got some leverage on the problem. I said:

23

"Answer me this. How much money do you suppose you've made doing all that scrogging?"

"I don't know. I don't keep books, or anything. Figure, ten or so scrogs a day for the last five years, at twenty bucks a scrog. What's that come to?"

I did some calculating. "Upwards of four hundred thousand dollars."

"Holy shit!"

"Here's my point: it isn't the *scrogging* that will send you to Hell. It's the *money* you got for doing it. That's what makes it whoring. It stands to reason, then, that all you have to do is give the money back."

Her eyes narrowed and she took a deep drag from her cigarette. Her nose was still running but she appeared to have gotten the worst of it out of her system. Finally I asked:

"Well?"

"Well, I don't have the money no more, that's all."

"You didn't save any of it?"

"No."

"Real estate? Mutual funds? Dow Jones industrials?"

"No."

"Just how much do you have?"

She opened her purse and emptied it into her lap. $1.77 and a couple of Marks in change, a cigarette butt with quite a bit left on it to smoke, and a dozen or so raincoats.

I asked, "What were you going to do for dinner?"

She folded her arms in an obvious attempt to conceal the needle marks.

I poured us both another Jägermeister. This was going to take some head busting, all right. You don't just pick up four hundred thousand dollars off the street. And if you did, you'd be one pious motherfucker to give it all to the church merely to stay out of Hell for eternity. Then an answer came to me.

"Look here," I said. "All you got to do now is scrog ten times a day for the next five years, for free, and that will cancel out all the scrogging you did during the last five years."

"It wouldn't cancel everything out, it would only reduce the average. It would mean I'd have scrogged ten times a day for ten years, and only made money for the first five. No amount of free scrogging would get it all the way down to nothing. And no self-respecting whore would take less than twenty bucks. So there's that damage as well."

"What if you continue to scrog, for twenty bucks, and give it all to the church?"

"How will I pay the rent?"

"You work overtime and increase your scrog rate. You keep enough scrog money to live on and give the rest to the church. Say, scrog fifteen, keep ten, and donate five. Donating five scrogs a day to the church, you'll need only ten years to pay it back for the last five."

"But then the scrogging I do for myself will be just the same as the scrogging that got me into this mess in the first place."

"Dammit, girl, you're making this hard. Do you want to stay out of Hell, or don't you?"

She started crying again.

"Oh, for Christ's sake, Melina."

"Wait a minute!" She jumped up, her face all lit up and wet. "What if I scrog fifteen, keep five, donate five, and do five for free? In ten years, the five scrogs per day that I donate to the church will pay it back for the last five years of scrogging, like you said, and the five I do for free will cancel out the five I keep."

I didn't want to put a damper on things, but I had to test the theory. "Can you live on only five scrogs a day?"

She thought about that. "I know. I'll make my first even-ing customer buy me cigarettes and dinner at McDonald's. It's the only regular meal I eat anyway. I don't think the church will mind."

"No, the church has to bend a little, too."

"Is it okay that the first one be an officer? They're more likely to take me to dinner."

"No. No officers."

"Okay, no officers."

That settled it. We went over to the bed, and after considerable negotiation about whether this one was a keeper, a donation, a freebie, or a dinner, we settled on a freebie on account of my helping her with her dilemma. Getting dressed afterwards was awkward, as the payment ritual was missing. She was fidgety and didn't know what to do with her hands. I told her she'd get used to it; I'd be by now and then to volunteer.

*

BACK AT THE BARRACKS, Cybulski and I dumped an unconscious Garrett onto his bed with his boots on. Then I had to steer Cybulski toward his room. The alcohol made him walk in circles with ever-shortening radii. Once in bed he opened a fresh bottle of beer. He said, "I'm a mite parched," took a long swig, and fell asleep immediately when his head hit the pillow. The bottle dropped to his side and emptied into the mattress.

I lit a cigarette and checked the view from his window. Amy's lamp cast a red glow on the sidewalk across the street. Clouds blotted out the stars, and a low rumble came from somewhere in the distance.

It had been years since I'd been to church. I'd entered on a whim and sat down in the rearmost pew. Nothing much was happening. About a thousand candles were burning; they seemed to be doing all the work. A handful of nuns occupied the pews, spread apart like they couldn't stand the smell of one another, muttering to themselves and fiddling incessantly with beads. I struggled to reconcile how this activity would impress God so goddamn much, whereas Melina's talents, which had earned her no small amount of respect in the community, would send her to Hell. It occurred to me that not going to church for the past five years might send *me* to Hell, and that if I started going now it would only reduce the average. On the other hand, the church owed me for saving a whore from certain damnation. All things considered, my account should have been balanced.

I was just putting out my cigarette and turning to leave when it began to rain.

"*Laus perennis,*" Cybulski muttered.

"What's that?" I asked. "Are you praying?"

He was quiet for a moment, then he spoke in a voice almost too low for me to hear: "There's nothing you can do about it. You can't alter your fate."

He was lying stiffly on his back with his feet pressed together and his hands clasped over his stomach. "Do about what?" I asked. "What are you talking about?"

But he was already asleep again. The rain came down in a torrent, and the noise of the big drops hitting the roof and the parked cars drowned out his snoring. They were warm rains, those that fell heavily in the late German spring. You could smell them, dense and moist, seconds before they came.

Chapter 5

DTG/Releaser Time 150800Z JUN 90
Precedence RR
Class UUUU
Orig/Msg Ident 1660830Z

U N C L A S S I F I E D NOFORN EYES ONLY

EYES ONLY//EYES ONLY//EYES ONLY//EYES ONLY

For: MG K. Carson Bundy, Cdr, 111th ID(M), Bad Karst,
Germany
From: LTG Roger Samson, ACofS, Operations,
Washington, D.C.

*Kit, I'm going to make it on time after all. In fact, I think a day
early. Margie wants to go to Prague again to do some shopping.
Like we need another hunk of crystal. Or one of those goddamn
impasto oil paintings. Margie's coming over MAC, but I'm getting a ride from an Air Force major, Barstow is his name, in a
new F-16 trainer he's delivering to Spangdahlem. He owes me a*

favor (I'll tell you about that one some other time). In Spangdahlem he's picking up an old F-16 for donation to a guard unit somewhere in Conus. Which is okay with the Air Force, he says, because they've x-rayed the airframe and it's got structural weaknesses.

Last time I got a ride overseas with Barstow we had I don't know how many refuelings and he couldn't wait so he crapped in his helmet carrying bag. After we landed at Mildenhall he dropped the bag in a dumpster and the customs peon almost cuffed us on the spot for suspected smuggling. That is, until he had a look in the bag—and got a whiff of it too.

I still don't know how I'm going to get my tackle there, the pole doesn't come apart, and Barstow doesn't think he can strap it to the underside of the plane, aerodynamics and all that. Kit, see where I can buy a new one in Germany, will you? One that comes apart. I'm glad this isn't a goddamn ski trip. If Joe Taxpayer knew what we were doing with his money he'd shit a brick. God I love being a general.

By the way, I've got a Beetle Bailey on his way to you to deliver a TS document the spooks want to store in your vault. I don't know what's in the document, and neither does the Beetle Bailey. Probably the spooks don't even know themselves. Maybe it's another one of those Castro things. Whatever. You're to keep it sealed and locked in your vault.

See you in a week. Keep a stiff one. Give my regards to Patricia. Don't forget the fishing pole.

Roger

*

THE MORNING THE DOCUMENT arrived was spent like many others: getting out of cleaning details while the barracks prepared for inspection. Not sweeping and mopping the hallway cost me two packs of cigarettes. Not scrubbing and hosing the showers cost me three. Not removing the lint from the dryers cost me one, which was too high a price to pay for so little effort, but protecting my record as a goldbricker was worth the expense.

"Ten-hut!"

Top entered my room, followed by Captain Ralph Brannigan, the new company commander. Brannigan ignored me at first and instead inspected the room while I stood at attention in front of my open wall locker. He had a crew cut and strong, athletic features, and although I had never seen pictures of his father or grandfather when they were in the army, I was sure he looked just like them. I wanted to impress Brannigan, a West Point graduate whom I was meeting for the first time, because I was up for promotion to corporal.

I had experienced a moment of panic, minutes before the inspection, when I discovered my TA-50 was missing. I couldn't for the life of me remember what I'd done with it. I knew better than to admit my loss to the captain, so I visited the laundry room, and in one of the drying machines, labeled "no TA-50" like all the others, was a personal set of web gear and canteen covers, spic and span and practically dry. On the floor next to the dryer were the rest of the components; someone had been overhauling his TA-50 before the inspection and had evidently gone back to his room to wait for the covers to dry. It would turn out to be a mistake.

TA-50 was combat field gear that included steel pot, sleeping bag, entrenching tool, and the like, as well as articles that hung from the webbing and utility belt: canteens, ammunition pouches, first aid kit, and so on. TA-50 was worthless in peacetime but we wore it to get used to wearing it. You wouldn't want your Beetle Baileys fumbling awkwardly with their TA-50 during a battle just because they were trying it on for the first time.

Captain Brannigan checked for dust on the windowsill while Top stood by with a clipboard. He lifted a corner of the rug and squinted at the floor. He examined each item in my store-bought mess kit, wrinkling his nose.

You never displayed your supply-furnished mess kit for inspection because it wouldn't pass, and you never cooked in your store-bought mess kit because it would get dirty. The army still believed the whole of its battle readiness was the sum of its countless trivial parts. Just like the classic story of the missing horseshoe nail that caused the loss of a war, a dirty mess kit was, according to army thinking, the first in a phenomenally unlikely sequence of failures that might somehow lead to the decline and fall of the American Empire. This way of thinking may have been relevant in a day when weapons were simple and discipline was a problem, but it had little relevance in a day when five-hundred-pound bombs fell from the sky and killed indiscriminately: all Beetle Baileys, those whose forks were clean as well as those who'd missed a spot, got blown into their constituent atoms.

Brannigan looked long and hard at my dress shoes placed neatly at the bottom of the locker, just given a fresh coat of liquid wax as I saw him coming down the hall. He stuck his lower lip out and nodded approvingly.

"Your field jacket is missing its zipper pull string," he said.

"Sir, that's always the first thing to go."

"I'm aware of that, private. See that you get it fixed. Today."

"Yes sir."

Brannigan was about to leave when he hesitated and looked into my eyes.

"Private Fisher."

"Sir?"

"Open your duffel bag."

Wearing my most crestfallen look, I grabbed the bottom of the bag and lifted it, spilling its contents onto the floor. A half-dozen bottles of beer tumbled out amid a pile of filth-stiffened socks and underwear.

Brannigan turned to Top: "Three days extra duty." Top made a note on his clipboard.

"Private Fisher, you're up for corporal, aren't you?"

"Just waiting for a board to convene, sir."

"As long as you are assigned to the 111th Infantry Division you will comport yourself with dignity. Otherwise there will be consequences. Do I make myself clear?"

"Crystal clear, sir."

"I'm told you're a valuable asset to the Plans office."

"I do my best, sir."

"Extend that effort to your domestic affairs."

"Yes sir. Thank you, sir. I appreciate your confidence, sir."

Brannigan left the room and continued down the hall to the next one. Top finished making his notes, shook his head sadly at me, and followed.

*

THE DOCUMENT ARRIVED, AS all top secret documents did, in a plain brown envelope. It struck me as funny that objects so mundane as specks of ink on plant fiber could prevent—or launch—events so calamitous as wars.

We stored hundreds of documents in the Plans vault, including some odd ones, such as those that gave battle instructions to the division should a space shuttle crash in our zone and be captured by foreign armies or terrorists. We stored general defense plans for all units in the division and for other units with which we would have to coordinate during war. We stored documents detailing the location and use of nuclear weapons.

This document, labeled Oplan 2357-90, was sealed with warnings not to be opened—by anyone. Pendergrass and I signed for it, and the courier watched as we put it in the safe.

"Someone will be by for it in a few weeks," the courier said.

"Whatever," I replied.

The courier was not happy with my remark and was about to lock me up when Pendergrass said, "That will be all, sergeant."

As soon as the courier left Pendergrass said, "You'd better lay low for a while. CID is cracking down on entrepreneurs."

"I don't know what you're talking about."

"Of course you don't. Just be careful from now on."

"Tell me, sergeant, since you're from the future: if, hypothetically, I peddle some wares tonight, will CID be watching me?"

He thought about it. "No, not tonight. What happens to you happens later."

"Nothing happens tonight?"

He hesitated. "You get laid. But not arrested."

The door buzzed and Colonel Riddell's face appeared in the window.

"Computer," I said, "end program!"

"Let him in," Pendergrass ordered.

"Danger, Will Robinson!"

The buzzer sounded again, repeatedly and impatiently, until Pendergrass wearily came over to the desk and pressed the button to unlock the door.

Riddell walked straight up to me. "Don't fuck with me," he said.

I shook my head vigorously. "Wouldn't think of it, sir."

"What just came in?" he asked.

"A document."

"I gathered that, private. What's in it?"

"I'm sorry, sir, but you are going to have to demonstrate a need to know."

"I'm the fucking G2 OIC. Therefore I have a need to know. Now quit obstructing and let me see it."

Pendergrass stepped in then and said, "Sir, it's sealed. No one can see it, not even us."

Riddell glared at me. "You could have told me that to begin with."

"Must have slipped my mind, sir."

He turned to leave. "You better hope you never get assigned to my section, son. You'll be scrubbing the carpets in my office with your pubic hair."

You better hope you never end up working for me, either, I thought. Most colonels, when they retire, land in jobs that provide nowhere near the authority, responsibility, or salary they enjoyed when they were active duty. On the other hand, many privates get out of the army, go to school, and eventually become important people. And it isn't hard to become more important than a retired colonel; I know some short order cooks who have succeeded.

Riddell's one redeeming asset was his daughter, a meltingly pretty teenager who had a part time job at the base library. Before I got to know Riddell I hung out at the library, checking out authors like Fyodor Dostoyevsky to impress her. Only to learn from talking to her that the space between the sun and the planet Pluto was but a whisker's breadth next to the colossal void inside her head. Which of course was fine with me.

By the time I'd gotten to know Riddell better I'd come to learn that the truest, most definitive suffering you could imagine would be yours for the banging of his baby girl. Mattingly banged her and bragged about it, and Mattingly ended up in the concertina wire after he was anonymously pushed off the roof of the Division Tactical Operations Center. It took them forty-five minutes to cut him out. It took the surgeons a year, I heard, to rebuild his dick.

When Riddell was gone Pendergrass asked, "Why do you always give him the big brown cloud?"

"He's an officer," I said. "I loathe him."

But I wish I'd given him the plan, instead of the cloud. I wish I'd given everyone the plan. I wish I'd stapled copies of the plan to every bulletin board in the building. I'd have been punished for it, severely. But no punishment could possibly compare to what was in store for me now.

*

THAT EVENING CYBULSKI AND I met in his room. He opened the closet for me. It was filled about one-third of the way up from the floor with cigarettes.

"How many cartons?" I asked him.

He told me.

"How many Marlboros? How many menthols?"

He knew that too.

"Let me see the receipts."

I shuffled through the stack, mentally checking off contributors. Each contributor had a ration card that allowed the purchase of four cartons a month. A pack of cigarettes cost a quarter in the commissary, if bought by the carton, and four Marks in the German cigarette machines. At the exchange rate of the time that was about a dollar sixty. We sold them for two Mark fifty in the bars in town.

"Where's Pierce's?" I asked.

"He's smoking them. He started again."

"Chadwick's?"

"Couldn't find him. I think he's hiding from us."

"They aren't moving very well," I said.

"You know why, don't you? There's a guy at Discom who's gotten into the business. He's selling at the back gate."

"I know about him. CID will get him before long."

"Jimmy, if we sold at the gate we could triple our sales."

"Yeah, and then CID would get us too. Let's stick to what we do. It's safer." I kicked around among the cigarettes. "How much gas we got?"

He told me: about four hundred liters. It was in a trailer in the motor pool.

"That isn't moving either, is it?"

"The canisters are too big to lug around."

I grabbed a laundry bag and filled it with cigarettes. "Come on," I said, "we'll work the Canape tonight. We'll have to find a way to unload the gas in bulk."

"We won't get as much for it."

"But at least we'll get something. By the way, you're delivering the gold teeth to Schäfer."

"Why me?"

"Let's just say, you have some makeup work to earn your keep." I handed him a piece of paper. "Take this. It's got the price written on it. If Schäfer doesn't give you that price, bring the stuff back." I reached into my pocket and handed him the envelope containing the teeth.

He looked at the paper. "You sure this is what you want to do? He's never paid this much before."

"I'm sure. Put the money in your mattress. I'll be by later tonight to split it."

"Does it have to be tonight?"

"He's expecting one of us. And Chuck?"

"What."

"Don't let him push you around."

We drank a few glasses of bourbon to oil ourselves up before going out to a bar where the drinks were more expensive. Afterwards I checked the hall to make sure no one was coming, then led Cybulski to the stairs. We looked like a pair of Santa Clauses with the laundry bags slung over our shoulders.

"We could break his legs," Cybulski suggested over his free shoulder.

"Whose?"

"That guy working the back gate."

"Ha. You know what that sounds like, coming from you? You, who would carry a spider outside to save its life?"

"Just trying to be a good businessman."

"Leave that kind of business to the Mafia."

"By the way," he said, "your TA-50 is still in the truck."

"My what?"

"Your TA-50. You left it there after the last field exercise."

I frowned at him. "I'm afraid you're mistaken. My TA-50 is in my wall locker, where it belongs. It passed inspection this morning."

"Then whose is it?"

"How the hell should I know?"

"Well, it's a good thing, I guess. Because somebody stole mine out of the laundry room. And if I ever catch the bastard—"

"You'll beat the living piss out of him, right?"

"Actually, I was sort of hoping you'd do it for me."

"Gladly, my friend. Find the guy, and I will."

Chapter 6

THE CANAPE WAS A subterranean loading zone under one of the dirty brick buildings on Bleichstrasse. It was a good place to get lucky. Cybulski preferred it over the other bars because the girls who patronized the place were better looking, which meant, as is generally the case, the men were better looking too. Cybulski liked men, and he liked getting lucky. As far as I was concerned, the uglier the men were, the better.

Cybulski also liked animals, but not for the same reason. He liked them so much that his goal in life was to rescue them from the laboratories of cosmetic companies and start a sanctuary call Beast Haven for all the furry orphans and refugees. Somehow this suited him; he had droopy eyes and walked like a tortoise on two legs. I could see him in my mind's eye, a kind of reptilian Moses, wearing a bed sheet and holding a staff, leading one hundred and one Dalmatians to the Promised Land.

As we entered the Canape we found Shane Garrett at the bar, so we joined him. He wore a crooked grin and his elbows kept sliding off the edge of the bar. He raised a glass to toast our arrival, spilling some of its contents into his lap.

Cybulski handed his laundry bag to me and sat down next to a good looking blond with fresh, smooth skin and a narrow waist who was drinking a high-ball with a straw. The blond introduced himself as Hansi and promptly bought Cybulski a drink.

I took the last empty stool and ordered an Apfelkorn. The bartender sighed heavily, then held up a half-empty bottle for me to see.

"This is all I have left," he said. "Nobody drinks the stuff anymore. It is, as they say, out. When this bottle is empty I will have no more. Do not ask for it again."

"You could buy more," I said.

"No. You are the only one who drinks it, and you do not come here often. You apparently prefer to spend your money in other establishments. No doubt they are fine and noble establishments, but still they are not this establishment."

"I'll buy some then, and supply you with it."

"No. It is out. When this bottle is empty there will be no more."

The man sitting next to me, one with a dark, closely-cropped beard and an earring, leaned over and spoke: "The Netz still carries it. Do you know the Netz?"

I nodded and leaned away. Cybulski had snubbed this one for the smooth-skinned blond.

The bartender said, "But does the Netz have specimens so fine as these?" He tilted his head toward a pair of women sitting together at a table. We turned to look. One of the women was a tall redhead with a strong, pretty face and just a few freckles. Her hair, parted in the middle, was lustrous in the dim light. She had been looking at me while smoking a cigarette, but now pretended otherwise. Her friend, a good looking brunette, continued to stare.

"Oh, tuna fish," the bearded man said.

"They are Amerikans," the bartender informed me.

"How do you know?"

"I overheard them talking. Maybe you should go over and introduce yourself, as you are their fellow countryman."

The redhead glanced at me again, then quickly looked away. The brunette locked eyes and smiled.

"The dark haired one is from Iowa," the bartender said, smug in doling out his knowledge. "They grow corn there, the kind you feed to cows and pigs."

A balding man at the other end of the bar, who until now had not said anything, said, "Excuse me, but I am afraid you have badly mispronounced a word." He said it with exaggerated politeness.

"What word is that?" the bartender asked.

"You said 'Iowa,'" the balding man explained, "and I happen to know the correct pronunciation is 'Ohio.' I do not mean to be rude, but I did not want you to embarrass yourself in front of the Amerikans here."

Suddenly even the small conversations at the bar halted as everyone watched to see what would develop. Garrett came over and stood behind me. Cybulski and his friend used the opportunity to leave together.

"I believe it is you who are mistaken," the bartender said. "You are mispronouncing the English word. It is pronounced 'Iowa.' That is precisely how the women pronounced it. If the word were pronounced 'Ohio' no doubt they would have said 'Ohio.' Instead, they did not. They said 'Iowa.' There is no such place as 'Ohio.'"

"You think not?"

"I am certain of it."

The bartender looked at me and raised his eyebrows. I nodded my assent. His expression relaxed into confidence and relief.

"Iowa," the bartender said loudly. "Imagine being so unsophisticated as to think it is called 'Ohio.'"

"Think what you want," the balding man said. "It does not change the truth. The state is pronounced 'Ohio,' and neither your opinion nor your insulting tone will change the truth."

Garrett nudged me with his elbow as if to say, Watch this. He cleared his throat and said, "The truth of the matter is, the state is pronounced 'Iowa.' I happen to know, because I grew up in the bordering state of Ar-Kansas."

The Ohio-man frowned. "You mean Kansas, do you not?"

"No," the bartender said, picking up the cue. "He means *Ar-Kansas*. Can you not hear?"

"There is no such place. I have traveled extensively in Amerika, and have never heard of it."

"Indeed there is such a place," Garrett said, "whether you who have never heard of Iowa have heard of it. Kansas and *Ar-Kansas*. They are two different states."

"Like North Dakota and South Dakota," the bartender said. "Like West Virginia and East Virginia." He looked to me again for confirmation.

"It's true," I admitted. "There is a state called 'Ar-Kansas.'"

"Oh, you mean *Arkansas*," the Ohio-man said.

"Don't you think we know how to pronounce our states?" Garrett asked.

"Oh, come now," the Ohio-man said. "You're not suggesting it's pronounced Ar-Kansas."

"Suppose I am suggesting it," Garrett said, a little too aggressively.

"Yes," the bearded man chipped in. "Suppose he is." He had been watching the exchange as though it were a boxing match.

"Have you ever been there?" the bartender asked the Ohio-man.

"Well, no."

"Then you don't know how the Ar-Kanasians pronounced their state, do you?"

The Ohio-man shook his head. "You dumb fools."

41

"Who're you calling dumb fools?" Garrett asked him quietly.

"Take a look in the mirror, my young friend, and ask yourself what it is that looks back."

The bartender was beaming. "Who ever said geography was boring?" He mumbled something about getting another bottle of Apfelkorn for the bar. I placed the two laundry bags of cigarettes on the counter and told him I had a business proposition. He looked inside the bags and asked, "How much?"

"Two Mark fifty."

He tapped the counter with his finger. "You leave them right here."

I looked back at where the two women were sitting. The redhead was pointedly ignoring me. The brunette, still smiling at me, got up and went to the bathroom.

Garrett was watching me watch them. He said, "You set your sights high, don't you?"

"Do I? I'm a sucker for red hair and freckles. Besides, I think I've just found the girl I'm going to marry."

He nodded approvingly. "She's pokeworthy."

"Hey, don't talk about my fiancée like that."

"What's your fiancée's name?"

"I'll find out. Meantime, you'd better be careful. That bald-headed dumbfucker looks like he means to kick the shit out of you."

I picked up the bottle of Apfelkorn and my shot glass and walked over to the redhead's table. I hadn't kept track of my drinks at the bar; the bottle was almost empty. Clearly I'd had one too many, counting the bourbons in Cybulski's room, because on my way to the table I began a roller coaster ride that would only get worse as the alcohol flooded my bloodstream. I made it to the table, bumped into the brunette's vacant chair as the room banked on a curve, and managed to sit down.

"Hello?" the redhead said. "Excuse me?"

"I was sitting at the bar," I told her, "and couldn't help noticing that you have the loveliest red hair I have ever seen in my life."

"How sweet of you." She smiled. "But I'm sorry, that chair is taken. If you don't mind."

"I don't mind." I got up and moved over to another chair, one that was closer to her.

"Was there something else?" she asked.

"Yes, thank you for asking. If you would be so kind as to give me your name and telephone number. I'm afraid that without them I might never see you again, and that would be a tragedy."

She smiled again. The smoke in the bar had made the room hazy, and the effect combined with the bourbon and Apfelkorn diffused her face.

"Now don't tell me you don't have a girlfriend," she said. "Surely someone as handsome as you must have a girlfriend."

"I *had* a girlfriend," I said, "until a few weeks ago, when I dumped her."

"How long did you have her?"

I counted on my fingers. "Three," I said.

"So, after three years—"

"No, weeks."

"—after three weeks you dumped her because . . ."

"I thought probably she was going to dump me."

"Oh. What evidence did you have for this?"

"Well, it was difficult piecing it together at first, it took some detective work, let me tell you. But I think the final clue, the one that connects all the others, was when I came home from work one day and found the lock changed and all my clothes and things on the lawn."

"So," she said, "having caught wind of something, you decided to dump her."

"It was the only humane thing to do."

"Obviously."

"I didn't want to hurt her by prolonging a hopeless relationship."

"No, of course not. How considerate of you. Tell me, what prompted her to cast your things onto the lawn?"

"Stubbornness, I suppose. She had a ridiculous, unsubstantiated notion I had slept with her best friend."

"Had you?"

"That's not the point. The point is she was unable to *prove* it, so she shouldn't have held it against me."

"How did she get the notion?"

"Her friend told her, which was stupid of her, but which nevertheless didn't constitute *proof*, only *hearsay*. I asked her, did you see us do it? Did you *see* penetration? No? Then you have no case! And even if I *did* do it, you could hardly blame me, all you have to do is take one look at the girl to see why. Who *wouldn't* do it? But I never admitted *I* did it. She was stubborn, though, and you might as well not waste your time on such people."

"I see." She lit another cigarette. The flame from the lighter made her brown eyes glow. I poured myself a final drink and set the empty bottle on the floor.

"So," I said, "if you would, please."

"If I would . . ."

"Give me your telephone number."

"Right," she said, "listen. Do you happen to know who my husband is?"

"No."

"Do you care?"

I thought about it. "No."

"He's a general."

"I'm impressed."

"A very big general. With lots of stars. Like this." She walked her fingers across her shoulder to show me how the stars were arrayed.

"Imagine."

"With but a snap of my fingers you could be surrounded by MPs."

"Golly."

"I just want you to know what you're dealing with."

"I'm grateful."

"So," she said. "Are you finished? Have you had enough of your little entertainment? I must tell you I am not in the habit of speaking to men who are in a drunken stupor. You *are* in a drunken stupor, aren't you?"

"It would appear to be the case."

"There you are. Now if you will excuse me."

"But you haven't solved my problem."

"Namely . . ."

"Namely, I'm experiencing the biggest hard-on of my life, one that would give you cause for marvel, if you bothered to notice. And I need someone to treat it, to care for it, to make it soft again."

"Direct communication isn't one of your weak points, is it?" She glanced behind me at the restrooms. "Tell you what. Did you happen to notice the young lady who came with me? She's in the toilet."

"I do recall there was someone."

"Good. Did you happen to notice she couldn't take her eyes off you? She's really quite taken in. I probably shouldn't be saying any of this."

"I hadn't noticed."

"Well, here's a tip. Ask *her* out, when she gets back. I'm sure she'll go with you. I'm willing to bet she'll even sleep with you, people do sometimes get what they deserve. Is that all right? I mean, it doesn't really matter which one of us you do it with, does it? As long as you have an opportunity to disperse your genes? It's been a pleasure to meet you, Private . . ."

"Corporal. Jimmy. Soon to be Corporal."

"Private, soon-to-be-Corporal, Jimmy. A pleasure to have made your acquaintance."

She held out her hand to shake mine, but I didn't go for it because the lag time on the alcohol had expired and I couldn't tell which hand to shake. Instead I said, "If I go out with your friend, then will you go out with me?"

There was a loud crash behind me that sounded like furniture shattering. I turned around. Garrett and the baldheaded Ohio-guy were going at each other. Garrett was getting the worst of it; he was still on his feet but teetering, his fists clenched, broken pieces of wood scattered at his feet. The baldheaded guy grabbed another chair, lifted it into the air, and dismantled it over the top of Garrett's head. To his credit Garrett remained standing, but his balance resembled that of a drunken tight rope walker. His fists valiantly carved up the empty space in front of him until a third chair brought him to his knees.

"Aren't you going to help your friend?" the redhead asked.

"If he needed help, he'd ask for it."

The baldheaded man lifted Garrett and slammed him into the wall. Then he pummeled him in the gut with his fists.

"Looks to me like he needs help," the redhead said.

Garrett slumped to the floor and toppled onto his ear. His eyes were closed and his tongue hung out.

"Not anymore," I said.

The brunette returned to the table. She was a little chunky, but she was pretty enough, so I asked her out and she said yes.

"I'll call you later," I told the redhead. "Did you mean it when you said I was handsome?"

On our way out, the baldheaded Ohio-man was explaining a pile of broken chair pieces and an unconscious customer to an angry bartender: "But you see, goddammit, the state of Oregon was *not* named after president Ronald O'Reagan!"

"Pipe down," the bartender said. "Here, buy some cigarettes. Only three Marks a pack. Cheaper than the machine!"

*

THE BRUNETTE HAD A suite in the BOQ. I plopped onto the bed and tried to convince myself the furniture was not, in fact, scuttling across the floor. She peeled off her top in one deft movement and her breasts oscillated like a pair of plumb bobs complying blithely with the laws of gravitation.

"Shit." I pawed at the blankets, trying to rise.

She stepped out of her pants and climbed on top of me. She was much heavier than I had realized. Although I was limp I somehow managed to take me in. I closed my eyes and tried to think of someone else. It took a lot of concentration with her grunting right in front of my face. Once I forgot myself and grabbed her ass. It broke my concentration. I let go immediately and tried to imagine having grabbed someone else's ass, but the damage was done. Finally, snorting like a buffalo, she came.

Pendergrass had been right: I'd gotten laid.

I rolled her off and asked, "That girl you were with tonight, what's her name?"

"Molly, why?"

"What's her phone number?"

"You asked me out, not her, what do you want her number for?"

"To tell her how much fun I had, and to thank her for bringing us together."

She smiled and wrote the number down on a piece of paper. As she passed it to me she gently squeezed my hand.

"Also," I said, "to tell her to put you on a crash diet, lickety split."

She left the room in a huff. I dialed the number and a man answered.

"Captain Brannigan."

General, hell. Holy shit! The new company commander!

"Hello Captain," I said. "May I speak to Molly?"

"May I ask who's calling?"

"Of course. This is Major Fisherman, one of the division chaplains. I'd like to speak to Molly about some volunteer work at the chapel. We have a load of frozen sausages we want to cook up for a fund raiser, and I wonder if she'd let us borrow her grill."

"Yes sir, one moment please."

After a moment Molly came on the line.

"Hello?" That voice.

"Hi. It's me, Jimmy, the guy who fell in love with you in the Canape tonight. Do you remember me?"

"Ah, yes."

"Well, I've just fucked Oinky. *Now* will you go out with me?"

Chapter 7

BACK IN MY ROOM I found no note from Cybulski, no envelope filled with money. I went downstairs to the second floor and knocked on his door. When he answered, clad in pajamas and blinking sleepily, I pushed my way in, sat down at his desk, and rummaged in the bottom drawer for the bottle of Asbach he kept there for me.

"Help yourself," Cybulski said.

"Don't mind if I do."

He went back to his bed and laid down.

"So," I said, "did you get any?"

"Now, now. I don't kiss and tell. You?"

"Unfortunately, yes."

"Hmm. The redhead you were looking at?"

"No, her friend. Did you know the redhead was Brannigan's wife?"

"As a matter of fact, I did. Maybe I should have warned you."

"Yeah, maybe you should have."

"Sorry. Guess I should have also warned you the friend was his sister visiting from the States."

"Shit."

I downed the brandy and poured another. "Now's as good a time as any to tell you," I said, "I don't expect to be living in the barracks much longer. I'm looking for an apartment on the economy."

He didn't say anything.

"I can't stand it anymore," I explained. "I can't stand doing the cleaning details. I don't want to pick up after anyone else. I don't want to scrub their sinks and toilets. I don't want to remove someone else's lint from the dryer."

"You always get out of it anyway," he said.

"That's not the point. It's the principle of the thing. I don't want to sweep or mop the hallway with its goddamn grooved tiles."

"When's the last time you did that?"

"I don't want to rise at oh-dark-thirty and stand in formation, freezing my ass off, doing jumping jacks and knee bends in the goddamn parking lot."

"You have to go to formation anyway, no matter where you live."

"I could get out of it if I didn't live here."

"What are you babbling about? You get out of it anyway!"

"But don't you see? I don't want to *have* to get out of it."

He sat upright in his bed. "Why are you telling me all of this? Are you trying to rationalize your escape? Is it because you think leaving the barracks would upset me?"

"Well . . . wouldn't it?"

He flopped back down on his rumpled blanket. "Not one bit."

I poured a fresh shot and handed him the glass. He placed it on the nightstand. He said, "A wise man once told me something: if you ever meet more than three assholes in one day, look in the mirror."

"What's that supposed to mean?"

"It means, if you must eventually run away from everyone you get close to, something must be wrong with *you*. It means, if you leave a trail of lost and forgotten friendships, something must be wrong with *you*. It means, if you're going 'right, left, right' and the rest of the battalion is going 'left, right, left,' something must be wrong with *you*."

"Is that what I do?"

"How long has it been since Silke dumped you?"

"Silke?"

"Your former girlfriend."

"Oh. She didn't dump me. I dumped her."

"Fine. How long has it been?"

I shrugged. "A month?"

"A month. Congratulations. You're moving out again. After only one month. Let's drink a toast."

"Do, let's," I said. I downed mine in one gulp. He didn't touch his. Instead he tried to cover himself with his blanket, but it was twisted into a lump, so he gave up and kicked it to the floor.

I walked over and stood above him. Something was wrong. He had that "I hope he doesn't ask me" look in his eyes.

"Where's the money?" I asked him.

"Jimmy, don't start in on me."

I grabbed him by his pajama lapels. "Where is it?"

"I didn't get any."

"Then where's the stuff? You brought it back, didn't you?"

He reached for the shot of Asbach on the nightstand but I knocked the glass from his hand.

"Well?"

"Schäfer kept it," he said.

"Do you mean to tell me—"

"Don't start in on me, Jimmy."

"—that you went down there, gave him the stuff, and came back with diddly?"

"Don't yell at me."

"Not even a goddamn cent?"

"He owes us the money. He's good for it—you know that. I know what you're going to say, but he's a hard man to deal with, Jimmy. He didn't agree with your price."

I picked the shot glass up from the floor and placed it on the nightstand. "You gotta learn how to deal with him," I said. "Like any other asshole in the world." I went to the door and opened it, then turned back around. "And maybe it's *your* mirror that needs scrutiny, not mine."

∗

DEALING WITH SCHÄFER'S WINDOW, I discovered, was more difficult than dealing with Schäfer himself would prove to be. Naturally the window was latched from the inside. The Rolladen was down, but I was able to push against it with the palms of my hands until it rolled back into its box and the pull-belt inside was slack on the wall. I took the sole of my boot and struck the glass once, hard, and the resulting crack went from corner to corner across the pane. Then I walked back out to the Fußgängerzone and sat next to the old well to wait and see if anyone had heard the noise.

The neighborhood was seldom quiet. Schäfer lived in one of the old houses on Brunnengasse, the narrow street leading from the Altstadt into the Schlosspark. He had once complained about the young boys who had to play in the street late into the evening because their homes were too small and crowded.

Brunnengasse was empty, and nothing had resulted from my blow to the window. I left the well, walked back into the darkness of the street, and stood before Schäfer's ground floor apartment. A stiff breeze blew from the Schlosspark, kicking tattered pieces of paper and empty cups past my feet. The apartment's first floor windows were so low you could step from the street into the living room. A sign on the front door warned, *Vorsicht—Hunde. Betreten auf eigene Gefahr!* Though Schäfer had cats, not dogs.

I worked the two pieces of glass, pushing and loosening them, until I was able to pull one out of the pane. Then I reached inside the window, unlatched it, and crawled into the house.

I had been inside Schäfer's before but now I wished I had studied it for just such an occasion. Squatting on the living room floor for several minutes, I let my eyes adjust to the darkness. I had a notion, and rejected it, to enter the kitchen and get something to eat out of the refrigerator.

When I found the bedroom I didn't hesitate—I didn't want to be shot—and turned the light on immediately. Schäfer and his wife were sleeping normally in their bed. Neither woke when the light came on. I went over to Schäfer's side, grabbed him by the hair, and pulled him out from under the covers. He thunked onto the floor like a sack of potatoes.

"*Ach, was ist . . . ?*"

I jumped on top of him and got a strangle hold on this throat. "Where's my money, cocksucker!"

"*Ahhhgh!*"

His wife was out of bed in an instant, throwing her robe on and tying it desperately with shaking hands, as if she couldn't bear to be robbed or raped or killed in only her nighty. When she had finished and had hurriedly smoothed her hair with her palms she stood wondering what next to do. Her husband meanwhile had turned a not unattractive shade of azure.

"*Ich rufe die Polizei an!*" the wife stuttered. But she didn't move toward the phone, she only looked at it. Perhaps she found my stern glare a formidable obstacle.

"*Nein!*" Schäfer managed to gurgle. "*Keine Polizei!*"

Of course he didn't want the police. I let go of his throat for fear of doing him serious harm; he had all the durability of blown glass.

"Where's my money?" I asked calmly.

He shook his head. The helpless look in his eyes told me there wasn't a penny in the house.

"Where's my stuff?"

He pointed under the bed. "*Kiste*," he said in a raspy voice.

I threw the blankets up and looked under the bed. Sure enough there was a wooden box. I dragged it out and tried to open it. It was locked.

"Key? *Schlüssel?*"

He made a feeble gesture toward the hallway. I lifted the box and slammed it down on the floor. It shattered, and hundreds of articles, mostly rings and findings, scattered across the room. Frau Schäfer, cowering in the corner, covered her mouth with her hands.

I started picking through the stuff, trying to sort out my teeth. Schäfer reached protectively for the pile, but I grabbed his face and pushed him back onto the floor.

There were hundreds of pieces of old gold; rings without stones, earring posts, rope and flat chains, broken and bent; some of it already hammered into oddly shaped clumps. And gold teeth. He'd collected them piece by piece over a long time. Altogether it was worth a lot of money. I realized it was Schäfer's life savings, his retirement nest egg. I scooped it up and filled my pockets.

"*Bitte . . .*" Schäfer pleaded.

When the pockets were full I unbuttoned my top shirt buttons and shoveled the rest inside my shirt. The metal was cold against my skin.

"Rent on the teeth," I said, patting the bulge.

Schäfer was in tears. As I left the bedroom his wife drew up the courage to confront me. Her fists clenched, her face shaking in fear and rage, she said:

"Fuck *du!*"

"Fuck *du auch*," I said.

On the way out I stopped in the kitchen long enough to raid the refrigerator of some wurst and dark bread. I would have enjoyed a glass of wine as well, but all they had was Dornfelder.

Chapter 8

SECRET (For Training Only)

SUBJECT: 111th Infantry Division (Mechanized) Operations Plan 105-90 (Orange Offense)

SEE DISTRIBUTION

Reference:

    Maps: Western Europe, 1:24,000 series M856, sheet numbers 6421, 6423, 6425, 6427, 6621, 6623, 6625, 6627, 6629, 6821, 6823, 6825, 6827, 6829.

    111th Infantry Division (Mechanized) Field SOP.

Time zone used throughout the order: BRAVO.

Task Organization: Annex A (Task Organization).

SITUATION

    Enemy Forces: Annex B (Intelligence).

    Friendly Forces: On order, 5th (US) Corps attacks, with 111th Infantry Division making the main attack in the south and 3rd Armored Division (simulated) in the north, to restore the integrity of the corps area of operations. Fourth Allied Tactical Air Force provides close air support and reconnaissance support for 5th (US) Corps with sorties allocated to 111th Infantry Division upon aircraft availability.

Attachments and Detachments: Annex A (Task Organization).

MISSION

111th Infantry Division (Mechanized) deploys on order; occupies Tactical Assembly Areas (TAA) Marquette, Joliet, and LaSalle; conducts corps main attack in sector to seize area vicinity objectives Diamond and Emerald; on order, prepares to defend.

EXECUTION

Concept of Operation: Annex C (Operations).

Maneuver: Division deploys and occupies designated tactical assembly areas: 1st Brigade, TAA Marquette; 3rd Brigade, TAA Joliet; 4th Brigade (simulated), TAA LaSalle; 2nd Brigade (simulated), OPCON to 5th (US) Corps. On order, division attacks with two brigades abreast to secure high ground vicinity objectives Diamond and Emerald. 1st Brigade conducts the main attack in the north to seize objective Diamond and 3rd Brigade conducts a supporting attack in the south to seize objective Emerald. 4th Brigade (simulated), division reserve, on order follows 1st Brigade and supports main attack.

Fires: Annex D (Fires).

*

WHEN THE SKY IS overcast and the sun is down and you are deep in the deciduous forests of Germany, forests so dark you can't see the ground beneath your feet, you use your one hand to hold the plan you just copied inside your field jacket to keep it dry, and the other hand you hold out in front of you to ward off sudden trees. For security reasons you're not allowed to use a flashlight.

You hope it's too cold and wet even for Jake. The task of avoiding trees keeps you busy enough; you don't have time to worry about Jake too. You recall the joke about the officer who was bitten by Jake and Jake subsequently died. You pray you find the concertina wire surrounding the Division Tactical Operations Center long, long before it finds you.

You have by now, of course, learned how to avoid field exercises. But you still underestimate the sergeant major. The Friday before deployment you go around to all the staff officers and ask them if they have any work for you, specifically typing. You tell each one you need to fill some idle time before deploying. They tell you they don't have anything critical, but can nevertheless give you something to type, if only to keep you busy. Making your rounds among the staff officers, you gather an alarming pile of work which you place in your inbox with the rest.

Sunday morning, outfitted in your TA-50, with your steel pot and gas mask on the floor next to your desk and your M-16 leaning against the wall, you type furiously while waiting for the order to mount up. When the sergeant major checks in to see whether you're ready to deploy, he discovers the pile in your inbox and observes you humping doggedly at it. He decides, reluctantly, that you must stay behind to get the work done.

But after a few exercises the sergeant major catches on; it's too coincidental that your inbox always fills up just as the trucks are starting their engines in the motor pool. Consequently, you and Jake and the invisible trees share a cold, dark, rainy night.

You can just see the soft glow of a light leaking out from under a tent and you believe the tent belongs to the DTOC military police. You hope it isn't just another forest illusion. The MP tent is the only place you can enter the DTOC without crossing the concertina wire, and the MPs who staff it are popular on account of the hot soup they offer to anyone passing through.

You work your way through the trees toward the glow of the light, and when the distance is about right, you reach out your hand. When you feel nothing you take one more step forward and reach again. Your hand brushes razor sharp strands of concertina wire. You follow the wire until it stops at the flap of a tent.

Once inside the MP tent you show your pass to the guard and fill your canteen cup with soup. Then you walk down the creaking wooden pallets laid between the two parallel rows of trucks parked back to back. The rear doors of the trucks are closed, but you can hear muffled voices and the distant clacking of typewriters. At the end of the walkway is the Plans truck where, inside, you find Cybulski and Garrett not smoking cigars.

*

"HOW'S THE WAR GOING?" I asked Cybulski. I set my soup on the table and unhooked my web belt, letting it drop to the floor.

He answered in a bored monotone. "Ivan is mobilizing his troops and rationing his food. He's revised all of his secret codes. Propaganda broadcasts have increased in frequency. G2 reports submarine traffic through the Dardanelles."

"Why aren't you smoking a cigar?"

"Jimmy, you know they make me heave."

"Would you rather the major sat in here with us? Light one up. You too, Garrett. What the hell do you think we buy these things for?"

We all lit cigars, and soon the truck was clouded in smoke.

"Your face looks better," I said to Garrett.

"Thank you." He smiled and blinked rapidly, pretending to relish the compliment. "I was hoping you'd notice."

"The bruises are clearing up, and I can hardly see the cuts anymore."

"The doctor did a good job with the stitches."

"I have to tell you though, the swelling in your jaw made it look stronger. To bad it's going away. For a while there you weren't half bad looking."

"I try a new look now and then, sometimes it works, sometimes it doesn't."

"Do you intend to start anymore fights like the one in the Canape?"

"I didn't start it. It was self defense."

"Clearly. By the way," I said, "where is the major?"

"In the theater," Cybulski answered. The theater was the mess tent with a screen mounted on one of its canvas walls.

"And the Three?"

"In the Ops truck."

"Will he stay there?"

Cybulski shook his head. "He's waiting for the Old Man to decide whether it's time for Third Brigade to up and over."

That made me queasy. By now Third Brigade had settled into their pup tents, had beaten back the rain and eaten a can of cold ham and eggs, had wrung out their socks. They were probably too tired even to go outside to take a piss, or to curse the bastards at division headquarters who choreographed these unspeakable circumstances. And yet unknown to them, in a few minutes they would be ordered to rise again and march twenty miles over sloppy terrain in the cold and dark and rain. The order, the kind of which drastically lowered the reenlistment rate, would be typed by one of us.

"Where's Pendergrass?" I asked.

"Asleep. It's not his shift yet. Or yours."

Pendergrass and I weren't due on duty for another hour. We took the night shift together, leaving the day shift to Skelton, Cybulski, and Garrett. I had added Garrett to the day shift, which was when most of the work got done.

"Jimmy, where do you want to be sent next?" Cybulski asked. "I mean, when you leave here?"

"Don't call me Jimmy when the major is here."

"I won't. Well?"

"I don't know. I guess back home."

60

"I want to go to Korea next," Cybulski said.

"Why?"

"It's someplace different. A different culture. Someplace I haven't been before. I've seen plenty of Europe, now I want to see the East."

"I hear the Korean whores make you do them like you're doing pushups," Garrett said. You're not allowed to touch them anywhere except the square inch you're doing them."

Cybulski didn't say anything. So I said, "The Korean whores in Korea can't be any better or worse than the Korean whores in Germany."

"After that," Cybulski said, "I want to go back to the States and join the animal rights movement."

"The what?" Garrett asked.

"A-L-F," Cybulski said. "The Animal Liberation Front. They break into experimental laboratories and free the victims."

"What kind of victims?"

"For example, L'Oreal, the cosmetics company, forces rabbits to keep their eyes open while chemicals are poured into them."

"Jesus. What the hell for?"

"To see what effect the chemicals would have on human eyes."

"Why don't they pour them into their own eyes, the fuckers?"

"Guess."

Garrett thought about it. "Right."

We puffed on our cigars for a moment, thinking about the rabbits.

"So I wouldn't object to going home now," Cybulski said, "if they sent me. Do you think there's going to be a complete draw down in Europe?"

I shrugged. "Hard to say. We'll certainly keep something here. Some air bases anyway. I think we'll have a much smaller total force and there'll be a greater percentage of aviation units in it. I don't think Hermann will tolerate the infantry units much longer."

"If Pendergrass were here, he'd say it's because there are too many black soldiers in the infantry units," Cybulski said.

"Be careful where you talk like that," I said.

"That's what Pendergrass would say. Hermann doesn't like black soldiers. He blames all the rapes on them. Remember when the mayor asked that all blacks be sent back to the States and replaced by whites?"

"He was accused of that," I said, "but he denied it."

"Of course he denied it. He had to. Would you admit it, if you had said it? There was an uproar and he had to deny it. But still it's what he wanted."

Garrett turned to Cybulski and said, "Are you sure it isn't the faggots they want to kick out?"

"Shut up," Cybulski said.

"*You* shut up."

"Hey," I said, "the both of you shut up." I pulled the copies of the plan out of my shirt and tossed them on the table. "The major wanted these. Lock them in the footlocker, will you please?"

"Why bother?" Cybulski asked.

"Don't give me any shit. Just do it."

I looked at Cybulski and wondered what kind of environment could have nurtured such a noodle. I could see him in the role of managing "Beast Haven," but I couldn't see him rescuing the animals; I couldn't see him busting into laboratories with a stocking over his head and a crowbar in his hand. The Pied Piper of mice and rabbits, yes. Breaking and entering, when the mere static electricity on a doorknob presented a barrier, no.

Garrett was more troublesome because I didn't understand him nearly as well. In fact, I wasn't sure I understood him at all. I asked him once what had brought him into the army and he mumbled something about the education benefits. That was bullshit, because if he was smart enough to go to college he was smart enough to avoid cleaning latrines and serving KP. You might think they'd cut a bright, hard working private a break now and then, but this was the army. Since Garrett never complained he was on latrine duty and KP duty nearly every day in the field. You had to wonder what kind of college would admit him and whether he would be eligible for a scholarship. Maybe some kind of fucktard scholarship for people who had no common sense.

Cybulski was saying to Garrett, "Why should I lock this shit up in the footlocker? Security is moot. The enemy knows everything anyway."

"What makes you think so?" Garrett asked.

"First, there are the spies."

"You think there are spies?"

"I think there are spies. I think there are swarms of spies. And I think," he pointed to the sheaf of papers I had thrown on the table, "our enemies have all of this anyway."

"That's training only," I said.

"You know what I mean. They have the General Defense Plan. They have it because surely somebody has sold it to them by now. Or they've watched our terrain walks and written it themselves."

"Terrain walks?" Garrett asked.

"You haven't been on one yet," Cybulski said. "Whenever a new commander, say a brigade commander, is assigned to the division, he needs to see the terrain his unit will occupy during the exercise of the General Defense Plan. We take him there by jeep or helicopter and stomp around for a few hours pointing importantly. It doesn't take a rocket scientist to figure out that if Colonel X takes command of Brigade Y—the change of command is published in the *Stars and Stripes*—and goes out to examine Terrain Z, then most likely Terrain Z is where Brigade Y, commanded by Colonel X, will be positioned, if and when the GDP is implemented. By collecting such information enemy spies can make—and I'm sure already have made—a pretty accurate facsimile of the GDP."

"Once we saw them taking pictures," I said.

"The ice cream truck!" Cybulski laughed. "For a while they followed us in an ice cream truck. Then a warning about it appeared in Annex B. Apparently soldiers had seen this same ice cream truck following them more than once. But as soon as the warning appeared in the annex the ice cream truck disappeared from the landscape, and was probably replaced by some other device. It doesn't matter. Whenever we're in the field, whether or not we're exercising the GDP, Hermann is always there in his Lederhosen and feathered cap, 'volksmarching' or bird watching in the woods. He's denied access to certain areas, of course, but the display of troops and trucks and generators and tents is so obvious, there's no mistaking the nature of the activity. Also, we all wear shoulder patches that identify our units. Even the most inept agent can see at a glance who and how many we are, what we brought with us, and exactly what we're up to."

"Then why buy anything from a spy?" Garrett asked.

"To confirm it," Cybulski said. "As a backup. What do you think, Jimmy?"

"I don't go in for all that cloak-and-dagger shit."

"You don't think there's a spy behind every bush," Garrett said.

"No." I picked up the copies of Orange Offense and put them in the footlocker. "Do you?" I asked him.

"Not especially," he said.

I glanced at my watch. "I still have time before my shift," I said to Garrett. "Go out and get the password for tomorrow. While you're at it, pick me up two Bratwursts with mustard and an order of *Pommes Frites* from the Imbiß across the road."

"It closes in a few minutes."

"Then you'd better hurry." I handed him five Marks.

"What's the German word for mustard?"

"*Senf*. And don't get beaten up by the goddamn cook."

"Bring me an order of Currywurst," Cybulski said.

"Give me the money."

Cybulski gave it to him.

"Anyone want to guess what the new password will be?" I said.

"What was it today?" Cybulski asked.

"Constant Compass."

"Jesus. They don't have a lot of imagination on the password committee, do they? What was it the day before?"

"Virtual Valor, or something stupid like that. Well?"

"I'll say Habitual Hard-On," Cybulski said.

"Perpetual Pussy," I offered.

We both turned to Garrett.

"Actual Asshole," he said.

"Huh?"

"Actual Asshole," Garrett repeated.

"What the fuck is that?"

"That's . . . my guess."

"Some guess," Cybulski said.

"Okay," I said. "Take off. Closest guess wins a suck on my dick."

As Garrett put on his field jacket and opened the door of the truck Cybulski said to him, "You don't have anything to worry about, because I promise you it won't be anything like Actual Asshole."

"*You* don't have anything to worry about," Garrett replied, "because one way or another you'll find a dick to suck."

Cybulski lunged after him but Garrett made it out the door.

"What do you make of him?" Cybulski asked, returning to his chair.

"I don't have the foggiest idea what to make of him."

"He reminds me of an officer."

"A what?"

"An officer. You know, the privileged species."

"What makes you say that?"

"Well, he looks like one, or at least he did when he got here. He talks like one, and he's stupid like one. The only thing he doesn't do is wear the rank like one."

"You're paranoid, you know that? If it isn't the MPs finding our cigarette hoard, or the gasoline stores igniting spontaneously and blowing us into atoms, or vigilantes randomly digging up graves to see if the bodies are still there——"

"Jimmy, quiet!"

"——it's officers masquerading like enlisted men to invade our privacy, or to get some choice latrine duty, or whatever the hell you think the reason is. You're saying this guy's a general dressed up like an E2?"

"No, I'm just saying he ain't no E2. Think about it."

I thought about it. Cybulski had a point; he wasn't no E2. I pictured him in an officer's uniform and the uniform fit. He was too stupid to be a captain; he hadn't been in the army long enough (he didn't even know what a terrain walk was). But he was smarter than butter bars so I pegged him as a first lieutenant. That was it; First Lieutenant Shane Garrett.

"You're paranoid," I told Cybulski.

"There's something else about him that bothers me. Remember that TS document that came in a while back, the one the courier brought, that no one's supposed to read?"

"Oplan 2357-90."

"That's the one. Garrett keeps asking about it. And about the TS safe combination."

"So he's curious."

Cybulski was quiet for a moment. "Yeah, you could say that."

The door opened and Lieutenant Colonel Arthur Flintlock, the G3, walked in. Cybulski and I immediately rose to parade rest. The Three seemed even shorter and stockier than usual; the TA-50 and steel pot did that to little men.

"Where's Major Skelton?" he asked.

"Asleep in his tent, sir." I saw Cybulski looking at me. Cybulski had told me Skelton was watching a movie.

The man we called "Little Howitzer" stared at the large, ace-tate-covered wall map on which we had marked unit positions. "He's asleep you say?"

"Yes sir. I heard him snoring as I passed the officers' tent."

He looked into my eyes for the first time. "How did you know it was him?" When I refused to blink he said, "Never mind, go and get him."

"Yes sir."

I grabbed my steel pot, left the truck, and went out through the MP tent and around the wire until I found the mess tent. Farther up the dirt road the generator was hammering painfully. I entered the mess tent, and after my eyes adjusted to the light I found Major Skelton sitting in the back row on a wooden bench, watching the movie. He had already been passed over once for lieutenant colonel and had the look of resignation on his face that is unique among passed-over majors: waiting for retirement and death.

"Three wants you to write a plan," I told him.

"Get Pendergrass to write it. It's almost his shift."

"Pendergrass is still in bed."

"You write it."

"Three says for you to write it."

"I don't like it in there with all that cigar smoke."

"But sir, you know how much they enjoy smoking cigars. Take that away and you'll lower morale."

"Is that a fact?"

"Yes sir. It is."

He stood up and stretched. "You know something, Private Fisher? For two years I've been trying to figure out just who the hell is really in charge, as they say, of this chickenshit outfit. And now I've finally narrowed it down. Tell me, how do you get away with it?"

"I don't know what you mean, sir."

"Yes you do. Oh yes, you do."

"Three's waiting, sir."

"All right. It wasn't that good of a movie anyway."

*

WHEN HE LEAVES YOU take his seat on the bench and watch the rest of the movie. It isn't bad. Patrick Swayze plays a ghost trying to prove his existence to Demi Moore. You are in love with Demi Moore. Her face is so pretty it almost hurts to look at it.

They don't need you back in the truck. Skelton will dictate the order, Cybulski will type it, and hundreds of Beetle Baileys from Third Brigade will rise wearily from their pup tents in the middle of the night. They'll don wet socks and trudge the remaining distance from Joliet to Emerald, two days earlier than planned.

You've already spent a week in the woods. During that week the Summer Solstice, the longest day of the year, came and went. And instead of strolling through the village with a girl, taking maximum advantage of the late evening light, you sat in the back of a truck with smelly men. The enemy can have Diamond and Emerald as far as you're concerned. They can have Garnet and Quartz too. You want to go home.

*

4. COORDINATING INSTRUCTIONS

 a. This plan is effective for planning on receipt and for execution on order.

 b. All non-brigade slice units initially deploy to and occupy designated sectors of TAA Marquette.

5. SERVICE SUPPORT See Admin/Log Plan.

6. COMMAND AND SIGNAL

 a. Signal.

  (1) Signal current CEOI in effect.

  (2) Annex H (Signal).

 b. Command.

  (1) Initial DTOC location vicinity MB 361136.

  (2) Initial DTAC location vicinity MA 496046.

Acknowledge: Bundy, Major General

Official: Flintlock, G3

Chapter 9

IT WAS THE FIRST real day of summer. You could tell not so much from the temperature as from the smell, which was rich in nectar and chlorophyll. You knew from the feeling in your nose, in a country that might have cold spells well into July, that the cold spells were over for the year.

As the Plans truck pulled back into town Cybulski and I cleaned up the back. The work tables were strewn with plans and messages, the garbage cans were full, and a mouse was chewing on one of Cybulski's leftover sandwiches. We took the map board down from the wall and tore off the sheets. The unclassified stuff would go into a motor pool garbage barrel. The classified went into a canvas bag for shredding and burning later.

I raised the security shade and watched the half-timbered buildings of Bad Karst roll by. Old women leaned out windows, beating rugs. Schnell-Imbiß vendors fired their ovens. Window dressers stood out on the red bricks, their hands in their pockets, surveying store fronts.

The flash of red hair was the first thing to catch my attention. But it was the way she walked, the nuances of balance and control, that made me recognize her. There are not many women who walk as sure-footed in high heels as they do in sneakers.

I banged on the wall of the truck and shouted for Garrett to stop. The truck pulled over to the curb. I jumped out the back and told Pendergrass, who was riding in the passenger seat, "There's something I have to do."

"Get your ass back in the truck," he ordered.

"Don't wait for me. I'll meet you at the barracks."

"Fisher!"

Molly Brannigan, the company commander's wife, continued her stroll into town. I didn't know what made me follow. I stood no chance with her; her station was too high. But she'd had a chance to turn me in as a masher and had elected otherwise.

I watched her pass before the Kaufhof show windows, her reflection in the glass growing larger as she approached the entrance. She kept glancing over her shoulder. I followed her to the store entrance, then waited half a minute before going inside.

The store was a forest of mannequins, salespeople, and customers. The mannequins looked so good I almost said "Excuse me" to one of them. When I found Molly she was circling the escalators in the middle of the ground floor. She didn't seem to be shopping for anything, and she had a harried look about her.

I ducked into the cosmetics section to the left of the main entrance. Molly streaked past the greeting cards along the wall and left the store without having bought anything or spoken to anybody. I was about to follow her out when I noticed the man.

He had not grown up in the country; he had a flat-nosed city look that suggested urban predator. But mostly it was the way he followed her. If you're tracking something in the woods you must remain aware of everything going on around you; the behavior of the birds, the changes in the wind, the freshness of the track; you must blend in. The man following Molly watched her with a tunnel vision that prevented him from noticing I had left the Kaufhof on his heels and was following only two paces behind. He was so intent on not losing his mark he leaned forward slightly with his chin jutting out and his fists balled up. He was so focused on his prey he didn't realize the prey was leading the chase.

Molly headed northwest along Mannheimerstrasse, walking in a straight line as if on a mission. The man followed her, and I followed the man. Then Molly slowed and window shopped on the right side of the street. Before the Fußgängerzone ended at the Café Kiefer, she abruptly turned and crossed the street and took an interest in the clothing displays in the shop windows beneath the cafe. When she turned she got a good look at the man.

I jammed my face into the display window of the Wirth jewelry store, and the man pretended to be looking at cosmetics in Yaska's, a couple of store fronts ahead of me. But she found him because she was looking for him and wouldn't find me because she had no idea I was there. You can hide from someone who passes by close enough to smell your breath if he isn't looking for you and doesn't expect you; if you stand still he won't be able to distinguish you from your surroundings.

Molly entered the Kornmarkt and evaporated into the crowd. The man bounced up and down on his toes, scanning over the bobbing heads like a prairie dog, but couldn't find her. Just as he gave up looking and dashed into the crowd, pushing and bullying to get through, someone tapped me on the shoulder. I turned around.

"Why are you following me?" Molly asked.

I looked back in Mugsy's direction, as if to share the embarrassment with him, but he had disappeared into the crowd. When I turned back to Molly I noticed she was holding her purse funny; she had her hand in it all the time.

"Well?"

"I'm not following you," I said. "*He's* following you. I'm only following *him*."

"Shut up. Here he comes again. Kiss me."

She pulled me close and kissed me, watching the man through one nearly closed eye.

"I love you," I said.

"Don't be stupid. Here, take my hand."

We continued down Mannheimerstrasse, passed the bridge houses and crucifix, and crossed into the Altstadt. All the while we held hands. When we reached one of the expensive jewelry stores in the Altstadt she stopped and put her arms around me and laid her head on my shoulder.

"Thanks for remembering who I am," I said.

"You would be difficult to forget."

"I take that as a compliment."

"You may take it any way you wish. I only meant it as a neutral observation, much as one would observe a violent storm that didn't destroy one's home or otherwise directly affect one's life, but that left a lasting impression nonetheless."

"That sounds ominous."

She glanced behind us briefly and said, "Kiss me again."

I did. I put my hands on the small of her back and pulled her hard against me. Her lips were eager. And then—not.

"That's enough," she said.

The man was watching us from the old well near the entrance to the Schlosspark and trying not to look like he was watching us.

"He's still there," I said. "We'd better kiss some more."

We held each other and kissed again and it felt good holding and kissing someone you suddenly knew you loved.

"I'll walk you home," I said. "Better yet, maybe we ought to check into a hotel room until the coast is clear."

"No, I'll be fine. Just walk me down to the river."

"To the river?"

"That's what I said—the river."

"He can mug you just as easily down there."

"Trust me."

"Suit yourself. But wait—there he is. We'd better kiss again."

"Okay, that's enough. I think he got the message."

"Shh. A little more. Just to be safe."

"Silly."

"I missed a spot. We mustn't leave any part of you exposed to the danger."

"You little shit. Stop it."

She had lost all concern for the man now and took a look at the show window of the jewelry store we had stopped in front of. Dozens of rings filled the window. I asked her to pick out a favorite.

"It would have to be eighteen carat," she said. "Or better."

"It wouldn't change the appearance."

"It would to me. I can tell the difference."

"That's what everyone thinks. But you can't. Fourteen carat is fourteen parts gold, ten parts other metals. Eighteen carat is eighteen parts gold, six parts other metals. But you can't tell the difference just by looking at them."

"What kind of other metals?"

"In yellow gold, mostly silver and copper. The more copper used, the darker the color. That's why you can't tell the difference at a glance; the appearance varies with the alloy content."

"You sure seem to know a lot about gold. Rare, I should think, among privates in the infantry."

"I told you: I'm going to be promoted to corporal soon."

"Oh yes, I keep forgetting. You're a high-ranking private."

"Do you still want my help? Shall I walk you to the river? Or do you want to just stand here and insult me?"

"I seriously doubt you feel insulted. Your hand is on my ass."

I removed it.

"Thank you," she said. "Now, escort me to the river, and you'll be rid of me."

"That's what I want," I said. "To be rid of you."

"Good."

"And no more kissing, either."

"Right."

We walked back to the bridge houses where she stopped and let go of my hand.

"Let me buy you a drink," I said.

"No. I haven't the time. But thank you very much just the same. You did me a great favor."

"Do *me* a great favor. Let me see you sometime."

She smiled and touched my lips with her index finger. "Don't be so brash with officers' wives. It will get you into very, very big trouble. Goodbye, Corporal Private."

"Jimmy," I reminded her.

"Jimmy."

She left me standing there and continued back into town. I leaned against the stone crucifix and waited for the man, but he never came.

When Sergeant Pendergrass told me, days later, that an unidentified body had been found in the river, I asked cautiously whether it had a mashed nose. Nobody knew, he told me; the face had been shot away.

Chapter 10

SCHÄFER WOULD HAVE COOLED off by now, so it was time to return his gold. The teeth and findings were packed in zip-lock plastic bags. They went into the pockets of my field jacket. I kept the wedding band, the one Cybulski and I got from our last dig, and wore it on my little finger.

I told the CQ I wouldn't be home that night, then ran back up to Cybulski's room and knocked on the door.

"It's open."

He smiled when he saw me but then frowned when he saw the expression on my face. "You're going out."

"Yes."

"Oh." He turned his back to me.

"Don't look so forlorn," I said. "We'll do something together tomorrow." I opened his desk drawers, looking for the bottle of Asbach.

"Who is it tonight?" he asked. "Brannigan's wife?"

"I wish. But she's not quite tuned up yet. So I've reserved Melina at Amy's."

"When were you going to tell me?"

"I just did."

"Did you pay Melina's bar fine?"

"Yes, I'll be staying the night."

He leafed idly through a book. "It's sure nice to be informed."

"Look, Chuck, I never know how you're going to take such things."

"Well, you still don't know, do you?"

"There is no you-and-me. There can't be a you-and-me."

He walked to the far side of the room and turned to face me. "Are you falling in love with Molly Brannigan?"

I closed a drawer but kept my grip on the handle. "Where the hell did that come from?"

"How long do you think it will take before she sees through you. Before she figures out she's with the world's greatest opportunist. Before she dumps you, like they all do."

"This one's different, Chuck."

"How so? She's going to do to you what all *women* do to you. They're all the same. You just don't see it."

I gave up on the search for the Asbach and slammed a drawer shut. "What the fuck do you want me to say?"

"Nothing," he said. "I don't want you to say a fucking thing."

I took the zip-lock bags of teeth and findings out of my field jacket pockets and set them on his desk.

"You know what to do with the stuff," I said.

He stared at the floor between his feet.

"We're still partners, right?"

He nodded.

"And friends?"

He nodded again, almost imperceptibly.

"Good." I turned to the door. "I guess I'll—"

"Wait." He opened the gray metal door of his wall locker and took out a half empty bottle of Asbach and two shot glasses. "One drink," he said, "before you go whoring." He made to put on a cheery face, but the light in his eyes was dim.

We sat on the rug in the middle of the room and drank from the bottle of brandy. We didn't stop at one drink, nor at two.

He told me about his former fiancée and showed me her picture. She was short and dumpy and had a plain face, but her long brown hair was pretty enough and her smile was fresh and alive.

"She's cute," I said.

He told me she was the only girl he'd ever had. Although it had been three years since she left him, it still hurt. I told him it would continue to hurt until he got another one and that one left him too. Then he would only associate hurt with the second one, and with the first he would associate either fond memories or shame, depending on how stupidly he had behaved when they broke up. I told him that was how it worked and the rules applied to everybody, but he seemed doubtful.

We listened to the radio until the bottle was empty. It was my cue.

I had trouble standing. Cybulski watched me get up, then followed me, hurrying to place himself between me and the door. He put his key in the lock, turned it, and shoved the key into his pocket.

"Don't go," he begged.

"Come on, Chuck. I have to go."

"Please don't. Please, please don't." He was almost crying. I realized I'd fucked up. I reached around him and took hold of the doorknob. It wouldn't turn.

"Unlock it, Chuck," I said.

"I've asked you *a hundred times* to move in here with me. You always say no, you always say you don't want to hurt everyone else's feelings. You always feed me that line of shit."

"This is a single room, Chuck. You only have one bed."

"Now you're going to sleep with that Melina cunt, and I bet you don't even know her last name."

78

"She's not a cunt. So don't call her one."

"Cunt."

My patience was gone. "Unlock the door, Cybulski."

"My room's not good enough for you? *I'm* not good enough for you?"

I went over to the window to look for a way out but Cybulski's room was on the second floor. I pressed against the glass anyway, in futility, like a prisoner testing his cell. I didn't want to have to hurt him. He'd been a good partner for a long time and it would be unfortunate to have to hurt him.

"I told Shane Garrett about the digging," he said.

"You did *what*?"

"Don't get mad at me, Jimmy."

I got into his face. "What the fuck did you tell him?"

"He wants in. He wants to join the business."

"You fucking idiot."

"He figures you'll say no, so he invited me to break away and form a partnership with him." Cybulski began to cry. "He says he'll treat me better than you treat me."

"Oh yeah?" I punched him in the gut and he crumpled to his knees. "Would he treat you better than that?"

Cybulski choked and coughed and sobbed. "Please don't hurt me anymore."

"Is Garrett a faggot too?"

"That word makes me very upset, Jimmy."

"Well? Is he?"

"I asked you *never* to use that word."

"Faggot. Now give me the key before you need a dentist."

He wrapped his arms around my legs and held them fast.

"Get up, faggot."

He buried his face in my crotch.

"I said, get up!"

I tried grabbing him by the hair, but it was too short. I slapped him several times about the ears.

79

"I'll kill you, you bastard!"

The alcohol had hit me and the room was spinning. I tried to walk away from him but he still had me by the legs. I grabbed the brandy bottle by its neck and slammed it against the side of his head. The bottle didn't break, but Cybulski fell back from his kneeling position and hit the floor.

He lay on the rug and whimpered. I stared at him for a minute, feeling the kind of loathing you feel when the person you loathe needs more pity than you can muster. Finally I yanked him up off the floor and dumped him onto his bed.

I had to reach into his pocket to get the key, and when the key came out so did a laminated photograph. It was a picture of the two of us, taken the previous fall as we finished a thirty kilometer Volkswanderung together.

I put the photograph on his nightstand, then crossed the room and opened the door. But I didn't leave right away; I hesitated in the open doorway and rested my head against the frame.

We'd had a lot of fun the day of the Volkswanderung. In the photograph our arms were around each other's shoulders and we had no cares in the world other than for each other. Cybulski had made mistakes, plenty of them, but in the end he was always there for me, always following me where I went and doing what I told him to do. If that's a reasonable definition of friendship, then Cybulski was the only real friend I had.

I closed the door again, returned to his bed, straightened his blanket, and tucked him in. Then I laid down on the floor next to the bed. After a few minutes he quieted and we both fell asleep.

Chapter 11

SUNLIGHT STREAMING THROUGH THE window woke me the next morning. I sat up, wiped beads of sweat from my forehead, and looked to see where I was. If my evening had gone as expected I would find Melina in bed with me, stretching naked in the sun, luxuriating in the tranquil realm between deeply asleep and wide awake. When I touched her she would take long, deep breaths and make little noises as freshly woken people do. That was the plan. Instead I found myself on the floor of a barracks room and the person occupying the only bed in the room was snoring. I rose and left quietly.

After showering and eating breakfast I went to the office. Half an hour later Cybulski showed up.

"You left without saying anything," he said.

"Yes."

"I would very much appreciate you not doing that again."

"Right."

I put him to work stripping the old topographic sheets from the wall and placing them in the shred-and-burn bag. I would escape the office by making a trip to the incinerator, as soon as the bag was full, and wouldn't return. We worked in the office for a couple of hours in silence, he with his brow constantly furrowed. Eventually the dense silence got to me and I asked:

"You'll run the stuff over tonight, won't you?"

"I said I would, didn't I?"

"Don't get touchy. I was only making sure."

"Well, now you're sure."

I pulled the drawstrings tight on the shred-and-burn bag and threw it over my shoulder. I had to get out of there. "I'm going to make a run," I said.

"The bag's not full yet."

"I'm going anyway. Tell Pendergrass I won't be back today."

"Where else are you going?"

"You know goddamn well where I'm going."

He pressed the buzzer for me and the door unlocked. I kicked it open and went down the hall. When I had gotten as far as the stairwell he leaned out of the office and shouted:

"When can I expect you home tonight, honey?"

*

THE INCINERATOR WAS A blackened potbelly stove enclosed within a chain link fence. If you were a spy and you wanted to get at the charred bits of paper in the stove you first had to gain access to the Kaserne, then you had to get through the chain link fence. From the looks of the fence, you had to want the charred bits of paper mighty badly. I was supposed to carry my bag to the basement first and use the shredder in G2, but it took too long to shred a large canvas bag full of paper, what with staples and paperclips and everything. I couldn't see how anyone could gather information from burned paper, so I simply opened the heavy hinged door of the stove and dumped the bag into it.

After the pile was finished burning and I had made sure there were no remnants of unburned paper in the soot I took a broomstick handle and stirred the mass until it was nearly powder. If a spy could collect any useful information from that, he deserved it. The life of a spy had to be a hard one, what with digging through garbage cans and sorting out charred bits of paper in the bottoms of potbelly stoves. I stirred and thought: I have not made their jobs any easier today. But I didn't think, as Cybulski did, that there were spies. Burning and stirring were just common sense precautions we took.

Garrett poked his head through the gate. I ignored him for a few minutes, during which he studied my work with all but his head hidden behind the chain link fence.

Finally I asked, "What are you doing here?"

"I thought you might need some help."

"I don't."

"Well, actually, Cybulski thought you might."

"Cybulski was wrong. And if he sent you here to check up on me, both of you need lives of your own."

Garrett entered the enclosure and stood with his hands in his pockets, watching me clean up. I brushed past him on my way out, shoving the empty canvas bag into his hands. "Return that to the office," I told him.

"Fisher." He grabbed my sleeve.

"What is it?"

"We need to talk."

I shook my sleeve loose. "You've already been talking. To my boy Cybulski."

"I was only trying to unlock a door. I want in. I want to join your business. I think I have a lot to offer."

"Namely?"

"You've already got cigarettes and gas covered. Bring me in and we'll do book."

I shook my head. "Book requires deep pockets. Maybe you haven't noticed, but we operate pretty much hand-to-mouth."

"I did notice. I could possibly solve that problem."

"If you can solve that problem, you don't need me and Cybulski."

"Fisher . . ."

"Stay away from him. And don't ever fucking follow me again."

*

MELINA MUST HAVE BEEN watching for me from her window, because she greeted me at the top of the stairs.

"I was expecting you yesterday," she said.

"I couldn't get away."

"Who were you with?"

"Private First Class Charles Cybulski."

"Oh. You have to pay the bar fine again, you know."

"I know."

She led me to her room and fixed dinner on the little stove. We had pan fried Schnitzel. She'd bought the meat the day before and had saved it when I didn't show up.

We ate in silence for a while, then Melina said, "I've always wanted to visit America." She said it a little too whimsically.

"It's a nice place," I acknowledged.

"You'll be going back someday."

"I suppose."

"Is there a girl there you'll return to?"

I chewed my food and kept my eyes on my plate. What would my mother think if I brought Melina home to meet her?

"Yes," I said. "There's a girl waiting for me."

When dinner was cleared away Melina sat with her hands in her lap and said, "Well."

"Well," I said.

We undressed and climbed into bed. Like most whores, Melina wasn't big on ceremony. She laid down on her back and spread her legs.

"Wait a second," she said. "It's a quiet night, let me check something." She reached for the phone. A minute later she hung up and said, "Kristin says it's quiet on her end of the hall too. I invited her to join us."

84

Kristin showed up in thigh-highs, wearing too much eye makeup. She was skinny and leggy with long blond hair and mousy features. She wasn't big on ceremony either.

The girls took turns sucking on me, sharing my dick like a popsicle. Then I mounted Kristin, and Melina squatted over her, facing me. As I fucked Kristin, Melina massaged Kristin's face with her pussy. We all came at once, but I was probably the only one who didn't fake it. Afterwards we lay together, one girl on each side with a leg draped over mine, their heads resting on my chest.

When the phone rang it was Cybulski making his one allotted call from jail. They had picked him up at Schäfer's house and charged him with trafficking stolen property. It had been a set-up; Schäfer had skedaddled, and the MPs were camped out in his house.

Cybulski was blubbering with fear. The "stolen property" included gold teeth. Only dead people gave up their teeth without protest, and there was only one ready source of dead people in town. It was just a matter of isolating recent burials and examining dental records to trace the teeth back to their original owners, owners now missing from their final resting places under the shady pines on Alzeyerstrasse.

Book Two

*From the first day to this, sheer greed has been the driving
spirit of civilization.*
—Engels

Chapter 12

ALL THE NEXT DAY they didn't come for me.

I waited in the office, pretending to concentrate on stamping manuscript pages Unclassified, Confidential, or Secret, depending on the highest classification that appeared on the page, but in fact I had little idea what I was stamping and knew the job would have to be repeated.

"What's gotten into you?" Major Skelton asked.

"Nothing, sir."

"You're not yourself. You haven't once asked to be excused for the day or have a four day pass. You haven't once commented on the girls passing in the hallway. Are you sick?"

"I'm just tired, sir. It's nothing, really."

Pendergrass and Garrett, inventorying the contents of the safes, made a steady drone with their voices as they worked. Once there was a long silence. When I looked up to see why, they were looking at me strangely; one of them had asked me a question I hadn't heard. They were talking about Cybulski mostly. Garrett wanted to know everything I knew and was disappointed to learn that I knew even less than he did.

Near the end of the day Riddell came to the office to tell us he was suspending Cybulski's clearance.

"He's a thief," Riddell said, "with no scruples whatever. He's going to hang by his nuts—if he has any nuts."

"They haven't even charged him yet," Pendergrass said.

"All I need is the suspicion. His clearance is *gone*. Do you understand me? Rip, rip." He made tearing motions with his hands. "Lock him out of the office. Change the combinations. Today."

"I need him in the office," Pendergrass argued.

"He's a faggot and a thief."

"He's a good worker."

"He won't be any good to you hanging by his nuts. Take Lamoureaux as a replacement. I can spare him; all he does is sit on his ass in the EAC. He's got a clearance so you don't lose any continuity."

"Sir . . ."

"Is there anything else I need to clarify for you, sergeant?"

After Riddell was gone Pendergrass said, "I knew this would happen. The same thing happened last time around."

I was turning to leave when a question occurred to me. "Sergeant Pendergrass, what happens to Cybulski? What happened . . . last time around?

He looked away. "Enjoy your holiday, Private Fisher," he said.

Because the next day was the Fourth of July the office cleared out at precisely five o'clock. Garrett was the last to go. He paused in the doorway, as if he wanted to say something but couldn't come up with the words. Finally he said:

"I'm sorry about Cybulski. I know he's your . . . friend."

I nodded.

"If there's anything I can do—"

"No."

"Well, good night."

"Good night."

I waited in the office to give them plenty of opportunity to come for me. It would be better to get cuffed at my desk rather than in the barracks, in front of everyone. But the National Anthem played and the flag lowered and another hour went by and still they didn't come.

At seven o'clock I finally left the office. I considered turning myself in. But the idea was muted by a sense of self-preservation, and was killed, finally, by the conditioning the army provided never to volunteer for anything, ever.

I wondered which car would stop for me. Jumping out of the passenger seat, flashing identification, a man in a dark blue suit would say, "A few questions, if you don't mind."

I didn't mind.

I went to the mess hall for dinner. The main course was meatloaf. I remembered that they never come for you while you're sitting at a table in the mess hall eating meatloaf. They always come after you've gone out to a bar and gotten drunk. That way they can ask around and find out where your local hangouts are and track you down in one of them. It's real detective work then, not just a routine pick-up because you happen to be sitting at a mess hall table eating meatloaf.

"We got him, all right," the man in the dark blue suit would say. "He was sousing himself in the Tenderloin. Don't ask how we found him—it was a real puzzle."

I went to the Canape. It was still early and I was the only customer.

"My friend," the bartender said. "It has been a long time. Why do you stay away so long? You have found another bar?"

"I've been in the field."

"I am sorry to hear it. You are alone now?"

"Not for long."

"Ah, good, you are expecting company. What will you have?"

I squinted at the clock above the bar. Time for two or three, anyway. "Something strong," I said. "I need to get drunk in a hurry."

"I have just the thing." He took a bottle from the rack and filled a shot glass. When he placed the shot glass in front of me I took hold of his wrist, making him wait while I swallowed the drink. He refilled it and I let go.

The lights were low in the room. Two Beetle Baileys entered the bar and started a Fussball game in the corner. A man with bushy eyebrows took a seat two stools away from mine.

"Survey," I said to the bartender.

"Eh?"

"*Noch ein Mal, bitte.* Leave the bottle."

I read the label on the bottle. Krabbeldiewandenuff, it said. I drank another shot and refilled my glass. The alcohol burned all the way down to my toes.

"Pretty good stuff," I said to no one in particular. The man two stools away looked at me and nodded politely.

"Wantsome?" I asked him, raising the bottle in the air.

He shook his head.

"Don't mind me," I said. "They'll be along any moment now."

I'd never been in an adult prison before, not even to visit someone, but I had a good idea from the movies what I was in for. You live in a barred cell that is one of many in a long hallway. Everyone has to be in their cells by a certain hour in the evening when, electronically, they close all the doors at once. The floors above and below are metal gratings so the guards can see through them, and you don't have any privacy and neither do your pet birds. You get some time every day in the exercise yard where you have to take care not to get stabbed in the back with a sharpened screwdriver or fucked in the ass by Vic Morrow.

Some prisons have libraries and craft shops and you can learn a trade or even go to college. At least there are books. I had no particular desire to read books but it would be impressive to be well read, or at least to have read one or two of the more important books. I thought about all the books and authors I had heard of and wished I had read. *Moby Dick* was one, and Faulkner was another. I didn't know who wrote *Moby Dick* or what Faulkner wrote, but presumably I would know if I had time to read them in my jail cell.

Some of my high school classmates went to college. I asked them how it was and they said, just like high school only harder. I asked what they meant by harder and they said you have to do a lot more homework. I had trouble gauging this since I hadn't done any homework in high school. I asked my father once whether I ought to consider attending college. He laughed so hard he went into one of his coughing spells and had to run to the sink to spit up phlegm.

All the time I was thinking, I was drinking. When it occurred to me that my sitting posture might result in a bad fall, I noticed, relieved, that there was a stool beneath me preventing just such an accident from happening. I noticed too that the bar had filled up with people. The man who was sitting two stools away had moved over and was speaking in my ear. I wondered how long he'd been there.

"You can never be confident of the Japanese brands," he was saying. "The label is used by the manufacturer but common watch guts are inserted. So to answer your question, I would strongly advise loyalty to the Swiss industries."

"What about Rolex?" I asked, trying to remember whether I had asked him about the Japanese brands.

"Always buy from a reputable, licensed dealer," he said. He spoke with a British accent laced with a German accent which meant he was native Hermann educated in England.

"I like the way the little second hand hums around the dial," I said.

"Hmm, yes."

"I take it you are a watch salesman."

"You already have my card. It is in your shirt pocket."

I pulled the card out of my pocket. "So it is," I said.

Burkhard Krupa, the card said. Handelsvertreter: Qualitätsuhren. The man had extraordinarily bushy eyebrows and an annoying habit of smacking his lips between sentences. He stank of age.

"Are you going to try to sell me a watch?" I asked.

"Oh no, my dear man. Whatever gave you the idea? We are having a drink together; we are not conducting business."

"That's good," I said. I had picked up a Rolex or two in my day but it had never occurred to me to go out and *buy* one.

"Travel a lot?" I asked him.

"Worldwide."

"Must be nice."

"It is. Except for . . ."

"Except for what?"

"I'm not fond of flying. You could say it was my greatest fear, and I have only partially overcome it to do my job."

"That's too bad," I shook my head sympathetically. "A traveling salesman who doesn't like to travel is in an awkward position, what?"

"Everyone has a greatest fear . . ." He stared at me following this comment, until I realized he was expecting a response.

"Some people do," I said.

"No, everyone."

"Well, that may be true," I admitted. "I guess my greatest fear is of salesmen."

"How very funny. Or very insulting, if that's the truth."

"No, it's not." I didn't want to insult the fucker. But every time he spoke to me he leaned close and I caught a whiff of

91

him. I tried to pour another glass from the bottle but it was empty. I glanced at the Rolex on his wrist. It was close to midnight. Still they hadn't come.

"Well, Herr Krupa," I said rising, "I have to go now."

"I'll be happy to give you a ride home, if you like."

"No, don't get up."

"You are in no condition to drive."

"I came on foot."

"Please, allow me."

"Good night."

I stumbled to the door, thinking, they must be right outside. They were waiting for me to come out of the bar so they could surround me. "Got him just as he was leaving," they would say. "Nabbed him just in the nick of time."

I climbed the steps to the sidewalk and leaned against the cigarette machine. The night was cool; I rubbed the goose bumps on my arms. Cars whizzed by in front of me. I waited for one to stop, but none did, so a moment or two later I headed for Amy's.

I had given them plenty of opportunity to come for me but obviously they wanted to play dirty. They wanted to cuff and manhandle me in front of my whore. I could see Melina now, sitting on her bed, the small room crowded by a trio of burly men. Nobody had anything to say. Melina's eyes darted back and forth between the men, and the men tried hard to look at anything in the room but Melina. They had already grown bored with the room and the view, had already stared at the music posters on the walls, had already gotten over the weirdness of being in a whorehouse, with a whore, and still wearing pants.

As I walked up the creaking staircase at Amy's I could imagine the men hearing me and perking up, reaching inside their poorly tailored jackets to unstrap revolvers from shoulder holsters. The leader motioning for the others to take their places on either side of the door. Melina leaning over the vanity with her face in her arms.

A few questions, if you don't mind.

I don't mind. Really I don't.

When I knocked on her door no one answered. One of the other doors opened and a lieutenant I knew came out. He tipped his cap to me and went down the stairs. The whore, a shopworn blond, stood in the doorway and asked if I wanted to go next.

"Is Melina here tonight?"

She shook her head. "Melina's doing a private party with some Japanese businessmen." She went back into her room, sat on the bed, and turned on the TV. She was vaguely pretty and I enjoyed watching her relax in her underwear, but it was Melina's company I wanted. That an officer had preceded me didn't help matters, either.

I went downstairs to the bar, ordered a beer, and sat watching the street traffic through a window that had never been washed. The accumulated dirt made the window almost translucent and spared the need to invest in frosted glass. Headlights flickered into the bar like weak flashlights aimed toward the bottom of a murky pool.

Some customers and a few whores on break were talking, saying the time was right for a draw down, but nobody was happy about it. One of the women, a blond with a long nose and waxy looking skin, lamented the loss of the Americans because of their cultural contribution. She was a permanent fixture in the bar, trying but always failing to get hired on upstairs.

"I think there will be peace," she said, "but I want the army to stay anyway. I'm sure the peace will last so long as the army stays."

"There will be war," said a worker from the Opel automobile factory whose hands were dirty. He lifted his beer glass to his lips with his dirty hands. "There will be war and millions will be rubbed out."

"Why do you say that?"

"There are too many countries in Europe. They do not get along well unless now and then they have a war."

"There is the economic alliance," the bartender said.

"The economic alliance will not stop a war. Likely it will be the start of one."

"The Amerikan Army will stay and keep the peace," the waxy skinned woman said. "I do not think we will see another war in our lifetimes. Perhaps Europe will never see one again."

"You are naïve," the Opel worker said. "When the Amerikan soldiers begin to go home, the Amerikan people will want to bring them all home. The army will leave just as it arrived, one unit at a time. The Amerikan politicians must bend to the will of the people."

"But the will of many of the people," I said, "is that some of the units stay."

"That will change. They will realize how much it costs to guard against an impotent threat."

The waxy woman smiled at me and patted my knee. "Everyone is sick of war. The governments consist of older men who remember the last one all too well. They will not have another one. They know it is cheaper to leave the army here than to have another war."

"The old men in government will grow old and die," the Opel worker said, "and younger men will take over, men who have not had war and will want a taste of it for themselves. Millions will be rubbed out. There will always be poor people, there will always be crime, and there will always be war. We are only waiting for the old veterans to die and for a charismatic leader to inspire the disgruntled masses."

"There will be a war, but it will not be in Europe." This from one of the whores who had been reading a book until the conversation distracted her. She put the book down on the bar and tightened her robe. "It will be in the Middle East."

"She has a point," the Opel worker said. "The war vacuum must somehow be filled, and the Middle East clearly wants to fill it. A war will start in the Middle East, Europe will get sucked in, and millions will be rubbed out."

"I am confident of a lasting peace," the waxy woman said. Her hand was on my knee. "I have confidence in the Amerikans."

We toasted the Amerikans for keeping the peace, and we toasted Ivan for having become an impotent threat. Even a pair of whores who were whispering among themselves at one of the tables got into the spirit of the moment and toasted the Israelis and Palestinians for not having sucked Europe in. But nobody thought to toast the Iraqis.

I stepped outside to get away from all the smoke and to have a cigarette. The waxy skinned woman followed me out. We stood next to her car, swigging from a bottle of Canadian whiskey she had brought with her and trying to keep our balance by leaning against the car.

I apologized that I couldn't take her home with me, as I lived in the barracks. She apologized that she couldn't take me home with her, as her husband was there. This was an acceptable predicament, since I hadn't drunk enough to neutralize her waxy skin and bad breath. I drank more, though, from her bottle, and the safety mechanism of passing out before you did something stupid failed to kick in. Her car was parked on the street in front of Amy's, and she made so much noise in the back seat with her pants hanging from one ankle that I had to tell her to be quiet.

Entering my room later I pushed the door open slowly, figuring I'd get jumped from both sides. But no one was there.

Fine, I thought. Have it your way. Don't arrest me. See if I give a damn.

Chapter 13

THE NEXT MORNING I went downtown to buy the local papers and the *Frankfurter Allgemeine*. I asked the vendor if he had the previous day's papers, and he did. He even had a couple of them from the day before and he handed them all to me, individually rolled, like sticks of firewood. I carried them to a bench in the Fußgängerzone near the Kaufhof.

There was nothing about Cybulski's arrest in the newspapers and nothing about grave robbing either. Cybulski's arrest was a trivial event and might go unnoticed, but evidence of grave robbing would make the headlines. And if it made the headlines it would only be a matter of time before they tracked me down. On the other hand, there was little chance either the MPs or the Polizei would merely assume the gold teeth had been taken from fresh graves. Somebody had to tell them. And the only somebody to be concerned about was Cybulski.

If I approached Cybulski about anything he might have said to the authorities he would go to pieces and deny having said anything. Then he would be so careful about what he admitted to me that I would never learn the truth. And the truth was worth learning; if Cybulski confessed that he and I were digging up fresh graves and selling the corpses to medical researchers, it would not be viewed as the kind of extracurricular activity that would earn us commendation medals.

*

AN E5 READING A Stephen King novel manned the desk at the MP station. When I told him I needed to see Cybulski he picked up a telephone without looking at me and spoke a word I couldn't make out. A moment later a corporal came up from the back and led me into the building. All the time the sergeant at the desk never even looked at me. I could have been carrying a LAW and he wouldn't have known it. Apparently a guard's attention to visitors is a function of the value of merchandise he's guarding.

In the movies the visitor and inmate talk to each other via telephone while separated by a sheet of bulletproof glass, but this MP station didn't have so elaborate an arrangement. The corporal led me into a room with a pair of stools.

"You his lawyer?" the corporal asked.

I looked at my collar; the PFC rank hadn't fallen off. "No," I said, "his priest." Marilyn Monroe could have strolled into the building and committed a crime, and these clowns wouldn't have gotten a description of the perpetrator.

"You have ten minutes." He left and I sat down on a stool. A minute or so later Cybulski entered the room through another door. There were circles beneath his eyes.

"Did you bring anything for me?" Cybulski asked.

I took some reefer out of my pocket and handed it to him.

"Too bad I can't smoke it in here."

"Why can't you?"

"It's a fucking police station, for Christ's sake. Or hadn't you noticed?"

I wasn't sure I had. "There's no safer place. Go ahead and light it up. How could you possibly get caught smoking a joint in a police station? Besides, he told me we only have ten minutes, so it's now or never."

"You have a strange way of looking at things, Jimmy." He lit the joint. "By the way, where the fuck have you been?"

"Remember when you told me that if ever I met more than three assholes in one day, I should look in the mirror?"

"I remember."

"Chuck, I'm surrounded by assholes."

He sat down on a stool. "Do you remember my plans for when I get out of the army, Jimmy?"

"Nobody gets out of the army."

"Be serious. Remember I told you about PETA, the People for the Ethical Treatment of Animals?"

"Sure. You're going to join some kind of delta force and rescue the bunny rabbits from the cosmetic companies."

"That's the idea."

"So?"

"So join me."

"Thanks. I have higher ambitions."

"Get me out of here, Jimmy. Let's go back to the States together and join the animal activists. You have a talent for breaking and entering. We need you. The animals need you."

"Do me a favor. As long as we're inside a police station, don't talk about my talents, okay?"

He quit the joint halfway and snuffed it out on the floor, then put the rest in his pocket. "You going in with Garrett?"

I shook my head. "He wants to do book. Book's not my thing."

"There's a rumor going around about him. Joiner was transferred out so Garrett could be transferred in."

"But you picked Garrett out of the replacement detachment. You picked him out yourself."

"True, but I may have been set up. It's all about aptitude scores, you know."

"Look, what's your point? Joiner left, for whatever reason, and Garrett replaced him. It happens a thousand times a day. What's the big deal?"

"The big deal is that Garrett lived in the replacement detachment for almost *three weeks* before I picked him."

I thought about that. Three days, maybe, on the outside. But not three weeks. If the rumor was true, something wasn't right.

"How sure are you of this?" I asked.

He nodded gravely.

We sat quietly for a minute. "What happened, Chuck?" I asked. "Tell me."

"Jimmy, you gotta take the rap with me on this one."

"You shut your fucking mouth."

He got up and paced the room with his hands clasped behind his head.

"They were waiting for me. I knocked on the door and then there were floodlights all over the place, and there they all were, they'd been waiting in the bushes. They grabbed the bag and opened it and said, 'Lookee what we got here.' They were real mean to me, Jimmy."

"What did you tell them?"

"I didn't tell them anything."

"What did they ask?"

"They asked about where the stuff came from, and I told them I found it on the sidewalk. They laughed, but I didn't know what else to say. They wanted to know why I was knocking on Schäfer's door. I told them I was lost and just wanted to ask directions. Schäfer set us up. He was furious about what you did to him." Cybulski sat back down on his stool and took a deep breath. "They got Dr. Fuchs, too."

"Shit."

"Fuchs is in German jail. Schäfer's disappeared, left town. The whole ring's busted."

I rubbed my eyes and tried to work it out. Fuchs wouldn't say anything, but Schäfer would, if they found him, and that would be enough to authorize a warrant to pick me up. They wouldn't find any evidence to connect me, though, and with Fuchs taking the fifth it would be necessary to corroborate the accusation with Cybulski. Once they did that, it was just a matter of time before they wrote a charge.

"You gotta take the rap with me, Jimmy."

I grabbed him by the arms, lifted him out of his stool, and slammed his back against the wall. "Now look here," I said. "You stop saying that. Putting me in here with you isn't going to make it any better for you. If you drag me in here I'll make sure you regret it."

"Jimmy, Jimmy." He started to sob. "Please don't do this to me. Please don't dump me now. Not now of all times. I beg you, Jimmy. I don't think I can take this one by myself."

"You think bringing me in here with you is going to make it easier? Chuck, I can help you a lot better from the outside. It's not my fault you didn't case the neighborhood before going in."

"I don't think I can do it by myself." He was choking on his words. "I don't. I really don't. I'm telling you, I just don't."

"Now you listen to me carefully," I said. "If you get a notion to sing, I suggest you do yourself instead."

"Oh, Jimmy, don't say that."

"It's the honorable thing, Chuck. Otherwise keep your goddamn mouth shut."

Chapter 14

A BMW PULLED UP on the curb in front of me as I was walking back to the barracks. In the driver's seat was Burkhard Krupa, the watch salesman I had met at the Canape. There was another man in the passenger seat.

"Fancy running into you here," Krupa said.

"Fancy," I said.

"Need a lift?"

I climbed into the back seat. "Take a left at the light," I told him.

"This is Wittlinger," Krupa said, nodding toward the passenger. The man he was introducing me to had thinning hair, greased down and combed from one ear to the other, in a pattern that was uncomfortably perpendicular to the vertical composition of his face. The grease was so heavy the grooves made by the comb were visible. His mouth was small and effeminate and his eyes were too close together. I was glad I wasn't sitting next to him.

"Nice to meet you," I said to him.

"Pleasure."

"Do you sell watches too?"

Krupa laughed. "Wittlinger cannot even tell the time, can you Wittlinger?"

"Hmm," Wittlinger said.

"Wittlinger and I are occasional . . . business associates," Krupa explained. He put the BMW into gear and pulled away from the curb.

"Left at the light," I reminded him.

"You know, we were just going to Wittlinger's place for a couple of drinks. Why don't you join us?"

"No, thank you." It was a military holiday, Melina was expecting me, and I had long before discovered that sex with a woman, even mediocre sex, was better than conversation with a man, even great conversation.

"We have much to talk about," Krupa argued. "I will show you my collection of early clocks and watches. I have some pieces I wager you have never seen."

"I've seen them all. This is it—left here." We were sitting at the light but he wasn't signaling a turn.

"Of course you have. There could be some interesting company, if you understand my meaning."

"How interesting?"

He turned around and looked at me. "Very interesting."

The light changed to green and the BMW passed through the intersection. Krupa obviously wanted me for more than he was willing to admit. I didn't trust him, and I certainly didn't trust his pathetic sidekick; something smelled funny. But if you avoid all the funny smells in life you miss all the opportunities. On the other hand, you miss all the hell and heartbreak too.

"Okay," I said, "count me in." What the hell.

"We did not have to twist the arm, did we?" Krupa said.

"Just don't try to sell me a watch."

*

THERE WAS A SWING set in Wittlinger's yard, but I doubted any children lived here. It probably served as bait to lure them. We walked a creek stone path to the front door and I could see through the windows. People filled the living room.

"You're having a party," I said to Wittlinger.

"Oh, a modest little July Fourth gathering."

"I don't want to intrude."

"You won't be intruding. I assure you."

I wondered why he happened to be driving past the MP station when there was a party going on at his house, but I knew better than to ask. Probably he didn't really live there. Probably Wittlinger was not his real name. I tried to remember whether the business card Krupa had given me contained his home address and phone number; at any rate, I had thrown it away. These two wanted something from me, and they wanted it badly enough to throw a party and pick me up as they pretended to be passing by.

I confess I was curious. With Cybulski in the slammer and the heat on all around me, I was lying low and operating, as they say, on a fixed income. I hoped whatever it was that it did not have anything to do with Wittlinger's apparent sexual preference. If so my evening was a waste.

There were a couple of girls at the party, as Krupa had promised. They were nice looking German girls which meant they were expensive. Krupa must have signaled to one of them when we entered the living room because she zeroed in on me. She had large breasts that preceded her like bumpers. She introduced herself as Gretchen. Of course; it had to be Gretchen. I told her mine was Jimmy.

"James?" she asked.

"No," I said, "Jimmy. My what big tits you have."

She laughed convincingly, as if she had laughed at her clients' stupid jokes a thousand times before.

She'd been to America once, she told me; to Florida. She saw Disney World and the Everglades and several alligators. She remembered it had been hot. In Daytona Beach she entered and won a wet t-shirt contest. All in all it had been a good trip. Next time she wanted to go to California and see the large red trees. Some of them, she had heard, were so big you could drive your car through them. Her speech was rehearsed; she'd had American clients before.

We walked around the living room together and I wished I knew more about art because there were many fine paintings on the walls. I'd spent a lot of time in the Art Institute of Chicago, killing time there because it was a good place to make sure no one was following me. My favorites were the Impressionists. The paintings on Wittlinger's walls were nice too and I admired the way he had arranged lamps to cast shadows on the brush strokes and give the paintings a sense of depth. It occurred to me to try my luck in the art business sometime, because it was such a noble profession and you met such interesting people. The pieces were a little large and therefore awkward to turn over, but the money was good.

Someone put a glass of champagne in my hand. Krupa started a friendly conversation about military defense against terrorism and called me into it. War planning was, he said, a favorite topic of his, as he had once been an officer in Her Majesty's army. A small group gathered around to hear him speak. They were men and women of his age, upper- to middleclass, and thoroughly uninformed about the military.

"With how many brigades abreast do the Americans plan to defend the Fulda Gap?" Krupa wondered. "At what point do they implement the passage of lines with reinforcements from Conus? Do they actually expect the attack will come through Fulda? Surely the Russians know of this defense posture and will simply maneuver around it. Straight to Hannover on the Helmstedt Autobahn. Down to Bonn. Get high of the river and poison it. What can the Americans do? All their forces are in the Rheinland, in Hessen, in Bayern, defending the Fulda Gap. The Russians need only go around it. Surround it. Cut it off.

Then attack through Fulda and crush what opposition remains—if any."

"The Amerikans will blow up the bridges," someone suggested.

"Nonsense. The Amerikans will blow up no bridges. The Amerikans pay for the bushes they damage, they will not blow up any bridges. Being Amerikans they will get permission from the Bürgermeister before blowing up his bridge, and the Bürgermeister will not give it. Besides, they need the bridges for their own retreat. The Russians will gain their objective by gaining air superiority with superior air forces, and the Amerikans will need all the bridges they can find to escape."

"But what about the forces on the ground?" someone said. "You must take the ground—you must occupy it. You cannot hold onto a territory with only a grip on the air."

"You only need take the air. The war is over when you have air superiority. When you have taken the air, taking the ground is mere corollary."

"The Amerikans will reinforce."

"With what? It will all be over forty-eight hours after it begins, and it takes at least that long to deploy units from Conus. The Amerikans will not have enough time to reinforce either men or materiel. They will call a truce and define new boundaries. The Russians will have achieved their objective: a new boundary pushed deeply into the territory of the west."

Several desperate plans for the defense of Western Europe were then proposed. Someone suggested that enor-mous trees—whichever species produced the greatest trunk diameter—be planted closely together along the East German border to form a natural fence, to hinder the passage of tanks. Krupa responded that what the suggester failed to realize was the bigger the tree, the more room it needed for its canopy. So if the trees were big enough to stop a tank, there would be plenty of space between them through which a tank could pass.

Not to mention that if the technology exists to move mountains and travel in space, probably a way could be found to knock down a tree or two.

Someone else suggested that everyone with a car should drive it into the city and park it—anywhere—just so it blocks the street. Create the world's biggest traffic jam. The rationale was that if the city were jammed Ivan couldn't navigate through it. Krupa pointed out the plan failed to address what would prevent Ivan from going *around* the city. And it failed to provide for the city itself, which presumably would have to go on functioning, afflicted with an endless traffic jam. The plan also tacitly assumed the city's inhabitants would not be hankering to evacuate it.

"Neither fat trees nor traffic jams will stop airplanes," Krupa declared, "and it is airplanes that will win the war. Can no one offer a better defense plan than these?"

Silence.

"Perhaps Mister Fisher has an opinion."

"No," I said, "Mister Fisher does not have an opinion."

"But he must. Everyone has one."

"No, he mustn't. If he had an opinion he would not be able to reveal it as he is privy to classified information."

"Of course, you are correct. Please forgive me. I have been insensitive."

"Forget it. How is it you are so concerned about American defense strategy?"

"I have many friends in the American community. We talk. Military war planning is my hobby. I once held Her Majesty's commission."

"So you said."

"You are not drinking."

I looked at my glass, which had been refilled repeatedly. "I am drinking."

"There is plenty; do not be bashful."

"I'm not bashful. But I can only drink one at a time. See?"

Krupa smiled and turned away to speak to another guest. The stiffness that comes with being in a strange house and mixing with strangers had gone. Gretchen—if that was her real name—glanced up at me occasionally from across the room. She glanced over at Krupa too, plainly waiting for a signal. Wittlinger was nowhere in sight. People were beginning to leave. Whatever was going to happen would have to happen soon.

I hoped it would be lucrative. I had grown tired of the graveyard work and at any rate had no desire to do it alone. The only real pleasure I'd ever derived was watching Cybulski scurry back to the truck when I had a body in tow on his heels. The cigarette and gasoline trade were drying up; everyone was being careful. I could really use some dough.

"Mister Fisher."

"Herr Krupa?"

"I wonder if you could do me a favor."

Here it comes. "I would be happy to do you a favor."

"I wonder if you could provide me with—"

Here it comes.

"—a telephone book."

"A telephone book?"

"Yes. I have business contacts in the American community. A telephone book of the American military community would be a great convenience to me."

What kind of bullshit is this? Drag me all the way here, screw up my entire evening, and ask me for a fucking telephone book?

"A corporate ladder, illustrating the chain of command in the division headquarters, would also be useful to me."

"That's it? That's what you want? A telephone book and a corporate ladder?"

He shrugged. "I would be willing to pay for them."

"No, that's not necessary. I'll get them for you." I shook my head; what the hell.

"When might I expect delivery?"

"Delivery?"

"When will I see you again, and receive the items?"

"Um, that would be, let's see, oh . . . sometime."

"Sometime soon, I hope."

A figure in an adjoining room caught my eye. The woman's back was to me, but her hair was familiar; it draped across naked shoulders and was more scintillating than any piece of jewelry she could have worn.

I handed my empty glass to Krupa and headed wordlessly in her direction, moving through the remnant guests like a polar icebreaker. When I was directly behind her I cleared my throat. She turned. It was a stranger.

"I'm sorry," I said to the woman. "I thought you were someone else." I felt stupid; obviously Molly Brannigan would not attend a gathering such as this.

When I turned to rejoin Krupa I almost collided with him.

"Some distraction," he said. "That is what you need. I alluded to it earlier, and now it is time to provide it." He glanced across the room.

Gretchen rose, smiling, and approached. She took my hand. "Let's explore the house," she suggested.

"Do, let's," I said. "Show me the bedroom first."

She giggled.

We waved goodbye to Krupa and followed her breasts into the bedroom. The room was dark, so I turned on a lamp. More impressionist paintings hung on the walls. The most striking was an airy, atmospheric rendition of a cathedral.

Gretchen sat on the edge of the bed and took her top off. Her breasts wobbled with energetic momentum as they came free of the bra. She put her hand behind my neck, pulled me close, and raked her eraser-sized nipples across my face. She had a sturdy body and when I got on top of her I relaxed and allowed my entire weight to rest on her. She straightened out her legs, and I felt the full length of her figure against mine. I rocked slowly as if on a water bed. It didn't take long to finish.

"That was quick," she said.

"Sorry."

"Don't apologize. It comes with the territory."

"You're a working girl, right?"

She looked confused. "Isn't that obvious?"

"I just wanted to make sure. Is Krupa paying you?"

"Yes. Didn't you know?"

"Yeah, I guess I did. Do you know what he wants from me?"

She shook her head. "He only told me to make you happy."

I got up and started getting dressed.

"Are you happy?" she asked.

"Very." I dropped a twenty Mark tip on the bed. She picked it up silently and folded it into a small square, then watched me finish dressing.

"Tell Krupa I had a good time," I said.

I opened a window and climbed out. As I was walking away from the house I heard the window close behind me. A few seconds later the bedroom light went out, and I assumed Gretchen was reporting to Krupa. She must have merely wrapped a sheet around herself because she hadn't had time to get dressed.

I had planned to get to bed early, and it was already close to midnight. Tomorrow the promotion list was coming out. If everything had proceeded in concert with the natural patterns of the universe, my name would be at the top of the list, and I would have seen my last day as a private in the Armed Forces of the United States of America.

A telephone book. Jesus fucking Christ.

Chapter 15

I WOULD HAVE TO wait to find out about the promotion. As soon as I arrived in the office the next morning Pendergrass ordered me to Discom to help with cartography. He claimed to know nothing about whether I was on the promotion list, but at the same time he was unable to look me in the eye.

When I returned to the office late in the afternoon I found the entire section empty; the staff had gone to the base theater to take a piss test. I spent the final hour of the day straightening and organizing documents in the safes. At five o'clock everyone returned from the theater and packed up to go home. Pendergrass still wouldn't look at me. He went behind the safes and pretended to be busy with something and couldn't be bothered. Finally as he was preparing to leave I took his cap away from him. You couldn't go outside without your cap, so this was like breaking his legs. He finally looked at me, and his shoulders slumped.

"You didn't make it," he said.

"Why not?"

"I don't know."

"You knew this morning I didn't make it, didn't you?"

"Yes."

"Why didn't you tell me then?"

"I didn't want it to distract you from your work."

"Bullshit!"

"All right, I didn't know how to tell you . . . I was hoping you'd hear it from someone else."

"Well, aren't *we* the big sergeant with the strong spine!"

"At ease, private."

"You also know *why* I didn't make it, don't you?"

He hesitated, then shook his head. "No."

"Fine." I wanted to grab him by his mug handle ears and bash his face on the desk. "I'll just go the IG," I said, "to get an answer. And I'll cite your behavior in my protest."

"Don't do that."

"Then tell me."

"I can't."

"You mean you won't. I'm going down to Bundy's office right this minute and have a little chat with him. You want to come along?"

He didn't answer.

I dropped his cap on the floor next to his feet and reached for the door.

He grabbed my arm. "Don't," he said.

"Then *tell* me."

"I can't. But if you guess, you might guess right."

Men got promotions from other men, so the only thing that could have stopped my promotion was someone who didn't like me. But everyone on my promotion board liked me—Pendergrass, Skelton, and Vance. So either someone who didn't like me got on my board, or he convinced someone on my board to blackball me. There was only one person in the entire United States Army who disliked me enough to do either.

"Riddell?" I said.

Pendergrass picked up his cap from the floor, dusted it off, and put it on. "Goodnight, Private First Class Fisher," he said, and walked out the door.

Garrett and Lamoureaux were lingering at the front entrance of the building, waiting for me.

"Fisher," Garrett said. "I'm sorry about the promotion. I wanted you to know." He had PFC stripes on his collar; he'd been promoted.

"Who was on your board?" I asked him.

"Pendergrass," he said, "and Skelton. And Riddell."

"Riddell?"

"Yeah. He bumped Vance. He said it was getting too easy to make rank in the 111th Division."

I turned to leave.

"I'm sorry, Jimmy. Really."

"Fuck it."

Melina had made a cake and decorated it with the word "Congratulations" and a crude illustration of corporal stripes. She'd also invited all the whores at Amy's to join us. There wasn't enough room in the bed for everyone, so some of the girls had to stand to the side and lean over to reach me. I didn't have the heart to tell Melina I hadn't gotten promoted. Also, I saw no reason to spoil the party.

Chapter 16

MY ATTITUDE CHANGED. I practiced "malicious obedience"—strict adherence to the rule or command without regard for consequences. For example, Pendergrass gave me a pile of documents to file. I noticed that his personal mail had been placed accidentally in the pile, and so I filed the mail under "miscellaneous" in the unclassified drawer. Later in the day, after Pendergrass had spent an hour turning the office upside down, he asked me point blank whether I'd seen his mail. I told him what I'd done.

"Why didn't you just give it to me when you found it?" he asked.

"Those were not your instructions, sergeant. You told me to file the documents, not to review them to determine whether anyone's personal mail happened to be among them." Malicious obedience.

Word got around that I had an attitude. "Fisher's in revolt," they said. "Fisher's got a hair." A couple of hours later it was "Fisher's going down," and people were avoiding me and averting eye contact as we passed in the hallway. When I tried to visit General Bundy that afternoon and his secretary told me he was too busy to see me, I realized my army career, such as it was, was over. Riddell had won.

At exactly five o'clock I stopped work, put on my cap, and left the office. For the first time in memory I was the first one out of the office at quitting time. As I passed through the Kaserne gate onto Alzeyerstrasse I noticed Wittlinger across the street, standing in front of Amy's. He was by himself, waiting on the sidewalk under the red lamp, holding a bouquet of flowers. It was the silliest thing I'd ever seen. No one brought flowers to whores.

I stopped just outside the gate and watched him for a few minutes while I smoked a cigarette. Although he noticed everything else happening around him, he didn't once look directly at me. I put out the cigarette and crossed the street.

"Are you trying to pick someone up?" I asked him. "Because if you are, you chose the wrong place. This corner of the world is frequented by girls who sell their bodies to men, and by the men who pay for the service."

"Krupa wants to see you," he said, still looking the other way.

"Krupa? What for?"

"He's waiting for you at the Weinstube."

Wittlinger's close-set eyes were looking at the flowers in his hand, at his shoes, at everything but me. His hair was plastered to the top of his head with grease and sweat. When he spoke his mouth hardly moved; he was apparently trying to conceal his words from passers-by.

"Is that what this is about?" I said. "This flower bullshit is a signal that Krupa wants me to visit him in the Weinstube?"

"Yes. And from now on, when you see me here, ignore me. Just go to the Weinstube." His words had the strange buzzing sound that comes from a mouth that's not moving when it speaks.

I shook my head in disgust and continued down Alzeyer-strasse. At one point I looked back and found him still there, holding his flowers and looking bored.

The window frames of the Weinstube were red and green, in keeping with the building's medieval character. Each floor covered a little more area than the one beneath it, giving the building a chesty, top-heavy look. I walked up the steep, narrow staircase, holding onto the rope railing, and found Krupa sitting at a corner table in a parlor-like room on the second floor. He had a glass of red wine in front of him that was about three-quarters empty and he was reading the menu absentmindedly. I stood in the doorway, watching him tap his fingers impatiently, until he noticed me. His face relaxed with relief and he motioned right away for me to join him.

"Nice of you to come," he said, rising. "Obviously you got Wittlinger's message."

"If 'message' is what you call it," I said. "Standing in front of a whorehouse with a bunch of flowers."

"You will have to excuse Mister Wittlinger's judgment. He leans toward the dramatic."

We sat down and I looked at the menu. A waitress appeared and took my order of a local Riesling. Krupa ordered another glass of red wine, something from a place called Pomerol.

"You Americans are all alike," he said. "At home you drink cheap California wines out of a jug, because that is what they serve you. When you come to Germany you drink the local white wine because it grows in the hills outside your window. Consequently, you think you are cultured."

"I drink the local wines because I like them," I said.

"Is it any wonder the better German wines do not export well? They slosh their low-end production together and call it Liebfraumilch. That is what they sell to the United States, and that is how the United States know German wines. The better material—and they do make some good material— stays at home and does not sell. Now the French," he said lifting his glass, "the French export their best wines and drink the plonk at home."

"If you hate Germany so much why don't you move to France?"

"I do not hate Germany. I merely prefer French wine. Many Americans enjoy Chinese food but that does not mean they should move to China."

He took a couple of deep breaths. Finally he smiled. His bushy eyebrows hoisted themselves up higher on his forehead.

"It is good to see you again," he said.

"Is this a fag thing?" I blurted.

"Excuse me?"

"Is that why you're so interested in me? Because you want to do fag things to me?"

He looked puzzled, then comprehension spread across his face. A second later comprehension was replaced by apprehension.

"No, of course not. No, my goodness, no. Is that what you think?"

"It had occurred to me."

"Oh my. I am terribly sorry. Whatever gave you the impression?"

"First, because there's no other reason for you to be interested in me, and second, because your friend Wittlinger obviously takes walks on the wild side."

He closed his eyes and shook his head. "I assure you, that is not what this is about."

"Then what *is* it about?"

He appeared surprised. "But my young friend, I thought I made that clear to you the other night. I am interested in obtaining a telephone book and a company ladder of the American military stationed here in town. I would like to have these articles to extend my contacts and sales into the American community. I am willing to pay for the articles. You had agreed to obtain them for me. If you have changed your mind I will request them of someone else. In either case I apologize for the misunderstanding and for any inconvenience I have caused you."

"Let me get this straight," I said. "Wittlinger stands in front of the whorehouse across the street from my office, holding a bunch of flowers, waiting for me to get off work. It's a cloak-and-dagger signal for me to meet you here, and all you want is a telephone book?"

"And a company ladder. I admit Wittlinger's methods are dramatic. However, all I instructed him to do was contact you and ask you to meet me. Nothing more is intended, nor is anything more requested of you."

"I don't believe it."

He raised both arms in the air. "Search me," he said. "Have I asked anything more of you than a telephone book and a company ladder?"

"No. Not yet."

He lowered his arms. "That is all I want. Really. The friendship was, as they say, icing on the cake. We can forgo that if you wish. I am willing to pay for the documents."

I sighed. "It's not necessary to pay for them."

After all, what difference did it make? Krupa could get that kind of stuff at his leisure. If I refused to help him he would merely ask someone else. The military telephone book was available to the public—many local business people and private citizens had a copy—so there was nothing wrong with getting one for Krupa. The company ladder was a little sensitive, but still a long way from being classified. It merely listed who worked for whom and in what office, and none of that information was, by itself, sensitive. Certainly none of it was classified. Giving a telephone book and a company ladder to Krupa would therefore break no law nor cause any harm to the United

States Army. It occurred to me, besides, that the United States Army had not been doing me any favors lately.

"I'll get them for you," I said. "I have no problem with that."

"Fine," he said, "good." He looked at his watch. "Today is Tuesday. Shall we say we will meet here two days from now, on Thursday?"

"That's the nineteenth."

"Right."

"I'll come directly here after work on Thursday, the nineteenth."

We ordered more wine. He was in a mood to talk. He spoke of *loyalty*, pronouncing the word reverently, as if it were the Prime Virtue. He admitted he didn't trust anyone and never would. But he nevertheless had to employ people who were as loyal as people could be; definitively loyal people, which is to say, people who would go to any lengths and make any sacrifice to protect him. From what he didn't say. He was not so naïve as to believe such behavior could be guaranteed, but the qualities were nevertheless what he had to seek in his employees and colleagues to be successful. At the time I assumed he was talking about success in the watch business.

Finally he played a question-and-answer game with me to discover the limits of my scruples. He asked whether I would do such-and-such or such-and-such, and under what circumstances I would go so far as to do such-and-such. His questions became more and more specific as he tried to pin down my moral character.

Would I rob a bank if I could be assured in advance I wouldn't be caught? Would I turn in a family member who I knew had committed a crime? An acquaintance? A known and dangerous criminal? An enemy? Would I kill an ant? A rabbit? A man? Would I return a wallet I found on the sidewalk if it contained ten dollars? Ten thousand dollars? Would I interfere if I witnessed a mugging? An animal being abused? A stranger beating his wife? How much money would I accept in exchange for not interfering? Did Jesus Christ exist, and to what extent did his teachings, as purportedly documented in the Bible, constitute my ethical premises? What did I respect most? Love most? Fear most?

He was clever at the game, and I felt like I was spread-eagle on a disk that was rotating in front of a circus knife thrower. The knives came ever closer until they outlined my body, my soul, my character.

Chapter 17

I HAD ONE MORE go at preserving the old lifestyle. Maybe if I could take charge of my personal life, charge of my professional life would follow. I contacted all of my cigarette suppliers one by one and asked them to bring their rations by for wholesaling. I acted as if nothing had happened, as if we were conducting business as usual. But one by one they either turned me down or hung up on me. Even Pierce and Chadwick, formerly my two steadiest suppliers, refused to do business with me. Pierce, who worked next door in JAG, said he didn't have the time to bring his cigarettes by. Chadwick hung up the telephone as soon as he heard my voice.

It was time to prostrate myself before Riddell. I asked Sergeant Pendergrass for permission to leave the office and visit G2. He looked at me respectfully, almost in awe, as if I had just volunteered for a suicide mission. Then he nodded silently, too choked up for words.

"The next hour was one of the gutsiest things you ever did," he managed to stutter.

G2 was in the basement of the building. I think all intelligence units are in the basements of their buildings, and the reason may be that intelligence officers believe the deeper in the earth they perform their work, the less susceptible it is to surveillance. A more likely reason, though, is that intelligence agents have always thought of themselves as operating below surfaces—whether of society, or of law, or of moral decency—and their affinity for subterranean offices, as well as for terminology such as "underground," "undercover," and "mole," is metaphorical.

The hallway in the basement was always dark, so you had to stop in front of each door and squint to read the name. Riddell's name—COL L. RIDDELL—was painted in block letters. A band of light was visible at the base of the door.

I knocked.

"Come in."

Riddell watched my entrance as if he knew in advance who it would be. He sat motionless as I stepped into the room. The moment I closed the door behind me I understood the meaning of peace of mind—for I saw it in his eyes—and realized I'd made an enormous mistake in coming to see him. The contentment that leaked from the deep creases around his eyes was one that could be enjoyed only after a profound accomplishment, following a lifetime of suffering. A mere handful of men in history had felt what Riddell was now feeling: David, when he slew Goliath; Columbus, when he made landfall; DiMaggio, when he saw Marilyn Monroe naked for the first time.

"What do you want?" Riddell asked. His voice was sultry; he knew damn well what I wanted.

"Sir," I said, "I am made to understand that your opposition to my promotion to corporal is the reason I am still a private." I pointed at one of the chairs in front of his desk. "May I sit down?"

"No."

"As you wish, sir." I shifted from one foot to the other; I was unable to control my body language. He settled deeper into his chair, as if he were about to watch a movie.

"Stand at attention," he said.

I stood at attention.

"I haven't got all day, private," he said with mock impatience. "You still haven't told me what the hell you want."

"What I want is—"

"Call me sir."

"Sir," I said, "I have come here to ask—"

"You haven't requested permission to speak."

"Sir, Private Fisher requests permission—"

"You haven't reported for duty. Don't you know anything, Private?"

"Private Fisher reporting for duty, sir." I saluted and held the salute while he picked his fingernails. A long minute went by. Of course it was inappropriate to report for duty to the OIC of another section merely because you wanted to have a conversation with him. But little of our encounter would come within a country mile of what could be called appropriate.

He returned the salute. "Now ask permission to speak," he said.

"Sir, Private Fisher requests permission to speak."

"Request denied."

He lifted himself out of his chair, puffing a little from the exertion, and maneuvered around to the front of the desk with patient confidence, like a cat approaching a bird with a broken wing. I could hear fabric swishing as his inner thighs rubbed against each other. When he got to the front of the desk he tilted his frame backwards against it and crossed his arms. I chanced a look at his face. There was both pain and revenge in his eyes. He looked like one of those trees that threw apples at Dorothy in *The Wizard of Oz*.

"Assume the leaning rest," he said.

I dropped to the floor and complied. The civilian world knows the leaning rest as the push-up position. Only the army would adopt such a euphemism, as if it betokened rest rather than discomfort and humiliation. Riddell sat on the edge of his desk and stared at my back. Another long minute went by; he was waiting for me to get uncomfortable. Finally he spoke.

"Are you able to recall all the times you treated me like shit, Private?"

"Like shit sir? Well, no, as a matter of fact I—"

"Try."

In the leaning rest you don't actually do push-ups, so your arms aren't the first parts of you to tire. Keeping your back straight becomes difficult after a short while. Your body begins to bow downward in a gentle arch until your crotch and thighs are millimeters above the floor.

"Um," I said, "I believe that on occasion you were unhappy with—"

"Call me sir."

"Sir, you weren't happy with—"

"You haven't requested permission to speak."

"Private Fisher reporting for duty and requesting permission to speak, sir."

"I did not instruct the Private to report for duty. I only pointed out the Private had not requested permission to speak."

"Sir, I just thought I'd be efficient and save us both some time."

"I appreciate your concern for my time management, Private. However, you still do not have permission to speak."

"Sir, Private Fisher requests permission—"

"You haven't reported for duty. Don't you know anything, Private?"

After a couple of minutes in the leaning rest your wrists hurt from supporting the weight of your upper body, and your back aches from trying and failing to remain straight. You raise your butt into the air, mostly to give your back a stretch. At this point the exercise becomes humiliating.

"Private Fisher reporting for duty, sir."

"You're supposed to salute when you report for duty, Private."

I balanced myself on one arm and saluted awkwardly. The rules require that you hold the salute until it is returned. Colonel Riddell didn't budge.

"Now you may request permission to speak," he said.

"Sir, Private Fisher requests permission to speak."

"Permission granted. Now describe—completely and in excruciating detail—all the times you treated me like shit. The sooner you complete your presentation, the sooner I'll allow you to recover from the leaning rest."

Recover is the right word. Eventually your upper torso begins to quiver. The quivering steadily increases until your whole body begins to shake convulsively. Surprisingly, you're able to remain in the leaning rest a long time after reaching the convulsion stage. It becomes a show for whomever is tormenting you.

"Sir, I intentionally placed Echo Company in swamps. My sole purpose in doing so was to piss you off."

"Excellent. Next?"

"Sir, I intentionally withheld documents from you, invoking the need-to-know principle, to piss you off. May I stop saluting now sir?"

"No, you may not. Next?"

I continued, scouring my memory for incidents of disrespect. The number was greater than I would have guessed. It shouldn't have surprised me; I'd hated Riddell for upwards of two years. Never before had I seen a man so happy listening to a confession.

When I ran out of material to confess I sensed he hadn't heard enough. He appeared cheated, like a child who has reached the bottom of the candy jar sooner than expected. So I made a few things up and took credit for a few pranks I hadn't pulled. Gradually the hard lines in his face softened and he appeared satisfied. By this time my left wrist and arm were numb, as were my shoulders and toes. My back was ready to collapse. Any minute I would lose my balance and topple over.

"You know, it took me three weeks to scrape the glue off my windshield," he said.

"Sorry, sir."

"It would have been more considerate of you to have used a weaker glue."

"Of course, sir. What kind of glue did I use?"

"Super glue. But you knew that—you've confessed to it."

"I'm sorry. I forgot. One uses so many glues."

"You've done well, Private," he said. "Very well. But there's just one little item you have so far failed to mention."

I blinked in pain and tried to think of what I might have left out. I drew a blank. "Sir, I've told you everything. I've even confessed on behalf of others who hate you even more than I do. I've confessed on behalf of people not yet born, who one day will—"

"Think, Private, think. You're leaving out something rather obvious."

"Sir, I'm sure that I . . ." Riddell had once had a clerk who every day for a year had urinated into his coffee. But apocalyptic horses couldn't make me take credit for that one.

"*Think.*"

"I *am* thinking, sir, I—"

Then it came to me, and I bit my tongue. Oh my God—if he was talking about what I thought he was, then I had a serious problem on my hands. My life was in danger, but I was in no condition to stand up, let alone run.

"Thought of it, did you?" he said, smirking. "I can tell by the sweat dripping from your nose."

"No sir, I am positive I have told you everything."

"*You fucked my daughter, didn't you, you little guttersnipe.*"

"Oh, no sir. No, no, no, sir. I would never, ever d-do such a thing, sir."

"She told me you did."

That dumb bitch! She swore she would never tell! But wait a minute; maybe he was merely trying to trap me.

"I didn't f-fuck her, sir. No matter what she said to you. I *swear* to you I didn't d-do it."

"She told me she promised you she would never tell me, because you believed your life would be in danger if she did."

Oh, f-fuck.

"Well?" he said. "Do you want to confess to having sex with a fifteen year old, or do you want to stay a private—and in the leaning rest—for the remainder of your natural life? It's your choice."

Some choice. I had a feeling the remainder of my natural life was, from his perspective, a trivial quantity. She had told me she was sixteen. Sixteen still wouldn't mollify her dad, but at least it was legal.

"All right," I said. "What the hell." I had nothing left to lose. And I was in such pain that I would have accepted death in exchange for a few minutes of rest. "I fucked your daughter. I admit it. Can I go now?"

"Call me sir."

"Sir, I fucked—"

"Request permission to speak."

"Sir, Private Fisher—"

"Report for duty."

"Private Fisher reporting for duty, sir."

"Salute."

"I am saluting, sir."

"Salute again."

I put my arm down, then raised it again to my forehead. It was all I could do to keep from crashing to the floor.

"Well?" he said.

"Sir, Private Fisher requests permission to speak."

"Permission is granted."

"Sir, I admit I fucked your daughter. However, I didn't do it to cause harm to her or to you. I did it because I thought she was beautiful. I still think she's beautiful, and I don't mind at all that she has the IQ of a mushroom, or that she has been fucked by legions of soldiers, including officers in your own command." I stopped to catch my breath. "If it's quite all right I'd rather not be pushed into the concertina wire. I never *bragged* about fucking her, sir, like Mattingly did. For what it's worth, I'm sorry."

The period of silence that followed was torturous. I concentrated on not falling and not crying. I was swimming in pain.

"Now you have just one opportunity to answer me," he said, "and you had better make it good. What do you want? Why are you here?"

It was his big moment; it was what he had set the stage for. It was also my big moment; I had paid a high price to reach this point in the conversation.

"Sir, I want to be promoted to corporal. I'm sure I deserve it. I want to do what it takes to get your support for the promotion. I ask that you don't let our personal differences stand in the way of what is right."

He slid off the edge of the desk and took his cap from the top of the coat rack.

"Take a brick about yay big," he said, holding his hands a foot apart. "Write your request on it with a crayon. Then shove the brick up your ass, sideways."

He left the room. I allowed myself to go limp, and my chest slammed against the floor. I may have cried, I don't remember, I probably did.

Someone once told me that no matter how far down you fall you can't fall off the floor. That there is indeed a lowest low from which point things can only get better. I lay on the floor for a few minutes, breathing deeply. Then I dragged myself up and sat in Riddell's chair. It took about five minutes before my circulation returned and all the numbness was gone. When I felt well enough to keep my balance I got up and walked home.

It was obvious why officers sometimes got fragged by their men: the greatest revenge you can take on your enemies is to outlive them.

Chapter 18

THURSDAY AFTER WORK I changed into street clothes, grabbed a bite at the mess hall, then went to the Weinstube. Krupa was sitting at the same table, in the same chair, as during our first meeting two nights before.

"Welcome, welcome," he said, standing up. "You brought the documents?"

"Yes." I handed him a telephone book and a corporate ladder I had lifted from Skelton's desk.

"I'm so grateful," he said. "Won't you have a seat?"

"I'm not staying."

"Oh, but you must. Have one glass of wine at least."

"Thank you, no."

"How much do I owe you for these?" He reached for his wallet.

"You don't owe me anything," I told him.

"Nonsense. How much?"

"I mean it. I don't want any money."

"I cannot accept them for free. I have to give you something."

"It's not necessary, really. They weren't mine to begin with."

"They weren't mine either," he said.

"All right," I said, "ten dollars."

He leafed through the bills in his wallet. "It seems I only have Marks. What is the exchange rate?"

"Don't bother. Ten Marks will do."

"No, you said dollars, so dollars it will be. And the rate?"

"Okay, call it two to one."

"Very well. Two to one. So good of you to know. Twenty Marks, then. Oh, but there remains a problem. I only have fifties."

"Then let's just not worry about it. Really."

"Nonsense. Gabi will have it." He switched to German. "Gabi, would you come over here for a small moment? I owe this gentleman twenty Marks, and it seems I have only fifties. Might you be able to assist us? Of course you can. I knew you would. Thank you. So, Mister Fisher, here are your twenty Marks."

"Thank you."

"And Gabi, please bring the gentleman a glass of dry Riesling."

"No," I said. "I can't stay, I really can't."

"Bring the wine, Gabi," Krupa said. "Please sit down, Mister Fisher, and do me the courtesy of allowing me to buy you a drink."

I sat down. The lights were low in the room and the background music consisted of soft violins. One drink was okay. Then I'd go somewhere else and have a bunch more.

"I have another business proposition for you," Krupa announced.

My heart sank. I'd had enough of him and wanted to end the relationship. The stench of his imminent liver failure was overpowering, and for some reason it was worse when he had a drink in his hand.

"Herr Krupa," I said, "if it's more office memos you want, I'd prefer you get them from someone else."

130

The waitress, Gabi, brought my wine and Krupa waited until she had left again. "Not office memos," he said. "This time I would like to buy something a little more interesting, and pay a little more for it."

"What, a desk calendar? To keep track of American holidays?"

"No, a terrain walk."

My wine glass stopped halfway to my lips. "A terrain walk?"

"Yes."

"What the hell for?"

"I have a client who wants to buy one." He took a sip of his wine. He was relaxed, waiting for my response, as if he had merely offered to buy a used lawnmower.

"They'd string me up," I said. "They'd give me life, if they caught me."

"Oh, pooh. Terrain walks are unclassified. They could not—and would not—do anything of the sort. Besides, how would they find out? It is no more difficult than the so-called office memo. You simply make a copy and bring it here."

I pushed my chair away from the table.

"Mister Fisher, there is no need to feel threatened or insulted. I have made you a proposition, that is all. Please, finish your wine."

"You're a spy," I said. "Aren't you?"

He winced. "I am a businessman. I buy and sell certain rare and unique commodities. I consider myself a specialist. My activities are harmless—and legal, I might add."

"Spying is legal?" I said. "Buying a terrain walk is legal?"

"Shh, there is no reason for you to raise your voice so. I can hear you quite adequately. Terrain walks are *unclassified*. Therefore anyone can read them. Therefore anyone can have them. Therefore anyone can buy them. So please stop with that spying nonsense. It makes me uncomfortable."

"It's not as simple as you say it is, Herr Krupa. Though they're unclassified they're nevertheless sensitive. What you're asking me to do is a violation of some kind of law—I just don't know right off hand which one."

He leaned back in his chair, folded his arms, and regarded me with mock criticism. "This thing about violating laws: it would be a new experience for you?"

I finished my wine in one gulp, then stood up. "Thanks for the drink," I said.

"Wait."

"Goodbye, Herr Krupa."

"You have not heard how much I am willing to pay for the document."

I hesitated. "All right, I'll bite. How much?"

"Five thousand dollars."

I laughed out loud. "If it's so legal, and so harmless, and so perfectly moral and upright, as you insist, then why is it worth so much money?"

"I have a client who cannot obtain it otherwise and is willing to pay the price."

"And you get a little something too, right?"

He closed his eyes, tilted his head and shrugged.

"What could your client possibly want with the thing?" I asked.

"That is his private business. I do not ask those questions. It makes absolutely no difference to me—nor should it to you. Frankly, I am surprised to find you so virtuous. That is not at all what I expected."

"Well, I'm now supposed to ask what it is you expected, and what the basis was for your expectation. But I know how salesmen work, and I'm not going to allow you to extend the conversation indefinitely until I finally surrender and agree to do what you want. I'm leaving."

"Ten thousand dollars."

"For a fucking *terrain walk*?"

"Please-keep-your-voice-down."

"You know what I think?" I said. "I think this is one of those bullshit internal system checks. I think you'll keep offering more and more money until I finally agree, and you'll learn just how much it costs to penetrate the system. Then you'll report to G2, or whoever hired you in the first place."

He shook his head. "No. You are way off target."

"Tell me, is this just a survey, or do you have the authority to arrest me for conspiracy to commit espionage if I fail the test?"

"This is no test, Mister Fisher. I do not work for G2."

"Riddell sent you, didn't he?"

"I do not know anyone named Riddell."

"Well, here's my answer. Take a brick about yay big." I held my hands about a foot apart. "Write your business proposition on the brick with a crayon. Then shove it up your ass, sideways."

He reached into his shirt pocket and removed an envelope. "Before you go, please have a look at these." He held the envelope over the table, turned it upside down, and shook it gently.

A thin stack of photographs spilled out of the envelope and slid across the table like a deck of cards. I picked one up and looked at it. It was a picture of Cybulski sucking Wittlinger's dick. I dropped it and picked up another one; Cybulski was licking Wittlinger's balls. The rest were the same: Wittlinger was fucking Cybulski in the ass, Wittlinger and Cybulski were doing the sixty-nine, Wittlinger and Cybulski were kissing passionately. And so on. Cybulski had a silly grin on his face in all the pictures; he appeared as though he'd been drugged. I sat back down in my chair.

"Gabi, please bring Mister Fisher another glass of wine. And one for me also."

"Who the fuck are you?" I said.

133

"I have told you my name, and I have told you what I do—I buy things, and then I sell them. It is the same activity millions of retailers, wholesalers, and brokers the world over engage in every day. There is nothing more to me that would interest anyone."

"This is blackmail."

"Now Mister Fisher, blackmail is such an ugly word. But yes, if you must, that is what it is."

I pointed at the photographs. "How did you get these?"

"We took them last night."

"Last night? How? Cybulski's in jail."

"Not anymore, he was released yesterday. Were you unaware?"

Gabi brought the wines and set them on the table. "*Zum Wohl*," she said, and disappeared again quickly. The Weinstube was filling up.

"With others I might be inclined to pussyfoot around, as you Americans say," Krupa said. "But with you one ought to get right to the point. So, let us get to the point, shall we? I could screw up your life. I would rather do business with you. I will pay you five thousand dollars for the terrain walk. If you do not sell it to me I will show these photographs to your friend, Mister Cybulski. The exhibition will destroy him. You may trust me on that matter. I have a knack for determining what makes people tick."

"You said ten thousand dollars," I reminded him.

"That was when you were less cooperative. The offer is now five thousand dollars. I suggest you accept it before it changes again."

"Tell me, Herr Krupa, what is it that makes *me* tick?"

"The most effective way to reach you is to threaten your friend Cybulski. If I threatened you personally you would only laugh and invite me to do my worst. But Cybulski—now, there is a soft spot in the heart."

"Don't do this."

"I do not *want* to do it. Do not *make* me do it. All I want to do is purchase a terrain walk. All you need do is copy one for me."

"It's not . . . right." The words felt strange coming out of my mouth.

"It is unclassified. You will not be doing anything wrong. We could just as easily be talking about a used car."

"Or a watch?"

"Exactly."

"The telephone book and the company ladder were one thing, Krupa. This—this is something else."

"Listen, my young friend. If you do not sell it to me, someone else will. Believe me, one way or another the terrain walk is going to pass hands. Now, you can profit from the transaction, or your friend can suffer. You know the old saying, you are either for us or against us? Well, that is the way I do business."

"It's an evil way of doing business."

"Is it? I never bothered myself with questions of good and evil, and I never understood people who did. To me it is only a matter of business. I am a successful businessman, and I do not mind saying so. And laugh if you will, but I have the highest moral standards. Yes—do not shake your head—I do. Cybulski had a wonderful time last night, and besides, he does not remember any of it today. Wittlinger certainly had a good time; ask him and he will tell you. You and I are both going to make some money. That is what we are about, is it not? My client will get exactly what he has ordered. And none of the NATO countries—yours included—will be harmed in any way by the transaction. So what is the difficulty? There is no evil going on here. At any rate, I cannot see any. But you are going to have to work out the right and wrong of it in your own head. I cannot make that rationalization for you. By the way, it is funny to hear you, of all people, talking about good and evil and right and wrong."

"You know me so well, do you?"

"Better probably than you are aware. The bottom line, as you Americans like to say, is that I will pay you five thousand dollars cash for an unclassified document that will do no harm in my client's possession. Or I will show these photographs to your friend Cybulski, and you can predict the consequences as well as can I. The choice is yours. I am not bluffing; long ago I discovered bluffing to be a waste of time. I will give you several days to work it out in your head, if that is what you need to do. I am sure that if you give it some thought you will see how uncomplicated—and harmless—the transaction is."

"This is . . ."

"Business, Mister Fisher. This is simply business. If it is *corrupt* business you want to see, take a look at your own lawmakers on Capitol Hill. If you think about it, there is a reason so many lobbyists thrive in Washington; it is because most of your congressmen are on the take. Every time an automobile plant ends up in one state rather than another, or handguns go uncontrolled for yet another year and kill yet more people, or tobacco smoke fills the lungs of yet more teenage boys and girls, you can be sure money has changed hands in Washington. In each of these scenarios—and in a hundred more every day—an inestimable number of lives is affected, usually adversely. Do you know where the most expensive prostitutes in the world ply their trade? In Washington, which is choked with bureaucrats who can afford them. If you are concerned with distinguishing between right and wrong in the eyes of your government—of behaving in a way that meets with your government's approval—then I suggest you first cast your eyes on the government itself. And then compare all of that with this." He rapped his knuckles on the table. "All we are talking about here is the sale of a harmless, unclassified piece of paper."

136

"I'm still not sure you're not an insider trying to do me," I said.

He held up one of the pictures. In it Cybulski was grinning stupidly, and Wittlinger's semen was dripping from his lips and chin. "Would an insider do this?"

"All right, what do I do?"

"Sunday is the best day to conduct this kind of business. Do you know the stone crucifix across the street?"

"Of course."

"Wittlinger will wait there from six to nine on Sunday. If you fail to show, he will do the same on Monday and again on Tuesday. If by Tuesday you still have not shown, then on Wednesday—that is the twenty-fifth—the photographs will go to Cybulski. By the way, copies will also go to everyone in his chain of command, to his 'fiancée,' as he calls her, and to all members of his immediate family—and he will know it. Not only will his personal life turn upside down, his military career will go splooey as well. If you do not want that to happen, do not call my bluff."

"When do I get paid?"

"Wittlinger will pay you cash at the crucifix."

"And what happens after this? What's the next thing you're going to want from me?"

"I will not want anything more of you."

"That's what you said about the phone book."

"I want to buy a terrain walk, Mister Fisher. That is all. I do not have a commission for anything else. I swear it."

"I don't believe you."

He raised his arms in the air. "Search me."

Chapter 19

I HAD TO KNOCK repeatedly at Cybulski's door before he would open it. He was obviously inside; I could hear him moving around in the room. I knocked and listened, then knocked louder and listened again, and finally the door opened. Cybulski looked at me briefly, as if to verify my identity, then turned away.

"Right on time," he said. "I knew it was you. That's why I didn't answer."

"Thanks," I said.

"Since the day's almost over you must have visited everyone else on your list, and saved me for last."

"Maybe I visited you last because I saved the best for last."

"Maybe you should go fuck yourself."

He went to his bed and flopped down on it. The room looked prepared for a siege: there was enough booze on his desk to keep a man drunk for a year.

"Mind if I have a drink?" I said.

"Not at all," he said. "Mind if I ignore you?"

"Be my guest."

I selected a bottle of Jim Beam. Also on his desk were several water glasses; one looked like it hadn't been used more than half a dozen times. I poured a couple of inches of whiskey into the glass and went over to where Cybulski was lying on the bed, looking at something. The something turned out to be a picture of his girlfriend back home. When he saw me watching he pushed it under the pillow.

"Where were you last night?" I asked him.

"I went out and got drunk," he said.

"Were you alone?"

"No, I made a friend at the bar, thank you very much. Why are you asking?"

"What did you do after you left the bar?"

"The police already interrogated me, Jimmy. What makes you think you also have the right?"

"Did you leave with the friend? Did you go to his house?"

"All right," he said, "I'll tell you." He planted his head on the pillow and covered his face with his hands. "I don't know. It's as simple as that; I just don't know. I've spent the whole day trying to remember what I did after I left the bar last night, and it's not coming to me. They let me out of jail, I went to a bar, I met a man in the bar, we drank, we talked, we had a good time—and this morning I woke up in my bed. I don't remember anything in between, and I have no idea how I got home. By the soreness in my... you know where... I can tell certain things were done to me, but for the life of me I can't remember letting anyone do them."

"What did the man look like?"

He removed his hands from his face and looked at me. "Why?"

I shrugged. "Just a hunch. Maybe I know the guy."

"No, I mean, why the fuck do you care?"

"I'm worried about you."

He snorted. "Deja moo," he said, covering his face again.

"What's that?"

"Deja Moo. The feeling you've heard this bullshit before. You've never before in your life worried about anyone else but yourself. Goddamn you."

"Chuck, listen to me. I think it's important we reconstruct the events of last night."

"What for?" he said, peering through his fingers. "What business is it of yours?"

"I think your lifestyle is one that invites people to try to take advantage of you."

He sat up in the bed. "What do you mean, my lifestyle?"

"You know what I mean."

"I'm not sure I do. Could it possibly be that you are referring to my liberal sexual preference?"

"Yes, in fact, that is exactly what I am referring to."

"Just once, Jimmy, I'd like to see some compassion in you."

"Some . . . compassion?"

"You heard me. For just once, I'd like to see you focus on the good things about me, the things you like about me. Don't just keep trying to make me something I'm not—i.e., you. Help me, just this once. Stop protecting yourself by using me as a shield."

"Ouch," I said. I took a couple of steps backwards to illustrate the impact his words had on me. "I'm sorry, Chuck, that you don't think I have any compassion, but I do. And I'm not trying to change you, or use you as a shield. I'm just worried that your lifestyle—your liberal sexual preference—is going to get you into trouble."

"How?"

"Well, what if someone revealed that lifestyle to members of your family, or to your chain of command? Or to your fiancée? What affect would that have on you?"

He stared at me silently for a few seconds. "Oh, I see. Very nice. You're threatening to expose my homosexuality if I tell anyone about your involvement in the grave robbing scandal."

"No, Chuck! That's not it. That's not it at all. Jesus H. Christ."

"Of course it is. What else could it be? Why else would you confront me with a hypothetical threat? Why else would you want a detailed narrative of my actions last night? My God, I think I'm going to throw up. Just when you think things couldn't get any worse."

"You've got it all wrong, Chuck," I said.

"Do I?" His face twisted in grief. He started to cry.

"Yes!"

"You come here and ask me how I will react if my family and my girlfriend find out I'm sexually attracted to men. Who else would tell them? You're the only one who knows me well enough to hurt me. And you're the only one in the world who stands to be hurt—very badly, in fact—if I open my mouth about the other thing."

"It's not me I'm worried about, Chuck; it's you."

"So, if you're not the threat, who is?"

I didn't answer right away. "Consider it hypothetical," I said finally. "And leave it at that."

"Thank you, Mister Compassion, for your hypothetical scenario. I'll keep it in mind. If anyone ever comes along and tries to blackmail me—unlikely as it may seem, considering I have nothing of interest to anyone—I will credit you with having predicted it and warned me. Now, please leave."

"Chuck . . ."

"Fuck you, you piece of shit."

"Listen. None of this is my fault, Chuck. It's Schäfer's fault. He's the one who set you up. So stop blaming me and start blaming him."

"I used to think it was Schäfer's fault. I don't anymore. I had lots of time to think about it in jail. Now I'm convinced the blame lies entirely with you. You got me into this mess in the first place. I was perfectly happy, and living a perfectly legal life, before you came along."

Once again he started to cry.

"Being weak isn't going to help, Chuck."

"Go to hell." He was sobbing.

"For God's sake, get a grip."

"Get the fuck out of here."

Chapter 20

THE NEXT MORNING THEY called an alert. The call came at four a.m., and it was the sergeant major on the line.

"Confident carbine," he said.

"Huh?"

"Confident carbine."

"Oh, are we having an alert?"

"This line is not secure, private. Act accordingly."

I took my time showing up. First I had to check my gas mask out from the NBC room, then I had to pick up my rifle from the armorer. Then I stopped by the mess hall and talked one of the cooks out of a ham and egg sandwich. By the time I reached the office Pendergrass was already holding on to one end of the classified footlocker. He'd been waiting for me.

"Where have you been?" he asked.

"I'm here now."

"Help me get this goddamn thing down the stairs. We gotta roll."

"Somebody ought to bring the truck around."

"Lamoureaux already did, he's waiting in the cab right now."

"Where's Cybulski?"

He looked at me funny. "Cybulski's in jail."

We carried the footlocker down to the truck and heaved it into the back. Then we sped off to catch up to the convoy. I drove the truck while Pendergrass occupied the passenger seat and Lamoureaux sat between us. Skelton sat on an office chair in the back, holding onto the table and map board as best he could to keep from tilting and falling as the truck went around curves.

As we passed a Tchibo shop I pulled over and stopped.

"What the hell are you doing?" Pendergrass asked.

"I'm getting a cup of coffee. Want one?"

"We don't have time for that shit. Get this truck back on the road and roll it up the hill."

"In a moment, Sergeant, in a moment."

I went inside the Tchibo and selected a coffee. It took the girl a minute to grind it. When I returned to the truck Pendergrass was in the driver's seat.

"Get in," he said, gritting his teeth.

He gunned it to catch up to the convoy. I drank my coffee. When we arrived at the top of Kuhberg, Pendergrass opened the back of the truck and let Skelton out.

There was nothing to do now but wait for recall. I looked around for Cybulski. It was unlikely he would have come in another section's truck, but just the same, it wasn't like him to miss an alert either, even if he'd been released from jail only two nights before.

Kuhberg was beautiful under the rising sun. The trees were fully green with summer and there was sap on the bark that glistened in the sunlight. It was peaceful to be so high above the town as the town came alive.

I was in a distracted mood and wanted to be alone. After strolling aimlessly for a few dozen yards I found an old stump under a break in the canopy. I sat down on the stump, watched the sky turn blue above the canopy, and listened to the birds. A red squirrel crept out along a branch over my head and looked at me curiously. If I'd had ammunition for my rifle I could have shot him dead.

There are no red squirrels in the States, and when Americans see one for the first time they're taken aback by the animal's beauty. The red is the color of a red fox.

I stared back at him. I'd heard of American Indians having totems, and I wondered if a red squirrel appearing now in my life had any significance. The squirrel watched me for a few seconds more, then scurried back along the branch and disappeared into the tree.

The rifle in my hands felt alien to me. Any other day, if I'd had ammunition I probably would have shot him. Because that's what I'd been taught to do—what most American boys are taught to do when armed and confronted with a wild animal, however harmless it might be.

I remembered something Cybulski had once quoted to me: how difficult life is sometimes, knowing that not everyone has to face it. Nevertheless, facing the difficulties in life is preferable to the alternative, and I realized at that moment that a choice on behalf of the squirrel, or any other harmless creature, was not mine to make. Nor was it anyone else's. And an opportunity existed to participate in preventing others from exercising such a choice.

Cybulski had invited me to join his mission to rescue animals from cosmetics and pharmaceutical laboratories. He suggested I would like that line of work when I got out of the army because it would draw on my particular talents. He also suggested we operate a shelter called Beast Haven to house the rescued animals.

The scheme would draw from my experiences as though I'd been training for it all along. My youth had been more or less devoted to entering places where I was not welcome, and such preparation made me the perfect candidate to conduct animal rescues. The army had trained me to cope with unwelcome human interference. And my various entrepreneurial enterprises were excellent potential sources of financing.

Here I was, a common Beetle Bailey, sitting on a stump in the woods, high on a hill in Germany, and of all times and places, this is when and where I would figure out what to do with my life. I'd been offered a mission and accepted it. Cybulski had been trying to communicate the mission to me for some time, but I'd refused to listen. It took a red squirrel to greet me with an automatic weapon in my hands to ensure the message was heard.

As for entrepreneurial enterprises, I had also just been offered a large sum of money to perform a trivial task. It was nevertheless an illegal task, and therefore dangerous. I faced a choice between my country and my friend.

Terrain walks were unclassified. Should I pass the material and technically commit an illegal act, albeit one that would really do no harm? Or should I refuse and allow my friend to suffer? My instincts told me Krupa wasn't bluffing.

What is one's country if not the citizens who comprise it? What sense does it make to betray one of those citizens to protect something so abstract as a boundary or a flag?

I decided to pass the terrain walk, but for the full ten thousand dollars Krupa had previously offered me, and no less. Not only would I protect Cybulski from harm, I would raise enough money to begin financing Beast Haven. I was worried I may have hurt Cybulski and was anxious to return and apologize. Also, I was eager to start planning the operation. My enthusiasm would infect Cybulski right off. Our relationship would return to what it was before. The score was friend, one; country, nothing.

And then, for the first time, I noticed the details of the ecosystem in which I sat. The stump I was sitting on was covered with moss. The ground, carpeted with leaves, was soft and spongy beneath my feet. I wished I could take my boots off and walk barefoot.

What I had previously classified as "birds" now became several distinct species, each making its own unique call. There was a musty, earthy smell in the air. Trees were my cousins. Never before had I experienced such a sense of identity and belonging.

Pendergrass whistled from the road, so the recall had come. Reluctantly I stood up and walked back, content with the world and my place in it. Pendergrass even let me drive the truck again; the visit to the woods had affected his mood, too. On the way back through town to the Kaserne I noticed a spider crawling across the windshield. I resisted the urge to crush it with the palm of my hand and wipe my hand on the seat cushion. I was a changed man.

When we reached the Kaserne we carried the footlocker upstairs to the office. Then we checked our masks and rifles back in at headquarters company and sat around waiting for lunch.

I pictured the break-ins and seizures that would be necessary to rescue the laboratory animals. The break-ins were no real problem; I'd had plenty of experience with that sort of thing. But we would need a van to carry all the animal cages and we would have to have Beast Haven up and running to take care of the animals. You couldn't just open the cages and expect the rabbits and mice to make a dash for freedom. Well, maybe the mice. The rabbits would probably sit in the middle of the laboratory floor until the technicians showed up for work the next day and returned them to their cages.

I couldn't wait to tell Cybulski of my new plan. I was sure he would be as excited as I was. With ten thousand dollars of start-up money, we could break into our first lab anytime we liked.

At noon some of the recreation staff tried to open the rec center but the doors were blocked. When finally they forced them open they found Cybulski hanging by his belt from a ceiling beam. He had locked himself in the rec center late the previous night and barricaded the door with dumbbells. An up-ended exercise bench lay on the floor beneath his feet.

Chapter 21

THE FOLLOWING DAY I borrowed Lamoureaux's car and drove to Rheinböllen. I parked downtown in the Marktplatz next to the Rathaus. It was a glorious day and I'd decided to walk to my destination. Also, I didn't want anyone to be able to identify the car.

Someone had once told me to come to Rheinböllen to see the bomb craters in and around which one could still find rusted shrapnel from the war. I kept my eyes open as I walked but didn't see any craters. Maybe I had the wrong town; I couldn't fathom why the allies would want to bomb Rheinböllen.

There's a small family-owned jewelry store in Rheinböllen, the kind that employs a soft sell. In Hermann's larger cities the jewelry salesman is a shark that circles you and tries to judge the fatness of your wallet. But in the small towns he's usually the store owner as well as the salesman, and maybe he's the goldsmith too. More often than not he's the only employee. He sold Hermann's mother her engagement ring and will eventually sell one to Hermann's daughter. He's a trusted friend who knows everyone in the community, has attended their weddings and funerals, and can inventory their jewelry holdings more accurately than they can themselves.

He's hurt and a little offended when Hermann goes to the big city to buy a piece of jewelry. He's not in a position to give Hermann a better deal or to offer him a better selection, but he's hurt nonetheless, and Hermann advises his wife not to wear the recreant jewelry when she visits his store.

Herr Nagetusch was one such jeweler. When I entered his store a cow bell rang and he came out of the back room and watched me suspiciously. I admired his wares and pretended to shop for an engagement ring. I told him I might be moving into the community if I could find an apartment—and did he know of any available?

He said no, but he would keep his eyes open for me.

I told him I might have some old gold to sell—and would he be interested?

Yes, he would always be interested in old gold and would pay the best price for it.

Was there, I wondered, another jeweler in town?

No, there wasn't.

But what about the jeweler I had heard about, the one who might have an apartment for rent?

Ah, so it was only an apartment I sought.

Of course; I wouldn't go to another jeweler, especially to one with a lesser reputation, to buy something or commission a repair.

Well, as it turned out, there was a woman who was the sister-in-law of a jeweler, and perhaps he was the jeweler I meant. I was welcome to the address. However, he knew nothing of an apartment for rent, and the woman was not herself a jeweler, but only related to one. He, Nagetusch, was the only true jeweler in town. Besides, the woman's brother-in-law was not a good jeweler. He didn't purify his metals properly, and the resultant product often came apart when it went under the next jeweler's torch for sizing. Nobody wanted to work on jewelry that this jeweler had worked on.

I assured him I was only interested in an apartment, and that I would come back to him when I was ready to buy the engagement ring. He seemed content. I gave him a false name and told him I was stationed at nearby Dichtelbach. I didn't want him sending the police after me when he learned the fate of the jeweler who was the woman's brother-in-law.

On a quiet street near the edge of town I found the small, single story house where the not-very-good jeweler's sister-in-law lived. And there, sure enough, tending the vegetables with spade and hoe, wearing denim overalls and orange rubbers, his knees stained with grass and his face flushed with effort, was Rolf Schäfer himself.

I got him face down on the ground with my knees on his shoulder blades and my hands clasped around his forehead. I yanked. The snap was crisp, like a dry branch. The convulsions that continued for a minute or so afterwards resembled a coordinated sequence of slow motion spasms. His breathing continued too, and pink froth bloomed about his mouth and leaked into the soil of the garden.

The corollary to Cybulski's quote now occurred to me: how terrible death would be if not everyone had to die.

That night a violent thunderstorm rocked Bad Karst and beat mercilessly against the windows of Amy's. Lightning made the night seem like day. At the climax of the storm the thunder clapped so loudly that Melina sprang up in bed and cried out.

I comforted her and told her there was nothing about the storm to fear. It only meant that a very bad man had died and was making his passage through the gates of Hell.

Chapter 22

THE PARTIAL SOLAR ECLIPSE that occurred the next day, July 22, didn't impress me. It seemed the moon had to cover all or most of the sun to darken the day, and if it covered only a piece of the sun you couldn't tell the difference.

Often you couldn't tell an eclipse was occurring unless you made a pinhole in one side of a box and pointed it at the sun: an image of the eclipse would form inside the box, on the opposite wall. The girl who showed me this trick noted that we were not actually looking at an eclipse, but rather at the image of one, and therefore it was like the analogy of Plato's cave. I told her I agreed with her—that the box more or less resembled a cave, and the pinhole the cave's distant entrance. She looked at me like I was an idiot. The solar eclipse was the last event we attended together. I guess some girls just don't like it when their boyfriends are insightful.

Eclipse or no eclipse, I was in a bad state that Sunday. I weighed my options: I could spend the afternoon in my room, pacing the floor, or I could visit Amy's and spend the afternoon in bed with a naked girl. I had to be careful that I wasn't developing feelings for Melina. Feeling a girl is one thing; feeling *for* her is another.

Sundays were always quiet at Amy's. In fact, on this particular Sunday the only girl working was Melina, and I had to wait behind a couple of Beetles who were ahead of me. When it was finally my turn and she looked up to see who was next in line, that I-don't-think-I-can-put-up-with-this-anymore look in her face melted away and she rushed over to hug me.

"Thank God it's you," she said.

"Has it been that bad?"

"How many more are behind you?"

"Only one. Unless some more are just now arriving."

"What does he look like? What does he smell like?"

I shrugged. "Like all the rest. Goofy, horny. His clothes probably haven't been washed since he left his mother and joined the army. What's the difference?"

"Do you think you could stay in here a while and give me a rest? I've got some cold beers if you want."

"Sure. What's going on? Are you alright?"

She paced the room in her lingerie. "Have you ever had a sudden flash that you should be doing something different?"

"Is this another one of those church-guilt things?"

"No. This is a career change decision. It came to me, exactly what I want to do with my life."

"As a matter of fact," I said, "the other day in the woods—"

"I finally know what I want to do for a living, Johnny."

"Jimmy."

"Oh, yeah. Sorry. I keep forgetting."

"Don't mention it." I began removing my clothes.

"I know what I want to be."

"What?" I asked, untying my shoes.

She stopped pacing for a couple of seconds, as if waiting for the trumpets to begin. The trumpets remained silent. "A banker," she said.

I had just unzipped my pants, and now, startled, I dropped them to the floor.

"You don't—you don't think I can?"

"Why a banker?"

"They're the ones with all the money. Why are you looking at me like that?"

"Melina, you can't even read. How can you be a banker?"

"Of course I can read!" She bit her lip. "As well as the other girls."

I looked around the room for printed material, but there was nothing in sight. There were some music posters on the walls, and they had the artists' names on them, but presumably Melina knew who the artists were. Finally I thought of my wallet. I took it out of my pants pocket and found my USAREUR driver's license. It was printed in both German and English. I handed it to her.

"Tell me what this is," I said. "Tell me what it says."

She looked at it for several long seconds, then handed it back. "You don't think I can become a banker, do you?"

"Of course you can, sweetie. You can do anything you want. Come on, take your things off, and let's get in bed."

"You think I'm going to be a whore for the rest of my life."

"Not at all. You'll probably be a whore for a little while longer, then you'll be a banker. I'm sure of it."

"You think I'm stupid, don't you?" The change in her tone told me my blow job was in jeopardy.

"Listen, Melina."

"Admit it. Say I'm stupid. I know you're thinking it. Say it." She lit a cigarette. Her hand was trembling.

"You're not stupid. But if you want to be a banker you're going to have to learn to read. There are people who can help. For example, my own father—"

"Stop."

"Stop what? We haven't even started yet."

"I don't wanna hear any more of this."

"I can help you, Melina."

154

"Please leave."

"Calm down, will you?"

She walked over to the door and opened it. I grabbed my clothes and left the room.

Sitting on the pews in the hallway were three other guys besides the one who had been next in line behind me. This latter stood and entered Kristin's room wordlessly, and the three others watched as I put my clothes back on.

"Christ," one of them said. "Don't they even let you get dressed?"

"She's efficient," I told him. "If you're already naked when you go in, and you're still naked when you come out, you get to spend all of your time scrogging rather than getting dressed and undressed."

All three stripped in the hallway as I headed down the staircase. When I reached the sidewalk I looked up at the windows of the headquarters building across the street. It was late afternoon but the sun was still high. I couldn't tell which office lights were on and which were off. I crossed the street, showed my ID card to the gate guard, and approached the building until I could see the ceiling lights in the upper story offices. Skelton's lights were still on. I would have to wait for Skelton to leave before I could do the job.

Church bells rang; it was five o'clock. I crossed the parade field and sat down in front of the mess hall. From this vantage point I could keep track of everyone coming and going in the headquarters building, but no one could see me unless they looked.

Three hours passed, during which I thought a lot about my future. The funny thing was, even with Cybulski dead I still wanted to continue with plans for Beast Haven. He had known where the animals were and what was happening to them, and he had relied on me to orchestrate the rescues. Now I was going to have to learn the plight of the animals.

Only one critical element was lacking: money. And yet, in my relationship with Krupa, I had stumbled on the solution. Because I was sure the terrain walk would not be the last document he'd want to buy.

Still it seemed a lonely business, being a vigilante force of one. I decided to invite Melina to join me. She was a diligent whore, we got along well together, and she didn't try to control me. She'd already been hinting about going to America. I would teach her to read. While I thought about her I remembered I was still wearing a wedding band on my little finger. I spun it around the finger absentmindedly. It surprised me that I would, in free association, connect thoughts of Melina to thoughts of a wedding band.

Finally Skelton's lights went out. A minute later he left the building and drove away in his car. By this time the sun had set, and although it was not yet dark I noticed that light was also coming from Riddell's basement window. But it was two floors below the Plans office and there was no reason for me to fear a visit from him this late in the day.

I didn't have much time. Wittlinger would wait at the crucifix only until nine o'clock. I entered the building and showed my ID card to the guard on duty.

"What is the nature of your visit?" he asked.

This took me by surprise. I'd never before been asked why I was entering my own building, day or night, weekday or weekend.

"I work here," I said.

"I gather that," he said. "What are you doing here on a Sunday night?"

"I have to type a terrain walk for distribution tomorrow morning. I just got the call from my OIC. He told me to go to the office and get right to work. If you'd like to confirm this with him, I can give you—"

"Sign here."

When I reached the Plans office on the second floor I first had to gain access to the vault. And quickly; I didn't want to be discovered in the building by anyone who knew I wasn't required to type or distribute a terrain walk.

I turned the dial on the vault door—right, left, right again—and pulled it open. Then I used my key to open the office door. Although no one was in the office I experienced an eerie feeling knowing that Skelton had just left and locked the doors minutes before. I didn't turn the lights on; I didn't want anyone outside to see them, wonder who was there, and investigate. The light leaking in from the hallway was enough to work by.

The unclassified drawers in the vault, despite containing only unclassified material, were locked and treated as classified like all the others. I counted safes around the room, starting with the vault door, to remember the combination of the safe I needed access to. I turned the dial, popped the drawer open, and removed the terrain walk. It was exactly where I had filed it.

The only copy machine in the section was across the hall in the admin department. They didn't keep a copier in the Plans office—to prevent precisely what I was trying to do. Fortunately it was a quiet Sunday night. As far as I knew, Riddell was the only person in the building other than the guard. On any other night of the week the G3 section might be filled with officers. Krupa had been right: Sunday was the best day of the week to do such work.

I turned the copier on and waited for it to warm up. I didn't want to get surprised at my task; I would have to be able to stop copying at a second's notice, in case someone walked in on me. So I brought some other legitimate work to the copier to use as a cover. It was a stack of unclassified copying Pendergrass had ordered me to do a long time before, but it was nevertheless legitimate. If I were caught, all I would have to explain was why

I had chosen this particular time to do the copying I'd been putting off for weeks.

When the copier had warmed up I checked the hallway to make sure no one was coming. Then I copied one page. I checked the hallway again, then copied the second page. I continued in this manner until all ten pages were copied.

On about page seven I heard a noise, so I shoved the terrain walk and the copies I had already made under the stack of legitimate copy work. Then I walked up and down the hallway, looking for the source of the noise. I checked the bathroom as well. There was nothing.

I folded the finished stack of ten copies into a rectangle that would fit into the bottom of my shoe. I packed up my things, turned off the machine, locked the doors again, and left the building. On the way out I noticed Riddell's light was *still* on.

That was easy, I thought. The easiest money I'd ever made, or probably ever would make.

As I approached the gate a tall man with an athletic build stepped out of a Saab parked next to the gatehouse and blocked my path. He had a crew cut, was ruggedly good looking, and wore a suit that was standard government issue. His face was vaguely ethnic; not quite Hispanic, perhaps a mix of Cuban with something else. When he spoke to me he did so as if we were about to become friends.

"I'm Special Agent Joe Montalbano," the man said. He held his identification card in front of my face. "Private First Class James Solomon Fisher, you are under arrest for conspiracy to commit espionage."

BOOK THREE

Patriotism is the passion of fools and the most foolish of passions.
—Schopenhauer

Chapter 23

"A FEW QUESTIONS, IF you don't mind."

He was bald as a cue ball, with little tufts of hair sprouting over his ears. His face was long and haggard. The circles under his eyes and the way his mouth curved slightly upward in a constant smile not only balanced the roundness of the top of his head, it completed the essential features of a natural clown outfit as well. He had introduced himself as Special Agent John Blackburn.

"I don't mind," I said.

The office contained a gray metal army desk, a scarred table, and a couple of wooden chairs. Special Agent Blackburn sat behind the desk studying some papers in front of him and smiled warmly with creased eyes every time our eyes met. That made me uncomfortable, so I quit looking at him. There was another man in the room who said little. He sat behind me and off to one side on one of the chairs. He took notes constantly, and I could hear his pencil scratching against the paper.

A briefcase sat on a table next to the desk. The way it lay open, with the back facing me so I couldn't see inside, I assumed it contained a tape recorder.

"Now, take your time," Mister Blackburn said. "Just tell me whether you recognize any of the people in these photographs."

He spread several pictures out on his desk. I recognized all but one.

"This one's Cybulski," I said. "This one's Pendergrass . . . Sergeant First Class Gerold Champney . . . Spec Four Leonard Martin . . ."

"And this one?" He pointed to the blurred image of a woman wearing sunglasses. It could have been anyone.

"I don't know that one," I said.

"How about this one?" He pointed at a photograph of Schäfer, garnished in his Sunday best. It was an old photograph and Schäfer looked good mugging for the camera. He didn't look that good now. It occurred to me that his wife might bury him with something and that I could dig him up in a couple of weeks.

"I don't know that one either," I said.

"Are you sure?"

"Yes."

"Are you absolutely sure?"

"Absolutely."

The man behind me went *scratch, scratch, scratch.*

"Tell me about this young fellow." Mister Blackburn pushed Cybulski's picture in front of me.

"What would you like to know?"

"The two of you were friends, weren't you?"

"We were friends."

"Close friends?"

"Yes."

"Lovers?"

"No."

"But he was gay."

"He was?"

"It has been suggested he was gay, and one must draw conclusions about the company he kept. The closest company he kept, apparently, was you."

"It has never been suggested to me he was gay. *He* certainly didn't suggest it."

Special Agent Blackburn appeared disappointed. He gathered the pictures and put them in an envelope. Then he smiled, his eyes creasing so much they almost closed. His face was a study in tensely interlocking curves and circles. He said:

"Did you kill Rolf Schäfer?"

"Who?"

"Rolf Schäfer. A pawn shop owner with whom you did business."

"I don't know anyone by that name, and I've never done business with a pawn shop owner. He's dead, huh?"

"Oh yes, he's dead. We found him in his sister-in-law's garden. His neck was broken."

"That's terrible," I said, shaking my head in pity.

"Do you think it's terrible?"

"Don't *you*?"

He made some marks on a document cover page. I tried to read what he was writing, but I couldn't make it out without leaning over his desk. Only the title of the document was visible: Canasta Player.

"Does the name Douglas Jordan mean anything to you?" he asked.

"Should it?"

"Or the name Michael Grosvenor?"

I shook my head.

"Please answer out loud," the man behind me said.

"I don't know either name," I said.

"You didn't use the name Douglas Jordan to gain employment in a business owned by Michael Grosvenor?"

"What kind of business was it?"

"A funeral home."

"No, I'm afraid I don't know either of those people."

"Were you sleeping with Charles Cybulski?"

"No."

"After all, you said you didn't know he was gay."

"He wasn't gay."

"How often did you and he visit Schäfer in his home?"

"I don't know anyone named Schäfer."

I turned and looked at the man behind me. He was concentrating on his notes. It was a little warm in the room so I loosened my collar.

"Where were you in April of 1988?"

"I don't remember."

"Were you in Chicago?"

"Hmm, let's see. No, I don't think I was."

"Try to remember where you were."

"I was in basic training," I said, remembering.

He looked at his notes. He wasn't smiling and his eyes weren't squinting. "You entered basic training in late April of 1988," he said. "What were you doing in early April?"

"I don't recall."

"You were in Chicago, weren't you?"

"Not that I recall."

"But you joined the army in Chicago."

"Oh, yes. I was in Chicago to join the army."

"Why didn't you join in your home town?"

"Hell, I felt like joining in Chicago."

"You weren't there on any other business?"

"Hmm, let me think. No, that's about all Chicago's good for. A place to join the army. That and that Picasso statue in front of the Civic Center. Have you seen it?"

"You weren't in Chicago in April of 1988, using the name Douglas Jordan, working in a funeral home owned by Michael Grosvenor?"

"If I was, it's news to me. All I remember is that Picasso thing."

"Tell me, why did you join the army?"

"For the educational opportunities."

"Have you been taking advantage of the educational opportunities?"

"Don't you know? It must be in your notes. You knew I was in Chicago."

"Answer the question," the man behind me said.

"I have not been taking advantage of the educational opportunities," I said.

I had joined the army because I needed to start a new life in a big hurry. Also I was hungry. I asked the recruiter how soon he could get me in, and he told me if I joined the infantry he could put me on a plane the next day. Sensing my trouble he reminded me that meals were served on airplanes.

"Did you kill Schäfer with your bare hands?"

"I don't know anyone named Schäfer. And I'm not good with my hands."

He took a look inside the briefcase, then turned back to me. "Does the name Hannelore Schneider mean anything to you?"

"Does she live in Chicago too?"

"No, she doesn't live at all, anymore."

"Oh. I didn't kill her either."

"I'm not suggesting you did."

"Well, it just appears you have a lot of dead people on your hands, and you don't know what to do with them."

Mister Blackburn put his pencil down. "We're ready for Mister Montalbano now," he said to the man sitting behind me. "You," he said to me, "may have a cigarette outside, and stretch a bit, if you like."

I DID BOTH. I stood in the hallway outside the interrogation room and smoked a cigarette. At the end of the hall I could see the building entrance, a sliding glass door that opened into a guard station. The door was locked electronically, and the guard had to press a buzzer to let anyone in or out.

The building was somewhere in the Abrams Complex in Frankfurt. Special Agent Montalbano had brought me there after the arrest and put me in a holding cell for the night. It was not a regular holding cell; they'd removed the furniture from an office, placed a cot against the wall, and locked the door. That's where I spent the night. I hadn't had an opportunity to shower or brush my teeth, and I hadn't been given anything to eat or drink. I also had not visited a bathroom. It was a dirty and uncomfortable arrangement, and no doubt part of a scheme to break my resolve. The makeshift cell and the treatment were irregular; if I were merely under arrest for an alleged crime, I would be in jail like any other alleged criminal.

I was familiar enough with the Abrams complex and the surrounding neighborhood to know I could make a bus or subway in a hurry if I could get out of the building. The Frankfurt skyline wasn't visible through the entrance, but there was plenty enough haze to prove my nearness to the city center. I would need a fake ID card and a passport to leave the country. Those were the least of my worries, though; the guard at the end of the hall presented the greatest immediate challenge.

The circumstances were looking grim. I'd been in some grim circumstances before but always in the States, not in Germany, not in the army, not in a secure building where the guard had to press a buzzer to let you out. I had to find some way out of the building. There was a window in the interrogation room, I remembered. It didn't have any bars. I would go back into the room when it was time and if it got looking really bad I would throw my chair through the window and jump out. I would have to knock the shards out of the pane, because the window was so small, and that would take some time. Therefore I would have to subdue the note taker before I threw the chair. Both the note taker and the interrogator presumably had handguns. I would have to subdue both men, throw my chair through the window, knock the shards out of the pane, climb through, and make it to a bus or subway station. I gave myself a ten percent chance of success.

The note taker came and got me. "We're ready for you now," he said.

*

AS AN INTERROGATOR, SPECIAL Agent Montalbano wasn't anything like Special Agent Blackburn. Their appearances couldn't have contrasted more, either; whereas Blackburn was a study in circles and convolution, Montalbano had the angular features of a Cuban boxer, and his approach to interrogation was likewise more direct.

The briefcase was still open on the table next to the desk but it had moved slightly. The note taker sat down in his chair behind me and as soon as Montalbano spoke the scratching began again.

"So," Montalbano said, "how did it feel?"

"How did what feel?"

"How did it feel when his neck snapped in your bare hands?"

"Whose neck? I've never snapped anyone's neck."

"Did it give you a rush?"

"Sir, I wish I could help you, but—"

"Come on, Jimmy. You can tell me." He leaned forward and rested his elbows on his knees, as if to demonstrate our intimacy. "He was a real bad dude and it felt good twisting his scrawny little noggin off, didn't it?"

"I don't know anyone named Schäfer."

"Who said anything about Schäfer?"

"Blackburn did. I only assumed—"

"You killed him. Admit it. Hey, we're proud of you, we really are. He was a nasty son of a bitch and the world is a better place without him."

"I didn't kill him."

"You were in a rage. I understand completely, given what he did to you. And you caught him in his sister-in-law's garden, grabbed him by the ears, put your knee to his back—"

"No."

"—and popped his spine in three places."

"No."

He turned a page in the document Blackburn had been reading from. I could hear raised voices coming from the room next door. Somebody else was getting his.

"We found your footprints in the garden," Montalbano said.

"No you didn't."

"What makes you think we didn't?"

"Because I wasn't there."

"Or is it because you covered them up?"

"I told you, I wasn't there."

"You were there. You popped his spine, then brushed your footprints away."

"I don't know what you're talking about."

"We also found one of your cigarette butts."

"I wasn't smoking."

Montalbano paused, then looked up at me slowly. Note taker stopped writing for a moment.

"*When* were you not smoking?" Montalbano asked.

"I wasn't smoking when I was doing whatever I was doing when I didn't kill the guy."

"What *were* you doing?"

"Not killing the guy."

He chuckled. "You wanna know something? You're not as good as you think you are."

"I didn't kill anyone."

"You're not very good at this. Not nearly as good as I thought you'd be." He shook his head in mock disappointment. "We'll move on to another subject, and give you time to think about what you were doing when you weren't murdering Rolf Schäfer."

He made some notes on the document. Behind me, note taker was scratching furiously. I looked at the window. It was a little higher than I had remembered during my planning in the hallway—and a lot smaller. I knew then why no one had bothered to install bars; it was not considered a security threat, at least as long as someone else was in the room. I was going to have a lot more trouble with it than I'd thought. I revised my estimate of my chances to around five percent. And that felt optimistic.

"You've killed before," Montalbano said.

"If you mean the reason I spent a year in juvenile detention, yes."

"What that a satisfying experience?"

"What, detention?"

"No, killing."

"It was unintentional."

"Yes, that's why you only spent a year in kiddy prison—because you wished you hadn't done it."

I didn't see any point in educating him, he obviously had my record. I'd gotten into a fight with a bully in high school and had won the fight. If instead the bully had won, the tables might have turned. I have no memory of the details of the incident, but witnesses said that after I got him down I pounded viciously on his chest and they had to drag me off, my fists still swinging. Several of his ribs were broken and they in turn punctured his lungs, which caused him to suffocate.

"They said you laughed at the boy while he died."

I shrugged my shoulders. He was a bully. All the boys for miles around breathed a sigh of relief when he died.

"Answer the question," note taker said.

"He didn't ask a question," I said.

"Did you laugh at the boy as he died?" Montalbano asked.

"Yes," I answered. "I laughed."

"You're responsible for another death, one for which you didn't go to kiddy prison."

"That's not true."

He squinted at the page. "It's described here as a hunting accident."

"That's what it was."

"I'm sure it was. It troubles me though that you leave a trail of dead people wherever you go."

"That's an exaggeration. One boy died unintentionally in a fight, and I paid for it. The other boy died in a hunting accident. The accident wasn't my fault, I just happened to be there."

"What about Schäfer? Is his death an exaggeration?"

"It's a false accusation."

"And Hannelore Schneider?"

"Who the fuck is Hannelore Schneider?"

Montalbano flipped to another section of the document. "She died on June first and was buried on June fourth. The next day the family brought fresh flowers to the grave and noticed the earth had been disturbed. In fact, somebody had been digging. They called the police, who ordered an investigation and discovered, to everyone's horror, that the body was missing. It was the first known case of grave robbing in the modern history of the town."

So that's who the fuck Hannelore Schneider was.

"Shortly after," he continued, "the German police raided the laboratories of one Dr. Horst-Dieter Fuchs at the University Neurology Clinic, here in Frankfurt. Guess who they found?"

"Hannelore Schneider?"

"Bingo."

"What's that got to do with me?"

"You're the man who sold Fuchs the body."

"Bullshit."

"He confessed."

"Oh, for Christ's sake. This is weak, Montalbano. Haven't you got anything better?"

"As a matter of fact, I do." His hand flipped rapidly through the document. "Michael Grosvenor, of the Hillside Funeral Home in Chicago. Have you heard his name before?"

"Other than from Blackburn, no."

"You worked for him as a mortician's assistant."

"I've never heard of him."

"He's heard of you. Only he knows you as Douglas Jordan."

I yawned. "Whatever."

"He has signed an affidavit claiming you routinely removed the gold dental work from the mouths of his clients before final preparations for burial."

"He's got the wrong man."

"We also have testimony from . . ." he scanned down the page, " . . . William Jameson, a goldsmith. Mister Jameson has sworn that you tried to sell him a jar full of gold fillings. Like Mister Grosvenor, he identified your photographs with utter certainty. Only with Jameson you used the name Howard Roark."

In reform school they made us choose an apprenticeship. When it was my turn to choose, the only ones left were plumber's assistant and mortician's assistant. I preferred dead bodies over pipes clogged with shit, so when I got out, all I knew, other than how to kill people, was how to bury them. That's why I ended up working at a funeral home. As for the gold teeth, they would otherwise have gone to waste.

"All this sounds like it would make a good novel," I said. "Why don't you write one?"

"Tell me," Montalbano said, "how many children do you have?"

"I don't have any children."

"None?"

"None."

"Hmm." He read something in the document. "According to this, you have several."

"I don't have any."

"None that you are aware of, you mean."

"*None.*"

"Let's see. Does the name Judy Dresher ring a bell?"

"No."

"Ms. Dresher had a baby when she was sixteen years old. How old was she when you started fucking her?"

I didn't answer. I hadn't known how old Judy was until the warrant was issued.

"According to this," Montalbano continued, "you like them all a little on the young side."

"I don't know what you're talking about."

"The tighter the better, huh?"

"Fuck you," I said.

"Shit, Jimmy, you got three underage girls pregnant in the space of two weeks! That must be some kind of record."

They all look the same in the dark, I wanted to say. Instead I said nothing. I didn't think any of it had been my fault; the girls were all waitresses at a Ramada Inn where I was a line cook. I couldn't help it if the management only hired underage girls.

"Was Cybulski's ass just as tight as Judy's pussy?"

"I have no idea what you mean."

"Isn't that what attracted you to him? He was a fag, and his ass was as tight as a fourteen-year-old pussy?"

"Go to Hell, Montalbano."

"You fucked him, didn't you?"

"No, I didn't."

"You *fucked* him!"

"I did *not.*"

"You killed Schäfer."

"No."

"Tell me, did you fuck Schäfer before you killed him?"

"I didn't kill him."

"You just fucked him."

"I didn't fuck him, either."

"Did you fuck him *after* you killed him? Is there anything in this world sacred to you? Anything you *wouldn't* fuck? Anything you *wouldn't* kill?"

"I neither killed him nor fucked him. As I have testified, I didn't even know him."

"I wish you'd at least admit you killed him. He was an enormous pain in the ass to the entire law enforcement community. Every German cop within a three hour radius is thrilled the old reprobate is finally out of commission. Why don't you take credit for it? You'll be a hero. What you did impresses the hell out of me. Come on, Jimmy! Just admit it, and make my admiration for you complete. We're all pals here. Hey Wedgewood," he said to the note taker. "You're a pal, aren't you?"

"I'm a pal," Wedgewood said.

"See? So why don't you confess to the murder, and we'll drop everything about your sex life. After all, another dead body on your list won't attract much attention. But if we bring all the sex charges against you we can bring, you'll go down in history as one of the monster criminals of the century."

"I want a lawyer."

"Right. Did you hear that, Wedgewood?"

"I heard," Wedgewood said.

"The boy wants a lawyer. You know what they say, Jimmy. Only guilty people need lawyers."

"I want a lawyer, and I'm not going to say anything else until I get one."

Montalbano leaned to one side and looked into the briefcase. "Let's take a break," he said.

*

I HOPED THEY WOULDN'T give me a polygraph. I knew how to beat polygraphs, but they're best avoided. My first experience was as a civilian, when I applied for a sales job in a jewelry store, and the owner made me take the test so he could predict whether I intended to rip him off. Of course I had every intention of ripping him off to the fullest extent of my considerable abilities. But I had to pass the test to get the job.

The theory behind a polygraph is that when people lie they experience discomfort, and discomfort usually manifests itself physiologically—as rising pulse and blood pressure, erratic breathing, and the so-called electrodermal response. The problem is that these reactions don't necessarily indicate a lie, they merely indicate discomfort, and the discomfort may result from the question itself or even a truthful answer to the question.

Professional investigators get around this problem by showing the subject the polygraph and presenting it as proof the subject is lying—and hoping the subject confesses. Confessions are what the investigators are after, and are the principal reason polygraphs succeed. Unlike the test itself, a confession is admissible in court.

The test I took in support of my jewelry store application revealed nothing to the technician other than I was high-strung and didn't like taking lie detector tests. The one question that gave me unexpected trouble was whether I intended to resign the job shortly after being hired. I explained that the cause of my trouble was the low salary being offered; I didn't know whether I was going to even accept the job. The technician accepted the explanation.

The jewelry store owner gave me the job, and a week later I skedaddled with bags of loot. A sketch of my face appeared in the jewelry trade magazines soon thereafter, so I was forced, after only one job, to pursue alternative career plans. I was a lot better looking than the sketch.

Halfway through my second cigarette, Wedgewood made me put it out and return to the interrogation room. Now Montalbano and Blackburn were sitting side by side.

*

"PRIVATE FISHER," BLACKBURN BEGAN in a formal tone, "we have enough on you to put you away for several lifetimes. Conspiracy to commit espionage, for which you were arrested last night, is sufficient by itself to earn a life sentence. Although you don't wish to believe it, we have enough evidence to convict you of the murder of Rolf Schäfer. We can also prove you're an accomplished grave robber, which will go a long way in establishing your character in the eyes of the jury and the public. This says nothing of five outstanding statutory rape warrants and three *in absentia* verdicts against you in separate paternity suits. Nor of the charges brought against you in Chicago, in support of which all the relatives of the clients of that funeral home are prepared to testify. We might as well add that you are a suspect in a jewelry store theft in Terre Haute, Indiana, and that your friendly neighborhood CID lists you as a black marketer.

"You are one interesting fellow. You lied on all of your paperwork when you entered the army and then again when you applied for a security clearance. We understand why you've procrastinated in your application for a top secret clearance: the background check is much more thorough. But we're curious about why you entered the army using your real name, given how often you've used false names in the past. We're confident that when we complete a more in-depth investigation into your past we'll uncover evidence of yet more criminal activity, and with such evidence—"

"Enough," I interrupted. "You guys are doing a lot of talking, but other than holding me illegally in a room without a toilet you're not taking any action. If you have everything you say you have, why the hell don't you just book me, charge me, and proceed? Why all the conversation?"

They were silent for a moment, then Blackburn spoke past me, "Mister Wedgewood, if you don't mind."

Wedgewood got up and left. Montalbano reached into the briefcase and pressed a switch. This is the time they either offer you a deal or kick the shit out of you. I looked up at the window. With Wedgewood gone I had a better chance of escaping.

"It's off now," Montalbano said to me.

"What's off?"

"Don't fuck with me."

I got up, walked behind the desk, and looked into the briefcase. There was a tape recorder, and it was turned off. No doubt they had another bug in the room, and probably even a video camera trained on me. But I nodded, pretended to be content, and returned to my seat. Montalbano folded his hands together. He said:

"We can do you, Jimmy. We have enough to permanently retire your two-bit ass."

"You haven't got anything on me."

"We've got enough in here," he said, tapping the document in front of him, "to put you away for life. There isn't a jury in the world that will let you walk free after they see this. Even a jury of convicts would be appalled."

"I haven't hurt anybody."

"This suggests otherwise. What we asked you about was only the tip of the iceberg, you know."

That was bullshit. They used what they had and bluffed about having more. They all went to the same school and did it the same way.

"All right," I said, "do it."

"What's that?"

"Go ahead, do it. Book me. Put me away for life. Retire my two-bit ass."

"We'd be happy to," Blackburn said. He leaned forward and pressed his fingertips together. "I've been in this business for almost twenty years, and thought I'd seen it all. But I've never seen anything that can shake a stick at you. Frankly, my reputation in the bureau would rise substantially if I brought you in; you are a prize. However." He paused for effect. "It's not you we're after. It's the person to whom you were going to pass the terrain walk."

"Burkhard Krupa?"

"No, he's just a middleman. We want the end of the trail, the man Krupa works for. We want him more than we want you. A lot more. That's why we're talking to you rather than booking you and charging you. But we had to make sure you knew what we had on you, to enlist your full cooperation."

He stopped talking. Both he and Montalbano were looking at me. They expected me to say something.

"So?" I said. "How do you want me to cooperate? You want me to catch the guy for you?"

"Actually, instead of giving him what he asks for, we want you to give him what we supply you."

"I see. You want me to feed him shit."

"We don't put it quite that way, but . . . yes."

"There must be more to this than meets the eye," I said. "You couldn't be going to all this trouble for a lousy terrain walk."

"Your insights serve you well," Blackburn said. He stood up and fiddled with a pencil. "Routine intelligence gathering has revealed that operatives are working the theater. What they're after is Oplan 2357-90, a top secret document recently deposited in your vault. Are you familiar with it?"

"Documents come and go."

"It's a plan to evacuate the remaining American agents working in Russia and former Eastern Bloc countries. Since the document contains the identities of the agents, it's valuable to Krupa—and to whomever Krupa reports. A fake document will eventually be passed instead, one identifying high ranking Soviet intelligence officials who are not, in fact, working for the Americans. We hope the scheme will put the Soviet intelligence network into chaos."

So that's what this is all about. They didn't give a hoot about Schäfer, or Hannelore what's-her-name, or gold teeth. They wanted me in the middle to pass some shit, and to take a bullet in the head when the shit started to stink. By that time the operation would be over and they would have no further use for me.

"You said you want the guy," I said, "and now you say you want me to pass him false information."

"Yes," Blackburn said. "If you pass him false information, and he accepts it, then in effect he works for us, and we have him. However, it's also true that we want to identify the man and eventually pick him up."

"How did you guys catch me?" I asked. "How did you know I was going to pass a document tonight?"

"That was simple enough," Montalbano answered. "We knew there were operators in the area, and we knew what they were after. We watched everybody in the office. When we saw you meeting with Krupa, a known operator, it was just a matter of waiting for you to enter the office on a quiet day."

"That means you know everything I've done during the past couple of months."

"Yes, pretty much. You are one interesting fellow. This assignment has been one of the more entertaining ones of my career."

"This operations plan: if that's what they want, why doesn't Krupa just ask for it? Why all the bullshit about phone book, corporate ladder, and terrain walk?"

"They're using a classic approach," Blackburn said. "These mundane passes get you into the routine of passing, so when the time comes to pass something critical you'll be conditioned, you'll be less prone to hesitate on grounds of national loyalty." He paused and watched me. "You still seem confused."

"I am. I don't understand why such people would approach me in the first place, since I don't have the necessary clearance to gain access to the document you say they ultimately want."

"We're not sure about that either," Blackburn said. "However, given your, shall we say, reputation, I'm guessing they believe you to be more approachable than any of your colleagues with the appropriate clearance. When the time comes to pass the plan, your clearance won't matter. We're going to give you a fake copy anyway."

"All right," I said. "What's in it for me?"

Blackburn, who was pacing and twirling a pencil, stopped and walked behind the desk. He tapped the pages of the document he'd been referring to during the interrogation. "All this," he said, "goes away. Cooperate, and you'll be treated leniently on judgment day."

"And if I don't cooperate?"

"Then we'll have to turn you in, if only to be able to say the operation produced something. Get it?"

"I could get my two-bit ass shot off, you know."

He shrugged. "True. However, you may be overlooking one small facet of the arrangement, Mister Fisher."

"And that is?"

"You get to keep any money they pay you."

I had not overlooked that facet. In fact, I was warming up to the idea. If I could keep the classic approach going long enough I could stand to make a pile of money. But there was yet another facet to all of this, and I had not overlooked it, either.

"Gentlemen," I said. "Thank you for the deal you have offered. I decline."

Blackburn, who had started pacing again, stopped again. "Why?"

"The terms you have offered are not satisfactory."

The two men looked at each other. Montalbano said, "Mister Fisher, I advise you to reconsider."

"Nope."

"You would rather spend the rest of your life behind bars?"

"Right."

The room got quiet. I lit a cigarette—against the rules—and watched the smoke drift up toward the ceiling. I put my feet up on the desk and waited. Finally Blackburn exhaled audibly.

"How much?" he asked.

"Ten thousand," I said. "To start."

"Ten thousand . . . dollars?"

"I need a new suit."

"Are you crazy? Do you expect me to pay you money when the deal I'm offering you is one that will keep you out of prison for life?"

"If you don't pay it, you won't get your bad guys, will ya?"

Blackburn went behind the desk again and gathered papers. The circles and curves on his face were skewed and twisted in troubled concentration. He closed the briefcase, locked it, and balanced it upright on the desk.

"It will take a bit of time to arrange," he said.

"Well, I have an appointment to meet with Krupa tonight—you interrupted last night's appointment—and my performance could be a little off, you know, without the incentive."

"You can't make the pass tonight. We need time to rewrite the terrain walk."

"How much time?"

He sighed. "A week. Maybe less. Tell him you need more time."

"What the fuck kind of excuse am I supposed to give him? The FBI needs time to catch up on their paperwork?"

"Demand more money from him. You have a knack for that. Since it's not his money, he'll have to delay the pass until he gets permission to pay it."

"And what about my ten thousand?"

Blackburn looked at Montalbano, who nodded: "You'll have it before you leave today."

I put the cigarette out on the floor, then stood up. "Now if you guys don't mind, I really have to take a piss. I mean *really*."

"Before you go," Montalbano said, "you should know we have reason to believe a member of the spy ring is inside the headquarters building—a mole. There must be a leak, because otherwise how would Krupa know Oplan 2357-90 is there to begin with? It must be someone on the inside, but someone without direct access, otherwise they wouldn't need to approach you. You must keep your eyes and ears open at all times, and trust *no one*."

I assured them I would be careful. As for the insider, I already knew who it was.

Chapter 24

MELINA WASN'T IN HER room, but I found her downstairs in the bar, working tables. She brought me a beer, then wiped down the table.

"I was kind of expecting you last night," she said. There was a tightness in her voice, and she wouldn't look me in the eye.

"They put me on Emergency Action Center duty at the last minute. There was nothing I could do."

"You couldn't call?"

"Not from the EAC. I didn't know I'd be there all night."

She nodded, apparently satisfied with the answer. I told her I had some cash and needed a place to put it. She asked how much; I said a lot. She suggested a local bank, but I said never put your money in a place you can't get to in the middle of the night. She told me there was a false bottom in one of her dresser drawers, and she could put it there for me if I wanted. That's where she kept all her valuables. I pulled the money out of my pockets and handed it to her in a stack.

"Where did you get this?" she asked.

"Here and there," I said. "Business has been good lately."

"Business has been *real* good, it looks to me."

I WAITED UNTIL EIGHT-THIRTY before showing up at the crucifix on the Mannheimerstrasse bridge. Wittlinger was already there, sitting in the now familiar BMW.

There was a telephone booth at the intersection of Mannheimerstrasse and Mühlenstrasse. I entered it and pretended to have an animated conversation. It was the farthest away from the crucifix I could get and still see a car parked in front of it.

The problem with sneaking up on the crucifix was that it sat at the junction of three visible approaches. You could either walk up from the Kornmarkt, or down from the Altstadt, or cut across to it along an alley that ran past the Pauluskirche—all of which could be watched from the crucifix, putting you in the sights of an observer a good two minutes before you arrived. Obviously this was why the place had been chosen.

Wittlinger had the window rolled down and kept sticking his head out as if trying to get some fresh air. He was paying no attention to pedestrians or passers-by; it was close to nine o'clock and he'd already given up on me. In just a few more minutes he would blow this thing off and go home to a double martini.

I waited until a couple of minutes before nine, then hung up the telephone and walked toward the car. Just as I came up alongside of it the motor started. Wittlinger was leaving.

I knocked on the glass of the passenger-side window. Wittlinger looked over, startled. When he recognized me his expression relaxed. He smiled as men do when they learn a piece of the puzzle does in fact fit, when for a long time they'd thought it didn't.

He pressed a button inside the cab and the passenger-side window rolled down. "Hop in," he said.

"No," I told him. "I'm comfortable right where I am."

"Did you bring it?"

"No."

"Why not?" A shadow of doubt crossed his face. His mouth remained open, as if that were where the answer would enter when it came.

"I don't think you're prepared to pay what it's worth," I answered.

He frowned. "We have an agreement."

"I disagree with the agreement."

"That," he waggled a finger at me, "can be dangerous to your health."

"Tell Krupa I want fifteen thousand dollars, which is ten thousand more than his first and third offers, and five thousand more than his second offer."

"He won't like it. He won't like it at all." Wittlinger looked down the street, as though Krupa were waiting out there, growing impatient.

"Tell him."

"I'll tell him. Meantime you need to start shopping for a good life insurance policy."

He roared off in his BMW. I walked to Amy's.

I had to wait in the hallway until the soldiers ahead of me were finished, and when I entered Melina's room she locked the door behind me.

"Closed for the night," she said.

She didn't make me wear a raincoat. She wrapped her legs around me and I buried my face in her neck and came hard, panting with effort. Afterwards she said, "Will you teach me to read?"

"Of course, sweetie, you know I will."

"You won't make fun of me?"

"Never."

She draped herself across me and kissed my chest, and after a little while began making soft sleeping noises. I gently eased out from under her and went over to the dresser, where I checked each drawer until I found the one with the false bottom. It was the lowest drawer, and the bottom lifted when I pushed down against its rear part. My money was there, as were several articles that belonged to Melina: a diary, some photographs, a few miscellaneous rubber-stamped documents.

I dropped the false bottom back into place, then returned to bed.

*

ON JULY 24 CYBULSKI flew home to Wisconsin. His mother was present at the airport, waiting for the casket to arrive. On the morning of the 24th they had a memorial service for him at the chapel before the casket left for Frankfurt and was loaded onto the plane.

The day should have belonged to Cybulski. But that same morning something else happened that overshadowed his departure. A man who had died more than twenty years before either of us was born was buried with full military honors in the cemetery on Alzeyerstrasse.

A couple of months prior, a German teenager had been searching the Hürtgen Forest with a metal detector and had found an American World War II helmet. He dug deeper and unearthed what looked like human bones, at which point he contacted the authorities. A German explosive ordnance team took charge of the site and excavated a ninety-five percent complete human skeleton.

Mingled with the bones was a pair of American dog tags belonging to one PFC Patrick Parnell, a native of Elizabethtown, Kentucky who had been reported missing on 7 December 1944. Dental records were checked and matched; it was Parnell, all right. He was no longer MIA, he was KIA. The damage to his skeleton suggested he died of chest wounds.

The Hürtgen Forest, near Aachen, saw some of the fiercest fighting of the war. Between September and December 1944 seven American divisions tried in monotonous succession to drive the entrenched German Army out of the forest. Hermann was under orders to hold his ground. He was planning a major counteroffensive, one we now know as the Battle of the Bulge. Had the Hürtgen Forest been lost, the Ruhr River and dams would follow, jeopardizing plans for the counteroffensive.

The 111th was the fifth division to attack. One of its regiments, the 121st, was ordered to capture the so-called Burgberg complex near the town of Bergstein.

Private First Class Patrick Parnell was a Beetle Bailey in Company C of the 121st. He was killed on 7 December apparently while crossing a ravine, and was covered with dirt loosened from the sides of the ravine by German artillery and mortar fire. After the battle his comrades searched for him in vain.

Parnell was twenty-two years old when he died. When his remains were found there were no relatives or friends left in Elizabethtown, Kentucky who knew him. If not for the boy with the metal detector, time would have forgotten him altogether. Headquarters and Headquarters Company were released from duty to attend his funeral. I chose instead to recognize Chuck's departure, and to do so from his favorite place, the Schlosspark. There would be so many people in the cemetery on Alzeyerstrasse that no one would miss me.

The violets were already gone from the banks of the pond; summer spoils the spring. I took off my boots and walked in the grass. Dandelions, cool beneath my feet, speckled the green lawn. The park was empty of people but for two women pushing baby strollers, and they were merely part of a greater fertility scene. I felt alone. By contrast, the cemetery would be crowded and buzzing with human voices.

The pond was still, a sheet of foiled glass. It reflected the clouds and swamp cypresses until ducks crossed it, disturbing the reflections with ripples like footprints in fresh snow. A pair of black swans followed me around the circumference. They swam silently, efficiently, elegantly, and the only evidence of their passing were the fractured, marquise-shaped ripples of hue left in their wake.

There was something about the "wild"—constantly churning with Darwinian battles, of consequence in proportion to the size of the creatures engaged in them—that was peaceful. The only civilized places that gave me the same sense of peace were graveyards. It seemed that the more death was present, the more peaceful the location.

They'd had a brief Catholic service for Cybulski before shipping his body to the airport. The priest didn't know him. But he knew how he died. The priest read, dispassionately, from a book.

Now as I sat on a bench in the Schlosspark watching the swans a squadron of F16 fighter jets from Spangdahlem Air Force Base screamed over the town in a salute to Patrick Parnell. At the same time, in Frankfurt, a Boeing 747 was lifting off with Cybulski's casket aboard. As the turbine engines of the F16s roared over the park I came to attention and gave Cybulski a proper military salute.

"Goodbye, Chuck," I said. "Don't worry about the laboratory animals, I'll take responsibility for rescuing them. I promise I'll save them all."

The noise of the jets sent the swans running for cover, which in turn upset the surface of the pond with a myriad interfering ripples.

One more thing: it was good, Chuck. It was real good. I look forward to next time. With any luck, next time will be even better.

*

AT THE END OF the day Wittlinger was waiting across the street from the barracks, in front of Amy's, holding a bouquet of flowers. He didn't look at me, nor did I approach him. Instead I went straight to the Weinstube as told.

Krupa wasn't in the building. I took a table alone and a waitress gave me a menu. I sat and waited, psyching myself up to stand my ground for more money, and worrying about what would happen if I demanded too much.

After fifteen minutes he still hadn't showed, so I opened the menu to order a glass of wine. A note fell to the table.

Okay, the note said. *You will receive fifteen. Try again Sunday. Same arrangement as before.*

Chapter 25

THURSDAY BEFORE THE BIG switch I bought a video camera at the PX. The saleslady kept trying to sell me up to more sophisticated features, like light adjustment, image stabilization, and so on. I could hardly tell her that all I needed was a simple device with which to photograph black type on white paper in a well lit military office on a Sunday afternoon. And that the frozen-frame images resulting from my photography needed to be just crisp enough for analysts to make them out. She was nevertheless a good salesperson and sold me a camera that had more functions than a Swiss Army Knife. I ditched the carrying case and replaced it with an Adidas gym bag.

I had decided to video the document rather than use the Xerox machine again because longer documents, when the time came for them, would consist of too many pages to run safely through a copier or carry out of the building.

Saturday in my barracks room I practiced with the camera on a dictionary, flipping the pages with my left hand while using my right hand to aim the lens. I adjusted the light up and down in the room to model various conditions in the office. Then I took the videocassette to the library where I could view it on a cassette player. The camera was excellent; it had made sharp images of the text at all levels of light.

Sunday afternoon I went to the AAFES bookstore to meet Montalbano, as ordered. The bookstore was off post, a couple of blocks southeast of the Kaserne on Alzeyerstrasse. Montalbano was already inside, perusing magazines. He wore a jogging suit and tennis shoes and didn't seem to notice me when I entered. He just kept looking at magazines. I started looking at magazines too. I was standing in front of the women's section and without thinking picked up *Cosmopolitan* and flipped through it. A couple of girls saw me and giggled. I put the magazine down and moved over to the military section, which is the second largest section, next to the comic books, in any military bookstore. There was nothing there that could compete with *Cosmopolitan*, but in the next section, where the car and motorcycle magazines were, were pictures of curvaceous, bikini-clad girls, the kind that always accompanied cars and motorcycles on magazine covers.

Gradually I worked my way down until I was standing next to Montalbano. He was looking through an issue of *Rolling Stone*. I was sure he chose this particular magazine because its format was large, rather than because he was a fan of pop music. After a moment he calmly reached inside his jogging top, took out a sheaf of papers, and placed the papers inside the magazine. Then he closed the magazine and returned it to the shelf. Moving over a few feet, he picked up a copy of *National Geographic*.

Without hesitating I picked up the *Rolling Stone* and walked to the cash register. The woman wordlessly rang the sale up and took my money. I declined the offer of a plastic bag and left the store with the magazine under my arm. Montalbano was still inside, reading the *National Geographic*.

It was a short walk down Alzeyerstrasse to the Kaserne. At the gate my heart was in my throat because the irrational fear had set in the gate guard might look inside my Adidas bag. But I had no reason for concern. Army gate guards, unlike their counterparts in other services, are ordinary Beetles dragged away from their regular jobs to stand guard in twelve hour shifts. They don't care who comes or goes or what's in their Adidas gym bags.

The guard passed me through without even looking at my ID card. Likewise, the two guards inside the headquarters building, a young man and a younger woman, were more interested in each other than in me. I took the steps two at a time and strode down the hallway through the G3 Section with obvious and deliberate purpose. But the display was in vain; nobody was there.

I had to video the terrain walk inside the Plans office to legitimize its appearance. Anyone scrutinizing the document would also scrutinize the background, as well as any sounds that might have been recorded, and it wouldn't do to have my bedpost make an unexpected appearance or my neighbor's stereo provide an unexpected soundtrack.

I turned the combination and unlocked the vault door. Then I took the key out of my pocket and unlocked the electronic door. In any ordinary jewelry store in any ordinary shopping mall, my actions so far would have alerted the police. But this wasn't a jewelry store in a shopping mall, this was a document vault in an army building in Germany. It's much easier to steal secrets from the United States government, it turns out, than to snatch a high school class ring from Zales.

Once inside the office I wasted no time. It was still light outside, so I had no qualms about turning on the lights. I opened the *Rolling Stone* magazine and removed the fake terrain walk. It was an excellent facsimile, exactly like any original except that names, units, and grid coordinates were invented. I turned the camera on and flipped the pages over one by one, taking my time to make sure a viewer would be able to extract frozen frames for transcription. When I was finished I merely threw the facsimile into one of the shred-and-burn bags, where it would never be found. Then I packed up the camera and left the building.

The building guards were still standing at their station inside the front door, whispering to each other as I came down the stairs. I could have been wearing an Ivan uniform and carrying an AK-47, and still they wouldn't have taken notice.

"*Dosvedanya*," I said to them on my way out. They didn't respond.

The gate guard who had so quickly passed me through on the way in barely glanced at me as I approached him from the opposite direction. But as I was crossing the painted line separating the territorial holdings of the United States of America from those of the Federal Republic of Germany, he held up his hand to stop me. He asked, in a bored voice, what was in the bag.

Gym clothes, I told him.

He wanted to know whether I had been working out.

Yes, I told him, I had.

He pointed out that I had come through the gate only half an hour before, and the workout session must have been a short one.

I told him I was just getting back into it and didn't want to overtax myself.

He asked what kind of machines I worked out on.

I told him the bench press and the stair master.

He said the barracks gym didn't have a stair master.

I told him I knew that; I had merely answered what machines I normally worked out on.

He asked me who was supervising the gym while I was there.

I told him I didn't know.

He asked who had signed me in when I arrived and changed into my gym clothes.

I asked him what the point of all this was, and whether he wanted to look inside the gym bag, since that's what seemed to have given him a problem in the first place.

He said yes, he would like to look inside. But first, if I didn't mind, he would like to check my identification again.

He was young looking, had closely cropped brown hair and brown eyes that watched me without expression. I asked him whether he would like to check the contents of my wallet for contraband at the same time he checked my identification.

He said yes, thank you, that would be a good idea.

I handed him the wallet. He went through it, removed about five hundred dollars in cash, then handed the wallet back. He asked whether it was a drug thing, or what.

I told him yes, it was a drug thing.

He said the money wasn't enough; next time there must be a thousand dollars in the wallet or he would search the gym bag.

I told him those terms were acceptable. Then I crossed the painted line and entered the Federal Republic of Germany. Officially, I was a spy.

*

WITTLINGER WAS PARKED IN front of the crucifix, in the same place he'd been the Sunday before. He was reading a newspaper. Once again I stepped into the phone booth on Mühlenstrasse and pretended to make a call, but it was for naught. Anyone who wanted to could watch the BMW from a dozen different angles, and there was no way for me to detect the surveillance. I would have to take my chances.

I left the phone booth and went up the street until I was standing next to the passenger-side door. It wasn't a newspaper Wittlinger was reading; it was a porn magazine. On the open page was a naked man standing with his hands on his hips and his dick hanging limply in front of him.

I knocked on the window. Wittlinger jerked, closed the magazine reflexively, and looked up to see who it was. Then he quickly shoved the magazine under his seat and motioned for me to climb into the back. I tried to open the door but it was locked. He pressed a button and unlocked it. I got in, and before I could close the door the car peeled away from the curb.

Wittlinger threw something in the back seat and told me to put it on. It was a ski mask with the eyes and mouth sewn shut. I stared at it amused for a few seconds until Wittlinger told me once again to put it on, this time in an aggressive tone. I put it on. It was slightly itchy and smelled of glove compartments. Then he told me to lie down on the seat, not to look up, not to take the mask off, not to say anything. Obviously he didn't want me to know where we were going. However, he failed to consider my intimate knowledge of the town.

The car turned left onto what had to be Rüdesheimerstrasse, then pulled over to the side of the road and parked for a few minutes. Wittlinger left the engine running, and I didn't know why he was stopping, but I guessed he was across the street from Montenegros, a Yugoslavian restaurant. Maybe he was waiting for a signal, maybe he was just making sure we weren't being followed.

Wittlinger then got back on the road again and a little ways down made another left turn, where I thought Hermannstrasse should be. But he was just trying to throw me, because he took a right shortly after, followed by another left, and we were right back on Rüdesheimerstrasse. The sharp right turn we made after that could only have been onto the Nördliche Umgehungsstrasse, which went above the town through the vineyards on the north side. We were on this road for a while and if I could lift my head and look out the window I would see Bad Karst laid out before me to my right.

I was lying across the back seat on my left side with my knees bent. My head was against the arm rest of the rear left door and my feet were pressed against the opposite arm rest. Since I couldn't see anything I concentrated on the forces that moved me around on the seat, forces that told me we were turning or slowing for a light. I could easily picture where the car was going.

At this point Wittlinger asked me where the document was. I told him it was recorded on a videocassette in the gym bag. He told me to put the bag next to the door. I asked him which door, the one next to my head or the one next to my feet. He said the one next to my feet.

If we kept going on this road we would pass the Feld des Jammers and enter Bretzenheim, but instead we turned right again, and the only place to do so was where the Östliche Umgehungsstrasse dipped down to Bosenheim. I realized then what Wittlinger was doing; he was taking me around in a large circle and would probably drop me off more or less where he picked me up. I felt the gentle slip as the car gradually turned to the right, then it straightened out and slowed down, and I knew we were entering Hackenheim. By this time I was anticipating turns; first a ninety degree right to take us back into Bad Karst, then a subtle choice of the right hand side of a fork to get us onto Alzeyerstrasse, where the barracks were. Right about where we should have been approaching the main gate, Wittlinger made a sudden left turn, then came to an abrupt stop. We were just outside the cemetery!

The back door next to my feet opened from the outside, and I felt cold air on my calves. Then I heard the zipper of the gym bag, and only a second later the door slammed shut again and the car was rolling. It swung counterclockwise around the cemetery, crossing back over to Alzeyerstrasse on one of the side streets, then continued downtown. The rest was easy. The moment we reached the crucifix on the Mannheimerstrasse bridge I braced myself for the braking action I knew would come.

Wittlinger told me to take off the mask, leave it on the back seat, and get out. I did, with my gym bag in my hand. After he pulled away and was out of sight I opened the bag. The camera was still there, but the cassette was gone. In its place was a sealed brown envelope. I opened the envelope and counted fifteen thousand dollars in one hundred dollar bills.

Not bad for an hour's work.

Chapter 26

MELINA BEGAN CLOSING HER door to customers as early as possible in the evening to spend time with me. It cost her, because the later the hour in a whorehouse, the looser the money. I usually worked late anyway, and when I locked up and crossed the street to Amy's Melina greeted me with an affectionate hug and a modest supper. She never told me about her day but insisted instead on hearing all about mine. I told her about my day but left out anything to do with spying.

We made love every night in front of the window. Soon after dark the temperature would drop abruptly and a cool breeze would blow into the room. We'd cuddle under a thin sheet, holding each other tightly, feeling the warmth of each other's bodies which was intensified by the contrasting sensation of the breeze. It made for stimulating lovemaking. Melina wouldn't make me wear a raincoat, and just at the right time she'd ask whether I wanted a baby. I said yes indeed yes I did want a baby oh please let's make one don't stop let's make piles of them. Afterwards, when she was asleep, I would lay awake staring at the white lace curtains billowing in from the window and wonder what we would do with a baby if ever one came along.

I taught her to read using flash cards. After memorizing words in the *Kleiner Eisbär* series she was able to read the books from start to finish. When done with a reading lesson she would wrap her arms around me in a way that said not only *I won't let you go* but also *I can't*. Sometimes she invited other girls over for dinner and afterwards we had fun.

I told Melina all about what Cybulski and I had been through, and about PETA, and that I intended to keep my promise to Cybulski, to PETA, and to the Animal Liberation Front. The money I was raising, that she was keeping for me in the false bottom of her dresser drawer, was for financing the animal rescues. Melina bought off on the idea instantly and enthusiastically.

When I gave her the fifteen thousand dollars from Krupa she counted it carefully, then hid it with the rest. "Think of all the animals we can save with that," she said.

It was a different feeling, having money. I started to get cocky about it. Whenever I recognized at least two people in a bar I bought the entire house a round of drinks. At work I started calling officers by their first names. Passing General Bundy in the hallway I said, "'Sup, Kit?"

One night at the Canape we saw Molly sitting at a table with her husband. If she'd been with anyone else I would have gone over and said hello. Instead I pointed her out to Melina. "That's the company commander and his wife."

Melina studied them for a few seconds. Apparently Molly wasn't aware of our presence. She was talking animatedly with her husband. At one point she leaned over and kissed him on the cheek.

"I don't like her," Melina said.

"Why not?"

"I just don't."

I bought the house a drink. You did this at the Canape by ringing a cow bell hanging over one corner of the bar. Afterwards Melina was quiet and when I asked her why, she said, "When you bought everyone a drink, you bought one for the redhead, too." We left without Molly ever having looked in our direction.

I had everything I wanted, yet I felt an emptiness, and after some study decided it was caused by a lack of romance in my life. Mind you, I had almost enough sex. More would have been better, but I didn't feel I had a right to complain. I was getting it a dozen or so times a week with a steady rotation of girls. I guess this level of activity is satisfactory if you aren't going for records or anything. But still, something was missing, and I think the feeling came from watching James Bond movies.

I asked Montalbano about this when he contacted me to see whether Krupa had gotten in touch again. I told him I hadn't yet heard from Krupa, and I asked him whether, since he was in the spy game, he routinely got laid by world class beauties. He was good looking, as guys go, and I figured if anybody'd get it, he would.

The question made him uncomfortable. He answered that promiscuity was detrimental to government professions, and besides, he was married. I asked him why he had chosen a profession that was detrimental to promiscuity, and what being married had to do with it. He suggested we change the subject.

I went on a dig one evening, but it wasn't the same without Cybulski. I hadn't appreciated how much he contributed to the experience merely by being afraid of the dark. The job took me much longer, working alone, but it was well worth the effort; the stiff was loaded. It was as though the family knew I would come for him and didn't want to disappoint me. I found a reasonably reliable fence in Wiesbaden who gave me a fair price. I put the money in the false bottom of Melina's dresser drawer.

There was no market for the stiff. After peddling it unsuccessfully for a couple of days I had to admit defeat and find a place to rebury it. Ironic thing was, the only logical place to rebury it was in its original resting place. So for the first time ever I dug up a grave to return a body to its coffin. I laughed as I dropped the lid: if it's come to this today, what's in store for me tomorrow?

*

"THERE'S A LADY ON the phone for you."

Pendergrass had stuck his face in the doorway of the war room where Lamoureaux and I were indexing topographic map sheets. It was a Friday afternoon in early August.

"What's the lady's name?" I asked.

"She wouldn't say."

There were three telephones in the Plans office: one in the war room, one on Pendergrass's desk, and one on Skelton's desk. Pendergrass had been sleeping with his feet up on his desk, and now he returned to that position and adjusted himself in his chair. I went into Skelton's office and shut the door.

The lady on the phone was Molly Brannigan.

"I need to see you," she said. She sounded out of breath and agitated.

"Is this a joke?" I asked.

"I'm serious. I need to see you right away."

"Why?"

"Please, just meet me, would you?"

I shrugged, bewildered. "Name the place."

"Dimitri's. It's a little Greek restaurant on—"

"I know the place."

"Say, six o'clock?"

I looked at the clock on the wall. It was four-thirty.

"Say now," I said. "It's close enough to quitting time."

"In that case, I'm on my way."

*

DIMITRI WAS A SHORT, plump Greek immigrant. He had a boy-ish grin and a dry sense of humor enhanced by his abominable German. When I arrived at his restaurant I found Molly sitting at a round table for five in the center of the dining room. She was smoking and her ashtray already had two butts in it. Dimitri took my cap, hung it on a hat rack, and winked at me.

"New girl," he said. "Good."

"Don't chalk this one up just yet," I said.

He grinned. "New girls good. Good for you." He patted his stomach as though we were talking about nourishment.

I took a seat next to Molly and looked at the empty chairs.

"Are we expecting company?" I asked.

"I don't like to feel cramped," she said sharply. There was none of the breathless urgency in her voice I'd heard on the phone.

"Is that a warning? Or just friendly advice?"

"Whatever you want it to be." She lit another cigarette. Dimitri placed menus on the table in front of us.

"I already know what I want," I said, and gave him the order.

"Same for me," Molly said.

"And a tranquilizer for the lady," I said to Dimitri.

He didn't understand.

"Nothing," I said. "Forget it. It was a joke."

"Oh," he grinned. "Funny." He left for the kitchen.

I turned to Molly. "So speak."

"So what would you like me to speak about?"

"Well, for starters, why are we here?"

"You called my house last night, didn't you?"

"What makes you think so?"

"I know so."

"How?"

"By your answer. You didn't answer in the negative, so now I know with certainty it was you who called."

"Molly, other than that night weeks ago, when we met, I've never called your house."

"You've called many times. Each time my husband answers, you hang up. He usually answers the phone anyway, but now, since this foolish harassment has begun, he answers it every time. He's sure something funny is going on. Nearly every day the phone rings, and when he answers it, no one is there. What am I supposed to tell him? That some silly-assed private in his own company is calling me repeatedly, waiting for the one time I might answer?"

"Private first class."

"Now, even when he gets a 'real' call, he snatches the phone up and growls his name. It's not good. I want it to stop."

"You could have told me this on the phone."

"And now you're following me. Wherever I go, I'm afraid to look at the people around me, I'm sure you'll be somewhere in the crowd."

"You could have said all this on the phone. Why are we meeting here for dinner?"

"I wanted to tell it to your face. I wanted to make sure you got the message."

"I don't believe you. You could have accomplished that by coming to the office, or meeting me on the sidewalk. Why are we *here*?"

Dimitri brought the drinks and salads. He placed a glass of red wine in front of me and a glass of white wine in front of Molly. "*Guten Appetit,*" he said, and returned to the bar.

"You are a sick, demented puppy," Molly said.

"Then why are we here?"

"You disgust me thoroughly, and you are endangering my marriage."

"*Why are we here?*"

She took a long swig from the wine, smashed her cigarette out in the ashtray, and stood up, dropping her napkin on the table with finality. She headed for the door. I followed her out. Dimitri was startled when he saw us leaving.

"The wine," he asked, "no good?"

"No." I patted him on the shoulder. "Just the girl. Keep the food warm, we'll be right back."

I caught up to her outside and reached for her shoulder.

"Don't touch me!" she said. "And don't follow me either, you puppy!"

"What the hell's eating you?" I said. "I don't know who's been calling your house, but it hasn't been me. And I haven't been following you either."

"Then what were you doing in the Canape the other night?"

"I just happened to be there. I didn't know you were going to be there too."

"Liar."

"Or maybe you want me to follow you. Maybe you're wondering why I'm not calling your house. You get lonely at night, and you wish Jimmy would call."

"Private," she said. "Lousy private in the lousy infantry. How does it feel to be the lowliest form of human life on the planet?"

"It feels just fine."

"Word's out you're a faggot too."

"Shut up."

"Oh yes! You're a faggot, and you shack up with that whorehouse slut just to hide it. You and that Pollack friend of yours, what's his name?"

"Shut up," I said.

"Private Faggot."

I grabbed her by the back of the neck and kissed her. She put her hands up to my chest and tried to push me away, but she wasn't strong enough. She clawed at me and pulled my hair and bit my lip. I pulled her body closer, until it was tight against mine, and planted my lips on her neck.

"Now's when you're supposed to scream," I said.

She tried kicking me. I placed my hand on her breast. Her resistance subsided, she went limp in my arms and began crying.

"Take me home," she said.

"You know I can't do any such thing."

"Take me somewhere."

"Dimitri's cooking our dinner."

"Take me somewhere. Anywhere."

Chapter 27

I FUCKED THE COMPANY commander's wife in an unoccupied barracks room above the company commander's office. I could imagine the captain himself sitting at his desk a few feet beneath us, writing up an Article Fifteen for some shit-head in his command, or perhaps requisitioning a replacement light bulb for the storage closet; whatever company commanders did while sitting at their desks, after hours, as their wives were being fucked on unmade mattresses in rooms above their heads.

Afterwards Molly lay her head on my chest and fell asleep. I held her and stroked her lustrous hair and felt the softness of her cheeks and lips with the tips of my fingers. Later I woke her so she could go home. She dressed in a drowsy state, and as soon as she had put on her shoes we held each other and I sensed a desperateness in the way she clutched me. She went home and I went to my room and sat by the window, listening to Beetles staggering in from their drinking sprees. It was Friday night.

The next morning, when Captain Brannigan and Top entered my room to conduct inspection, it occurred to me how good it felt gazing on the figure of a man I loathed whose wife

I'd just squirted. The parallel silver bars he wore on his collar wouldn't ever have the same affect on me again.

There was apprehension on Melina's face when I showed up at Amy's that morning. "EAC again?" she asked.

"Yep. And wouldn't you know it? They want me to serve all day today too. I just came by to get a bite to eat." I gave her a hug and a kiss.

After finishing eating I noticed she'd hardly touched her food.

"Not hungry?" I asked.

"Not much."

I kissed her on the forehead. "Be back tonight. Maybe we'll go out. You'd like that, wouldn't you?"

She smiled. "Sure."

*

MOLLY PICKED ME UP at the Heilig-Kreuz-Kirche in an old maroon Citroen and we left town on Salinenstrasse, passing the Kurviertel and its open air vaporizers, then climbed up the Naheweinstrasse to Rotenfels.

Rotenfels meant "red rock." However, stare as I might, I couldn't find a single speck of red in it. It was an intrusive igneous body that had weathered the storms and resisted the river. Or maybe the river, which could cut anything it wanted to, given enough time, chose not to bother. Molly had selected Rotenfels as a meeting place because it was out of the way without being far away; she would not likely run into anyone she knew.

From the parking lot we walked up a gravel path to the top. There were other tourists on the path, and Molly eyed each one carefully. But she recognized no one. For my own part, I didn't care if the whole world knew I was spending the day with Molly Brannigan, the company commander's wife. Nor did I think she had any cause for concern, as the German geological formations didn't draw the same crowds as the German castles, cathedrals, and beer halls did.

We reached the edge of the rock and gawked at the view like the other tourists. One couple nearly fell off with excitement when they saw their hotel in the town below. The drop was steep—I guessed about five hundred feet—but manageable to an experienced rock climber. I was not such a climber. I had a fear of heights I kept under control by avoiding heights and by never approaching the edge of anything, ever.

"Come on up and look," Molly said.

"Thanks," I said. "I can see fine from here."

The incline was littered with moss- and lichen-covered boulders and populated by scrubby, do-or-die trees. We had a good aerial view of the towns of Bad Münster and Ebernburg. I could see far up the Nahe valley until it disappeared in the mist.

Most of the tourists went to the right and followed the edge of the cliff to the west, where the rock was steeper and the view more spectacular. We went east, following a path into the woods that here and there was tangent to the edge of the rock. Eventually the path wound down the hill, so we left it and went into the woods, continuing until we could no longer distinctly hear the voices of the other hikers. We found an arrangement of trees and shrubs planted in a rough circle with branches extending over the center, creating a space that, with a modest stretch of the imagination, resembled a cathedral. We took off our clothes, laid down on a bed of pine needles and oak leaves, and made love.

I was vaguely and absentmindedly aware of a jet flying overhead, and of pine needles pricking my back, but otherwise nothing in the universe existed but myself and Molly. She let down her long, lustrous hair. It fell around my face and created another small cathedral with room enough for our two faces, and neither the jet nor the pine needles intruded. I felt the full length of her bare legs against mine and soon no longer considered them distinct from mine.

Afterwards we both smoked cigarettes. The laughter of the other hikers seemed closer now. We might have been away for hours, maybe days. Finally I asked, "Why me?"

She shook her head and exhaled smoke. "Why *not* you?"

"Come on," I said, "that's no answer."

"To tell you the truth, I don't know." She finished her cigarette and ground it out in the leaves. "I've been thinking about it myself. If anyone had asked me a month ago whether there was any chance I'd cheat on my husband, I'd have said no chance at all. If anyone had told me I'd do it with a junior enlisted soldier in his command, I'd have thought him crazy."

"Rank really is important to you, isn't it?"

"It's a fair prejudice, you have to admit."

Yes, it was. The gentlemen were mostly in the officer corps. The enlisted ranks consisted largely of animate biomatter.

"But that made it all the harder to come with me," I said.

"Yes, it did."

"Then why did you?"

She shrugged. "Like I said, I don't know. All I know is, my instincts tell me this is right. It feels right, doesn't it?"

"Yes. It has never felt righter. But why suddenly now?"

She lit another cigarette. "I've been thinking about you a lot. It's been hard to get you off my mind. I've known a great many people, but I've never known anyone like you. I just couldn't stand it anymore. I had to get closer to you. A lot closer. I always was impulsive. I guess I just never knew how impulsive I really was."

We talked for a while longer, then got dressed and returned to the path and headed back to our starting point. When we reached it I turned toward the parking lot, but Molly stopped me and insisted we keep going and see what lay in the other direction along the cliff edge. I already knew what lay there, which is why I wanted to return to the parking lot.

The path turned into steps that rose to the top of a pinnacle. Although there was a wooden rail fence, I kept to the far inside of the steps.

Molly asked, "You okay?"

"Yep, fine."

We walked a little ways further. I could see the gentle rolling hills in the distance that comprised the Rheinland's eroded Schist Massif. A moment later we were looking straight down past a sheer rock wall that plummeted five hundred feet to the river.

Molly posed the question, "What do you suppose would happen to someone if he fell from here?"

I looked. He'd try to hold onto something, try to grab onto some shrubbery on the way down, but the drop was too steep. He'd tumble to the edge of the rock, then fall straight down to the river. He'd die. And he'd be stricken by unspeakable terror all the way down.

"What's the matter?" Molly asked.

"I can't do this."

"Why not?"

"I just can't." The path continued around the edge of the cliff, winding its way to another sheer pinnacle, but I'd had enough.

On our way out of Rotenfels we elected to have a beer in the Gasthaus on the hill. The beer tasted so good we elected to have a few more. Then we climbed into Molly's Citroen and drove back down the hill. We were both giggling, and Molly took great pains to avoid oncoming traffic by swerving off the road and into the trees.

*

AT AMY'S THAT NIGHT Melina had already turned in and there was nothing for dinner. I climbed into bed next to her, trying not to wake her, and just as I was getting comfortable she opened her eyes.

"I called Harold Lamoureaux," she said.

"And?"

"You weren't on EAC duty today. Or last night."

"I see."

"Or ever. Only Ops people, he said, get EAC duty."

"Is that a fact?" I made a mental note to educate Harold Lamoureaux the moment I saw him again.

"Just promise me one thing, Jimmy."

"What?"

"You weren't with that redhead you pointed out to me in the Canape."

"I wasn't."

"Promise?"

"Promise."

Then, after a long pause, I said, "What made you think of her?"

"Just a hunch. There's something spooky about that woman. I didn't like her, Jimmy. I didn't like her at all."

Chapter 28

DURING ONE OF MY nearly daily conversations with Blackburn I asked him why the approach was going so slowly.

"They want to give you time to accept your role," he told me. "Time for you to get over the revulsion of spying, then accept your status as a spy. Then—hopefully—relish the fact, as so many eventually do. At that point they have the greatest chances of success getting you to pass what they want, whereas before that point they risk refusal."

This made sense to me, but: what revulsion?

On Saturday, August 18, I stayed in my room all morning. That afternoon I happened to glance out the window: Wittlinger was standing on the sidewalk across the street with a bouquet of flowers clenched in his fist.

Finally.

I opened the window and waved at him, to acknowledge I had gotten the message, but he pretended not to see me. Five or ten minutes later he ambled away.

Half an hour after that I was joining Krupa in the Weinstube. He sat at the same table, in the same chair, as the last time I'd seen him.

"I took the liberty of ordering for you," he said. "I hope I behaved correctly."

A glass of California cabernet sat on the table. I tasted it and told him yes, he had behaved correctly.

We completed our usual greetings, argued about each other's tastes in wine, then settled into a conversation that by now I knew was necessary before he would get down to business.

"Did you know," he said, "this building was a house of ill repute before it became a restaurant?"

In fact I had known. I told him it had first been a private residence, and later a corset shop. I pointed out aspects of the decor dating back to its whorehouse days. "If the story is true," I said, "then everyone who ever got laid here is probably now dead."

"Interesting."

"If only these walls could talk."

"Indeed."

"Think of all the moments of intense pleasure that might have occurred over the years right where we're sitting."

"It boggles the mind."

"Think of the moaning—all of it brought forward in time to this instant—so that it echoes all at once off these walls."

"You have a vivid imagination."

"Picture the fountains of sperm that might have erupted right here." I touched my index finger to the center of the table.

"I get the picture. Now if you don't mind—"

"It's like being in a haunted house, except, no ghosts. Or at least, no unhappy ones."

"Suppose," he said, "someone wanted to buy the General Defense Plan?"

The sentence startled me; we had barely begun our small talk. I took a long gulp of wine and stared at him, blinking. "That," I said, "would be a tall order."

I had waited weeks to get another offer from him, and now he was squirming in his seat with impatience to deliver it to me. What's the rush? I wondered.

"It is a tall order, yes," Krupa said. "Nevertheless one that you would be able to fill."

"Possibly. Theoretically speaking, how much could one expect to receive in exchange for filling such an order?"

"A modest sum, theoretically."

"How modest?"

He shrugged. He wanted me to start the bidding.

"Suppose," I said, "someone didn't want to provide the document for less than three times the amount he'd been paid for the previous document he had provided?"

Krupa looked up at the ceiling. "That would probably be high. Two times would be more in the ballpark."

"Suppose he wouldn't do it for less than three times?" My previous fee had been fifteen thousand dollars, and three times that would support me for years, as long as I didn't stock *Haut-Médoc Premiers Crus* in my wine cellar.

"If that were the case," Krupa said, "whoever was making the offer would have to report the condition back to the buyer."

We both took sips of wine, stared into our wine glasses, and assessed our positions. He was asking for the General Defense Plan—the GDP—which, other than Oplan 2357-90, the one Blackburn and Montalbano had told me he was ultimately after, was probably the most important document in the vault. There were other documents that contained bigger secrets, including a dozen or so classified as top secret; the GDP was only classified secret, and was therefore easy for me to get. But in terms of mere bulk of classified information, much of which was quite sensitive, the GDP probably outweighed everything else. The top secret documents in the vault disclosed, among other facts, where nuclear weapons were stored in the European theater; but only the GDP described what we intended to do during the conduct of war. It was a detailed plan of troop movements, reinforcements, and line passages that, in the hands of the enemy at the moment of their attack, would make the division vulnerable.

The GDP was constantly under revision, which meant any version Ivan bought would soon be out of date. But the premises remained unchanged from version to version.

Eastern European armies, supported by Ivan units, especially his fighter jets, would lead a blitzing attack through the Fulda Gap in numbers that would overwhelm allied forces in place. The plan assumed forces in place would hold their ground at least until Conus units could deploy to Europe, a contingency those units practiced annually during Reforger—Return of Forces to Germany. A passage of lines would then occur, as forces in place retreated to the west and Reforger units attacked to the east. The plan preposterously assumed the aggressor armies would retreat to their starting points and the integrity of Western Europe would be secured.

Every sentient officer privately considered the GDP to be bullshit. Popular opinion held that forces in place would in fact die in place. That was their mission. And when Reforger units were successfully deployed and ready to attack, Ivan would sue for peace and draw new boundaries at the front, incorporating his captured ground.

It didn't take me long to convince myself I would do little or no harm passing the GDP. Not only because it was preposterous, but also because Ivan had no design to warm up Cold War again.

"Report the condition back to the buyer, Mister Krupa," I said. "I won't sell you the GDP for less than fifty thousand dollars in cash on delivery."

"You will not get fifty."

"Then you won't get the plan. It's that simple. Discuss the matter with your client, and we'll talk again."

"I am afraid there is not enough time. It is now or never. You have until Sunday, the 26th, to deliver the document to the Mannheimerstrasse bridge, after which Wittlinger will wait only two more days."

"Then what happens?"

"Then we buy it from someone else."

"What's the rush?"

"My client wants it as soon as possible."

"Same client as before?"

"No."

Of course not. He would say that regardless.

"You know, Fisher," he said, "we are not hurting anybody by doing this. In fact—"

"Save it, Krupa. I don't have a philosophical problem with the transaction. So let's get on with it. Do I get the fifty, or not?"

"You will get what you get."

"Well then, let me put it to you this way. I'll bring the document to the bridge, as before, but I won't hand it over unless there's fifty thousand dollars in the bag."

"I will do what I can."

"See to it that you do. In fact, if you can do better than fifty, do that."

Krupa emptied his wine glass and said, "What do you soldiers say? The eggs are in the beer?"

"You're a generation or two behind, but yeah, that's what they said."

"We could become friends, if you would allow it."

"I can't be your friend. Not after what you did to Cybulski."

"I did not make Cybulski a homosexual, Mister Fisher. It is what he chose to be."

It was probably pointless to inform him that, physiologically speaking, Cybulski didn't have a choice in the matter, either.

"There is one more thing," Krupa said. He took a five Mark bill out of his wallet and tore it down the middle. Then he handed one of the halves to me. "Bring that to the bridge."

"Why?"

"No exchange will be made unless you have that in your possession. When the two halves fit together, each party can be confident it is exchanging with a proper representative of the other party."

"Fine. Tell your client: fifty thousand dollars, or else all the guy's going to receive during the exchange is a torn five Mark bill."

*

I CALLED MONTALBANO AND told him of the arrangement.

"The 26th? Are you crazy? The GDP is over five hundred pages long. How are we going to prepare a fake by the 26th? Why didn't you tell him that was way too soon?"

"Uh, sorry. I didn't think about the length of the document. They seem to be in some kind of hurry for it."

"Of course they are, asshole. They have to get through this stage to get to the next, and they're in a hurry to get to the next."

"Then why did they wait so long to get to this stage?"

"Blackburn explained that to you. They needed to give you time to get used to—"

"Yeah, yeah. Revulsion and all that."

He sighed exaggeratedly. "We'll do what we can, we have no choice. We'll have a fake GDP ready for you by the 26th. That motherfucker. By the way, how much is he paying you?"

"Twenty-five thousand dollars."

"Sounds like you did pretty well."

"Problem is, I need fifty."

"So why tell me?"

"Because you're going to give me the other twenty-five."

"The fuck I am."

"Tell Blackburn."

"Tell him yourself."

"Tell him I need twenty-five thousand dollars from you cheapskates or the deal doesn't come off."

"You'll get twenty-five of something—years, not dollars."

"Good plan. Then you'll have to start the project all over from the beginning with someone else."

"That's my vote, if you want to know."

"Fortunately, you're not in charge. Tell Blackburn. Twenty-five or nothing."

"I'll tell him. Meantime you need to be on the lookout for the mole. We've tapped Krupa's telephone, but he employs a voice scrambler and we haven't been able to unscramble our recordings of his conversations. Krupa knows that no matter how visible he is, he's safe as long as the control is safe; nobody is really after Krupa."

"I have an idea about all of that," I said.

"What?"

"Colonel Leslie Riddell."

Montalbano was silent for a moment. "I don't think so."

"I do."

"Good for you, Fisher."

"Pass it on to Blackburn, will you?"

"I will, and he'll give it due consideration, but I don't think you're on the right track."

"Tell him anyway. And by the way, fuck you."

"Fuck you too."

Chapter 29

MONTALBANO WAS IN THE AAFES bookstore Sunday afternoon, looking at the magazines, just as I had left him the last time. With a small stretch of the imagination I could picture his entire twilight zone reality consisting only of the magazine rack in the bookstore. As before, he took no notice of me, he just flipped pages. He was dressed in shorts and a t-shirt and looked like an FBI agent trying not to look like an FBI agent. A gym bag hung from his shoulder.

Instead of a *Rolling Stone* magazine he had a copy of *Life*, but it wasn't going to make any difference; you couldn't put a facsimile of the General Defense Plan inside a magazine. I wandered up next to him, picked up another copy of *Life*, and waited.

Montalbano replaced the magazine in the rack and turned around, so he was standing in front of the opposite rack where the office supplies were on display. He removed the gym bag from his shoulder and set it on the floor, then took out a rectangular cardboard box, the kind reams of typing paper came in. He placed the box on top of a stack of several other identical boxes in the office supply rack. Then he straightened up and walked away, as though people did such things in bookstores all the time. I waited until he was on the opposite side of the store, perusing the bibles, before reaching down and picking up the box.

It was indeed a typing paper box, complete with cellophane wrapping and price tag, just like the others beneath it. I was on my way to the register when something occurred to me. I went back to the magazine rack and picked up the copy of *Life* Montalbano had been reading. Sure enough, planted inside was an envelope: my twenty-five thousand dollars. The fucker was hoping I'd leave without it, then he could pocket the money himself and claim he had delivered it to me.

I took the box and the magazine to the register and paid for them.

"The cellophane's torn on that one," the girl said.

"That's okay," I said. "I don't care."

"Suit yourself."

The next phase required getting past the gate guard and onto the post with a facsimile of the General Defense Plan in my possession. But as I rounded the corner on Alzeyerstrasse I saw that it wasn't the same guy as before. If it had been, the trip would have cost me a thousand dollars on the way out.

The same two guards as the first time—a young man and a younger woman—were posted just inside the main door of the headquarters building, and once again they paid no attention to me. I noticed that whereas the last time I saw them they behaved as though they were about to begin a sexual relationship, this time they looked as though they'd made measurable progress toward completing that goal. They had the relaxed presence in each other's company that comes when two people have experienced the ultimate intimacy. Apparently they routinely volunteered for Sunday duty to spend time together.

I climbed the stairs to the second floor, turned the corner, and froze. The vault door to the Plans office was wide open. I cursed under my breath. Approaching the electronic door, which was closed and locked as usual, I looked through the window, but couldn't see anyone. That meant whoever was there was either in Skelton's office, in the war room, or positioned behind the safes. Or had left for a few minutes to go elsewhere in the building. I took out my key and opened the door.

"Hello?" I said. "Hello?"

I looked behind the wall of safes in the main office, and I checked Skelton's office and the war room. Someone had been there, but had left for some reason. It was five-thirty, so maybe whoever it was had gone to dinner. If that were the case he should have closed the vault door before he left.

This was a dilemma. Should I continue and hope to finish before he returned? Or should I just leave? The former was dangerous because someone was bound to walk in on me. The latter wasn't that much more appealing because I would then have a large piece of sensitive contraband in my possession for another twenty-four hours. Also, if I waited until the next evening to film the document I might face an entire section full of officers, because on week nights they usually worked late.

I chose to shoot the thing then and there. It just so happened there was a stack of copies of the GDP in one of the secret drawers waiting to be stamped. It wasn't a rush job, because spare copies were not in demand at the time. Nevertheless the job needed to be done, and the sooner the better; there was some kind of regulation that disallowed classified documents to sit in storage for very long without classification stamps.

I opened the drawer and took out the stack. There were, in fact, an even dozen copies, which provided me with at least several hours of work. I would have to spread them all out on the tables in the war room and check each page of an arbitrary master copy. The problem was, I didn't have several hours. On the other hand, it would look suspicious if I stamped only one copy. I compromised with three, because there was room for three on a table behind the safes. I had to work behind the safes; if I worked in front of them, anyone peeking through the window of the electronic door would see me with a video camera in front of my face. And if I worked in either Skelton's office or the war room, I might not hear someone entering the main office: it was possible to open and close the electronic door without making much noise.

Clearing off the table, I laid out three copies of the GDP, and returned the other nine to the drawer. I got out my camera and set it up. For the sake of appearance I stamped the documents as fast and efficiently as I could until I was about one-fifth of the way through. Then I turned on the camera. If I heard anyone opening the electronic door all I had to do was stuff the camera and the facsimile into the gym bag and continue stamping.

The reason the cellophane on the typing box was torn was because Blackburn and Montalbano had opened the box to replace the blank typing paper inside with the facsimile. They had cut the cellophane as carefully as they could along the edge of the box, but in handling it later Montalbano had messed it up; that's why the cashier noticed it. I tore it away and threw it into a garbage can. The facsimile, likewise, would go into one of the shredding bags when I was through.

I was familiar with the contents of the GDP because I had typed it, stamped it, copied it, organized it, and to some extent even written it, especially in places where staff officers had struggled for clarity of exposition. So as I turned the pages of the facsimile and watched fake secrets pass through the lens of my camera I noticed a couple of things were amiss. Presumably there had been too little time to do real justice to the document.

Entire sections had been rewritten, even though they contained nothing classified or sensitive. Several annexes were missing altogether, and the idiosyncrasies of the layout and organization were different.

Every army plan follows specific guidelines governing organization, structure, even punctuation. But grand old plans like the GDP, plans that have been rehashed countless times and fingered by hundreds of people, take on odd characteristics and employ unique conventions.

For example, because there were so many subparagraphs in the document, the usual convention of indenting every new subparagraph yet deeper than the previous one was discarded because paragraphs were beginning near the right margin of the page. This copy resumed the standard indentation convention. I wondered why they didn't just use the genuine GDP and change some grid coordinates. I guessed either they wanted to make it more realistic by making it more conventional, or perhaps there were subtleties in the document about which I had not been aware.

Nevertheless, although the essential content was plausible, with crucial information such as grid coordinates changed, it was disconcerting to pass a facsimile that did not do justice to the *appearance* of the genuine document. An insider employed to confirm or deny the authenticity would immediately see it was not in fact the GDP. It was, in espionage parlance, shit.

As I flipped the pages with the camera pressed against my eye the feeling gradually came over me I was being watched. I calmly turned the camera off and returned it to the gym bag. Then I turned around and looked.

Garrett was standing next to the end safe, looking at me. I had no idea how long he'd been there.

"What are you doing?" he asked.

"Stamping," I said. "Why are you here?"

"I just stopped by to see if anyone was in the office. When I found nobody here I went to check my mail." He scanned my work area until his eyes rested on the facsimile. "What's that?" he asked.

"Nothing. Something that came in while you were out. It's Sunday, you know. You should go home."

"I'm going now." He looked out the window and yawned, and the incredible reality sunk in that he hadn't seen the camera—my body had blocked the view. I had survived a dangerous encounter.

"Enjoy the day off," I said.

"Right."

After he had gone I waited ten or fifteen minutes, then opened the electronic door and looked down the hall. No one was there. I resumed filming until I was finished. Then I had to finish stamping the three genuine copies of the GDP. This took longer than I thought. I couldn't screw it up by stamping just anything on the page, because someone would eventually notice. And I couldn't quit in mid-effort, because in case Garrett raised an alarm I needed to be able to show that I had in fact completed a job.

It was eight-fifteen when I was done. I had forty-five minutes to make it to the Mannheimerstrasse bridge, where presumably Wittlinger was waiting. Otherwise I had to keep the cassette on my person, or hidden in a safe place, until the next night.

I didn't want to take any chances with the cassette. Things had gone well so far, but Garrett's appearance might have been the beginning of a streak of bad luck. Instead of carrying the cassette through the gate I wandered along the inside perimeter of the Kaserne until I found a part of the fence, near the chapel, that was partially hidden by weeds. The fence was chain link, painted green, with four strands of barbed wire stretched across the top. I sat down and leaned against it, like I was taking a breather. When I was sure no one was watching I nonchalantly took the camera out of the gym bag, reached around behind my back, and slid it under the fence. The camera and cassette were now outside the Kaserne, buried in a bunch of weeds. The odds of anyone finding them during the next few minutes while I exited the Kaserne and walked around the perimeter to the chapel were next to zero.

My instincts turned out to be correct. While I had been inside the Plans office taping the facsimile the guard shift had changed, and, lo and behold, my old friend was back on duty: the young looking military policeman with short brown hair and utterly bland expression.

As I approached the gate he recognized me and a Mona Lisa smile appeared on his face.

"I see you've been working out again," he said.

"Indeed I have."

"Well, let's have the money."

"What money?"

"You know, the thousand dollars I told you to bring if ever you walked through here with a gym bag again. It's either that, or I look inside the bag."

I handed him the bag. He opened it and shuffled through the contents. I had thought to pack some gym clothes in advance, because an empty gym bag is suspicious. When he didn't find anything he snooped around the sides of the bag, looking for pockets or secret compartments. Finally, giving up, he handed the bag back to me. Then he held out his empty hand, palm facing up.

"One thousand dollars," he said.

"What for?" I said. "What can you possibly do to me if I don't pay you? You've got nothing on me."

"Here's what I'll do: I'll pick up this telephone and order an immediate search of the fence perimeter. I'll detain you here until the search is complete."

I opened my wallet, removed one thousand dollars in one hundred dollar bills, and handed it to him. "You win," I said.

"I always win."

"We ought to form a partnership. You and I seem to—"

"No," he said, "thanks. I work alone. Every time I see you pass through this gate on your way out, during duty hours, during off hours, gym bag or no gym bag, drugs or no drugs, you owe me one thousand dollars."

"Got it."

"See to it that you do. And don't try to fuck with me next time. Just give me the fucking money."

"Okay."

What that meant was, from now on I would have to jump the fence. Which was dangerous, because if anyone saw me and reported it to the MPs I would be chased down. Jumping the fence was about as suspicious as it got.

*

I HAD TO HOOF it to reach Wittlinger on time. In fact, I didn't make it. It was two minutes after nine o'clock when I came pounding up the sidewalk to where he was parked on the curb in his BMW. He had already started the engine and was getting ready to pull away from the curb. I knocked on the window of the BMW just as it was shifting into gear. Wittlinger looked at me impatiently, then shifted back into neutral and thrust his thumb toward the back seat, signaling for me to get in. I got in.

We sat for a moment, then he said, "Aren't you forgetting something?"

I thought about it, then remembered. "Oh, yeah." I reached into my pocket and took out the five Mark bill Krupa had given me. Wittlinger snatched it out of my hand and held it up against one of his own. Satisfied, he tossed a ski mask into my lap, the same one I had worn the first time. We were on our way.

I was sure he would pick a different route to confuse me, but clearly he thought the route he had chosen the last time was a mystery. At any rate, when he turned onto Rüdesheimerstrasse, parked for a few minutes, then continued and turned left onto Hermannstrasse, I knew we were connecting the same dots as before.

Once again I was lying across the back seat on my left side with my knees bent. By concentrating on the gentle forces that nudged me around on the seat I could imagine the path of the car. Since it was the same path as before, I was able to predict each turn and stop before it happened.

"Where is it?" Wittlinger asked gruffly, about halfway through the trip.

"I assume you mean the cassette. It's in the gym bag, same as before."

"Put it next to the door, next to your feet."

"Aye aye, sir. Have you got my fifty?"

"I haven't got anything."

"How much do *they* have, whoever has it?"

"That's not my department."

"It'd better be fifty, or the deal's off."

"Take a look at yourself. You're in no position to negotiate. If I were you I'd keep my head down and my mouth shut."

A few minutes later we parked once again next to the cemetery on Alzeyerstrasse, although neither Wittlinger nor his cohorts were aware I knew. Not that it mattered; I was convinced the cemetery was merely an arbitrarily selected public place, not the headquarters of the bad guys. They just didn't want me alerting a third party that might take pictures. I assumed the route included check points, probably manned by other team members, to make sure the car wasn't being followed.

The back door swung open. Once again the switch occurred wordlessly. Then Wittlinger drove me back to the bridge. When he had dropped me off and was out of sight, I looked inside the gym bag to confirm the presence of the camera and the money, and the absence of the cassette.

I counted the money. There was only twenty thousand dollars.

No matter. Altogether I had made forty-five thousand dollars in one day. I knew what Krupa was ultimately after, and he would have to pay me in advance for it—including the thirty thousand dollars he still owed me for the GDP.

Chapter 30

MISSION

111th Infantry Division (Mechanized) deploys on order; occupies Tactical Assembly Areas (TAA) Descartes, Fermat, and Pascal; conducts corps main attack in sector to seize area vicinity objectives Galaxy and Nebula; on order, prepares to defend.

EXECUTION

Concept of Operation. Annex C (Operations).

Maneuver. Division deploys and occupies designated tactical assembly areas: 2nd Brigade, TAA Descartes; 4th Brigade, TAA Fermat; 1st Brigade (simulated), TAA Pascal; 3rd Brigade (simulated), OPCON to 5th (US) Corps. On order, division attacks with two brigades abreast to secure high ground vicinity objectives Galaxy and Nebula. 2nd Brigade conducts the main attack in the north to seize objective Galaxy and 4th Brigade conducts a supporting attack in the south to seize objective Nebula. 1st Brigade (simulated), division reserve, on order follows 2nd Brigade and supports main attack.

Fires. Annex D (Fires).

*

WHEN IT'S DARK AND the windows of the truck are wet with dew as you roll out of the motor pool and find your place in the convoy, you're cheered some by the light on the horizon but dismayed by all the stars still in the sky. Not that the sun, when it rises, will improve this day. You're on your way to the field, the last place in the world you want to be, and when you arrive it will be dark again. So it might as well have stayed dark the whole trip, because it's easier to concentrate on your misery when there's no scenery to distract you.

Mind you, you did try to get out of deploying. During the two or three days before deployment you stacked your inbox so high the tower of documents threatened to topple over. But the sergeant major is no longer fooled by the ploy. A field exercise beginning Sunday, September 2, the day before Labor Day—an army holiday—is enough to piss everyone off, including the sergeant major, and he'll be damned if he's going to let anyone get out of this one. Even the pregnant girls—the ones who put on maternity uniforms the moment they learn they're pregnant—are taking part in this one.

On its way out of town the convoy runs into a traffic jam. No one knows why there's a traffic jam on this particular Autobahn access road so early on this particular Sunday morning. Except of course that massing the division headquarters in a string of lumbering trucks and sending them all through the gate at the same time might have something to do with it. No one thought to post MPs along the route because no one thought there would be a traffic jam. As a result the convoy begins to break up. This means some vehicles will get lost because only the driver of the first vehicle and his passenger—the sergeant major—know exactly where they're going.

As the Plans truck sits in the jam with its motor idling you get a hair, open the door of the cab, and climb out.

"Where the fuck are *you* going?" Pendergrass wants to know.

You tell him you have an errand to run, that the truck is going to be sitting there for a while, and you therefore have the time.

He says, "Get the fuck back in here, Fisher. *Now*, goddammit!"

"That's *Private First Class* Fisher," you say, "Sergeant Pendergrass." You start walking down the road back towards town. Some of the drivers of the other trucks honk and give you the thumbs-up sign. They apparently figure you're going to do something about the traffic jam, although you can't imagine what that would be. Or maybe they think you're deserting. You give them the thumbs-up sign in return.

You hear Pendergrass yell from the truck: "That's *Sergeant First Class* Pendergrass, Private First Class Fisher!"

The lights are on in Molly's house, as you knew they would be. She had to get up early to help her husband get ready for the deployment. You know he's sitting somewhere in the stalled convoy, probably in a jeep behind the sergeant major.

Molly opens the door only wide enough to see who's there. When she recognizes you she lets you in. The two of you embrace wordlessly. You tell her you need one for the road.

You follow her into the bedroom and make love in the company commander's bed, which is still warm from his sleeping in it. Or at least you imagine it to be. Afterwards you hold each other under the blanket and she plays with the hairs on your chest. The light is out in the bedroom but the sun is coming up and the sunlight leaks through the blinds. You trace the curve of her chin with your finger.

"What will we do?" she wants to know.

"What do you mean?" you ask.

"I mean, about us. What will we do?"

You think about that for a minute, then you say, "Whatever we can."

Molly drives you back to the edge of town. The convoy is moving again, and you can't see your truck. She drops you off near the rear of the convoy and you hop a jeep that is on its way to the front. You can see Molly watching from her Citroen as you drive out of sight.

A few minutes down the Autobahn you see your truck parked in the emergency lane. You tell the jeep driver to let you off. When you climb aboard, Pendergrass starts the engine up without saying a word. He just stares through the windshield and drives back onto the Autobahn. People with large protruding ears, you observe, look particularly stupid when they're pissed off.

*

JUNIOR ENLISTED BEETLE BAILEYS assigned to the Division Tactical Operations Center have little to do between the time they set the center up and the time they tear it down. The only work that takes place is war gaming, and such is the sole province of officers. Not that enlisted men wouldn't mind making a command decision or two. Problem is, they'd opt for nukes the first night out to end the conflict quickly and go home.

In the Plans truck the enlisted men smoke cigars to keep the major away. So the major spends his time in the mess-tent-converted-to-a-movie-theater, watching movies he does-n't care to watch, because anything is better than that nasty cigar smoke. What he doesn't know is the men smoking the cigars hate it almost as much as he does. But they hate his presence even more.

You're grateful the advance team found a good spot for the DTOC. It's a small clearing surrounded by a circle of trees, and the MPs strung the concertina wire from tree to tree, rather than merely rolled it out on the ground. Not only is this more aesthetic, but when returning to the DTOC in the deep dark of night you stand a finite chance of finding one of the trees before the concertina wire finds you. The environmaniacs thought this might itself constitute maneuver damage, but the MPs pointed out that concertina wire doesn't have the same affect on bark as it does on human flesh.

Late one night a squad pretending to be Ivan creeps out of the woods and lobs a couple of training grenades—metal balls with fuses but no shrapnel—over the concertina wire. The loud pop the fuses make wakes everyone up in the compound. No one stops to wonder how Ivan got there in the first place, and the question of why he only brought a squad of men with him and armed himself with only a couple of grenades is best left to military philosophers. At any rate, the MPs shoot him to pieces.

One would think Ivan could launch a more sophisticated attack. Normally a few zealous privates would repel it while the rest of you drowsed in your tents or smoked cigars in the van, and one of the privates could be counted on to fall into the wire. But with the draw down underway and the likelihood increasing that Ivan is in town not to kamikaze the DTOC but rather to find some good Bratwurst, it's difficult to get even the zealous privates to come out. So the MPs have to do the dirty work.

"Put that in the log," the Three would say to Skelton. "Enemy attack repelled. DTOC secure."

Of course if enemies did attack they would do so from the air. Your World War II camouflage technology would not fool their infrared cameras. It would only make them snicker as they dropped wave upon wave of napalm and turned you and your comrades into crispy critters. The general would have already high-tailed it out of there. What he didn't know was the rest of you, from the Three down to the newest buck private, would be on the pussy's heels.

When you were a zealous private you once asked Pendergrass what you could do to survive a genuine enemy attack, what with being hemmed in by a ring of concertina wire and sitting under a net of artificial camouflage that acted much like a beacon to the reconnaissance technology of the day.

"Cut a hole in the wire," he said, "and run like a mother-fucker."

You realized then the wire was not there to keep the bad guys out. It was there to keep you in.

There's always a place outside the wire, away from the tents and generator, a small cluster of trees that's quiet and peaceful and in which you can be alone. You can always find such a place early in the field problem, before others have found it and have come to regard it as a good place to pinch a loaf. There's ample warning of such pinching, even in the dark, because you find the white toilet paper littering the ground, toilet paper the young privates will have to police up at the end of the exercise. The toilet paper comes with the C-Rations in little napkin-like packets. You store the packets in the ammunition pouches on your web belt because you have not been issued any ammunition. It's a cheap, sturdy toilet paper, not the soft, expensive kind that tends to get left behind when you wipe.

If you find a place that isn't filled with pinched loaves you can have some time to yourself and think about one of your girls, or maybe about the village you live in and how stupid you were to take it and its showers, beds, and restaurants for granted. You swear you'll appreciate the village exponentially more than you did before, if ever you make it back, and that you'll tell your girls how much they mean to you. But of course you'll do neither. It's not the village that makes you homesick for the village. It's the field. It occurs to you to fall into the concertina wire just so they'll send you home. But you're afraid of what the razor-sharp blades in the wire might do to the dearer parts of your anatomy.

While sitting on your steel pot, leaning back against a tree, you wonder how you came to be here. You have no formal education to speak of, nor have you achieved any particular professional distinction, for example election to public office. Instead you're a private in the infantry and you're sitting on a helmet in the woods and your ammunition pouches are stuffed with toilet paper.

For dinner you had cold scrambled eggs and "juice." You have not washed your hair in a week. You don't have much hair. In the morning, when you're off-shift and settling down in your cot to sleep, Top will order you to take off your socks so he can inspect your toes for fungus.

There are no bullets in your rifle. Your gas mask could not, at its peak performance, hinder a dense fart. If you want to jack off, you have to do it inside your sleeping bag, which itself became soaked with rain the first night out, because there hadn't been time to erect the barracks tent after traveling all day in the convoy. You've gotten good at push-ups and little else; you have therefore made no dent on the world, with the possible exception that doing push-ups changes the orbital speed of your planet in some infinitesimal way.

No amount of planning, no orchestration of cause and effect in your environment, could possibly bring about this state of affairs. Yet here you are.

One morning after crawling into your sleeping bag you wait until everyone else on your shift has fallen asleep, then you retrieve the bag of Oreo Cookies you hid beneath your cot. You eat them, savoring the rich chocolate and cream flavors, reminding yourself of the civilization you will no longer take for granted when you return to it. There's something funny about the texture of the cookies, but you can't put your finger on it, so you keep on chewing. You think of all the wonderful food you're going to eat when you get out of the woods, including, by golly, enough chocolate to turn your shit a spectacularly dark hue. You eat some more Oreo Cookies, and you continue to notice something funny about them. You dig out your flashlight and shine it on the cookies. They're covered with ants.

Everyone below E5 has to take his turn doing KP, and since the job is considered punishment for merely being junior enlisted, a vicious cycle develops. KP duty is an all-day assignment: to wash the pots and pans soiled while preparing three hot meals for a company of Beetle Baileys. Since the cooks don't have to wash the pots and pans themselves, they don't have to bother making sure the bottoms don't burn or that they get rinsed out after use. The result is the pots and pans come to the KP tent caked with hardened food residue and need much scraping and cursing. In fact, chisels are regular issue in army field kitchens.

Of course, the KP workers say, "Fuck that shit." They give the pots and pans a once-over and send them back to the kitchen still dirty. The cooks in turn don't give a rat's ass, because as well as not having to wash them, they don't have to eat out of them, either. So they take them as they come and use them again for the next meal. By the end of a typical field exercise some of the pots are so encrusted that the fresh food, if ever there is such a thing in an army field kitchen, never meets so much as a square inch of metal. Word gets around as evening meals are served: "I wouldn't touch the gravy if I were you. I washed that pot myself two days ago, and it was already disgusting when I got to it."

When it's your turn to do KP, no matter how conscientious a worker you are, you're not going to get stuck removing a week's worth of encrusted filth that a couple dozen of your buddies have left for you. So you give the pots and pans a once-over like everyone else and eat lettuce the rest of the week. On your second and all subsequent field exercises you take enough candy bars with you to make up the nutritional deficiencies of a lettuce-only diet.

Then, of course, the time comes when you slip and say, "Aw, hell, let me try the creamed corn." Half an hour later you run into the woods and aim for a place to toss your cookies where you didn't pinch your loaf the night before.

You've brought a stock of cigarettes with you to the field. You're generous with your cigarettes early in the exercise, handing them out a pack at a time, graciously, and everyone comes to know you as well supplied. Late in the exercise, when the new privates, careless NCOs, and stupid officers run out of cigarettes, you sell your packs at a thousand percent markup. You also carry a supply of earplugs you lifted from the dispensary because there are always one or two fools who can't find theirs minutes before going on the range. You sell earplugs for ten dollars a pair, and if the exercise includes a significant range activity you do a corking business.

You've learned it's expeditious to carry a couple of Jake-bite kits for sale to new privates whose eyes widen at your handy stories about the tender young E1s and E2s that Jake got on "just such a night." You tell the stories like ghost stories and sell the kits for twenty dollars. You paid four-fifty for them in the PX. You've never heard of anyone getting bitten by Jake. Jake is terrified of the trucks and the generator and the stomping of a thousand men. But the young E1s and E2s are even more terrified of Jake. Sometimes you feel shame when taking their money becomes too easy, but you have your ethics to uphold and your part to play in natural selection.

You miss Molly terribly, and when you need a break from her, you miss Melina terribly. It's good to have at least two serious romantic interests, in addition, of course, to a generous number of casual ones. Although there are relatively few girls in the field, there's at least one who will set up shop in one of the tents and take on any comers. She isn't the best looking of specimens, but the darkness inside her tent stimulates your imagination. You feel her warm, soft flesh, her rapid breathing on your cheek, and you pretend she's someone else. Each day you try to be one of the first in line but it's hard to keep abreast of show times. By the time word reaches you someone is putting out, the girl is usually exhausted.

As the exercise enters its third week you become loopy with boredom. Boredom so maddening you could scream. But if you become a screamer they'll kick you out of the army. And the only thing more humiliating than being in the army is being kicked out of it.

Chapter 31

KRUPA ASKED ME TO meet him at the Weinstube for lunch. Wittlinger had stood fruitlessly in front of my house day after day and had caught the sniffles. I told Krupa there were worse things Wittlinger could catch on the street.

"Where have you been?" he demanded to know.

"In the field. What is it you want?"

"You know what I want."

"I'm afraid I don't. You're going to have to spell it out for me."

We were sitting at our usual table, sipping our usual wines. Krupa's loss of composure revealed his menacing side.

"What is the most important document in the vault?" he hissed.

"I suppose it's one of the top secret documents."

"How clever you are." His voice got low and sultry. "And which of the top secret documents is the most important?"

"Hmm. Now that I think about it, I suppose it might be Oplan 2357-90. It's the one most shrouded in secrecy."

"Good. *Very* good. I want it."

"That's going to be something of a problem. I don't have the combination to the top secret safe."

"That will not be a problem. I will get it for you."

"How?"

"Never you mind how. I will get it."

"Suppose"—I laughed nervously—"suppose one were to express one's desire to quit the operation."

"There will not be any more transactions after this one."

"But—suppose one wasn't all that keen to participate in *this* one."

Krupa pushed his wine glass slowly toward the center of the table, almost out of reach, as though he were afraid an act of violence might knock it over. He crossed his arms and said, "Grave harm could befall such an individual."

"Well, as a matter of fact, dangers being what they are—"

"There are no dangers."

"—as I said, dangers being what they are, I think a significantly larger payment is in order."

He shrugged. "A larger payment is in order. I don't know how much *significantly* larger."

"The payment for the last job was fifty thousand dollars. At least, that's what we *agreed* on."

He hesitated. "Yes . . ."

"The payment for this one will be one hundred thousand dollars."

He smiled.

"Plus," I said, "the thirty thousand dollars you stiffed me on the last job."

"Listen."

"*Also*, I will need to be paid in advance, to avoid being screwed by you again, since this will be my last job."

"How far in advance?"

"When do you want the document?"

He looked at the ceiling. "Day after tomorrow."

"That's Sunday."

"That's right."

"Well, I think that's probably way too soon."

"Why? What is the impediment?"

The impediment, of course, was that Blackburn would need time to prepare a facsimile, and two days wouldn't be enough. But I could hardly tell that to Krupa.

"A week from Sunday," I told him. "That's the soonest."

"You know," he said smiling, "I used to have a Dachshund, and he only had one ball. My veterinarian told me reproduction was not possible. Nevertheless a neighbor of mine wanted to use him as a stud, and I did not see any need to deny my pet some pleasure. Of course, the activity failed, shall we say, to take, but I told the neighbor he could keep on trying; try as often as you like, I told him. Every Saturday night my dog came home with a grin on his face."

"What's the point, Krupa?"

"You know, I do not even know if I have a point. I was just thinking about how you would get along in the world with your nuts cut off, and the thought reminded me of my little puppy."

"Oh, come on. You can't be serious. You're threatening physical harm merely to finish this thing a week earlier, after having spent months setting it up?"

"Listen to me carefully, my young friend." He leaned forward, clenching and unclenching his fists. "I can and will do far worse than threaten. I want the document day after tomorrow. I do not want any ifs, ands, or buts."

He stopped and took several deep breaths. "We are friends, you and I."

"I'm not your friend."

"We enjoy each other's company. We *think* alike."

"Hardly."

"I need a friend. Someone I can trust."

"You can trust me to get the job done, if you pay me what I'm worth and what you already owe me."

"Do you know what trust is? What it *really* is? I will tell you. You can never trust a person to do anything differently from what *he* thinks is the best or right thing to do. I predict you are going to deliver the document on schedule."

He paused and lit a cigarette. "I like you, Jimmy."

I didn't say anything.

"I need that operations plan. The day after tomorrow. I absolutely must have it. Do not disappoint me. For your own sake, do not dare disappoint me."

*

GARRETT AND LAMOUREAUX WERE in the war room pretending to be busy. After appearing for the sake of appearance, I left the headquarters building and crossed Alzeyerstrasse to the phone booth next to Amy's. I needed to call Blackburn and report my conversation with Krupa. But when I got there I remembered I'd forgotten to tell Garrett not to bother stamping a training plan because it was still in draft. So I called the office first.

"He ain't here," Lamoureaux said.

"What do you mean, he ain't there? I saw him not two minutes ago."

"He left after you did."

"Where did he go?"

"He didn't say. He just watched you leave, then packed up his stuff and walked out the door, almost on your heels."

"Why that motherfu- ... when he gets back, tell him I went home for the day."

"Okay."

I called Blackburn and told him Krupa had made his play for Oplan 2357-90. I also told him Krupa wanted it the day after tomorrow. Blackburn said that was no problem: he'd been expecting the request, so he was ready for it. I told him the transaction was going to cost him one hundred thousand dollars. He laughed and said he would do the best he could, which would, he was sure, fall measurably short of one hundred thousand dollars. I warned him the best he could do would have to be one hundred thousand dollars, in advance, or I wouldn't carry through with the switch.

"By the way," I said, "I know all about your boy."

"What boy?"

"The guy who's been following me, and not doing a good job of it."

"Listen, Fisher. Whoever he is, he's not one of ours. He must be one of theirs."

"So maybe you could get him off my back."

"We can't do that; we can't get directly involved. It could compromise the whole operation. You'll have to take care of it yourself."

"How?"

"Neutralize him."

"What does that mean—neutralize him?"

"It means just what it says."

*

MELINA WAS SITTING ON her bed, her eyes swollen and red. There was no food ready for me, nor was any cooking on the little stove. She just sat there, staring vacantly, wiping her runny nose.

I sat down next to her. She looked at me, blinking, as though trying to remember who I was.

"You promised me it wasn't the redhead," she said.

"And I've kept my promise. It wasn't."

"Jimmy, stop lying to me!"

I stomped my boot against the floor. "I haven't laid a finger on the redhead! What more can I tell you?"

"The truth! I just want the truth! I can forgive anything but a lie, Jimmy. Just tell me the truth and we can go on with . . . whatever we were going on with. I can take just about anything. As long as it's the *truth*."

"The truth is, I didn't fuck the redhead."

"Jimmy, someone saw you go into her house at the beginning of the field exercise. You were in her house while her husband was absent. If you weren't fucking her, what were you doing?"

"Delivering a message."

"That took forty minutes?"

I kicked one of the bed legs. "Do you have spies following me?"

"It's a small community, Jimmy. You can't just wander from bedroom to bedroom without somebody knowing about it."

"I didn't fuck her."

"You did. Admit it, and we can move on."

"I didn't."

"You *did*. Please just this once, grant me the truth. You owe that much to me. I can take it. What I can't take is your stubborn lying."

"*I didn't fuck her, goddammit.*"

"YES YOU DID!"

"All right! To hell with it! I did!"

She started crying.

"Oh, for Christ's sake, don't do that."

She cried louder. She cried as though she had lost everything.

"Come on. It's not that bad."

She flung herself across the mattress, her body convulsing in sobs. I laid down beside her and put my arm around her. She didn't resist. I turned her around so her head was resting on my shoulder.

"Shh," I said. "It's okay."

Gradually she became quiet, and after a few minutes of heavy breathing she buried her face in my neck. "Whatever I did to drive you to her, Jimmy, I'm sorry."

"You did nothing."

"Do you love her?"

"Of course not."

"But you fucked her."

"Yes."

"You're not just saying that to please me."

I laughed. "No, I actually did truly fuck her."

"More than once?"

"More than once."

"More than twice?"

"Three times, total."

"Do you intend to fuck her again?"

"No. Never."

"How can I believe you?"

After a pause I said, "You can't."

She sniffed. "That's honest. That's a start."

I kissed her and pulled the blanket over us. We held each other for a while until I reached a decision. "Melina, would you consider going to America with me?"

Her eyelashes fluttered against my neck. "Are you serious?"

"Yes."

"I don't know if I can get a visa."

"We'll get married."

"Really?"

"Really. We'll get married. Then we'll get you a visa. Then we'll blow this place."

"But when do you get out of the army? I mean, when will they let you go?"

"Just as soon as you get the visa."

"But they won't just let you go. Not just like that."

"They won't have any say in the matter."

"Oh, I see."

"It's time to move on, Melina. I'd like you to come with me. Will you?"

She climbed on top of me and wrapped the blanket tightly around the both of us. "I'll go wherever you go. I love you."

"I love you too."

She remained on top of me and eventually fell asleep with her face in my neck. I stayed awake a while longer and worked out the details. When I had all the questions and most of the answers I gently pushed her aside and tucked her in.

The one answer I didn't have was what to do about Molly.

Chapter 32

I SPENT THE NEXT day, Saturday, fretfully preparing to leave the country. The army had made Saturday a work day because Monday was a holiday. That's the way the army did it: you could have a holiday, all right, but you had to sacrifice another day to compensate.

For the first time in my life I carried a weapon on my person. I tucked a bayonet inside my belt, under my BDU shirt. I had always gotten by in the world without carrying a weapon, but I figured the time had come to change that habit.

I would need a passport to get out of the country, since I had no military orders, but I didn't have enough time to apply for one. So I bought one. There was a staff sergeant in Discom who sold them for two hundred dollars. It was the same staff sergeant who made passports legitimately, the difference being if you attached two hundred dollars to your application he would take the photos and make the document without recording the transaction or notifying the consulate. Or, for that matter, caring whose name happened to appear inside.

I had to figure out how to get my payments from Krupa and Blackburn in advance. Krupa owed me $130,000 and Blackburn owed me $100,000—assuming, of course, I made the final switch, which I had no intention of doing. I was pondering this problem in the war room when Lamoureaux came in and told me I had a call.

It was Melina: "Hello, Jimmy, I just wanted you to know I'm at peace with what happened between us last night. I forgive you."

"I'm glad."

"When you get home tonight I'll have a surprise waiting for you."

I found that endearing—referring to her room at Amy's as our "home."

"What surprise?" I asked.

"Shh. My secret. See you tonight."

"I love you, Schatz."

"See you."

I hung up, then picked up the receiver again to call Blackburn—and the line was still open.

"Melina?"

"Yes?"

It meant somebody else was listening to the conversation on my end.

"Gotta go."

"Me too."

There were only six telephones on my side of the G3 section: three in Plans, one on the sergeant major's desk, one on the Three's desk, and one in Ops. Training and the EAC were on different lines.

I made sure nobody was in Skelton's office or the war room, then I ran down the hall to the sergeant major's office. Nobody was on his line, and the Three's office was empty. I opened the Ops door, and that's when I saw him: Garrett was working his way through the cubicles, trying to escape through the door on the other side of the room. I let him go.

*

IT COST ME A carton of cigarettes to get the key to Garrett's room from the company clerk. I found the room neat and trim, but also bare: no stereo, no posters, no odds and ends. It had the look of temporary quarters. I opened the locker—nothing but uniforms and boots. Then I looked under the bed and found cardboard boxes. I pulled the boxes out and opened them. There were cameras and other electric appliances I couldn't identify. There was also a small parabolic mirror.

When Garrett entered the room twenty minutes later I was hiding behind the door. He stopped halfway through the room and stared at the open cardboard boxes on the floor. At that moment I tackled him from behind and put him in a headlock.

"Who the fuck are you?" I said. "What the fuck are you doing here?"

"Arghhss!"

"Out with it, pissant, or I'll snap your neck!"

"Air," he croaked. "Breathe."

"I'll give you air, you spy motherfucker."

I dragged him over to the window and shoved his head out; he was looking down at a two story drop. I guessed that this distance would scare him much worse than would a greater one, as it was much more likely he would travel it.

"Out with it—or you go down head first. Who are you? What are you doing here?" I let go of his throat and held him by the hair.

"You know me!" he said.

"Who do you work for?"

"Same as you! I'm on your side!"

"Bullshit!"

I lifted him by his belt and pushed him out until his stomach was on the window ledge. He was balancing on the ledge like a see-saw.

"What's with all this shit under your bed?"

"What shit, man?"

I grabbed him by the ankles and let him hang out the window. He scratched the outer brick wall of the building with his fingernails.

"The electronic shit, you fuckhead. What's it for?"

"I'm on your side," he cried. "I'm here to watch over you, to make sure nothing happens to you."

"Who do you work for?"

"The FBI," he sobbed. "I work for the fucking FBI."

"Wrong answer, motherfucker!"

"Ask them!"

"I *did*."

I let him go. To his credit, he didn't scream on the way down. On the other hand, there wasn't much time.

Chapter 33

I NEEDED A DRINK. It wasn't every day you threw a man out of a second story window, and whenever you did, you needed a drink. I left the barracks and headed for the Netz.

I hadn't made it far down Alzeyerstrasse when Wittlinger's BMW pulled up on the sidewalk in front of me. The right rear window lowered and Krupa stuck his head out.

"Need a lift?"

"No."

"Get in anyway."

His tone suggested I ought to obey. Wittlinger drove us up to Kuhberg where the air was crisp and the leaves were already changing colors. Visiting this sacred place with Wittlinger and Krupa was a desecration. We traveled about half a kilometer into the woods, then stopped and got out. I followed the two men behind the car where we stood next to the trunk. Krupa expected me to speak first.

"Don't drag me into anything else," I said. "I quit."

"You cannot quit," he said. "It is not finished."

"It's finished after this job."

"I will decide when you quit."

"No, I'll decide. You said this would be the last one."

"It *is* the last one. For now."

"Forever."

"For now." He nodded to Wittlinger, who opened his jacket and let me see a large hunting knife strapped to his belt. I could feel the sheaf of my bayonet pressing against my back, under my BDU shirt, but didn't think now was the time to reveal its presence.

"You can cut me," I said. "It won't change anything."

"We will not just cut you," Krupa said. "We will cut your girl."

I thought of Molly, ripe and warm and beautiful, and I imagined Wittlinger standing over her, rending her flesh with his knife.

"What is his girl's name, Wittlinger?"

"Melina."

"Ah, yes. Melina. The whore. Herr Wittlinger will cut her into little pieces. If you believe, as I do, the whole is greater than the sum of the parts, you will work for us as long as we need you."

"I'll do one more job," I said. "That's all. You won't cut anyone. You're not beasts."

Krupa nodded again to Wittlinger, who turned a key and opened the trunk. There was a body inside. Wittlinger tossed a sheet aside, grabbed the head by the hair, and pulled it up for me to see. It was Major Skelton. His eyes were open, staring vacantly. His clothes were soaked in blood.

"We are not beasts," Krupa said. "But we do cut people, when necessary. We will cut you. And your girl. I want that operations plan. I do not want any shit like what you passed before. That is right, I know the terrain walk and the GDP were shit. Do that to me again and I will do to you what I did to your spineless major here."

"The plan is in the TS safe," I said. "As I told you before, I don't have the combination."

He handed me a slip of paper. "You do now. Skelton gave it to us. He thought maybe doing so would save his life."

I took the paper and put it in my pocket.

"You will use that combination," Krupa said. "And you will get me the plan. And you will make sure the document is genuine."

And then you'll cut me.

"And you will not say a word to Blackburn and Montalbano," he continued. "Yes, yes, I know all about them, too. Are you surprised?"

"No, I suppose not."

"Good. Whatever piece of shit they give you, just throw it away. I want a cassette with Oplan 2357-90 on it, and nothing else. Give me something else, and you will end up like the fertilizer in the trunk of this car. And so will your girl. Understand?"

"Yes."

"Good."

*

THE NETZ HAD BEEN redecorated with stuffed animal heads. The owners apparently thought it would contribute to the atmosphere, and perhaps attract a different kind of clientele, one that might spend a little more money. They weren't big game trophies, just small woodland animals that inhabited the local forests: several deer antlers, a fox, some small creatures I couldn't identify nor could I imagine took a lot of skill to bag, and one wild boar with fierce looking fangs that curled up menacingly from its lower jaw.

The boar looked even more furious as a result of being made to spend the remainder of its modest existence on the wall of the Netz. The other animals had the dazed look of bewilderment they'd been wearing the moment they were shot. The heads were dusty and the antlers were threaded with cobwebs, so the owners must have bought them off another barkeep who went out of business—no doubt because he surrounded his clients with artifacts of death.

The effect of the dust and cobwebs was to make the room seem unclean rather than woodsy. If I wanted to look at dead animals I preferred to look at clean dead animals. But at the moment I didn't want to look at any dead things at all.

There were only four customers in the Gasthaus, blue collar workers sitting together at a table, drinking beer. Their conversation had stopped upon my arrival. I took a stool at the bar, and one of them said, just loud enough for me to hear, "I'm told Amerikans wear their wedding rings on their left hands because the right hand is the one they jack off with."

I could feel the four of them looking at me, but I pretended not to have understood. Most Beetle Baileys don't take the time to learn German when they're stationed in Germany, even if they're stationed there for three or four years, so it comes as no surprise to Hermann when a Beetle cannot even order a glass of water in a restaurant or say "excuse me" when he bumps into someone on the sidewalk. I was obviously an American because I was in uniform, and the factory workers were testing to see whether I understood.

When the bartender came to take my order I asked for a bourbon and coke in English.

"I once had an Amerikan girlfriend," another of the workers said. "I was thinking of putting her to work—on her back. Some girls have a job on the side. Mine would have one on the back. Ha ha!"

This same worker, secure in his confidence that I couldn't understand him, flashed me a cocky smile. He had a crazy look in his eyes. I smiled back. He leered at the others and said, "If this specimen sitting at the bar is what Uncle Sam is sending to the Gulf, no wonder the land of the free and the home of the brave is getting its ass kicked."

"The Amerikans have had the fight knocked out of them," the first worker said, the one who had made the comment about wedding rings. He was a burly blonde with a mustache that grew down over his upper lip. "Time to cut and run."

"Come on, guys," a third worker said. "There's no need to taunt the soldier. He might pick up some of what you're saying."

The burly man looked at me briefly, then cast his eyes at the ceiling.

"Amerikan soldiers are pussies," he said, too loudly. "They come home with stress disorders because somebody went bang-bang at them."

"Don't do this again, Klaus. Please. Remember what happened last time."

"There is only one place Amerikans feel safe, and that is under their mothers' skirts."

"Maybe," I said, turning to face him, "it is the German soldier who is the pussy."

My German was accented but good. I had made it obvious to the workers that I'd understood every word they said. None of them looked at me.

"The American soldier and the German soldier have met twice on the battlefield," I continued. "The German soldier has lost both times. Perhaps it is the German soldier who should hide under his mother's skirt."

The burly man swirled the remaining beer in his glass and calmly drank it down. Then he looked at me, smacking his lips. The frayed bottom of his mustache was wet with beer. The worker with the crazy eyes glanced back and forth between us, his lips twisting into a cruel grin.

I finished my bourbon and coke and left the building. When I got around the corner I put my hand on the handle of my bayonet and waited.

Seconds later the burly man sauntered around the corner. When he saw me waiting for him he shook his head. His friends remained at the table, probably because they thought he would dispatch me with so little effort that it wouldn't be worth watching.

As he got closer he rolled up his right sleeve and balled his fist. His arms were meaty and his fist was like the head of a sledgehammer.

The instant he was within range he took his first swing, but I quickly stepped out of the way. The momentum of the swing turned him ninety degrees to his left. I pulled the bayonet out from under my belt, and when he turned around again to face me I stuck him in the gut.

We both stared dumbly at the knife protruding from his abdomen. It was too much like a movie scene. I pulled on the handle but the wound had closed and the blade was stuck. I pulled harder and he helped me, cooperatively pushing at my hands while I pulled on the handle, which by now was slippery with blood. Finally I gave it a jerk and it came out.

He watched the blood spread on his shirt and tried to stop the leakage with the flat of his hand. Then he lifted his arm as if to strike me, but changed his mind and put his hand back on the wound. A look of inconsolable regret came over his face. He dropped to his knees, blood dribbling through his fingers, and said, "*Meine Güte.*"

I wiped my hands on some grass but couldn't get all the blood off. It was already drying under my fingernails and in the wrinkles under my knuckles. I wiped them on my pants but the blood continued to dry and wouldn't come off. I rubbed my hands together to ball up the dried blood and that helped some, but I still couldn't get it out from under my fingernails.

Directly across the street from the Weinstube was a concrete staircase that wound down from the Mannheimerstrasse bridge to a narrow wooden dock on the river. I knelt on the planks of the dock, rinsed my hands, and got all the blood off. I tossed the bayonet into the river. On the way home my hands dried slowly in the cold air. When they were finally dry I smelled them and could still smell the blood.

*

I THOUGHT ABOUT WHAT I had said to Melina the night before. I had proposed marriage and invited her to accompany me to the States. Now I was having second thoughts. If there was anyone I wanted to marry, it was Molly, not Melina, and Molly was already married. Besides, I wasn't sure I wanted to marry anyone who so readily wanted to marry me.

I figured I would just tell Melina straight out I was indeed having a romantic relationship with Molly. That one thing had led to another. And from now on I was going to be with the redhead, who I believed was better suited for me. I felt if I broke this to Melina in a simple, straightforward manner she would understand and appreciate my concern for her feelings. We could remain friends and possibly more. We certainly didn't have to end our sexual relationship. Melina had been sweet to me and I was going to carry a torch for her for a long time. I reminded myself to tell her that.

When I knocked no one answered, but when I tested the door it was unlocked. I checked the stove to see what was cooking. Nothing was cooking. I noticed that some of Melina's personal affects were missing: the slippers on the floor next to the night stand, the nightgown draped across the bed. The music posters were gone from the walls. I opened her clothes Schrank and found it empty.

I wandered around the small room, opening drawers and shoving furniture, looking for evidence of occupation. There wasn't any. She had left. Then, with sickening dread, I opened the bottom dresser drawer and lifted the false bottom. The money was gone. The bitch had taken me for every penny I had.

Chapter 34

FOR THE LAST TIME in my life, I entered the AAFES bookstore on Alzeyerstrasse and posted myself next to Montalbano in front of the magazine rack. For the first time in my life, I was sure of what was going to happen next.

Instead, Montalbano dropped the magazine he was pretending to read and grabbed me by the collar. Half leading me, half dragging me, he kicked open a storage room marked "Employees Only." When we were inside the room and the door was closed he pulled a revolver from his jacket and stuck it in my face.

"Now you listen," he said. "You're going to pass the real document. Do you hear me? Krupa told you what you would get if you stiffed him with a fake. Well, you'll get the same from me, if he doesn't reach you first."

"So," I said. "You're the mole."

"Yeah, I'm the mole. And you're not going to get a dime until after the switch. You just tell Mr. Blackburn you passed a fake I gave you, according to plan, and I'll pay you then. You understand? You're going to pass the genuine document to me. Be a good boy and make a shitload of money. Fuck up, and die."

He let go of me with a shove and I tumbled into a pile of cardboard boxes. Then he holstered his revolver, left the storage room as though he had merely entered it in error, and walked out of the store.

On my way to the Kaserne I considered my options. The most relevant fact was that I was broke. Therefore I had to make a switch of some kind, to have any chance at all of getting my hands on some money. The question was, should I switch the real plan or pass something else? Montalbano hadn't given me a facsimile to copy, so any cursory viewing of whatever Krupa ended up with would immediately reveal the truth.

I had to copy the real document, if for no other reason than to create some insurance. If I should come to need the document after having bolted I didn't think I would be able to regain access to the Plans office. But dangerous as it sounded, my instincts told me to pass a fake instead, and hold the real plan in reserve. I was sure they would kill me, rather than pay me, as soon as they had the real plan. As long as *they* didn't have it, I had a good chance of living and escaping. On the other hand, as long as *I* didn't have it, I had little chance of getting any money out of the deal. It would be difficult to leave the country without money.

Just my luck, the thousand dollar gate guard was on duty. The duty had become so lucrative, he was obviously volunteering for it. I showed him my ID card and he smiled the smile of one who knows he's going to get a wad of money in a short while.

I'll be waiting for you, his eyes told me. "Thank you, have a nice day," his voice said.

Once inside the office I first tried to call Blackburn. But an answering machine responded after five rings. That figured. It also occurred to me to contact Riddell, since I now knew he wasn't the inside man I'd pegged him to be. But Riddell hated me with such passion he probably would have uncorked a bottle of champagne on learning of my predicament.

I unfolded the slip of paper Krupa had given me and turned the dial of the top secret safe to the combination he had written down. The combination didn't work.

That didn't surprise me. Skelton never could remember the combinations, and a knife pressed to his jugular wouldn't have improved his memory. It was also possible that Skelton, a field grade officer in the United States Regular Army, was too loyal to his country to surrender the real combination, even under threat of torture and death. He knew he was fertilizer either way, so he gave them the wrong number.

Somehow I had to figure out the combination. I counted the locks starting at the vault door until I got to the safe next to the TS safe. I had always suspected the TS safe combination was simply another one in the series, so I added seven to the last increment and tried it. It didn't work. I added fourteen, twenty-one, and twenty-eight, and they didn't work either.

I sat down on one of the shred bags. Crowbars were sold in the PX, but I was familiar enough with the safes to know that trying to force the door open would be a waste of time. Drilling, likewise, would get me nowhere. I had to discover the numbers. Skelton had been terrible with numbers and had often asked me to open the safes for him. But when it came to the TS safe he opened it without hesitation.

He had three daughters, whom he loved dearly. How old were they? Thirteen, twelve, and nine. No, eight. I tried thirteen, twelve, and eight; then eight, twelve, and thirteen. The drawer held fast. If all else failed, I could leave the office with a blank cassette. But the rest of my life might turn out just as blank.

My fingers twirled the dial to random numbers in the irrational hope they would stumble on the right sequence. In frustration I picked up the logbook lying on top of the safe and threw it. It sailed across the room, into Skelton's office, and knocked the lamp on his desk to the floor.

That gave me an idea. I went into Skelton's office and rummaged around. A photograph of his wife and daughters sat on his desk, and plaques given to him during previous assignments covered the walls. I opened drawers, looking for a crib sheet he might have left for himself.

One drawer was locked. I jerked at the handle without result, then got a screwdriver out of Pendergrass's desk and pried it open. It was full of pornographic videos.

My watch told me Wittlinger wasn't yet waiting for me on the Mannheimerstrasse bridge, that I had at least three hours to solve the problem. I sat down at Skelton's desk and buried my face in my hands. I had to gain access to the safe. The only security I had was possession of a copy of the genuine document.

On the top of Skelton's desk was a planning calendar. Staring at the calendar, wondering what to do next, I noticed the doodling. In one corner he had drawn a neat sequence of three major insignias. I went to the TS safe and dialed 04-04-04. It didn't open.

Then something else occurred to me: the TS safe was new. It had been ordered to replace one whose drawer kept getting stuck. And on the day it had arrived, Skelton himself had transferred the TS documents to their new home, because Pendergrass had not been in the office. That meant *Pendergrass had not been present to change the combination from the preset factory configuration.* And in all likelihood Pendergrass never got around to the task because here, finally, was a drawer Skelton could open all by himself.

The factory setting always appeared on the instruction sheet that came with each new safe. I needed to find the instruction sheet—any instruction sheet, since all of our safes came from the same manufacturer.

I searched Pendergrass's desk. I rummaged around the office, hoping a sheet might have been left in a drawer somewhere, until I allowed myself to admit there wasn't any reason for anyone to keep the things.

Sitting in Pendergrass's chair, wondering how I was going to get out of the country without any money, I found myself looking at the disposition orders taped to the back of each safe. These were required on all safes, filing cabinets, and drawers that contained sensitive materials. Should an emergency evacuation of the office become necessary, the evacuators would need to know what to do with the documents—take them, destroy them, or leave them—without having to waste valuable time sorting through them.

The disposition order taped to the back of the TS safe told evacuators its contents must be secured and evacuated with the staff.

I grabbed the corner of the disposition order and ripped it off the safe. Underneath, still glued to the metal casing, was a small slip of paper. The slip instructed the new owner to change the factory preset combination immediately after installation. The preset combination was printed in a rectangular box at the bottom of the slip: 0-50-100.

Holding my breath, I went around to the front of the safe and reached for the dial. If the combination didn't work, it was going to be a long walk home, with a lot of water between me and my destination. I turned the dial to 0-50-100 and pulled on the drawer handle. It opened.

Oplan 2357-90 was in a brown envelope like all the others. Only eight pages long, with a one page annex, it was an abbreviated standard operation plan that made numerous references to other plans. The annex was a list of names and addresses. The names were all Ivan, and most of the addresses were in or around Moscow.

It took only minutes to videotape the document, which I then returned to the drawer. I still needed a fake cassette, so I took one of the pornographic movies from Skelton's desk and peeled off the label. The name of the movie was "Blow Dry."

My wallet didn't contain a thousand dollars. So I couldn't leave the Kaserne through the main gate. Instead I went to the quietest part of the Kaserne, where a chain link fence separated Headquarters and Headquarters Company from the base chapel. It was the same place I had slid the fake GDP under the fence during my last switch. I stood around the HHC building, acting bored, until no one was in sight. Then I climbed over the fence.

It was about ten feet high and covered with four strands of barbed wire, but there was enough room between the fence and the bottom strand of wire to squeeze through. When I hit the ground on the other side I found myself in full view of about forty people just leaving a chapel service and conducting social amenities before going home.

They stopped talking, froze in the middle of their smiles and gestures, and stared at me.

I stared back. The chaplain himself emerged from the crowd and confronted me.

"May I ask what you're doing?"

"Security check," I said, and started walking away.

"Wait just a minute, son."

I started running, confidently, until my legs were clamped by a pair of strong arms and I fell full-length on the ground. The chaplain had tackled me. Not bad, I thought, for a man of the cloth. We both stood up and he grabbed my arm.

I hit him square in the nose. He fell back, covering his nose with his hands, and when he removed them blood was dribbling down his upper lip.

The congregation gasped in shock.

I took off down Alzeyerstrasse. A half dozen men followed at full gallop. I raced down Steinkaut and turned right onto Töpferstrasse. The men, dressed in their Sunday best, soon gave up the chase. They stopped on the sidewalk at the head of Steinkaut and shook their fists at me, shouting promises of God's retribution. I weaved through the residential district south of the Ringschule, making sure no one followed, then worked my way back to the cemetery, entering through the northwest gate.

The timing of my plan couldn't have been worse. Sunday was the busiest day of the week in the cemetery. But it was already early evening; the burials were over and the plots vacant except for old people grieving over fresh mounds of earth. The regular cemetery visitors had finished planting or watering flowers and were trickling out.

I went to the caretakers' tool shed and selected one of the shovels leaning against the wall. The metal blade of the shovel was still wet from having been hosed clean.

The cemetery was divided into chronological sections. When you died, you got buried next to the person ahead of you in line. When a section filled up, a new section—typically the one planted longest ago—was replanted with fresh bodies. Over time there was a turnover of occupants in a checkerboard pattern.

I found the section planted that summer, then the particular tombstone I was after. Patrick Parnell, it said. 9 June 1922 - 7 December 1944. Parnell was the division World War II casualty who had been buried the same day Cybulski's body flew back to the States.

Nobody had been caring for the grave. It was covered with a flat bed of soil, with no flowers or flagstones typical of German graves. There was only a headstone and a small, green oval tag—a kind of toe tag planted in the soil—that listed Parnell's name, critical dates, and grave registry number.

It was the first time I had ever dug up a grave in daylight, on a Sunday no less, but nobody took any notice. I dug as if it were my job to do so, figuring if anybody saw me working they would assume I was a cemetery employee preparing for a burial to take place the next day.

The ground was still loose, even though a thin carpet of grass had grown over it. I dug patiently and deliberately, tossing the shovel-loads of dirt onto an adjacent plot, one occupied by a man named Wilhelm Kaiser. When my shovel thudded against the wooden casket I brushed the rest of the dirt away with my hands, then used the blade of the shovel to pry the top off.

There wasn't much of Parnell in Parnell's casket. Only his bones had returned from the Hürtgenwald, and they were lying in a jumbled heap on the bottom on the box. The bones were stained brown after so many years in peat soil. I was surprised to see dirt still clinging to some of the joints, and one part of the skull was green with moss; it had obviously been exposed to the weather at least briefly before disinterment.

I dropped the cassette containing Oplan 2357-90 into the casket. Then I refilled the hole, retraced my steps to the tool shed, and hosed the shovel down before leaning it against the wall where I had found it.

Wittlinger watched as I approached his BMW. I could see his unblinking eyes in the rear view mirror. It was still daylight when I arrived at the bridge, but barely; the castle above was already glowing orange under its floodlights. A sunset was in the making, and the angular, blocky crucifix jutted into a pastel sky.

The BMW's engine was off. Water swirled in the river below and spilled over the rapids. An Opel was parked on the other end of the bridge, in the opposite lane. It was facing us, but its windows were dark and I couldn't tell whether anyone was inside. Wittlinger watched me out of the corner of his eye as I walked up to the passenger side of the car.

"Get in the back," he said, through the open window.

"Give me the money," I said, "and I'll give you the cassette."

"That isn't the way it works." His hands gripped the steering wheel tightly even though the car was inert.

"I'm not going for a ride with you," I told him. "We do the switch here and now, or we don't do it at all." I set the camera bag on the sidewalk and took out the cassette.

"How do I know the cassette is good?" he asked.

"You don't. How do I know the money is good? I don't. I'll take the chance, and so will you. You're just going to have to believe I wouldn't be stupid enough to pass a fake."

He looked down the road at the Opel and made a frustrated face. Then he turned to me with a sneer.

"Give me your half of the five Mark bill," he said.

This caught me off guard. Montalbano hadn't given me half of a bill.

Wittlinger leaned on his horn, and the Opel at the other end of the bridge sparked to life. Its headlights came on and it revved into forward motion, swerving over into our lane with a squeal.

I ran to the metal railing next to the crucifix, paused just long enough to regret what I was about to do, and dove into the river. I had time on the way down to wonder how cold the water would be, but was shocked at how cold it was. I exhaled reflexively under the surface and came up choking and coughing.

Men were shouting. I held my breath and went under again, swimming downstream as fast as I could with the cassette still in my hand. After what seemed like a minute I had to come up for air. When I did, I heard shouting, then staccato sneezing noises, and the water around my head was slapped and ripped several times.

I dove under again. This time I held my breath so long I flailed wildly to get back to the surface, which was farther above me than I'd thought. I looked back; the bridge was out of pistol range. There were four men at the railing, and when they saw me they fired again, this time with rifles. The shots sounded like the dull bang of a hammer hitting an anvil. The ripping slaps on the water were farther apart, and none came near my head.

The current was carrying me toward the Wilhelmstrasse bridge. The men ran to get into their cars.

Fuck me, it was cold. I mean, *fuck me*, it was cold. I swam as hard as I could downstream, but the cold was already sapping my strength. I stayed in the center of the river because I wasn't sure what obstacles were ahead. The Wilhelmstrasse bridge was a flat, uninspiring work of architecture with three arches supported by two massive pillars. I aimed for the part of the river that flowed between the two pillars; the last thing I wanted to do was butt my head against one of them.

Between the bridges were two feeding streams, channels of the river that went around linear islands, and past this point the speed of the current increased. I was only dogpaddling now, and thankful for every natural contribution to my forward motion.

The railroad bridge, my next milestone, was twice the distance again past the Wilhelmstrasse bridge, and was also supported by massive pillars. Despite its name it accepted foot and car traffic as well, so I prepared to dive beneath the surface again should anybody be waiting. It was hard to tell how much time had passed, and I was afraid they'd had enough time to beat me there.

On either bank was shrubbery and scrawny, scruffy old trees and bushes. I searched the banks carefully for any men who looked like they were keen to shoot people floating downstream, but the growth obscured my view.

It was getting dark. A surprising amount of light leaked on-to the river from the buildings overlooking the banks, and it was casting me as an easy target. I could clearly see the swirls and eddies of the current in front of me as I dogpaddled, and when I got close enough to the bridges I could see well enough to avoid their pillars. The lights made silhouettes of the scrubby trees. Fully half of them looked like men aiming rifles.

As I passed under the railroad bridge I looked up at the ties and could see stars between them. The current seemed to be moving faster, but it might have been my imagination. I was so tired and numb I didn't care anymore. I was expending just enough energy to keep my head above water. I turned to look behind me, thinking maybe I was going to see a motorboat or something chasing me, like in a James Bond movie, but there was nothing. I could still see the Wilhelmstrasse bridge, but the Mannheimerstrasse bridge had disappeared around a bend. The castle was still glowing orange on its hilltop. It would be my last view ever of the landmark.

When I reached the Jahrmarktsbrücke, about half the dis-tance again from the railroad bridge, I figured I had better get out of the water. The Jahrmarktsbrücke was only for foot traf-fic, just a sidewalk with aluminum railings. A single narrow pil-lar supported it, and it was here, next to the pillar, that I dropped the cassette. It sank to the bottom of the river.

At this point I was so numb and weary I could hardly move my arms to swim. It was all I could do to keep my nose above water. The shrubbery on either bank was dense. Sticks and logs in the current competed with my effort to reach dry land. I crawled up the shallow bank and rested for a moment on my hands and knees. Then I stood, shaking and dripping, and slogged through the weeds to the side of the bridge.

Fifty meters or so ahead of me was Heidenmauerstrasse. Across the street was the Gymnasium am Römerkastell. I made sure the street was clear of BMWs and Opels, then ran across, through the thorny bushes surrounding the school lawn, and chose one of the ground floor windows facing Heidenmauer. The ledge was only waist high; I broke the window with my shoe and climbed through.

Once inside the classroom I took my clothes off, wrung them out, and draped them over a radiator. The radiator wasn't on, but the state of mind I was in allowed me to imagine the clothes would dry faster on it anyway.

I squatted in the opposite corner of the room and stared at the window. Twice a car circled Heidenmauer, shining a spotlight north at the river bank. I was sure the men would search for me all night, and if they saw the broken window they would storm the room. But the school was large; I could run down a hallway or two and escape out the other side. It was therefore necessary to stay awake and watch the window.

On the other hand, they had no idea where I had left the river, and no clue where to begin their search. For all they knew, I was still in the river, trying to make my way up to Bingen where the Nahe joined with the Rhein. They could-n't have known how cold the water was—and how silly the idea was I might make it all the way to Bingen—without jumping in themselves.

Occasionally I heard, or imagined I heard, cars patrolling the neighborhood. Once I heard drunken Turkish voices. I don't know how long I gazed through the broken glass before I fell asleep.

*

THE VOICES OF YOUNG boys and girls woke me early the next morning. They clustered in the hallway outside the door of the room. Someone rattled the door handle; it was locked.

I grabbed my clothes and left through the window. The clothes were dry except for the jeans which were tolerable. I dressed on the school grounds, in the shadow of the building, then walked up Heidenmauer to the intersection of Gensingerstrasse where there was a bank of public telephones. Molly answered on the first ring.

"Where the hell are you, Jimmy?"

I told her. I said, "They're after me."

"Who's after you?"

"I'll explain later. You have to come and get me. Take me someplace, someplace safe, anyplace far away from here."

"What the hell is going on?"

"Molly, please."

"Come on, Jimmy. I can't just walk out."

"*Please.* I need your help. If you don't help me, I am in some very serious shit."

She was silent for a moment, then said, "Okay, I'm on my way."

"Thank you."

"Stay right where you are. Don't go *anywhere.*"

"Bring some money, pocket change, anything. I love you, Molly."

"I love you too. I'll be right there."

While I waited near the telephone booth a train crossed the railroad bridge. The train was loaded with armored vehicles. It was not an uncommon sight, but the significant difference was that this train was traveling toward Bremerhaven, rather than Rheinland Pfalz. The army had begun its draw down.

A wind came down from the hills and chilled me. Winter was coming.

BOOK FOUR

If you gaze long into an abyss, the abyss will gaze back into you.
—Nietzsche

Chapter 35

WITHIN MINUTES OF MY call Molly arrived in her Citroen. I looked up and down the street to make sure no one had followed her, then stepped out from behind the bank of telephone booths.

We embraced passionately, her fingers digging into my back. She released me and walked around to the passenger side of the car. She wanted me to drive.

I aimed the car toward Autobahn 61, and when we reached the exit Molly pointed toward the southbound lanes. The vineyards, dull and brown, hastened past us as I pushed the car down the highway. The villages drifted by subdued and tranquil, with brief splashes of sunlight reflecting from their red tile roofs.

"Any chance you'll tell me where we're headed?" I asked.

Molly rolled her window down an inch, lit a cigarette, and settled comfortably in her seat. "Stay on this road for a while."

I rolled my window down too, and the roar of the wind drowned out the music on the radio. I couldn't help wondering why Molly had offered so little resistance to my suggestion that she run away with me, and why she wasn't asking for the specifics of my predicament.

And why she wouldn't reveal our destination.

We crossed the Rhein into Baden-Württemberg and got on Autobahn 5 south toward Basel. To the east were the low, densely wooded hills of the Black Forest. The hills stayed with us until Molly told me to exit west toward Strasbourg. We had our passports ready at the border—mine still damp from the river—but the customs booths were empty. The entire checkpoint was deserted. We drove uninhibited into France. Coming the other way, I had a feeling, would be different.

Molly seemed more alert in France. She sat up in her seat and paid attention to the scenery. Strasbourg sprawled on the Alsace Plain. Even in the haze the city was a kaleidoscope of colors. The cathedral, the jewel of the city, rose above the old buildings in the heart of the Altstadt, on an island formed by canals. The cathedral looked much like other European gothic ornaments: an anachronistic brooch that made the rest of the city's architecture seem simple and elegant by comparison.

It was hot in the car, so I turned the heater down and closed the window. Molly asked if I wanted her to drive.

"Is it much farther?"

"No. Maybe half an hour. We'll take the scenic route."

"This place we're going to . . ."

"It's a hotel on a mountaintop. It used to be an abbey and they've converted it. I stayed there . . . once. You'll like it very much. The view of the valley is spectacular. We'll have to get you some reading material, though, because there won't be a television set or any other distractions."

"No TV?"

"I told you, it's a converted abbey. No television, no telephone, nothing. It's the definition of quaint. But you'll have me."

"We'll have each other."

"Yes. We'll have each other. I'm going to make you happy." She leaned over and kissed me on the cheek. Her manner of speaking had changed in a way I couldn't categorize. I concluded it must have been France. Being in France made people act more . . . French. I let it go at that.

Now we had a clear view of the Alsace Plain and the Vosges Mountains. They were beautiful mountains, highly eroded but not so denuded as the Hunsrück, still tall enough to be mountains yet low enough to climb without equipment. The peaks paired off with saddle-shaped depressions between them and were covered densely with deciduous and coniferous woods and ferns. As they receded into the distance their mottled browns and greens variegated through turquoise to dull blue.

From far away they gave no hint about the fighting that took place there during the world wars, nor the oppressive German occupation, nor the spirited French resistance. They looked like a gloomy, distant background in a landscape painting. Their shadowy haze and lack of detail contributed to my growing sense of foreboding.

A narrow and sometimes tortuously winding road took us up one of the mountains and deep into the woods. I had to slow nearly to a crawl around the bends for fear of meeting a not-so-slow car on its way down. The forest became more dense and coniferous as we approached the summit. Beneath the canopy of evergreens it grew ever darker, turning the road into a ribbon of light. Weathered sandstone boulders littered the shoulders. A bright green moss grew prolifically on the boulders and on the fallen trees and stumps. The combination of death, darkness, and exotic color made the landscape look ancient and mystical.

As we arrived at the top of the mountain the low sun emerged from the clouds and struck us bright and warm. And there, at the peak, was the pink sandstone cluster of Romanesque and gothic buildings that comprised the thirteen-hundred-year-old abbey of Sainte Odile, the Daughter of Light.

The abbey nested atop enormous sandstone blocks, some of which looked like weathered sculptures of grotesque faces. A nose still jutted out here, a mouth still snarled there, as if time hadn't yet erased an age-old warning to those who had come for the wrong reason.

I parked the Citroen in a lot in front of the abbey and tried to shake off an ominous dread. Molly flicked her cigarette out the window in a long arc. "We're home," she said.

*

WE CHECKED INTO A room under the names Mr. and Mrs. Ulysses S. Grant. The abbey was made of brick and stone and was cool inside, like a cave. But the heat was turned up full in our room. We were fortunate to have gotten a room with a private bath and toilet, as many didn't have them.

The room was small. The window opened to the courtyard where some older couples and priests and nuns were sitting on benches watching the fountain or looking over the wall to the valley two thousand feet below. Beyond the wall I could see the valley and the tiny villages dotting the landscape and fading into the haze. Like all villages in German-speaking lands, these reminded me of Indian campgrounds. Instead of teepees the shelters were picturesque houses with tile roofs, otherwise the shelters grouped haphazardly around narrow passages that ignored the cardinal directions. Their occupants had scouted the valley floor for the choicest spots near streams and in the shadows of the mountains.

The bathroom was clean and modern, and included a bidet. The toilet had a wooden seat. The bed was short and stubby; I laid down on it to test it for length, and found that with my head on the center of the pillow my feet rested on the top of the footboard. I would have to sleep on my side with my knees bent. Most nuns, after all, were shorter than me.

271

Unframed prints of tacky alpine scenes decorated the walls. It was, as Molly had promised, quaint. A brochure on the nightstand illustrated the history of the abbey in poorly translated English. While Molly took a shower I read the brochure.

Odile was born in the seventh century, and according to legend came into the world blind. Her father, the Duke of Alsace, intended to kill the handicapped infant. But her mother whisked her away to a convent where, during her baptism at the age of twelve, she miraculously regained her sight and thus earned the title Daughter of Light.

Dad reluctantly invited Odile to return home, then insisted on choosing a husband for her. She refused the suitor, hiding from him and his henchmen inside a rock she claimed God had opened for her. Seeing the writing on the wall, Dad then built an abbey on the summit of the mountain above Obernai and installed his daughter as its first abbess.

Catering to the poor, the sick, and the blind, Odile recruited nuns and populated her abbey. The miracles continued: at the touch of her fingers a fountain sprang from the rocks below the summit, and the blind who doused themselves in it regained their sight. It was no fountain of youth, however, and the abbess herself died early in the eighth century.

*

"WOULD YOU LIKE TO take a walk around?" Molly asked as she stepped out of the bathroom, drying her hair with a towel. "Or did you have something else in mind?"

"You're the boss," I said. Sunlight streaming through the window highlighted the curves in her figure, and I was reminded of Greek and Roman sculptors who had imparted the texture of pliable flesh to rigid marble.

"As a matter of fact," she said, "I had something else in mind."

She climbed onto the bed, kissed me, ran her fingers through my hair. I stroked her breasts until her nipples were hard. Then I laid diagonally across the double bed, and Molly went down on me. A couple of minutes later I warned her to come up, but she stayed.

"You see?" she said. "I told you I would make you happy."

We took a nap in each other's arms and an hour later woke and made love again. Molly got on top and straddled me, gyrating her hips almost imperceptibly, her hands grasping my kneecaps, her nipples hard and pointed. When I came I pulled her down and kissed her and felt the full length of her body against mine.

"Come again," she moaned.

"I can't."

Turning around into the doggy position, she raised herself for me. I mounted her and said, "I wonder if this is how Odile went blind."

She cried out and clawed at the blanket. I cupped her breasts in my hands, watched the gentle wobble of her butt cheeks as they bounced against my hips, and came a third time, gasping for breath.

"So you couldn't do it again, huh?"

"Don't ask me now. I really can't, now."

We dressed and Molly said I should take a walk while she put our things away in the room. She also said she must talk to the desk clerk about the dining arrangements and the bill, which she called "tarif." I went for a walk along the abbey wall.

Down in the valley a cluster of villages sprawled comfortably in the early evening light, as vacationers might recline in lawn chairs to watch the sunset. When dusk came the city lights blinked on one by one, and by eight o'clock, when it was dark, the landscape glittered with thousands of warm windows and street lamps.

I sat on a bench near the wall and watched the lights. Eventually Molly found me. She wrapped her arms around me from behind and kissed me softly on the ear.

"I love you, James Solomon Fisher," she said.

I guided her around the bench and sat her beside me. We held hands silently. The horizon was a deep cobalt blue. On the winding road that snaked up the hill to the abbey an occasional pair of headlights worked its way up through the woods.

"Want to go up to the edge and look down?" Molly asked.

"No, thank you."

"Still afraid of heights?"

"Still, and always."

We returned to the room, undressed, got under the covers, and made love lying on our sides. We slept, then woke and did it again. Molly fell asleep with her head on my shoulder.

I stayed awake and listened to the muffled conversations of people still milling in the courtyard below our window. I was out of cigarettes, so I extracted myself from Molly without waking her, got dressed, and went downstairs.

The light was on over the desk but no one was about. I rang the bell. The clerk, a middle-aged woman, came out from a back room rubbing her eyes.

"Yes, Monsieur Grant?"

"I wonder whether I could buy some cigarettes."

"Not at this hour, Monsieur. In the morning, when the tourist stands have opened, you may purchase some there."

"Thank you."

"Oh, Monsieur!"

"Yes?"

There was a telephone message for Madame this afternoon the clerk failed to give to her when she arrived. Will you take it?"

"Of course."

She removed a note from a narrow rectangular box.

"It only says, on the Rue des Maroquins, in Strasbourg."

"What does it say happens on the Rue des Maroquins, in Strasbourg?"

"It does not say, Monsieur. You will give the message?"

"I'd rather not. Please give Madame the message, when she comes down in the morning. And please do not tell her you gave it to me first."

"As you wish, Monsieur."

Molly woke when I climbed back into the bed. She stretched and looked at me with half-open eyes. I held her in my arms.

The last of the tourists had finally evacuated the courtyard and the top of the mountain was quiet. Molly played sleepily with my shirt buttons.

"Want to do it again?" she whispered.

"How long have you been a spy?" I asked.

She didn't answer right away, but continued to undo the buttons.

"How long?" I repeated.

"Shh, sweetie," she said. "Shh."

"How long, Molly?"

She sat up and straddled me, rubbing my bare chest down with the flats of both hands. Her eyes didn't meet mine. "All my life."

"When are you going to kill me?"

She lowered her head and playfully brushed my torso with the tips of her silky red hair.

"When, Molly?"

"We have some time together," she said. "Let's enjoy it."

"Why me?"

She stifled a laugh. "Your nefarious activities made you a definitive candidate for approach. You, my love, are one for the books."

She lifted my right arm and made me hold her with it. Then she laid down on top of me and covered us both with the blanket.

"When do I get rubbed out?"

"Shh. I'm going to make you happy."

"*When?*"

"Soon. But we have time. Now go to sleep."

I stayed awake. Late in the night I heard a noise at the window. It was only the branch of a tree the wind had brushed against the pane. There was a sparrow in the tree, making soft, inquisitive noises. But no one was in the courtyard to answer it.

Chapter 36

JUST AFTER DAWN I got out of bed while Molly was still sleeping. She slept beautifully, as if she knew someone was watching.

Our window opened into the courtyard but also offered a good view of the valley to the northeast. A patch of fog had settled between the mountains and blanketed the valley floor. The mountain peaks were green with firs. Where the sun struck them they shone like uncut emeralds.

The sparrow that had made inquisitive noises the night before was making a racket now, but the courtyard was otherwise quiet because the tourists hadn't yet begun arriv-ing.

I woke Molly and she blinked as if she didn't recognize me. Then she closed her eyes, smiled broadly, and said, "Hmm."

Before the day warmed up, while the frost still clung to the grass, we left the room in our coats, scarves, and walking shoes and made a tour of the abbey. The coat I wore was one Molly had brought with her. It belonged to her husband and fit nicely. It also made me feel like an impostor.

As we left the hotel I walked out ahead of Molly so she could receive her message privately at the front desk. She caught up to me shortly and took my arm as we walked past the lime trees to the Convent Church.

The buildings that comprised the Mont Sainte-Odile made a tight circle on the top of the mountain and reminded me of a military compound. In fact, aerial views revealed a fortress: the designers were plainly more concerned with protecting the nuns from the riffraff below than providing them a platform from which to praise the God above.

The Convent Church was a squat, lichen-covered sandstone structure designed to intimidate the Pagans. A statue of Odile herself stood on a tower next to the church and commanded the highest view on the mountain. With a halo around its head and a staff cradled in its left arm, its right arm reached out to bless the inhabitants of the Alsace Plain.

Judging by her various likenesses, Odile was not a pretty woman. The statue on the tower had a nondescript face and lifeless eyes.

Odile herself was buried next door in a sarcophagus of rough-hewn stone. Except for a missing souvenir or two, she was still in it—Charles IV had visited in the fourteenth century and removed some of her bones. Outside in the courtyard was another statue. This one depicted her with a long nose, a petulant mouth, and a soulful, penetrating gaze.

At lunchtime we stopped by the restaurant kitchen to pick up a sack filled with sandwiches and soft drinks, then followed a path down the hill. The path was wide and open but the woods on either side were deep and dark. Every few minutes we met French people on their way up the hill. They were always polite and said "*Bonjour*" to us as they passed.

We stopped at the little spring in the rock whose source was attributed to Odile and we ate the sandwiches the kitchen staff had made for us. According to legend the rock, which had been dry for centuries, sprang with sweet curing waters the moment Odile touched it. It was her idea the spring water would cure the blind, as baptismal water had cured her own blindness.

Molly and I waited to see if any blind people would regain their sight, but none loitered around the spring. Everyone seemed to know where he was going. After a while we threw the paper sack and plastic wrappings into a garbage can and started back up the hill. On the way we passed families en route to the spring, and we said "*Bonjour*" to them.

We found a quiet place in the woods, away from the paths, and took off all of our clothes in the October chill. There is no heat more sensual than that produced by two people making love outside on a cold day.

*

THE WOMAN AT THE front desk recommended dinner in the cafeteria. It was inexpensive, she said, and would give us the full flavor of abbey life. Molly said she hoped it would be quaint, and the woman assured her it was.

A pretty French girl seated us at a table and smiled invitingly at me, ignoring Molly. All the other customers were old. It was going to feel like eating in a retirement home.

"Why is everyone so goddamn old?" I asked Molly.

"Usually only old people stay at the hotel."

"But there are zillions of young people outside, on the grounds."

"They're only visiting for the day. Most of the people staying at the hotel are making some kind of religious pilgrimage, and few young people make such pilgrimages."

"Are we making a religious pilgrimage?" I asked.

Molly smiled and said nothing.

The silverware was actual silver. The soup spoon was as big as a shovel. Molly ordered a half bottle of Beaujolais after fending off the girl's strong suggestion that she select something more local.

"The Clevner from Heiligenstein is remarkable," the girl said. "Also famous Sylvaners are produced in Gertwiller and Goxwiller."

"I'll have the Clevner," I told her.

"An excellent choice, Monsieur."

She looked again at Molly.

"Beaujolais," Molly repeated.

When the girl brought Molly's wine she plopped it down on the table, already opened. The girl didn't speak directly to Molly again, but instead asked me, "Will Madame require . . . ?"

The entrees arrived family-style in china bowls: smoked ham, potato salad, and dark, crusty bread. For dessert we were offered our choice of apple dessert, pear dessert, banana dessert, orange dessert, or kiwi dessert. I ordered the pear dessert and Molly ordered the kiwi dessert. Molly asked whether one might order a mixed fruit dessert, but the girl, speaking to me, answered that what Madame had suggested was not possible.

The desserts came as advertised. I got a pear on a plate, and Molly got a kiwi on a plate. I ate mine like an apple, but Molly had to peel hers first. I was amused by the simplicity; Molly was not amused. She might have liked the meal better if the girl had not treated her so coldly. Under different circumstances I might have slipped into the kitchen and given the girl my room number.

After the quaint dinner in the cafeteria we walked the terrace around the abbey, watching the city lights glitter in the valley. When we returned to our room it was dark except for the courtyard light shining through the window.

Molly did a striptease in front of the open window, gyrating slowly, lifting her blouse rhythmically over her head, letting the lamp light glow on her naked skin. There were still people sitting on benches in the courtyard, including several priests and nuns, and if they had looked up at our window they would have treated themselves to a sight.

I took her hair down and watched it bounce slowly to her shoulders in the near darkness, one lock at a time, and felt like I was freeing a captive goddess. I turned her around and pushed her over the window sill, so her breasts were hanging freely in the cold night air. Then I entered her from behind, watching her hair dangle down on the frosted sandstone bricks.

"Fuck me," she whispered.

"Say it louder," I said.

"Fuck me."

"Louder. Say it loud enough for them to hear you."

"Fuck me, fuck me, fuck me!"

Afterwards we left the window open and curled up together under the blankets for warmth. Molly's skin was smooth and when I kissed her eyes her eyelashes fluttered against my lips. Her hair slid like liquid across my shoulders. We were quiet and held each other closely for a long while.

"Sweetie?" she said.

"Yes?"

"It will be better for you if you tell me now where you hid the cassette."

I didn't answer, but held her even closer and felt her body against mine and the warmth our bodies shared. I didn't think anyone so close to me could hurt me, and I felt safer than I had ever felt before.

"It will be very bad for you, sweetie, if you wait for them to come. Tell me now, and there will be no need for them to come. I'll make it easy for you. It's easier and simpler than you can imagine."

Her feet were cold, so I pressed them between my legs to warm them. I was happy to be able to do this for her.

She whispered, "Tell me, and I'll make sure it doesn't hurt at all."

The courtyard was quiet now, the only noise coming from the curtains tossed and rustled by the breeze. I wondered where the sparrow had gone. I couldn't see the village lights from where I was lying, but I could see the stars. I pretended the clusters of stars were only reflections in the sky of the city lights that burned in the plain far below.

"It doesn't have to hurt," Molly said. "When it's done right, it's just like going to sleep."

She kissed me and caressed my hair, and when her hand was still I knew she had fallen asleep, and I went to sleep too.

Chapter 37

MOLLY TOLD ME HOW she became a spy. The years of training, the selection of a mate. The fake American village outside Moscow where she passed her final exams before going to America. How to follow people, take expert photographs, evade capture.

Molly was a "sleeper" who had been activated for this assignment. Following her formal spy schooling and marriage to a U.S. Army officer she'd been instructed to wait until her husband gained sufficient rank, after which, at some point in the future, she would capitalize on her position at the discretion of her Eastern controllers. Oplan 2357-90 was important enough that her controllers decided to activate her much earlier than expected.

She happened to be at the 111th Infantry Division. There were, after all, sleepers everywhere, near and far, high and low. She just happened to be married to a captain and stationed—sleeping—in Bad Karst, Germany.

Her first instructions, when Oplan 2357-90 became an issue, was to evaluate the staff of the Plans office, identify a target, and compromise him.

Through Molly, my nefarious activities, as she called them, came to Krupa's attention. Krupa had also considered Garrett, because of his inexplicable behavior, but Garrett was a recent transfer whereas I had been on the job for two years. Garrett was also less interesting to Krupa, according to Molly, because he had an ordinary past. On the other hand, I couldn't be anything other than what I appeared to be. The problem that neither of us had a top secret security clearance would, he'd figured, meet with a solution.

Molly's real name was Natasha Taganov. After her formal training she courted a West Point graduate who showed promise of rising in rank. His name was Ralph Brannigan. The controllers mulled over Brannigan's Irish ancestry, then decided to give it a go and let her marry him. He was of no importance at the time, but he already had the eyes of military dedication and the tight-lipped smile and strong jaw that somehow, maybe by carrying rucksacks a lot, career military people tended to acquire. He had done well at West Point, and he looked like what a general should look like twenty-five years before making general. So he had as good a chance as anyone to become one—and would be important to the controllers when eventually he did.

She was told merely to wait until then. A lieutenant in the infantry is of no importance to anyone, not even to the infantry. But since unmarried generals are in rather short supply, they have to be targeted and married while they're still lieutenants.

That's the mission of the sleeper. Nobody believes it happens anymore, even though it happens all the time, and the term sleeper has taken on a cloak-and-dagger connotation and fallen into disuse. Although she didn't know how many senior officers were married to sleepers, it was Molly's impression the number was higher than the CIA would guess.

Her first assignment, before going to New York to mingle with West Point cadets at their dances, was in the mailroom on the third floor of the KGB building in Moscow. She and the other girls would use slender, split bamboo canes to remove letters from envelopes for copying and analysis.

On either end of an envelope sealing flap is a portion of the flap that isn't glued, allowing a letter opener to be inserted. The girls inserted their bamboo canes through that opening, caught a fold in the letter with the slit in the cane, twirled the cane until the pages inside were tightly rolled, then pulled the whole thing out through the opening. It was harder, Molly said, to get the letter back in when they were finished with it.

She graduated from the mailroom and was transferred to the passport section in the basement. It was a prestigious assignment, awarded only to the best. Across the street from KGB headquarters was Detsky Mir, a toy store. She would run over there once in a while, in a pinch, to buy water colors or maybe a camel hair brush for one of the artists.

Her department was devoted to the serious and successful business of duplicating American passports. This was easier than one might think, she told me, and it was foolish of the Americans to believe their passports were counterfeit-protected. The passports were almost as easy to copy as the money, which was done in another room by less talented printers and graphic artists.

As an example she showed me the new American twenty dollar bill, with its off-center portrait of Andrew Jackson. She assured me that although she had been out of the business for some years she was confident this bill was being duplicated with great authority in a basement room in Moscow, across the street from a toy store. The only hindrance to production, she said, was not to flood the market.

The technique was simple. To make American money you take a one dollar bill, wash it carefully of its ink—a process Ivan had perfected—and use the paper to print a twenty dollar bill. The paper was, after all, the most difficult part to duplicate.

American passports were manufactured at the time by the Payne-Jones company of Lowville, New York. The dark blue cover was a synthetic plastic called lexide. The manufacturing process was secret, and the Lowville plant operated under tight security, but it was all just chemistry, and anything that could be made could be copied.

The passport paper came from the American Writing Paper Corporation in Holyoke, Massachusetts. If you held it up to the light you could see water marks of the Great Seal. Why they bothered with that, Molly didn't know; water marks were easy. There were a hundred other details, such as the codes perforated on the front cover. An "A" number was used at the start of the decade, "Z" for those issued abroad, "X" for diplomat, "Y" for the maroon official passports, and so on.

Molly taught me some vocabulary they had learned from one of their agents, a successful spy who had gotten hired to work in the Lowville plant, and later for Crane & Company in Dalton, Massachusetts, where money paper was made. Later still he had gotten himself hired in Washington to duplicate Russian passports, then he returned home to duplicate American passports. It was part of his grooming, she said, but hardly routine; the man was famous. He taught them the vocabulary of the American passport duplicators, and from then on they used these terms when speaking to one another. They were supposed to practice their English anyway, and besides, it was fun.

A KGB technician who specialized in duplicating passports was called a "cobbler." They found this amusing, and delighted in calling one another "Comrade Cobbler." A passport was a "shoe." They themselves, to the Americans, were "neighbors," and the communist party as a whole was known as "The Corporation." There were many others. A radio transmitter was a "music box," a front was a "roof," prison was "hospital," an arrest, "illness." When they went on trips abroad they were told, "Take care not to get sick."

Although she had not been trained as a graphic artist or printer, Molly made a name for herself in the basement of the KGB building and was trusted to do some of the duplicating, particularly the water marks. Eventually she became supervisor of the binding process. She had a keen eye for flaws. By the time she was promoted out of the department she was inspecting every foreign passport manufactured in the Soviet Union before it was issued to its user.

It was time for advanced training. Her colleagues threw a party with cake and champagne. When Molly unwrapped her gift she found herself in possession of her own Walkman radio, an expensive gift in Russia. She was touched.

The eleventh commandment of covert activity was Thou Shalt Not Get Caught. It was to this purpose that most of the balance of the training was devoted. The philosophy had all been taken care of in school; had Molly not already had the philosophy, she would not have been recruited for the mailroom.

After decades of experimenting with breakable codes and ciphers, Ivan, like the Americans, had decided the only safe way to communicate was with onetime pads. Pads were the size of postage stamps and made of nitrated cellulose, which burned completely and instantly when exposed to flame. They consisted of any number of pages, sometimes several hundred, and each page contained rows of five digit randomly generated numbers. Each pad was unique, except that Control retained one duplicate. Half of the pages were printed in black; these were for enciphering outgoing messages. The other half were in red, for deciphering incoming messages.

The initial transmission was a group signaling the page. Following was a sequence of five digit groups the agent added in succession to the numbers in the columns of his pad. The modular sum was then translated to letters, and each group formed a word or a string in the message.

Of course, sometimes an agent got "sick" and his pad was confiscated. But there were ways to know that, Molly told me. Also, words and phrases were abbreviated, and vague references and allusions were employed as much as possible, to obscure the meaning of the text to any outsider who might read it.

They experimented with hiding messages inside coins, but gave it up because the coin, usually a nickel, looked fat when put back together. Besides, if you dropped it, it tended to come apart on the floor and roll in two directions. They made a lot of jokes about the American nickels when no one important was listening.

If a message had to go out to everyone in the field they would use Radio Moscow. The station would play certain oldies in a sequence to carry out a prearranged plan. Since not everyone in America could safely conceal and monitor a ham radio, they acquired programming control in small but strategically selected radio stations around the country. "I Want to Hold Your Hand," followed by "Strangers in the Night," then by "Crimson and Clover," might, for example, direct all agents to report their present positions without delay.

The general purpose of all the secret communication was to keep tabs on sleepers, activate them when necessary, and to direct other agents—those who were wide awake—in the business of gathering information about American military and industry. Such agents gained employment in key technical industries and defense contracting firms. They spent their free time watching, photographing, listening, reading—and reporting. The KGB, according to Molly, had inventoried the American military-industrial machine down to the last M16 bullet.

The final stage of training took place in a secret town on the road from Moscow to Kiev. It was an imitation American town, complete with road signs, traffic lights, cops with billy sticks walking their beats, McDonald's restaurants, rusted Ford Galaxy 500s, a supermarket stocked with Doritos and Coke, and a

Baskin-Robbins ice cream parlor. The grocery store even had a life-size cardboard cutout of Mr. Whipple.

Only English was spoken, and several American and British defectors worked in the shops. If you could go about your business shopping, banking, renting an apartment, applying for a social security number, and having a cocktail with "the ambassador," without tipping the instructors off you were Russian, you graduated.

Molly stayed on as an instructor for several months, handling an ice cream scoop at Baskin's and speaking amiably to the nervous clientele.

Now a certified spy, Molly—Natasha Taganov—was shown how to select a cover ID from a recent burial and was slipped secretly into the United States via Fort Francis, Ontario. The true Molly Delaney, a purebred Irishwoman who died in a car accident, rested under a quiet grove in a Poughkeepsie cemetery.

*

WE SPENT OUR DAYS hiking through the firs on the mountain, often stopping on a ridge to eat sandwiches and squint through the blue haze at the distant hills and plains. We dressed warmly and kept walking, so we didn't get cold but only red in the nose. Sometimes we drove the narrow roads around the mountain but soon gave that up because the roads became icy. Besides, we liked to walk.

When the sun was low it cut through the haze and highlighted the great sandstone cliffs in ways I had often seen in paintings overdone with highlights. While in the Alsace I learned to appreciate landscape painters more, who I had always believed exaggerated the intensity of their colors. Now I was convinced no painter had ever quite captured the beauty of a French landscape.

Here and there on the mountain were rock falls, the rocks covered with moss even in the splintering cold. The evening sky had the clarity that only happens in the coldest air, and if we stayed out after dark we could see the lights of the villages on the plain leaking through the firs like fire flies.

The deciduous trees never completed the slow winter death characteristic of other cold regions I had visited. They were naked of their leaves, but their trunks shone wet in the sunlight, and the paper birches were stunning, especially at dawn and dusk. The mix of conifers and deciduous trees formed a textured pattern that retained much of its color through the winter.

They were old forests; we found no evidence they'd ever been cut. The middle and upper canopies were well developed and there was plenty of dead wood on the ground. The moss, the sunlight streaming through the foliage, the haziness and frequent fog, all made for a surreal landscape, one Tolkien fans would find suitable as a model for Middle Earth. I wouldn't have been surprised to see a troll or goblin wander out from the deep shadows.

Sometimes we rose early to watch the feeble sunrise. The winter dawn came late beneath the upper stories of the forest. A lot of sun had to shine before the forest floor received any light, so the night survived the better part of morning. At forest's edge the dew rose from the shrub layer like steam, and down in the valley, where the air was still, smoke climbed in columns from countless chimneys.

We spent the nights in bed together, shielding each other against the cold that crept through the open window. In the morning I had to clean the frost off the window before I could get it to close. There was no one in the courtyard now. We were the only clients in the hotel.

We took walks around the abbey grounds at night. The wind was stiff and sharp, driving even the priests and nuns from the property. We had the abbey to ourselves. Stars saturated the evening sky. We could trace the outline of the Milky Way, the backbone of night.

The village lights made the horizon glow, and the farther away they were the more they shimmered, as if the light were passing through a liquid medium to reach us. The view reminded me of night flights in airplanes: so much to see, so much man-made beauty, yet too far away to hear any of the clamor or make out any of the dirt.

No television or radio in the room meant the evenings were painfully quiet. If a worker did something in the courtyard, or a female employee merely clopped in her high heels across the flagstones, it was enough of an event to draw us to the window.

When a man and a woman are together for long periods of time in a room that is bare but for a bed, they spend much of their time bare, making use of the bed.

"You want to do it?"

"We just did it."

"I know. Want to do it again?"·

"Okay."

We got to know the staff. The desk clerk treated us as a mother would treat her teenage children. When we came home she addressed us without looking at us, using the eyes in the back of her head.

A couple of nuns seemed offended by our presence, the cold months being the only ones that offered respite from the tourists. But a couple of the others went out of their way to cross the courtyard and speak to us. A priest who was bald and never wore a hat or coat made a point of blessing us each time we ran into him. We accepted the blessings knowing they didn't so much as scratch the surface of our sins.

We soon tired of eating the quaint dinners in Herrade's Hall and began visiting a grocery store in Obernai, buying bread, cold meats, and condiments, and making picnic meals in our room. We also launched a serious, incremental survey of the Alsace family of wine. Following each increment we rolled the empty bottles under the bed, thinking we would clean them out before they got out of hand. But soon the bottles leaked out from under cover, and eventually they were too numerous to dispose of covertly. We summoned the maid and asked her to please—finally—remove the mess made by the previous occupant. Flushed and embarrassed, she collected the bottles into a large plastic garbage bag while we watched with our hands grimly planted on our hips. She begged us not to inform the management. We agreed in exchange for a microwave oven loaned from the kitchen.

One afternoon the temperature rose and it rained steadily. Molly shopped for some English language magazines but could only find women's magazines. We stayed in the room that afternoon and I read them, taking my time to read all the articles and carefully examine every advertisement. When we were done with those we had nothing more to read. So we undressed and did the only other thing there was to do.

"Tell me how to act like a French girl," Molly said.

"Just be yourself," I said.

"What would a French girl do, that you wish I would do?"

"Well, for starters, a French girl wouldn't talk so much about French girls."

That night the temperature dropped again and the rain froze on the roads and the branches of the trees. The trees, encased in ice, glistened under the next morning's sun, and all day we heard branches cracking and falling because they couldn't support the weight.

At one point when I thought Molly was already asleep I heard her whisper, "Join us, Jimmy."

I turned to face her, and found her staring at me.

"We could use you," she said. "And you could use the salary that you're worth to us, that the United States isn't paying you."

I imagined living in Russia, and learning Russian, and eating cabbages, or whatever they ate in Russia, and abandoning and betraying everything I had ever loved in my life, other than her, and I said:

"Will you marry me?"

She nodded and smiled and answered, "Of course I will marry you."

"Tomorrow?"

"If you like."

"Tomorrow, then."

"Do you think we can?"

"We'll try."

The trees went on cracking and Molly became restless.

"I hope it doesn't snow," she said. "I'm sick of snow."

"But it hasn't snowed even once," I said.

"It will. And I'm already sick of it."

Chapter 38

THE NEXT DAY MOLLY and I were married in the Convent Church of the Abbey of Sainte Odile.

We had gone to Obernai to speak to the authorities about formal arrangements, but were told there were too many papers to be written on and that it would take much longer than a day. The clerk in the town hall held up the sheaf of papers for us to see.

"Perhaps in some of your American cities," he said. "Las Vegas, I believe. Also Mexico. Copenhagen too has the method, I remember. But not in France, Monsieur."

"There is no way it can be hurried?" I asked.

"No, Monsieur."

"On account of all the papers that must be written on."

"Yes, Monsieur."

We drove back up the mountain to the abbey, entered the Convent Church, and sat together on a pair of wooden chairs next to one of the massive stone pillars. The only other occupants were two men kneeling before the altar, sharing in the Perpetual Adoration. I took Molly's hand in mine.

"I take you to be my wife," I said.

"And I take you to be my husband."

"You're already married," I reminded her.

"No longer. This washes it away."

I removed the wedding ring from my little finger, the ring I had taken from Hannelore Schneider, and tried to place it on Molly's ring finger. But it was too small. I moved it over to her little finger, but there it was too loose. Molly suggested I keep it and wear it for the both of us.

We kissed self-consciously. Then we left the church and went up to our room to consummate the marriage. I undressed and got into bed, but Molly remained in her clothes. She pulled the blanket up to my chin.

"I have a wedding present for you," she said. "Wait just a minute, I have to go and get it."

She left the room, and about five minutes later a girl came in and locked the door behind her. When she turned around I recognized her as the waitress who had served us the quaint dinner in the abbey restaurant. I started to speak but she raised a finger to her lips and got into bed with me.

She had full lips and wonderfully shaped thighs and shiny black hair that spilled in disarray across the pillow. We made love with her thighs wrapped around my waist and her heels dug into my back. She bit her lip and moaned and her breasts shook with the rocking of the bed.

Shortly after the girl left, I left the room too, and took a walk alone around the abbey grounds. In the Chapel of the Cross next to the Convent Church was a door to a small sacristy. The door was open, and I watched as a nun helped a priest on with his garments. He wore bright green robes. When the nun was finished and had left, the priest stood with his feet apart, leaning forward against a table. He bowed his head in silence.

Church bells rang. The bells were mistimed, and the result was a continually changing cacophony. All over the valley bells were ringing; it wasn't a good place to live if you didn't care to hear them all the time.

The organ struck up a hymn in the church next door. The priest, who had been leaning against the table with his eyes closed, stood up straight and walked calmly out of the sacristy and through the narrow passage into the Convent Church. The choir rose in song as he entered, and I could hear his voice above theirs, leading the song.

I turned the other way and entered the Odile Chapel. No one else was around, since everyone was now attending the service next door. I squatted before the sarcophagus and looked through the brass grillwork to where the stone coffin, brightened by lamps, encased Odile. The coffin tapered off toward the feet, mummy style.

"Tell me what to do, Lady Odile," I whispered.

The singing stopped and I heard the priest's voice over a loudspeaker. He was speaking French and I didn't understand any of it.

"Tell me what I'm facing next, Daughter of Light."

Odile was silent in her sarcophagus. It was too much, I supposed, to expect someone who'd been dead for twelve hundred years to help me with my problems.

I went out into the garden behind the chapel, sat in front of the fountain, and looked down to where the villages camped on the valley floor. Here and there on the Alsace Plain the sun broke through the clouds and illuminated a patch of farm or village.

Blocks of sandstone protruding from the cliff aimed stubby fingers at the hazy place where earth met sky. I understood then why abbeys and monasteries were often located so high. It wasn't for the isolation; you can get that in the desert. Rather, the greater one's religious convictions, and the greater one's consequent revulsion for the Here and Now, the higher one places himself above others.

When the short service ended and the only people left were a pair of prayer-givers taking their shift, I entered the Convent Church and knelt in the rear-most row of chairs.

"You don't know me," I whispered. "I've never knocked on your door before."

I waited for some sign of outreach, welcome, or anything else one might expect from a hospitable host. But the only sounds in the room were the mumblings of the prayer-givers and my own knees scraping the floor, adjusting to the unaccustomed position.

"You see, I've never needed anyone's help before either. Until now."

I gave him a few minutes to acknowledge my presence. Maybe he was busy.

"Have I been that bad? Aren't there many people worse than me? Aren't you supposed to love them all, no matter how bad they are?"

A nun entered the chapel and "reloaded" the candles. They were mere casings, and the parts that burned were tea lights replaced after each service. Light streaming through stained glass windows cast colorful swirls on the vaulted ceiling. Chandeliers hung down between the pillars; they would have crashed to the floor had they not been suspended by iron chains—manmade chains.

Everywhere was evidence of man. Nowhere was evidence of God. God would not hang gaudy chandeliers or employ fake candles. Or make such hideous art. Or insist that people remain silent in his house, or grovel in humiliation on their knees. No, this was man's work, not God's.

*

WHEN I RETURNED TO the room Molly was already in bed, reading a magazine.

"Did you like your present?" she asked.

"Yes," I said.

"Did you really? I want to know."

"I liked it a lot."

"I'm glad." She threw the blanket off. She was stark naked. "Now, do to me what you did to her."

I did.

Afterwards we held each other and she said, "It's so vast, isn't it? The gulf between ecstasy and agony? I hope, for your sake, that you don't require an appreciation of both extremes of the scale."

"Molly, true love is worthy of a greater conviction than is loyalty to one's country or to any cause."

She thought about that for a moment. "I suppose. But remember that I love my country, and I love my cause. I love you too, but I cannot stop what has been put into motion. If you don't reveal where you hid the cassette, what you will experience is more unpleasant than anything you can possibly imagine."

Chapter 39

IT WANTED TO SNOW. Gray clouds filled the sky and the temperature dropped to near freezing. Molly kept looking out the window, waiting for flurries to block the view. She had spoken with the desk clerk the previous evening while I was enjoying my wedding present and the desk clerk had said it would snow.

Finally she looked at her watch and suggested we visit Strasbourg. She wanted to show me the city, and she knew a good café on the Rue des Maroquins. She didn't look at me when she suggested it.

"Are we leaving Mont Sainte-Odile?" I asked. "Should we pack?"

"No, leave your stuff here, we'll be back."

We drove to Strasbourg in her Citroen, using the same route we had taken on the way from Strasbourg to Odile. We didn't speak a word during the trip. I knew from having intercepted her message that whatever was going to happen to me was going to happen in Strasbourg. I didn't think we would make a joy excursion to the city, then follow it with another for more ominous purposes. It would be difficult for Molly to explain the need for making a second trip. Whatever she and

Krupa and whoever had in mind, they would carry out some-time in the coming hours.

We parked near the cathedral and had just enough time to tour the interior before lunch. Molly insisted we visit the top and enjoy the view. Halfway up I was already regretting the de-cision. I had climbed most of the towers in most of the cathe-drals in Europe, and this one would surely prove to be no less effort nor less frightening. We had to lean against the wall to make room for people coming down. It was claustrophobic. The last staircase in the sequence was so steep, it was more lad-der than staircase. When finally, legs weary, we reached the top, we enjoyed a view like any other from any other tower in any other cathedral in any other European city.

Molly pointed to the twin spires of Saint Paul's Church. "Isn't it beautiful?" she said. Incomprehensively far beneath us was a forest of rooftops.

"Yeah." I knew what was coming and couldn't take any pleasure in the view. Standing at death's edge nauseated me. What was coming was a spray of barf that would rain down on the rooftops and pedestrians below. The source of the barf would be my own mouth. At this elevation the buildings didn't hinder the wind, and our bodies were pitiful challenges to the high altitude jet streams.

"Can we go now?" I asked. I was getting dizzy and could feel the bile rising in my throat.

"Tell me where the cassette is," she said. "Then we can go."

I stumbled like a drunk toward the staircase, but she grabbed my shirt in her fists and held me. That's when I barfed. It dribbled down my shirt and onto Molly's arms.

The other sightseers on the small platform made a quick exit, pushing one another and glancing over their shoulders to avoid any stray eruptions. I heard someone on the next level down say to a group on its way up: "There's a guy heaving all over himself up there."

"Let me go," I said. The world was spinning vertically. The spires of Saint Paul's were rising and puncturing the sky.

"Where's the cassette?"

I could hardly remain standing. I tried to force my way toward the exit, but Molly pushed me toward the railing and made me lean over the edge. I barfed again, watching bits of breakfast scatter randomly in an ever-widening cone.

"Tell me, or you go over the edge."

"You wouldn't."

She pushed as hard as she could. Only my grip on the railing prevented me from going over.

"Molly, I beg you, don't." This was more gurgle than English. The pedestrian zone at the foot of the cathedral was swarming with ant-like people, and I could imagine their shocked expressions as I plummeted face first into the pavement.

"The cassette."

"At the bottom of the river," I said. "Directly beneath the Jahrmarktsbrücke." I started doing the dry heaves, because by now my breakfast had all come up. Molly put her arms around my waist and helped me to the stairs.

"See? That wasn't so bad, was it?"

The group waiting at the bottom of the stairs watched as we stumbled down, my shirt and Molly's arms covered with barf. The same man who had warned the others a couple of minutes earlier said, "That's him." If I had been able to see their faces through my tears I'm sure I would have seen expressions of intense disgust.

Molly took me to the café she had mentioned on the Rue des Maroquins, in sight of Notre Dame. We washed up in the bathroom, then took a table in front of a window facing the street. I looked at the menu and ordered the most harmless sounding dish: the gourmet salad. When it came I picked through goose pâté, whole shrimp with eyes bulging, unidentified raw fish filet, and suspicious strips of gray meat to get to the limp, discolored lettuce that lay beneath.

"I think I made a mistake," I said.

"Why did you order it if you didn't want it?"

"I ordered the most expensive salad on the menu. I thought it was the most expensive because it was the biggest. I didn't know it would be populated with bottom dwellers."

"Then it's your own fault. Look, at least eat the shrimp."

"There's nothing in here but slimy sea critters and weeds."

"Be quiet and eat the shrimp."

"I can't. Their little black eyeballs are staring at me."

"What kind of meat is that?"

"Beats me. Kangaroo maybe."

"Silly. Go ahead and eat the meat. At least you don't know what it is. Or would you like me to ask the waiter?"

"No, no. I'll eat the meat. Just let me cover the little shrimp eyes with the lettuce."

The church bells of Strasbourg struck noon. Molly wiped her mouth with a napkin and looked up and down the Rue des Maroquins. I stood up and told her I was going to the bathroom.

"Don't be long," she said.

"Want to hold my hand?"

"Sorry."

I left my wallet and passport on the table. "If the waiter comes looking for money, take some Marks out of there." There wasn't any money in the wallet, but Molly didn't know that.

A service entrance next to the restrooms led into the kitchen. In the kitchen were stacks of dirty plates on the floor. The leftover food on the plates had dried hard, so they must have been from the day before. No one was in the kitchen, and obviously no one was washing dishes. I went out through the back of the café and jumped into a cab on the Rue du Vieux-Marche-aux-Poissons.

"Train station," I told the driver.

"Eh?"

"*Bahnhof.*"

He turned his meter on and pulled away from the curb. I remembered I had no money.

"Stop," I said.

He pulled back over to the curb.

"*Ich habe kein Geld.*"

He turned around and looked at me as if I were a dog turd on the sidewalk. "*Ihre Uhr,*" he said.

I handed him my watch, and he sped back into the traffic.

The Place de la Gare was on the west side of the city. The station was a large, imposing building with bas-reliefs and stained glass windows. The French had to make even their train stations appear grandiose, as if Louis XIV had built them. I asked a ticket salesman for the correct track, then took an escalator up to the platform and waited for the train.

I wouldn't need a ticket to board. The conductors only checked for tickets after the train was underway, if they did at all. There were many people waiting for the train. Most were young and looked like students. Some were punkers. When the train came I got on with the punkers in second class, because I figured the conductors would start in first class, and because second class would be more crowded.

I had chosen the first available train to leave the city as fast as possible. Other trains left Strasbourg in other directions, including one that ran due east, into Germany. That would have been a better train, but I would have had to wait over an hour for it, and didn't think it prudent to sit that long in the station.

In the hallway of the rearmost second class car I stood waiting for people to fill the compartment. When the seats were all taken I sat on the floor in the hallway with the others who hadn't gotten a seat. I didn't hear the train or sense its movement when it started, but knew we were underway when I noticed the platform leaving us in the opposite direction.

I watched through the window to see if anyone was chasing the train, but no one was on the platform. All activity was normal. I was on my way. It had gone much easier than I had dreamed.

Chapter 40

THE CONDUCTORS BEGAN CHECKING tickets as soon as the train was underway. It wasn't an express train; it would stop at every village and dorf, and tickets would be checked repeatedly. I had to get off at the first stop on the other side of the border.

I studied the route posted above one of the doors. There were nine stops before the border: Suffelweyersheim, Wanzenau, Kilstett, and so on. The track paralleled the border until it arrived at the French town of Beinheim, then it turned east and crossed into Germany between Rastatt and Baden-Baden. I didn't think I should sit through nine stops. I would have to get off at one of the early stops and find a bridge across the Rhein, one I could cross on foot.

A conductor entered our car. He started in the back and worked his way toward the front. I went through the doorway between cars and headed for the front of the train. The conductor called to me as I was opening the door, but the door was rattling and wind was gushing into the space between the cars. I pretended I didn't hear him.

I went up through second class cars until I saw another conductor working his way back from the first class section. Then I sat down on the floor, mussed up my hair, and pretended to sleep. When he asked for my ticket I kept my eyes closed and my head on my knees.

He asked again. He touched me with his foot, then gave a little kick. I grunted. He kicked me a bit harder. I made incoherent noises and kept my eyes closed. He uttered some words that sounded like cuss words, and moved on.

A fat woman with straight black hair stood at the window in the hallway of the car. All the other passengers who couldn't get a seat were sitting on the floor, but she remained standing. She was shaped like a block and was probably just as comfortable standing. It occurred to me as well that the idea of her sitting on the floor was comical: her torso wouldn't bend enough to allow it.

When the conductor had left the car and gone into the next one, the woman spoke to me.

"You are in trouble," she said.

"No."

"I can tell you are. Let me help you."

"I'm not in trouble."

"You have not a ticket. You pretended to be drunk when the agent came through."

"I was only asleep."

"Let me see your ticket," she said.

"You are not the conductor."

"As you wish. But I think I can help you."

"I don't need any help."

"I could give you some money."

I looked at her face. It was square and solid, and her hair hung from it like a mop. "Why would you give me money?" I asked.

"I am going to Runzenheim. I will buy you a ticket and you will get off with me there."

"I don't need the money. Not that badly."

"The agent will return. He will not let you sleep again. You will show him a ticket or he will throw you from the train. If he does not arrest you."

"There are worse things than getting arrested."

"Are there worse things than getting thrown from a train?"

"Yes, there are. Fucking a pig, to name one."

"Do not say that. That is not nice."

"If the shoe fits."

"Are you hungry? I could feed you."

"I had the gourmet salad in Strasbourg."

"A comfortable bed for the night. And some company."

"All right. Give me some money."

She handed me some francs.

"That's not enough money," I said.

"It is enough to get to Runzenheim."

The conductor came back with a fellow conductor, and they stood on either side of me as I handed them the money.

"Runzenheim," I said.

*

I COULDN'T SEE THE Vosges for the compartments that blocked the west-facing windows. But the hills of the Black Forest were clearly visible to the east. I missed them and couldn't wait to cross the border. As long as I was in France I felt like a fugitive.

I didn't speak a word of French. I had to get back to Germany to find a way to get back to America. I missed America very much. Germany was on the way to America, so I missed Germany very much too. When I returned to America I would miss every place I had loved in Europe, and I probably wouldn't return to any of them.

The hills rolled slowly by and we weren't getting any closer to them, but only moving northeast through France. The fat woman offered me some chocolate from her purse. Her accent was heavy and her voice was throaty, almost sultry. If I didn't look at her while I listened to her I could imagine the waitress in the quaint restaurant on Mont Sainte-Odile. But the waitress wouldn't say the things the fat woman was saying.

"Did you fight in the Southeast Asian war?"

"I haven't fought in any war."

"But you are a soldier. The muscles in your arms and shoulders are prominent."

"I'm a tourist."

"Years ago we had soldiers come to France from Germany who did not want to fight the Southeast Asian war. They do not come anymore."

"The war ended a decade and a half ago."

"Did you kill many of the Southeast Asians?"

"Hundreds. I was in elementary school, but what the hell, they let me enlist anyway. I mowed gooks down in droves." I held my fists before me as though they were gripping a fifty-caliber machine gun. "Ratta-tat-tat."

"Now there is another war." She smiled and her eyes widened. I wondered whether I ought to go all the way to Runzenheim and get off with this woman or just jump the train at an earlier stop. I tried to imagine having sex with her, spreading her ponderous thighs enough to achieve penetration. I tried to imagine it, gave up, and opted to jump off the train.

"I have several friends who would be interested in meeting you," the woman said.

"Are they pigs too?"

"I have a garden where I grow vegetables. You will be comfortable. There are men who work the fields if you require masculine company. They inhabit the Bistro in winter. You must not spend too much time in the Bistro, but if you occasionally require such diversion I will understand. I have been told my cooking is excellent. In the spring the garden will produce again."

"How much money do you have?"

"I cannot give you any more money. I have given you enough money for the ticket and now you must come to Runzenheim. If I give you more money you will get off before Runzenheim and I will have lost my investment. You must honor the investment."

*

AT WANZENAU THE TRAIN waited at the platform longer than it would ordinarily need to. I stood up and looked out the window. Two men with their backs to me were arguing with a conductor wearing a red cap. The three of them were several cars back and I had to press my face against the window to see them.

The countryside was low, flat, and scrubby. There were no evergreens, only deciduous trees that had lost their leaves, contributing to the look of winter death.

Finally the conductor raised his hands in a gesture of defeat and walked away. The two men boarded the train. As they turned I caught a brief glimpse of their faces; they were Krupa and Wittlinger.

Without saying anything to the fat woman I tried to open the door to escape to the platform. But the train had already started moving and the door was locked. I considered pulling the emergency brake, but then we would all stop together—Krupa, Wittlinger, the fat woman, and me. Instead I hurried toward the front of the train.

Once I entered the rearmost first class car I waited just inside the door and watched. After a few minutes I saw Krupa and Wittlinger push their way through a door two cars back. They were searching methodically from rear to front, examining every passenger. I moved on, until I reached the forwardmost first class car, which was nearly empty, and locked myself in the bathroom.

The train was moving too fast to jump off, even if I could get the door open. I would have to wait until it stopped at the next station, Kilstett, and try to get off without the two men noticing. It was my only chance. If they caught me, either on or off the train, I was sure they would kill me.

Someone tried to open the bathroom door. He rattled the knob, then yanked at it and kicked the door. I sat quietly on the toilet. A few minutes later the train slowed down. We were entering Kilstett.

The bathroom was directly across from the car exit. I waited until the train had stopped, then opened the bathroom door, took several quick strides across the walkway, pushed the button to open the hydraulic doors, and watched as they swung open. There was nobody else in the walkway.

I stepped down to the platform.

The train station in Kilstett was nothing more than a brick shack. I rounded the corner of the shack and range-walked down a sidewalk toward the edge of town. I didn't look back. I needed to find transportation across the border, but I had no money nor any articles to trade. I had left my passport on the table when I abandoned Molly, and I couldn't remotely afford a new one. Now I was wondering how alert that would turn out to be.

A couple of hundred meters from the station was a sign informing me I was exiting Kilstett. Only when I reached the sign did I allow myself to turn around and look back. Krupa and Wittlinger were only fifty meters behind. They were wearing bulky coats and staring at me as though their noses were gun sights.

I jumped off the sidewalk and raced down a steep embankment into a grassy field. Beyond the field was nothing but plowed dirt as far as the eye could see. There was no place to hide. I ran as fast as I could for the open field, jumping a low fence and landing hard on the frozen dirt. The men started running too. My plan was to get out of range as quickly as possible, but the dirt was frozen in clods that behaved like jagged stones.

A shot was fired and I heard a sharp *crack* as the bullet whizzed past me. Another shot was fired and I fell in the dirt. I got up and tried to run but fell down again. My left leg wouldn't work. I looked at it and saw a hole in the jeans over the calf. I tried to get up again but then the pain hit me. My calf felt like it had been skewered by a hot poker. I could only crawl. I pushed dirt clods out of my way, clearing a path, and dragged myself forward.

Krupa and Wittlinger caught up to me. Krupa placed himself in front of me, blocking my path, and laughed. I never saw Wittlinger.

Chapter 41

THERE WAS ONLY ONE possible solution, but I didn't know how to tell him. I think he knew it too. Out on the gravel road where I'd gone to wait for a car I checked the blade of my pocket knife. It was sharp, razor sharp. So sharp you had to be careful when you touched it, because the slightest bump, any accidental pressure, even a strong gust of wind could make it slice your finger to the bone.

No cars were on the road. None were coming, either. Perhaps one car a week came this way, and even that estimate was optimistic. A few tire tracks were visible, but it was hard to say how long ago they'd been made; the marks were almost filled with sand and gravel. That morning's rain with its oversized drops had obliterated most of the evidence this road had ever carried a vehicle.

They were warm rains, those that fell heavily in the late Illinois spring. You could smell them, dense and moist, seconds before they came.

I put the knife back into my pocket, left the road, and walked the fifty yards back into the woods to the place where he still lay, leaning against a tree, staring at his left ankle. He had short red hair, freckles, and an annoying habit of blinking his eyes rapidly with his mouth wide open and his front teeth sticking out like a chipmunk. His nickname was Red. I figured I'd be able to recognize him as an old man, even if I never saw him again until then. And assuming he ever became one. This latter condition was growing less likely with each passing hour.

"Were there any cars?" Red glanced at me briefly, then focused again on his ankle.

"No."

"Will there be?"

"Sure. It's just a matter of time."

"Maybe soon?"

"Maybe."

Sunlight cascaded through a break in the canopy and lit up a patch of moss under his leg. The moss was red and slippery.

"What if no cars come?"

"Billy will tell them."

"It's too far. It's twenty miles. Billy won't make it in time."

All the while he stared, transfixed, at his leg. It was stretched out before him and the ankle was wrapped in a bandage made from my spare shirt. His right knee was drawn up near his chest. He held on so tightly to the knee that his knuckles were white.

"Yes he will," I said. "He'll stop at the blacktop. There'll be lots of cars on the blacktop."

"What if there aren't any? Billy doesn't have the sense to wait. He'll just keep going."

You got that right, I thought. If there were no cars on the blacktop at the moment Billy reached it, he would be across it in two seconds and would continue skipping through the woods on the other side. We should have given him specific instructions. Billy would need exceptionally good looks to make it in the world.

I said, "You don't have any confidence in him because he's your little brother. You should give him more credit."

"Grasshoppers deserve more credit."

"He'll make it, one way or another."

"It's twenty miles if he crosses the road."

"He'll make it. You just hang on."

I sat down to wait. He looked like he was going to be quiet again. He had been quiet after it happened, and had spoken only in short outbursts since. I had tried to make him comfortable with a blanket, a canteen of water, and the magazines. But he didn't touch anything, he just stared at his leg. I had made him comfortable, but there was only so much he would let me do, and besides, it was pleasant there under the pine tree on a makeshift bed of needles and wood chips. I should have worried about him, but all I could think was: no more camping trips. And they had all been so good, until this one.

We had left early the previous day in the rain with backpacks filled with the usual stuff: C-Rations bought at the army surplus store; a tent with a large patch in the shape of a teardrop; a compass that was broken and pointed permanently to fifteen degrees east of north; a hatchet for cutting firewood; select magazines, the ones I kept hidden at home between the mattress and box springs; and my pocket knife. I carried a whetstone with me and honed the blades of the knife and hatchet every night before the fire.

We put Billy on the point so we wouldn't lose him. The creek we followed into the woods meandered so much that we had to cross it repeatedly to travel in a straight line. Finally the brush on either bank grew so dense we decided just to remain in the ankle deep water and wade upstream, following the meanders through lightly foaming whitewater and over a sequence of low waterfalls. I stopped at each fall, placed my hand under the center, and felt the force of the current deflect off my palm.

As we went up the creek the falls became steeper and the whitewater boiled more vigorously. We were careful walking here because this was ankle breaking country. There were many natural potholes and in some of them we found the original pestle rock, rattling around inside, digging the hole deeper as the current scoured and stirred.

Finally the falls became so steep we had to climb around them. We maneuvered in single file between boulders the size of compact cars, our sneakers squishing as we walked, avoiding whitewater that tunneled through the rocks like fire hoses whipping out of control.

At the top of the knick point was the steepest fall of all. Behind the wall of rushing water was a cave big enough for the three of us to sleep in, and we would have done so, had it not been for Jake. We climbed massive slabs of broken rock to reach the top. I leaned over to place my hand under the center of the flow and braced myself. The current was muscular, pulsing.

This was my favorite place. The canopy was high, creating the impression of a large room with the fall as its centerpiece. The stream flowed down over the rapids and under a lofty arch of tree branches that served as an entrance.

Once we were over the top and above the fall, Billy threw a stick into the stream. We watched it tumble down and be devoured by the froth. Then we turned into the woods.

The rain was intermittent, and when it didn't rain, it dripped. I would remember this trip for the rain, and for the red moss. The moss was the red of maple leaves in autumn, the red of a blazing sunset. I had never seen such color in moss before.

We followed a deer path into the woods. By midafternoon we passed the place where we had found the arrowhead last summer, and just before dark we crossed the blacktop and looked for a site to camp.

We had seen the arrowhead two feet off the side of the path, half buried in the soil. Its conchoidal fractures had been worked to a knife edge that was still sharp after perhaps centuries in the soil. Red and I lunged for it simultaneously, and both of us closed our hands on it, but it came up in his. He lifted it jubilantly above his head as if he had just used it to slay a dangerous beast. It was a classic bow-and-arrow type arrowhead, made of gray chert, with notches cut into its base for lashing to the shaft of the arrow. Red agreed to share ownership with me but it stayed at his house.

It turned dark quickly after we crossed the blacktop. We set up camp out of sight of the road. I put Billy to work gathering all the dry, dead branches he could find, but we would need logs to sustain the fire.

"Whose turn is it to cut wood?" I asked.

Both Red and Billy shrugged. So we flipped coins. Red, outmatched in the toss, took the hatchet out of my pack and trudged into the trees.

I zipped my sleeping bag up to my neck and fell asleep quickly. It was hard work walking through ankle-deep water.

The next morning we set out at dawn to make the most of the day. We wanted to go deep into the woods, and if possible, reach the gravel road. I put Billy on the point again, but he couldn't hold the pace. He faded back and eventually fell too far behind for us to see him. We took a break to wait for him, whistling at intervals so he would know how far ahead we were, and when he caught up we set out again without letting him rest.

"That's what you get for falling behind," Red told him.

By early evening we made the gravel road and decided to camp there and do some fishing in the stream on the other side. I leaned the hatchet against a tree. Red picked it up rather carelessly and scratched his head in mock thoughtfulness. "*Now* whose turn is it to cut wood?" he asked.

And that was how he came to be where he was, sitting in the pine needles and wood chips, with his back against the trunk of a tree and his gaze fixed obsessively on his leg.

Chapter 42

"... HE'S COMING TO," I heard Molly say. "Here, help me lift his head. He's going to choke on his tongue."

I felt my body being moved and soft hands on my face.

"Let him choke." It was Montalbano's voice. It sounded frightened.

"You'd like that, wouldn't you?" It was Molly speaking again. "That would be convenient for you. You fucked up so bad, it would be better for you if the target died."

"I don't understand why *she* had to get involved," Montalbano said. "We had everything under control until she took him to France to recruit his dick. Look at all the time we've lost."

"There is no benefit whatever in quibbling about it now."

This last voice was Krupa's. I could smell his pipe smoke. I opened my eyes, but the room was blurry and spinning, so I closed them again.

"I don't understand what the problem is," Montalbano said. "Let's get it out of him, or else croak him. This waiting around is a bunch of shit."

"That is enough complaining, Mister Montalbano," Krupa said. "We do not need any advice from you. The target was behaving precisely as expected until you turned him into a rabbit."

"Fuck you, you sniveling kraut. I'll give you a little demonstration of my advice."

I heard scuffling, then felt a pair of hands on my throat.

"Tell me where the fucking cassette is, or I'll croak you right now!"

"Stop it!" Molly said. "You'll kill him."

"That's the idea."

"Stop that immediately," Krupa ordered, "or I will have you shot."

The hands left my throat.

"He needs a doctor," Molly said. "He's going to be worthless to us unless we get him a doctor. Would somebody *please* call a doctor?"

"No doctors," Krupa said.

"I say we croak him."

"No, let us give him a little more time."

"He's going out again."

"Then get some fucking water. I'll keep the fucker awake."

"Let him go. He will come back, and when he does we will apply a screw or two."

"It's botched. Can't you see it? Croak him!"

"Herr Krupa," Wittlinger spoke for the first time, "indeed we are running out of time."

"We still have time."

I heard someone moving, and the smell of Krupa's pipe smoke became strong. "Do you see this?" his voice said, close to me. He was tapping against plastic. "Open your eyes. Look at it. You will recognize it. It is a pornographic movie called 'Blow Dry.' We picked it up from the bottom of the river, at the location you gave Ms. Taganov. We know you copied the real document and hid it somewhere. We know because we lost you after you ran from the chapel, and it was almost two hours be-

318

fore you showed up on the bridge. During those two hours you hid the cassette somewhere. There is no other way to account for the time." He lowered his voice nearly to a whisper: "Where?"

I didn't answer.

He slapped me once, hard, across the cheek. "Where?"

"Herr Krupa," Wittlinger said. "If I may put my training to good use."

"Leave him alone," Molly said. "Don't you touch him. Not you."

"I am a patient man," Krupa said. "But as time passes I will come to favor Mister Montalbano's approach to the problem, and Mister Wittlinger's techniques." I could smell his breath. It was the breath of an old man and a pipe smoker.

"You need to exercise some of that patience right now, Krupa," Molly said. "Because you're forgetting who's in charge here. You will *all* do as I say." She paused. "You—go and get a doctor. And don't fuck it up."

"Stay where you are, Herr Wittlinger."

"I said go!"

"My dear Natasha, is it necessary for me to remind you how far from home you are?"

"Can he at least have something to eat? Some soup, some broth? Is that too much to ask?"

"Herr Wittlinger," Krupa said.

"On my way."

"There there, sweetie," Molly said. I felt her fingers stroking my forehead. "Just lay quiet."

"There he goes again."

"Get some fucking water! I'll keep the motherfucker awake."

"No. Let him go . . ."

319

Chapter 43

AND NOW, UNDER THE tree, Red felt his ankle and said, "Maybe we should change the bandage."

I knelt above his ankle and probed the wound. The cut had gone almost all the way through the leg. The bone was shattered. One little tug might take the foot off altogether. It was kind of funny when I thought about it: me standing there holding up his detached foot, saying, Hey, look at that!

"I don't think we should take the old bandage off," I said. "I'll put another one on over the top of it."

But it wouldn't do. What he needed was pressure on the stump. And to do that we had to take the foot off.

I dug through Billy's pack and found his spare shirt. I wrapped it around the ankle and tied it as tightly as I could. "Does it hurt?"

"No, it just feels numb."

It was still early enough in the afternoon. If Billy stopped a car on the blacktop he might bring help by nightfall. I looked at Red's face. It was chalky. He wasn't going to make it.

"Look," I said. "I have my pocket knife."

"So?"

"You know how sharp I keep it. It'll only take a second."

"No."

"It's the only way we can stop the bleeding. And it has to be stopped. I can't put enough pressure on it, with a bandage, as it is."

"No."

"But the foot's going to come off anyway. It's only hanging by a thread. You know that, don't you?"

"They can put it back. I've heard of it being done."

"If they come in time."

He bit his lip and tried to fight off tears. "Go to the road again."

"Why?"

"If a car comes I don't want you to miss it."

"I can see the road from here. I can run out in time to stop any car that comes."

"Just go, will you?"

"Fine."

I walked back through the thick brush that grew where the woods ended and the road began, and I sat in the gravel and waited for a car that wasn't coming. He sat under the tree, the picture of doom, holding his good knee with both hands.

So there would be no more camping trips, after this one. And they had been good, until this one.

We had seen some things that were so beautiful they couldn't be captured in words: a deer in a clearing, just as it detects your scent, pricks its ears, and lifts its head to look, then springs off into cover—and a second later you wonder whether it had been there at all. Tree branches encased in ice as though polished and shellacked. Autumn sunsets spreading warm colors on leaves already raging in orange and red.

As for the arrowhead, I would just ask Billy to retrieve it from Red's room for me. Their mother didn't have to know. I was, after all, the first to have laid eyes on it.

Now I could just see him through the trees but I couldn't make out any movement. There was an abrupt stillness in the canopy, the hush that comes when the birds know something is about to happen.

I walked back toward him slowly and quietly through the brush and looked at his face. But he was just being still, and as I approached he turned his head to watch me.

His face was startlingly white. I stopped in my tracks. It was horrible to look at. The sun had found a new break in the canopy and was shining on the moss beneath his leg. The moss was even redder than before. And the face, Holy Jesus.

"How do you feel?"

"Dizzy."

"Does it hurt now?"

"No."

"Are you afraid?"

"A little."

"Want some water?"

He nodded, and I held the canteen to his lips. He took several quick gulps. I wiped the mouth of the canteen and screwed the cap back on. He licked his lips. The combination of red hair, freckles, and bleached skin looked ghoulish.

"Stop staring at me," he said.

I looked away.

He noticed the hatchet still lurking at the scene, a couple of feet in front of him where it had been dropped, and tried to kick it away with his good leg. I reached over, picked it up, and tossed it into the brush.

"They're not coming, are they?" he asked.

I moved the canteen out of reach. "You know, you shouldn't have stood where you did. That was stupid. If you had just stood someplace else, this wouldn't have happened."

"Well, I'm sure sorry about *that*."

"Fat lot of good it does you now."

I sat and waited. The sun went down some more and the color of the moss faded and his grip on his knee relaxed and he rolled over on his right side and landed in the wood chips. The most exquisite action he had taken in his short life was to let go of it.

I went around to see the eyes. They were half open, as I was afraid they would be. I knew I should close them, but I didn't want to touch it. A moment ago it was him, but now it was a dead thing and I didn't want to touch it. I took my jacket off and covered his face, then walked back to the road again and sat in the gravel to wait.

They came just after dark. The pickup rolled up in front of me and stopped. The headlights stayed on. Billy jumped out, chattering excitedly, pointing into the woods, urging his father to follow him. The father trotted behind him after glancing sharply at me. He was wearing the same old blue flannel shirt he always wore.

I remained sitting on the road. They had to see for themselves. Billy's chattering continued until they reached the place. Then there was silence.

Many minutes passed before they returned to the road. The father approached and towered above me. His fists were clenched and his jaw was quivering. His eyes, wide with pain, drilled two holes right through me. I didn't hold it against him. I would probably have been just as upset if my son had done something just as stupid. He stood seething, but not speaking, fearful probably of what would come of it if he did.

I wrapped my arms around my knees. He was waiting for me to say something. I shrugged and said, "It rained all day—the handle was slippery."

He just stood there. He wanted to hear it all.

"I had my knife," I continued. "I could have stopped it, if he had let me. It just went on and on, leaking into the ground, into the moss, and he wouldn't let me do anything about it."

He looked up at the stars and his entire body relaxed as though in resignation. Then he turned and shuffled back to the pickup. His head was high but his arms dangled at his sides.

I called after him: "He shouldn't have been standing where he was. If he'd moved out of the way it wouldn't have happened. None of it would have happened."

He climbed into the truck and covered his face with his hands.

"Better this way!" I shouted. "Better now than later. Better me than an anonymous bully!"

He wasn't listening. Like son, like father. Well, at least there was Billy. Today he finally did something right.

I lifted my foot in the air. "Hey, look at that! Look at that!"

The rain was coming again, with promise of large drops. I smelled it seconds before it started. It was a thick, choking smell. When the drops came they were warm and heavy on my face.

Chapter 44

IT WAS DAYTIME WHEN I opened my eyes. Sunlight streamed through the window, and although I couldn't see the ground outside I judged the brightness to be the effect of snow.

Wittlinger was asleep in a chair by the wall. His hands lay loose in his lap and his cheek rested on his shoulder.

I tensed the muscles in my arms, legs, and back, to see if everything worked, and except for the stiffness everything felt fine. But there was no feeling in the lower half of my left leg. It felt like an artificial limb.

My vision was still blurred, so I tried to relax and focus on the window. But the sun reflecting off the snow was too bright, and I couldn't make out any detail beyond the window pane.

I recognized the room as Wittlinger's bedroom. I had escaped from a party months before by climbing out that same window. The bed was gone and I was flat on the floor with only a thin blanket underneath me. That explained the stiffness. But the wallpaper was the same. At least I knew where I was.

I remembered the field, and the dirt clods that felt like rocks when I fell on them, and the shot that dropped me. The latter accounted for the numbness in my leg. My stomach growled.

Hunger wouldn't slow me, but the leg would. And the dizziness.

The door opened. I closed my eyes. The footsteps were heavy and I heard the chair being kicked, and Wittlinger saying "Hmph!"

"You are not supposed to sleep," Krupa's voice said.

An audible yawn and smacking lips, then a drowsy response: "He's not going anywhere."

I heard the footsteps coming near me and I smelled the familiar smell of Glühwein. I opened my eyes.

"Good," Krupa said. "You are up. Here, take some of this."

He held a mug to my lips and I sipped from it. The Glühwein was hot, and immediately I felt the warmth go down through my chest.

"Could you take some food?"

I nodded.

"Good. We will have some conversation, then I will see about getting you something to eat."

"Food first."

"No, conversation."

He held the mug to my lips again and I swallowed too much and it burned my tongue.

"More."

He held the mug again and I finished it. My stomach was empty and the alcohol went to work straight away.

"How much did it snow?" I asked.

"It has not snowed."

"I thought it did."

"It did not."

"Well, this has been a pleasant conversation. May I have some dinner now?"

He chuckled. "It is good to see you still have your sense of humor." He turned to face Wittlinger. "Please bring the tools of conversation into the room."

Wittlinger left. Krupa pulled the armchair away from the wall, positioned it next to me, and sat down. He clasped his hands and waited patiently. Presently Wittlinger returned with Montalbano, carrying a small, three-legged table. The table was covered with a towel.

"Can you sit up?" Krupa asked.

"I think so. Is that the food?"

Wittlinger placed the table at my feet. I didn't smell any food.

Krupa said, "Where is the cassette, Mr. Fisher?"

"The one . . . you found . . . in the river—it's the only one I had." I looked at the table. Something projected up from the center, making the towel look like a low tent.

"I could go back and make another copy," I said. "That is, um, if you wanted me to."

"This is a game, my young friend," Krupa said. "It is only a game. But even games must be played earnestly, because they are metaphors for life." He was speaking to me as though I were a child. "You will therefore understand if we play hard and try to win. Certainly I would understand your doing the same. But consider this: are you willing to sacrifice your life for the sake of winning this particular game?"

"Are you willing to kill me for the sake of winning it?"

"Indeed, yes. But it does not have to come to that. Tell me where the cassette is, and I win the game. And you save your life."

Wittlinger and Montalbano helped me up to a sitting position. My legs were spread out before me and I was leaning back against the wall. I felt dizzy again and was afraid I would pass out. I forced myself to breathe deeply and fought to keep the room from going gray.

Wittlinger lifted the towel from the table and dropped it on the floor. A large, flat-headed nail had been hammered into the

327

center of the table. It protruded two or three inches above the table top. That explained the tent.

The only other object on the table was a meat cleaver.

"Where is the cassette, Mr. Fisher?"

Wittlinger grabbed my right hand and placed it on the table. He pressed down roughly to flatten it against the surface. Montalbano came around the other side and held my left arm. Then Wittlinger strapped my right arm to the top of the table with a belt. I looked at Krupa.

"Where is the cassette?"

"I'll get it for you. I'll go and get it and come right back."

Wittlinger crooked my thumb away from my hand by pressing it against the raised nail. Then he picked up the meat cleaver.

"Don't," I said. "Oh God, please don't. I'll tell you everything."

He raised the cleaver over his head and brought it down swiftly. I heard the dull thud of the blade going into the wood of the table. I didn't feel anything, and thought at first the show had been a bluff—that he had purposely missed. But then Krupa leaned over and picked something up and held it in front of my face. It was my thumb.

"Secrets are the cause of wars," he said. "It is safer for all involved to divulge them. If we had no secrets we would have nothing to fight about, nothing to kill each other for. People who divulge secrets are the true peace keepers of the world."

Montalbano was bandaging my hand. I still couldn't feel anything, but Krupa was holding the thumb in front of my face. It was curling slowly, like something from a carnival freak show.

"Think about it," he said.

*

LATER WHILE I WAS alone Molly came in. She knelt down on the floor and held my head in her arms. I buried my face in her breasts.

"Was it okay?" she asked. "I couldn't bear to be here."

"Help me," I said.

"I'm with you, sweetie."

"It smells like shit in here."

"You've soiled your pants."

"Oh God, please help me."

"Shh. You can do it, sweetie. Shh."

Chapter 45

SHE STOOD NAKED ON the rocks above the river, singing to the boat captains on the water below. I watched the way she stood with one knee bent, her arms hung loosely at her sides. The way her chest swelled as she sang. Her voice was clear and sweet, and no other noise competed with it, as if all the world had stopped to listen.

Her face was angelic, her hair fell in golden curls to the middle of her back, and her flesh radiated a warmth that could only have come from the Earth itself.

She finished the song, looked at me, and smiled. And I knew there was no cause for worry. If something that beautiful smiled upon me, even if only in my dreams, I was safe.

*

A NOISE AT THE window woke me. I squinted at the glass until a pair of hands came into focus; they were trying to push the window open from the outside.

At first I didn't believe my eyes. Then as the cobwebs of sleep cleared I realized the image wasn't an illusion. Somebody was trying to break *into* the room.

I rolled onto my stomach and raised myself up so I was resting on my hands and knees. Then I peeked over the top of the window sill. It was Special Agent John Blackburn. He was inching the window up a centimeter at a time, trying not to make any noise.

I crawled over to the window, reached for the sill, and pulled myself up to his level. We were face to face, with only a flimsy piece of glass separating us. But I didn't have the strength to help him. I could only watch as the window opened by small, screeching increments. When it was open far enough I reached through and grabbed his hand.

"Get me out of here."

"Shh! Help me get the window open. And if you hear anyone coming, just lay down on the floor."

Now the prospect of escape gave me energy I didn't know I had. I pushed up from the inside of the window while he did the same from the outside. After a few more minutes, during which we made so much noise I was sure everyone in the house could hear, there was enough space for him to crawl through. He rolled into the room, assumed a crouched position, and removed a small revolver from his jacket.

As he stared at the door, watching for any reaction to our noise, I sobbed quietly with relief. "It's Montalbano," I whispered. "Not Riddell."

"I know."

"Get me out of here."

"I will. Just tell me where you hid the cassette."

"Get me out of here, and I'll show you."

"Very well. I have a car about two blocks away. Do you think you can walk?"

"If I have to, I will. But I've got to get to a doctor right away. And we've got to call in some cops. A whole bunch of cops."

"Of course. After we recover the cassette."

"Check your priorities, mister! Look at me! Get me the fuck out of here, and get me to a doctor, and then you can have anything you want!"

"The cassette, Jimmy. Where is it? We have to settle that first."

"The cassette is safe. I'm not. Doctor first. Cops second. cassette third."

"Cassette first."

"Listen, knucklehead. No doctor, no cassette."

"You're making this awfully hard, Jimmy."

"If you're not going to help me, then get the fuck out of my way." I stood up painfully, balancing on my right leg, and tried to squeeze through the open window. At that moment someone kicked the door open.

Montalbano entered the room. Blackburn just looked at him.

"Shoot him!" I shouted. "What are you waiting for? Shoot the fucker!"

Molly, Krupa, and Wittlinger followed, entering the room in single file. All five watched me try to escape through the window as they would watch a fly struggle to free itself from a spider web.

"There's no cavalry coming to save you," Blackburn said, pocketing his revolver. "You're going to die—you know that. I promise you'll die painlessly if you give us the location of the cassette. Otherwise this goes on, and believe me, we can make it go on for a long time."

My arms were through to the other side, clawing at the air, trying to drag the rest of me to freedom. But the rest of me was too dizzy to follow. My head kept bumping against the window pane.

"We're going to give you until tomorrow," Blackburn continued. "After that the pain becomes unbearable—but you'll be made to bear it. Parts of you more dear to you than your thumb will be hacked off. We have a lot of experience at this kind of thing. We can keep you alive, suffering excruciating and unbearable pain, for months, perhaps even for a year."

One by one, Blackburn, Montalbano, Krupa, and finally Molly, left the room. Molly looked at me with an expression of great pity before she closed the door behind her.

Wittlinger stayed. His shirt was unbuttoned and he had a bottle of cognac in his hand.

He grabbed me by the collar, dragged me away from the window, and shoved me onto the floor. Then slammed the window shut. He smelled strongly of cognac. I watched him watch me, and I saw the message in his eyes. He took a swig from the bottle, unzipped his pants, and stroked himself.

"This cover sheet," he said, "is unclassified when separated from classified documents." He giggled.

I closed my eyes and tried to picture the Lorelei again, but the smell of cognac was too strong and the grunts too loud. I kept my eyes closed the whole time. I tried to make the hands into hers. But they were too large, too rough.

Finally I passed out. My mind just turned off the switch.

*

MOLLY CAME IN LATER with a bowl of beef broth. She put the bowl on the floor and examined my crumpled pants and underwear.

"Wash me," I said.

She left with the pants and underwear, and I heard her arguing loudly in the next room. A few minutes later she returned with a bucket and some clothes tucked under her arm.

She washed me all over with a sponge. The water was warm and soapy and felt good. My right hand ached. I could move my left leg a little now and could wiggle my toes, but there were bright red infection streaks radiating out from beneath the bandage on my calf. They spread down to my ankle and up to my knee.

Molly dressed me in the clothes. From the fit of them I guessed they belonged to Wittlinger. She spoon-fed me the soup, which by now was lukewarm. It was the first food I'd had since the gourmet salad in Strasbourg.

"You're dying, sweetie," she said.

"Please help me."

"I can't help you. You can only help yourself."

"I love you."

"I love you too. But I can't help you. I'm only serving my country. You understand that, don't you? Don't you, sweetie? You know you would do nothing less, or expect anything less from me."

I had been sitting up, but now I became dizzy so I laid back flat on the floor. Molly propped my head up with a pillow. She took a small metal box out of her shirt pocket. It looked like an old fashioned Sucrets box. She opened it and removed a capsule.

"I can make it easy for you," she said. "The choice is yours."

The capsule was gray and about the size of a vitamin pill.

"Give me the pill," I said.

"You have to earn it. Be a good boy, and tell me where the operations plan is."

"Please give me the pill."

"In a few minutes, Krupa and Wittlinger are coming back to have another conversation."

"The pill, please."

"Wittlinger is an expert at what he does. I told you about my training; Wittlinger was trained, too. He spent years in school, learning how to inflict agony while keeping the victim alive. He practiced on political prisoners. He loves his work. The first conversation was dull compared to what the next one will be like. You'll soon reach the point where death is your only ambition, and he'll keep you there for what will seem like an eternity. There are a lot of people looking for Heaven on earth. Wittlinger has found the key to the gates of Hell."

"The cemetery on Alzeyerstrasse," I said. "In a grave. The name on the tombstone is Wilhelm Kaiser."

"That's better. That's so much better. I'm proud of you, sweetie. I knew you could do it."

"The pill."

"No."

"Please."

"No."

Chapter 46

KRUPA WAITED AT THE house that evening while the others went out. He didn't enter the bedroom. I heard classical music coming from the living room and I smelled the smoke from his pipe.

I tried once to stand up, but as soon as I got to my feet the room spun and I fell back to the floor, making a racket. The music went off for a minute, then came back on again.

I inventoried the room. It was bare except for the two chairs, one simple and wooden and the other upholstered and overstuffed. I thought of the nails in the upholstered chair, but they were too short. I thought of how a splintered piece of wood might make a good weapon, but I barely had the strength to sit up, let alone snap a chair leg.

I thought of the window, too, and how a sharp weapon could be made from broken glass. But not only would the noise of breaking glass cause a general alarm, I wouldn't be able to hold such a weapon in my hand without getting the worst of it myself. As for climbing through the window to the outside, it wasn't clear what I would be able to do once I got there.

When the other four returned to the house there was some lengthy discussion in the next room. Then all five came in. Molly remained in the doorway, leaning against the frame.

"I have lost my patience, Mister Fisher," Krupa said.

"How should we do him?" Montalbano asked.

"As you wish."

"Hold on," Wittlinger said. "I just need a little more time. I thought that's what we brought him here for. Give me a couple of more days and I'll have him singing at the top of his lungs."

"No," Krupa said, "I am afraid we are out of time. Also, something tells me your methods will not work on this one. We need to convince him he will die if he does not open up, and the way he will die will be the way he most fears."

"Now we're talking," Montalbano said.

"Okay," Blackburn said. "But how?"

Krupa looked at Molly. She hesitated only a second, then said, "He's afraid of heights." She crossed her arms and watched me stonily from the doorway.

"That is right," Krupa acknowledged. "We knew that all along, did we not? We probably ought to have employed that from the beginning, and saved ourselves much trouble."

"He tossed his cookies from the top of Strasbourg Cathedral," Molly continued. "It was there he revealed the location of the first cassette."

"Well, well, well," Krupa said. "Strasbourg is a little far away, but I think we can come up with a convenient alternative."

"I'm going with you," Molly said. "So you don't fuck it up."

"I will not fuck it up."

"Nevertheless."

"I'm going too," Montalbano said. "I've been waiting for this."

"We will *all* go," Krupa said.

*

337

WITTLINGER TIED MY HANDS and feet, then gagged and blind-folded me. He carried me like a sack of potatoes out to the car and dumped me in the trunk. I passed out briefly from the movement, then woke in the darkness of the trunk and listened to the engine starting.

The night air was invigorating. It increased my alertness. The noises the car made were amplified in the trunk. I could hear the passenger doors slamming shut as if my ear were pressed against them, and the sound of tires scraping the gravel as though I were right above the road. I could also hear muffled conversation coming from the cab in front of me, but I couldn't make out what anyone was saying.

I timed the car between turns and tried to gauge its speed. We followed Salinenstrasse out of town, and when I had to brace myself from sliding back and forth in the trunk I knew we were entering the Kurviertel. We slowed at the outskirts of Bad Münster, then turned right onto what had to have been Nahe-weinstrasse. It was then I realized where we were going.

The road steepened as we climbed toward Traisen. After leveling off on a flat hilltop we stopped briefly with the engine running, and someone got out. Rotenfels was closed this late at night and the entrance would be barricaded. Someone was re-moving the barricade. He got back in, the door slammed, and the car started up again.

The sound the tires made on the road changed as we left the pavement and went onto gravel. Moments later the car stopped, the engine went off, and all four doors opened. I heard the trunk being unlocked and felt the cool air come in when the trunk door opened.

Rough hands dragged me out of the trunk and threw me on the ground. Then two pair of arms lifted me by the armpits and half carried me, half dragged me along a gravel surface.

"Take the shit off his face," Montalbano's voice said. "I want him to see this."

The gag and blindfold were removed. Wittlinger un-sheathed his hunting knife and cut the rope binding my wrists. "Don't make a fucking sound," he said. I balanced on one wobbly leg, rubbed my wrists, and glanced down at a steep drop. The lights of Bad Münster and Ebernburg twinkled on the other side of the river, far below. It was the same view I had shared with Molly during our visit earlier that year, only now it was nighttime. Five hundred feet down was a bed of jagged boulders.

"We will hang you over the edge until you talk," Krupa said. "Or until our arms get tired, after which you will fall. It is that simple, Mister Fisher. It will appear to be an accident. With all of your nefarious activities, who will be able to say what you were doing at the top of Rotenfels in the middle of the night? Looking for buried treasure, maybe? There is not a single person who knows you who will be surprised by your death, nor a single person who will devote himself to the discovery of its true cause."

Montalbano grabbed me by the shoulders and forced me to my knees. With both hands clamped on my shoulders he shoved me toward the edge, and I had to lean backwards as hard as I could to keep from sliding over. I threw up in a thin gruel, and everyone but Molly laughed.

"Now beg," Montalbano said.

"Oh, for Christ's sake," Molly said.

"Beg!"

"Mister Fisher," Krupa said, "your time has run out. Give me the correct location of the cassette, or Mister Montalbano and Mister Wittlinger will hang you over the edge by your ankles."

"He's not going to talk," Molly said, "until you actually hang him over the side. Why don't you stop tormenting him and just do it?"

"Not yet," Montalbano said. "I like to see him on his knees. I like to see him barf with fear. I want to hear some begging. I didn't put up with all this shit not to hear some fucking begging. Beg, motherfucker."

Suddenly the area was flooded in light. A half-dozen spotlights shined at us from equidistant points in a semicircular perimeter around the cliff edge. For a moment we stared at them in stunned silence.

Then a single shot was fired, and Wittlinger fell. He didn't fall gracefully, as people do in the movies; his legs buckled and he flopped to the ground.

More shots were fired. Krupa limped toward the woods. Blackburn pulled a pistol, stood his ground, and returned fire. Montalbano fretted about his decision, then ran toward the woods, passing Krupa, who was holding his left thigh as he ran. Dozens of Beetle Baileys stormed the scene, and there was shouting everywhere. The night filled with gunfire.

Molly reached into her bag, took out a handgun, and pointed it at my head. A Beetle who had been rushing our position stopped, dropped to one knee, and emptied his clip on automatic.

Molly twitched several times as though from electrical shock. But she didn't pull the trigger.

Several other Beetles closed in, firing on the run, and her body jerked spastically as she was hit from various angles. She sank to her knees, gasping in pain, the gun still pointed at me.

The Beetles hit her several more times as they got closer and improved their aim, until finally she dropped the gun and laid face-down on the ground.

Blackburn, struck by a hail of bullets, fell backwards over the edge of the cliff. One moment he was there, the next moment he wasn't.

I picked up Molly's pistol and put it in my pocket. Then I rolled her over to examine her wounds. So much blood was leaking from so many holes there was no point trying to stop it.

Her eyes fluttered open.

"Private Jimmy," she whispered, "soon to be Corporal. You were right about love." She went into convulsions.

Garrett came down the path, surrounded by a squad of men. His arm was in a sling. The squad carried M16s and had that flushed, exhilarated look of men who have crushed the opposition in dangerous battle.

He crouched over Molly. From the woods we heard automatic fire that sounded like a platoon in combat. After a few moments of silence there was a whistle, followed by boisterous cheering; Krupa and Montalbano were dead.

Garrett turned his attention back to Molly, who was writhing in a futile struggle with death. He removed his 9mm handgun, placed it against her head, and fired.

I leapt at him, but there was little I could do in my weakened condition. Garrett gently forced me back to the ground.

"You shot her," I cried.

"We could only get her on conspiracy," Garrett said. "This is simpler."

"You killed her."

"It's over now. We got them all."

"But she was beautiful. She was so goddamn beautiful."

He looked at her face, which was truly at peace, perhaps for the first time in her life.

"Yes," he answered academically, "she was."

Chapter 47

IT WAS DAWN BY the time the battlefield was cleaned up. Garrett drove me to the cemetery on Alzeyerstrasse, and I led him to the grave of Patrick Parnell, where the cassette was buried. He needed it, he said, to close the case. Next to Parnell's grave was Wilhelm Kaiser's, the soil freshly exposed because it had been dug up the night before. I wondered what the relatives would think.

"Happy Thanksgiving," Garrett mumbled. "Did you know?"

"No. I didn't even know what month it was."

I was too weak to dig, so Garrett had to do all the work himself, even though his arm was in a sling. I felt like Cybulski, merely standing by, while Garrett labored over the shovel. His feet did most of the work, pushing the blade of the shovel into the dirt; when the shovel was full he placed the handle under his armpit and used his whole body to leverage the weight of the load. While he dug he talked.

"Oplan 2357-90 was a fake. We wrote it and planted it to uncover Blackburn. A couple of days ago we followed him to Wittlinger's house, then waited until yesterday, when every-body went on a late joy ride to Rotenfels. Although our line of sight was poor, we figured the body tossed into the trunk of the car was yours. At that point it was just a matter of calling in the cavalry."

He stabbed at the bottom of the hole with his shovel, hoping to measure the rest of the work. Then he sighed and went on digging.

"We had no idea the operation would be so successful," he continued. "We got two spies, not one. We got both of the local operators. And we even got a sleeper we didn't know existed. She was gravy."

"Skelton's dead," I said.

"Yes, I know. We found him."

"Cybulski's dead. Krupa and Wittlinger are dead. Blackburn and Montalbano are dead. Molly's dead. You've got a broken arm, and my thumb's been hacked off. And you're telling me the operation was a success? You planted some bait and attracted people to it who, most of them, were otherwise living normal, purposeful lives. Now they're all dead, or maimed, and the United States of America proba-bly isn't any safer than it was when you started your 'suc-cessful' operation."

"Think what you want. I did my job."

His shovel struck the coffin. He climbed into the hole and removed the remaining dirt by scooping it out with his one good hand. I had already pried the lid up, so it clattered off when he jerked at it.

I walked unsteadily over to the grave and looked in. Sitting on top of a pile of brown-stained bones was the cassette, just where I had left it. Garrett blew the dirt from the plastic and stuffed it inside his shirt.

"We'll get you to a hospital now," he said. "Then, I'm afraid, I'm going to have to place you under arrest for conspiracy to commit espionage. You have the right to remain silent . . . you know the rest, don't you?"

"It's been quoted to me a few times."

He unhooked a pair of handcuffs from his belt. "Do I need these? In your condition they seem like overkill."

I shook my head. "It's funny, isn't it?"

"What?"

"They don't take up nearly as much space after they've decayed. In the long run, most of the space is wasted."

He blinked a couple of times before he realized what I was talking about, then looked down into the coffin and wrinkled his nose. As he bent over to pick up the shovel I removed Molly's revolver from my pocket and pointed it at his head.

"This is for everybody," I said.

As the sun rose in the sky it was obscured by clouds, so the day was not going to be a bright one. A cold wind swept across the graveyard. When I finished filling the hole I left Garrett's car where he had parked it on the gravel drive and limped down Alzeyerstrasse toward the train station. As I passed the barracks it started to snow.

Acknowledgements

I am grateful to the following friends and colleagues who read the manuscript in whole or part, at various stages of its growth: Kevin Aicher, Aerin Bender-Stone, Marsali Classon, Jude Hardin, Sarah Hina, Joy Johnson, Cheryl Kauffman, John Kauffman, Wendy Russ, Heike Specht, and Mark Terry.

No classified information was consulted for this story. Grid co-ordinates and other map designations are arbitrary. Military war plans are boilerplates. Defense strategies are either invented or were common knowledge at the time. Characters are entirely fictional and are not modeled on actual persons, living or dead.

Some of the opinions or attitudes expressed could be considered disparaging to the Armed Forces of the United States. Such opinions and attitudes are not mine. I served with pride in the U.S. Army Infantry and heartily recommend military service to all eligible Americans.

Made in the USA
Lexington, KY
08 May 2014